OCT   1998   LT
FiL
PARKER

S0-AWV-867

*Also by T. Jefferson Parker
in Large Print:*

The Triggerman's Dance

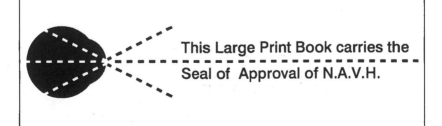

This Large Print Book carries the
Seal of Approval of N.A.V.H.

Where Serpents Lie

Where
Serpents
Lie

T. JEFFERSON PARKER

Thorndike Press • Thorndike, Maine

Published in 1998 by arrangement with Hyperion.

Thorndike Large Print ® Cloak & Dagger Series.

The tree indicium is a trademark of Thorndike Press.

The text of this Large Print edition is unabridged.
Other aspects of the book may vary from the original edition.

Set in 16 pt. Plantin by Juanita Macdonald.

Printed in the United States on permanent paper.

Library of Congress Cataloging in Publication Data

Parker, T. Jefferson.
  Where serpents lie / T. Jefferson Parker.
    p.   cm.
  ISBN 0-7862-1526-7 (lg. print : hc : alk. paper)
  1. Police — California — Orange County — Fiction.
2. Children — Crimes against — Fiction.   3. Orange County
(Calif.) — Fiction.   4. Large type books.   I. Title.
  [PS3566.A6863W54   1998b]
  813'.54—dc21   98-7892

For Rita
On This New Morning

Acknowledgments

I sincerely thank the following men for their help in researching this book: Sgt. Toby Tyler of the San Bernardino Sheriff Department; Rex Tomb, Neal Schiff and Douglas Goodin of the FBI in Washington, D.C.; Deputy Gary Bale of the Orange County Sheriff Department; Larry Ragle, retired director of the Orange County Crime Laboratory; Dr. Gregory Robinson of the Social Science Research Center of California State University Fullerton; and not least, Laguna Beach artist Mark Chamberlain. The facts are theirs; the mendacities are mine and mine alone.

Prologue

I am the champion of the little people.

Their shield.

Their sword.

I live in the world of men and women, because I have to. But my eyes see what the little people see; I hear what they hear. They are my constituents, all the children who are ignored or abandoned, damaged, hurt, exploited, hated, used. They are a secret society and I am their ambassador to the world. Their friends are my friends and their enemies are my enemies. Their dreams are mine, too. We are one.

Crimes Against Youth. CAY for short. It is my unit, within the Orange County Sheriff Department, and I am credited with starting it. There were just three of us, in the beginning. Then four, due to some of the things I accomplished. Now there are only three again, due to one thing at which I failed.

My name is Terry Naughton. I am forty years old, divorced and childless. Once, I had a son. And it was he, Matthew, who first invited me into the world of the small ones. He was five when he left here, and I was very close to him when he went away. That was two years ago. He is the not-so-secret reason for everything that I have done since that day. He is closer to me now than he ever was when he was here. Then, Matthew was living in a body of his own — a perfect, brown, strong little body that delighted me more than anything on earth. Now, he has only mine to live through, because I am the jealous protector of his soul. My old man's body is a far cry from his beautiful new one, I know. But heaven won't dare try to claim him until I have met The Horridus. I need Matthew inside me for that. I need his strength, his innocence, his laughter, his love.

One

"She'll like you."

Fathers, always proud of their girls.

Chet Alton was proud, with good reason. I'd seen Lauren's picture — a skinny ten-year-old with innocent eyes and a smile that looked just a little reluctant. Fair student. Well behaved. Quiet, observant, gentle.

"Makes up her own mind," Chet was saying, "on who she likes and who she doesn't. And she makes it up fast. But sometimes I have a talk with her, you know, because friends are friends."

Chet turned onto Tustin Avenue. I saw the white sedan in a parking lot, Johnny Escobedo and Frances White watching us go by before falling in. It was a clear, breezy April day, and inland Orange County passed across the windshield of Chet Alton's car with a hard specificity: blue sky, black asphalt, a white Transit Authority bus with an orange band around it, a row of tan palms with their heads bent.

Not far from here is where The Horridus abducted his first victim. She was found later out in a wilderness park — wearing a black velvet hood without eyeholes; a tunic of gauzy white netting that suggested the angelic; hands taped behind her back; wearing clothes not her own; bruised and dazed — but alive. She was five. I can't get within a few miles of a place where The Horridus has taken a girl without feeling the hairs on my neck bristle and a cool tightening of my scalp. He had taken his second by the time I was sitting in Chet Alton's car, and we didn't have a suspect. Few leads. Little evidence. And no suspect. Yet. Agent Mike Strickley at the FBI was due in with a profile for me the next day. And here I was, riding around with a small-time shit-wrap like Chet, doing what I could to get him off the street. It's hard to keep from getting furious.

"You okay, Art?" he asked me. "Seem kind of quiet."

"Thinking."

"Second thoughts kind of stuff?"

"Not that."

"May as well get the money part over with, then."

I was hoping to do this at the house. But I took the envelope out of my sport coat and set it on the gray plastic console between us. He let it sit there a minute, then picked it up and gave it a confirming squeeze.

"No reason to count it," he said. "This is about money, sure, because money makes things happen, but it's more about friends. Friends are all that matter. People like us."

Chet looked at me and gave me his fungoid grin, the Chet-likes-Chet grin he uses when pleased by himself. He's dark haired, pale and soft, has those fingernails that are manicured into hard little flips at the ends. A very clean man, physically. Well groomed. Suits, white shirts, bright ties. Dimples, and a smile that's morally bankrupt. He sells phone systems to businesses and made a little over sixty-five grand at it last year. Thirty-six, married twelve years, father of one. His real name is Alton Allen Sharpe. Priors for exposing a minor to harmful matter — his own obscene phone calls — pandering and lewd conduct, but nothing in his jacket for the last ten years. That was about to change.

"I'm glad we met, Chet."

The meet was accomplished months ago through "Danny," one of Chet's old friends, who ratted out Chet and his daughter in exchange for the DA's leniency in charging him. We got to Danny through an eavesdropping bartender, some long surveillance and a hard-earned phone tap. I'll lobby hard to have Danny's leniency deal revoked, once I've stripped him of every useful thing I can strip him of. I intensely dislike these people. And that's nothing, compared to what we'll throw at Chet. My mouth was dry and I had to keep from looking for Johnny and Frances in the side view.

"Me too, Art," he said.

11

For right now I am Art Means, an unemployed trust-funder with appetites not sanctioned by society, a man more curious than evil. It was a good cover, one I'd used before. I have the CDL, the credit cards, the initials engraved on an old pen I carry for Chet. He has not connected Art Means with Terry Naughton, and there's little way he could. He doesn't trust me, as a matter of course. There is, in fact, hardly a shred of honor among thieves.

Chet made a left on Collins. We were headed for a rented house with a pool that he and his wife, Caryn, maintain for people like me — the friends of Chet. Caryn furnished it. She will be there, with Lauren, when we arrive. So will Danny and one other man. Chet's program is, Caryn will barbecue and Lauren will maybe help a little, but mostly stay in her room. That's how she likes it. The men will eat, drink themselves ready and talk. After that, Caryn and Lauren will take over. Chet says we'll end it by ten, because Lauren's got school in the morning. He told me it was $1,500 for my first time, a "taster." After that, $2,000.

My program was different. We had the whole house wired for sound. The backyard patio and garage, too. The outside team had earphones and radios. Johnny, Frances and Louis would make their move as late as they could — we wanted Chet and Caryn and their

12

friends as deeply committed as we could get them. We'd have four uniforms out front for backup, two more on the street behind the house. The helicopter patrols were on orders to stay out of the sky around us unless we called them in, but if we did, they'd streak down like hawks. I also had my contact at County News Bureau — CNB — on standby, because I like to get my unit all the credit it deserves. The CNB cameras have been kind to us so far. There were also two state Youth Services officers, females, to take custody of Lauren. Lauren's real name is Linda Elizabeth, by the way. I was somewhat concerned about Chet's other friend — Marlon — who Chet says has a gun and an attitude. Usually, these child rapers aren't the type to carry. Usually, they're a friend of the family. Usually, they are precisely the kind of giggling pukes you would expect to find involved in something like this. Guys like Chet.

"This is a good time of year," said Chet. "All this sex in the air — the birds and the bees and the people. We got these sparrows at home, building a nest up in the eaves. Every spring they come back and do it. And every year, the birds grow and get feathers and look just like the adults — you can hardly tell them apart. Then they leave the nest. It takes them about four hours. One at a time. And while one is out at the edge of the sticks, checking out the world, getting ready to go, the other ones watch to see how he does it. I swear. And every year, the dog sits there and waits for the first bird to take off and fall into the bushes on his maiden voyage, and eats him. That first try at flying, you know, they hardly ever get it right. Then, when the next one tries, the dog eats him, too. Ate three out of four, last year. I set up a screen, but the dog pushed it down. Then I figured I'd go with the program — let nature do things her own way. You interfere with the natural world and all you do is make things worse. You interfere with natural desires and you get somebody like The Horridus."

His logic escaped me, but I agreed. "Yeah. Seems like you could put the dog in the garage or something."

"It's full of junk."

"Or the house."

"She's got fleas."

That's one thing you learn fast about creeps in general, and kiddy-sex creeps in particular: they've got an excuse for everything, a reasonable explanation why they can't do this, or have to do that. They're great rationalizers, and at some level they're convinced by their own arguments. On a deeper level, most of them are aware that their actions are shameful and repugnant. But their actions, of course, are never their fault, because they build these little reason-structures to justify and explain what they do, and the shame they should feel

14

runs off the roofs of those structures, just like rain. Inside, the creep stays dry. They've always got an angle.

Chet turned off the radio. I looked at his soft, pale fingers and the manicured little flip of his nails. They looked aerodynamic. We headed right on Lilac and left on Daffodil. Daffodil was a cul-de-sac and Chet's house was on the right, the first of three that made up the curve at the end of the street. The upside of a cul-de-sac is you know the exit route and it's easy to cover. The downside is it's hard to work without being obvious. Johnny and Frances were going to park on the other side of the wall that ran behind the houses, and listen in from there. They'd have to jump the wall when the time came. Louis was already parked near the entrance of the street, inside a van with a two-foot-long black plastic ant and the words "Countywide Pest Control" on each side. The ant is magnetized and removable. We have another set of signs for carpet cleaning, but I like to use the ant for busts because it's been lucky for us. Chet looked at the van as we drove by.

"Could get them to spray for fleas, maybe," he said.

"It really stinks up the house," I said. The less attention Chet paid the exterminators the better. "Probably not worth it for a couple of sparrows. I guess Lauren must be an animal lover."

"Yeah. Wanted a horse once. Looking forward to seeing her?"

"Got to be honest, Chet — I am."

"That's what it's all about, friend."

Chet hit the opener on his visor and up went the garage door. We parked inside, next to a Chevy, and the door closed behind us. Coming in from the sharp optics of springtime, it was a little hard to see. In the corner stood a set of golf clubs in a red and white bag with red-knit head covers. Chet had met Danny in the country club bar. There were five large cardboard boxes, neatly stacked beside the clubs. A few garden tools on wall hangers. *This* garage was not full of junk at all, I thought: the privacy of pulling his car in and out is much too important.

We went into the house. The living room was newly carpeted in light blue and had plump, oak-accented furniture that was heavy and graceless. The couch was beige. There was a tin vase on the coffee table with silk or paper daisies inside. There were brass-framed prints of flowers on the wall. The wall was papered in wide vertical bands of white with little flowers in it, separated by narrower stripes of dark blue. Homey and trite, cheaply cheerful.

A sliding glass door opened to a backyard charged with sunlight. A woman with yellow hair and two men reclined on chaise longues with drinks in their hands. A low table beside the woman had bottles and an ice bucket on it. The pool glittered light blue and silver. A woman's laugh, uncannily piercing, bounced off the water and through the screen door to us. The men chuckled. When Chet slid open the door, all three heads were already turned our way.

Chet introduced us. Danny, an associate professor of mathematics at a local private college, was fifty and distinguished looking, slender from a diet of cigarettes and gin. He gave no sign of knowing me. Marlon was sad faced, big shouldered and slow. A bright green and yellow Hawaiian shirt with parrots on it hung over him. Late twenties. Beneath his lugubrious eyebrows, his blue eyes were fast and anxious. We didn't shake hands: sex criminals generally don't like to touch or be touched by strangers. Neither do I. Caryn was mid-thirties. Her yellow hair was cut big — blown and sprayed back from her face like the *Cosmo* models of some years ago. She had smooth skin and a receding chin made worse by big teeth. After she smiled she closed her mouth down pretty quick, like her teeth might get away. She was short legged and full in the chest, and all the hair made her look topheavy. Her voice was a rasp, vaguely southern.

"Well, nice to finally meet you, Art. Chet here's been telling me all about you." Her voice was friendly and open while her dark brown eyes narrowed to study me hard. "Whatcha drinkin'?"

"Scotch and soda, if you have it."

"We can handle that." She started making the drink. "Chet tells me you're an investor?"

"I do have a few investments. Conservative stuff, mostly just mutual funds. Some munis, so long as the Fed rates stay down. Some company stock."

"Like it strong?"

"Please."

"She's going to like you."

"I'm still a little —"

She handed me a clear highball glass with a silhouette of the Manhattan skyline on it.

"— Drink up, Art. It's a good way to get yourself comfortable. Drink all you want, just so's it doesn't make you mean."

"Thanks, Caryn."

Her dark little eyes bore into me suddenly. "No rough stuff, Art. I mean none."

"Chet told me."

"Now I'm telling you again."

"That's not me."

Her eyes stayed hard but her teeth escaped into a smile. "I'm not gonna win any mom-of-the-year award, but I keep a close eye on my girl."

"That's the way it should be."

"That's the way it is here."

Caryn's hard gaze dissolved as she looked over at Danny. He nodded and lifted his drink.

"You know, Art," she said, "you're going to have to give me some tips on investing. I want to make some good money. I got to thinking about starting an emu ranch. They're worth a lot of money. You know, those big birds they got out now?"

"Steer clear of that, Caryn. It's more like a pyramid scheme. Plus, who the hell's going to buy an emu from you?"

"One egg feeds a family of five."

"Where you going to find a family that eats emu eggs?"

"Internet, maybe? Beats me."

She crunched some ice from her drink. "I've been wanting to get into stocks my whole life. Something safe, but something with a good payback. My bank CDs are getting like, well I'm not sure, but those stocks I hear are going up 20 percent and all."

"Well, some of them are, Caryn. The thing to remember is a lot of those stocks weren't up at all last year. Stocks should be long term. If you want to play them short for a big return, well, that's where you get burned. Still beat emus, though."

She seemed somehow burdened by this idea. "The little guys, like Chet and me, we ought to have some way of getting profits like the big boys. He works hard. I work hard. Get to the end of the year and what do you have? Same as you started the year off with. Lauren's chippin' about college already. I don't even know if she's smart enough. But it costs real bread."

"There's a couple of education trusts that are —"

"— Want to see her?"

"Uh . . . yeah."

Caryn led me back into the living room and down a short hallway. We stood outside the door on our right. Caryn raised her fist and knocked as she pushed open the door. "Sweetie? Lauren? This here's Art, one of our new friends?"

Chet had said she was ten, and he wasn't lying. Pedophiles usually round the age down. Lauren was cute in a plain, wholesome way, slender and rather tall. She stood there beside the bed at loose attention, her hands folded behind her back and her feet turned in, looking not quite at me and not quite away. She had her mother's dark eyes and nice skin. Dad's dark hair. Caryn had dressed her in a simple blue smock dress, white socks turned down and red canvas tennies with cartoon characters on them. Her hair was parted in the middle and tied off in two opposing pigtails that fell to her shoulders. The pigtails are a well-known deviant's delight, and I was instantly furious at Lauren being turned out by this woman next to me, her mother. Lauren was the picture of innocence, and I wanted to run out of the house with her and take her someplace where her childhood could be removed like a bad part and replaced with a new, better one.

One of my faults is that I feel children are precious. There was a TV going in the corner — music videos — and an open textbook on the bed. Dangling from the closet door were a couple of clothes hangers with a skirt and blouse on them, still packaged in clear plastic from the cleaners. In another corner stood a full-length mirror framed by those makeup lights you see backstage.

"Oh. Hi."

Chet had told me he "started her" when she was two, taking pictures of her naked, getting her "used to things." He gradually escalated the touching to include himself. He turned her to friends for profit when she was six — more pictures, more touching. She really took to it. Anything you wanted. Chet had ruined an entire life. In that moment, if he had been there with us, I would have had to restrain myself from pushing him into the hallway out of his daughter's sight and killing him bare-handed. I knew there was no way that Lauren would ever have her childhood replaced with a better one. It would be her foundation for-ever, a nightmare from which she could never quite awaken, a painful haze through which she sleepwalked the daily thing called her life. Lauren had the resigned eyes and the aura of passive invincibility found in nearly all chil-dren who have escaped to the last place they can go — to the private, silent cave of their own selves.

She looked at me very briefly, and I looked very briefly back, trying to tell her with my eyes that I was not what she thought I was. But I could tell by the way she looked away that she already knew who I was, and why I was here. There are few more heartbreaking expressions in the world than that of a child who has given up hope on you.

"Your dad tells me you're a good student," I said.

She shrugged, her gaze fell to the carpet and she mumbled, "Pretty good."

"What's your favorite subject?"

"Art."

"His name is Art, honey. Isn't that nice?"

"I know," Lauren answered, with a slow glance at her mother and just a hint of impatience.

"You like that," I asked, "the drawing and painting?"

"It's all on computer. I made a picture."

"Show him," said Caryn.

Lauren stepped over to her dresser and took a piece of paper off the top. It was kind of a montage, like kids used to make with construction paper and clips from magazines. There was an image of desert sand dunes at night, blue in the light of a full moon, one of those mood shots used to advertise perfume, or maybe a utility vehicle. I guess she'd scanned it in first. Then there were small smiling faces within the dunes — models and movie stars. At the bottom was a candle in a shiny gold candleholder, and the flame seemed to be reaching up into the desert and lighting the faces looking out of the sand.

"That's really something," I said. I didn't have to fake my admiration at all — I was truly befuddled that a ten-year-old could make such a sophisticated piece of work on a computer. I held the piece out and studied it. I told her I had a computer at home, but it was always giving me problems and flashing up options I didn't call for and didn't know what to do with.

She looked at me with her calm, subdued eyes. "Click help."

"Help?"

"On the toolbar. Help. Then do what it says."

"Well, thanks. I'll remember that."

She took back the sheet and set it on top of the dresser. Then she hiked herself onto the bed and looked at me, then at her mother. "I've got the stomachache," she said.

"Ah, honey, I'll get you something for it. Don'tcha worry about a thing. Come on, Art, let's go make up something good for Lauren's tummy. See you in a while, sweetie. Say good-bye to Art for now."

" 'Bye, Art."

"Good-bye, Lauren."

In the kitchen, Caryn mixed up Lauren's medicine: a big mug of whole milk, with a shot of chocolate liqueur, a shot of cheap bourbon and some cinnamon sprinkled on top. She put it in the microwave to warm it up.

"Settles her stomach," said Caryn. "She . . . really likes it."

Not even Caryn could look at me as she said this. I watched her quick little smile come and go, and she opened the microwave and handed me the cup. "Take it to her, and don't touch."

I knocked on her door and waited for her to say something. I heard the book shut, then the rustling of fabric on fabric. She opened the door and looked up at me. I held out the mug to her and tried again, with my eyes, to tell her I was not who she thought I was. She took the cup in both hands and sipped some, her eyes focused down at the liquid like a kid will do. Then she looked up at me again and smiled just a little. A smile of invitation. She cocked her head and closed her eyes slowly, then opened them again about halfway in a sleepy, bedroom look — a gesture so startling I wanted, again, to just grab her and make a run for it. Daylight. Freedom.

"Hang in there," I said.

"Why?"

"Because I'm asking you to."

I had to wonder what my team, picking up every word that was said in here, made of this statement.

"You have to talk to Mom."

"I will. Believe me."

"I do what she says. And Dad says."

"It's going to be all right."

She looked at me with her dark dead eyes and shut the door.

An hour later the men were drunk and eating hamburgers and store-bought potato salad. I drank right along with them, but I can hold a lot of booze and not show it. The evening had turned cool so everyone had on light coats or sweaters. The sun was still a half an hour from setting and I pictured Johnny and Frances sitting in their car, just beyond the cinder-block wall that ended the backyard. I pictured Louis in the black antmobile, dressed in his exterminator's costume with his automatic in the big radio holster. I pictured Lauren sitting on her bed, watching videos, drinking milk and bourbon to dull her nerves against the things to come.

Marlon drained his fifth or sixth highball. He finished grilling me about stock market ideas and asked if the Brandywine Fund is really all it's cracked up to be. He paused, then laughed overloud when I told him it was a good fund, but too much of it could impair his ability to drive or operate machinery. His face was covered in a light brown beard that matched his hair, and the whole thing kind of crinkled in on itself when he laughed. His eyes were nervous again when he stopped.

"What do you do, Marlon?"

"Caryn, can I build another one of these?"

She looked at him and told him to build away, and another one for her, too — rum and Coke, mostly rum. I watched him lumber to the drink table. When he reached out for a bottle I saw his shirt catch on something at his hip.

"I'm a supervisor at the school district," he said. "Got about thirty janitors under me."

"Sounds like good work."

"Pays the bills."

This talk is nearly all lies, and we all know it, but that is how things are done. The names are false, the occupations invented, the interests faked. It's partly for security — in case any one of them is popped or propositioned by law enforcement; it's partly the logical stance from men who, on one level, are deeply ashamed of what they do. Occasionally, you'll find a deviant who feels no shame at all, no remorse for his acts. Danny, whom we flipped quite easily, is not one of those. My guess is that Marlon is not, either, and that the handgun under his shirt is just another compensation for his profound and thorough inadequacies. I didn't make him for the kind of guy who would have the nuts to use it, but I've been wrong before. Chet is the real catch here, the sociopath, the only one cold enough inside to turn a profit on perversion, with his daughter as the product. Caryn is driven by greed, low intelligence and by hatred of the girl her husband prefers over her. Like most people who do this kind of thing, both Chet and Caryn were probably used sexually as youngsters themselves, came from measurably terrible childhoods that they will never outgrow. They're passing down the legacy to Lauren now, and, in the spirit of free enterprise, making it pay.

Danny kept to himself and no one said much to him. He seemed to feel superior to us all, but from the nonreaction of the others I gathered it was his usual way. My little Judas, counting down the minutes, guzzling down the gin. I had assured him that if he failed me even in some small way, his leniency deal would be shot and I'd personally see to it that they threw the book at him and plastered his picture all over the newspapers and TV. This guy's got a wife and two grown kids, and a tenured position. I'd never dealt with a more agreeable subject. All he had to do now was wait. He looked distressed, though. Maybe he just wanted to be in Lauren's room one more time in his life.

Chet reclined, gulped his drink and watched us. He smiled slyly at me a couple of times, a can-you-believe-this smile, trying to welcome me to the club. Caryn waited on him, bringing him his dinner on a real plate — the rest of us had paper and plastic. She moved mechanically, like her responsibilities could quickly overwhelm her if she didn't stay in control. I tried to guess how many times they'd done this. And I sensed it was time to make my move.

I rose and slid my chaise next to Chet's. He gave me a not-in-the-program look. I wanted to get the heart of this transaction for the tape for the DA. I sat on the edge and leaned toward him confidentially.

"I'm afraid Lauren won't like me," I said.

Chet's eyes narrowed as he vetted my intentions. "She likes who I tell her to like."

"But, well, are you sure she'll like me?"

"What's wrong with you, Art?"

"I just told you."

"Look, if it's you you're worried about, just let her do her thing. She knows what to do."

"I'm thinking that fifteen hundred is going to seem pretty expensive if she's scared or not turned on."

"Art, we covered this already. If you're scared then I'll take you home right now. But this is a professional operation here, so I'm going to keep that money of yours either way. You need to have this kinda shit settled before you come over."

I nodded and looked down at the patio. "I'm all right."

"You're all right, Art."

"Just . . . you know . . . first-time jitters."

"Make yourself another drink, man. Relax. We're adults doing adult things. Nobody's doing anything they don't want to. Fuckin' relax, man, you're making me nervous."

"Got it."

I stood up and dragged the chaise longue back where it was, regarded the pool for a moment, then started making another drink. Chet was looking at me and I didn't like the silence around it.

Caryn was eyeing me, too.

And then Marlon.

Danny was trying hard not to.

"Hey, babe," Chet said to Caryn.

"Yeah, babe?"

She had just sat down with her paper plate of food. He nodded his head toward the house and she got back up, setting her plate on the drink table.

He grinned at me. I grinned back.

Caryn walked toward the house with an air of self-conscious drama. It was her gait, I think, that suggested the importance of what she was doing — deliberate and measured but not slow, like she was walking between walls of flames, like this was a mission only she could accomplish, like the world really needed her now.

She went inside for about twenty minutes, and when she came back, Lauren was with her.

They'd dressed her in a short black skirt and red heels. Her face was made up and her lips painted, and perhaps most revolting of all, they'd left her little pigtails alone and they stuck out from her whore's paint job as a monument to her childishness. No, what was most revolting was the change in her personality now, the way she changed like any girl trying on her mother's clothes, playacting her vision of womanhood, performing her concept of how a woman acted and how a woman walked and how she looked at you. And I could see that Linda Elizabeth Sharpe, age ten, had been trained to believe that a woman was an object to arouse men. A painted, alluring item. A fuck in red heels.

She walked past me. I could smell perfume and a trace of booze on her. She stopped at the drink table, sloshed a little bourbon into a plastic cup, twirled and drank it.

"Wooh!" Marlon yelped quietly. "Hot stuff!"

Lauren smiled and set down the cup. She walked over to Chet and pecked him on the cheek.

Danny stood up then. He swayed a little, but he had a matter-of-fact expression on his face. I should have seen it coming, but I hadn't.

Suddenly it was over, and it was too late.

"Chet," he said loudly. "Art's a cop."

My heart was slamming in my eardrums.

"Not funny, my man," I said.

Chet froze a look at me.

Marlon shifted his big body around and his

30

hand came out with a revolver. "I thought he was a cop the second I saw him. Chet?"

"Boys," said Caryn, her rasp brittle with nerves. "*Boys?* Put up that thing, Marlon, for godsakes —"

"— Shut up!" said Danny, stepping to Marlon. "Give me the gun, fatso. I'll prove what he is."

Chet stood up. "One — Marlon, put that thing away. Two — Caryn, get Lauren in the house. Three — Art, you stay exactly where you are, friend."

"Lighten up, Chet," I said. "You too, Marlon. If I was a cop, the last thing you'd want to do is bring out a gun."

But Marlon, red faced now and sweating hard, pointed the big revolver at me, right at my chest. *"Cop!"*

"Come on," I said. "What is this, something you guys pull on the first-timers? Marlon, don't point that thing at *me*. Chet . . . what's going on here? I didn't pay good money to —"

"He's a cop!" hissed Danny. "Tapped my phone. Made me set you guys up. Said he'd get me on the news if I didn't, wreck my whole family. His name's Naughton."

Chet looked at me, then at Danny. His gears were meshing.

It all happened at once. Johnny grunted to the top of the cinder-block wall on the far side of the pool. Marlon turned his head to the sound and Danny smashed his fist down onto

31

the big man's wrist. Caryn whispered *shit* and ran. Danny picked up Marlon's revolver and looked at me, slurred *I'm gone* and blew a hole in his temple. His head jerked one way and a spout of dark blood wobbled out the other. He slumped over on the pool deck. Chet had already jumped the drink table and disappeared inside the house. Marlon held his wrist and lumbered toward the screen door, his eyes big and his mouth open in a silent O. I grabbed Lauren on her way by and fell on her. She screamed, then sunk her teeth into my face. I got my hand over her mouth. When I looked up Chet was hauling back out of the house with a little automatic in his hand. Marlon trailed him, blubbering. Louis the exterminator screamed from behind them — *Sheriffs, freeze!* Chet stopped at the pool and looked at Johnny and Frances, drawn down across the water from him. Then he reeled back for a look at the house. Marlon had already proned himself out, his arms over his head. Chet looked at me. *Don't shoot,* he said. He dropped the gun and put up his hands. *I want my lawyer.* Caryn's vulgar rasp grated from inside the house and then I could see her — all hair and flailing fists — thrashing in the grip of Louis, who pushed her through the open screen door, down to the patio deck, and cuffed her.

Underneath me, Lauren was crying. I could smell the bourbon on her breath and feel her wet face against my neck. I cradled her head in my hand, but I was careful not to hold her too tight. I knew that I had done something good. I couldn't keep from thinking of Matthew.

Two

I watched us on County News Bureau that night with Melinda. CNB gave us the good spin, playing the suicide like an incident that tarnished an otherwise heroic op. I was warm with pride, though my cheek was throbbing from Lauren's teeth and the six stitches it took to close the two punctures. Bites hurt. CNB was careful not to show my face on camera, but not because of the blood. Our arrangement is that I am not to be revealed. That's how I can continue to get away with things like today.

The reporter was Donna Mason, and she was her usual lovely self, calm and somehow dignified in her role as a digger of dirt. For the last two months, since The Horridus started his campaign here in the county, the media's been eager for anything with kids and sex. That old taboo has been broken, or at least suspended for a while. So Donna Mason really let the Sharpes and Marlon have it. Her cameras ambushed them being led from the house, and of course, you can't cover your face when your hands are cuffed behind your back. The CNB shooters tracked the miserable trio all the way to the Sheriff van. Got an angle on Marlon crying like a child. I had told Donna not to tape Lauren, and she had been good to her word. She always has been. So far.

Melinda brought me another tequila on ice. My drink of choice. She curled onto the sofa a few feet away from me, and gently brushed my cheek with her fingertips.

"That's good work, Terry," she said.

"Well . . . thanks."

"How close was Marlon to shooting you?"

"I don't think he would have."

"The girl going to be okay?"

I looked at her and sighed. "No."

CNB started in with a sidebar on Danny — Dr. Christopher Muhlberger, professor of mathematics — and the shocking secret life he might have led. I thought of his family and felt bad. I thought of him taking his own life in the backyard of a rented house and felt bad about that, too. I am long on compassion for the innocent, but there is always a little left for the guilty, too. Maybe this is a flaw in my character. But it's not to say I wouldn't tear the lungs out of any criminal who harms a child. I have and I will again. It's my reason for being. But after the death of Matthew two years ago, everyone and everything became, to me, somehow forgivable. I can't tell you why.

"That didn't have to happen to him," I said. "I could have disarmed the fat guy and it wouldn't have gone down that way. The prof didn't even have the guts to bring his own piece. Drunk. Scared. I could have seen it coming."

"You did what needed doing. He blew out his own brains, Terry. You didn't."

"I still think there was something I could have done."

"Precious little, Naughton."

As an investigator — Fraud and Computer Crime — Melinda's judgment of me can cut deeply. She knows my world and its limitations, and she can flatten me not only as a woman but as a professional equal. In fact, she is not my equal: she's a sergeant 4, one grade above mine of sergeant 3. She's two years older and at least ten wiser. More to the point, Melinda feels no compassion whatsoever for the wicked or the inept. I believe this comes from her own sense of victimhood. Her mother died when she was young and her father abandoned her when she was six. She feels the pain of the innocent. And she feels the fury of the wronged. In fact, in our year of domestic life together I have seen her almost consumed by that pain and fury. Maybe the fact that she can feel so much for the innocent reduces her pity for the guilty. I can be touchy about her comments on me and my work. Melinda is a hard woman to please in most ways, so success with her is all the sweeter.

"Thanks, Mel."

"Don't beat yourself up."

"Am I a liberal?"

"A real do-gooder."

"A pinko?"

"A commie."

"A poet?"

"A queen."

"You pour a mean drink, Melinda."

"Got to keep you up with me."

"You keep me up."

"I'll bet she could, too."

Donna was on-screen again for her wrap. I looked at Melinda, then back to the tube. I will mention now, then forever hold my peace, that Melinda is a jealous companion. In some ways this pleases me. And she can joke about it now. Like this crack about a TV reporter. But it never hurts to set things straight.

"Not my type."

"Too young and beautiful?"

"It's not the youth and beauty. She's just not you."

"You're a world-class liar, Terry."

"I know."

"At least you're honest."

"Look at Louis and Johnny there, see how long they . . ."

On-screen, Johnny and Louis stood at the curb until they realized the camera was pointed their way, then hustled off-screen. Frances did most of the talking for us — she's well spoken, credible and unabashedly ambitious to rise in the ranks. Truth be told, though, it was hard not to look at Donna Mason. Maybe that's why they gave her the job.

"Freshen up that drink, Terry?"

"Thought you'd never ask."

Penny, Melinda's daughter, came out of her room around nine. She'd been doing homework. She's a natural student, very much like her mother in the long, silent intensities she can bring to things. She's nine, chunky and pretty like her mom, with straight blond hair and placid gray eyes. Penelope Anne. A year ago we began the hesitant dance of getting to know each other closer than friends, but not as father and daughter. She has a continuing relationship with her real father, and I would never try to compete or interfere with that. He's a loving, if self-serving soul, and she needs him. My son, Matthew, would have been seven. Well, in August.

She sat down between us with her laptop computer and shook her head. "Microsoft Word sucks."

"Don't use that word," I said.

"But it's *called* word."

"You know what I mean, young lady."

Her mother pulled the little machine onto her own lap and looked at the flip-up screen. She tapped in a few commands and tilted the screen toward Penny. "It's the Windows that's throwing you, not the word processing program. See, you've got too much open, the thing just got clogged. You've got to go through and close them, one at a time, or, you can use this."

She showed Penny the right command and set the computer back on her daughter's lap. Frankly, I'm amazed that any nine-year-old can learn to operate a computer at all, not to mention two word processing programs, three data operating systems and God knows how many different keyboards, printers, CD readers and floppy backups. I wonder if they stock the classrooms with these things to educate kids or just to sell them similar gadgets when they're adults. I asked Penny what subject she was on.

"Science," she answered. "I'm learning the planets. Before that, I finished my report on slavery."

Computers. Planets. Slavery. The world of a healthy, somewhat privileged American nine-year-old.

"Your face looks sore, Terry," she said, looking up from the screen. "It's turning blue, like a bruise."

"It is a bruise."

"Did they arrest the girl who bit you?"

"They'll put her in protective custody. Later, depending on what happens to her parents, she'll go with relatives, or maybe to an institution."

"What did she do wrong?"

I thought about that a second. "Nothing, really."

Melinda looked over, her eyes condemning me over the tops of her reading glasses.

"Then you try," I said to her.

She shifted her body and reached out to touch Penny's hair.

"*Don't,* Mom. What did the girl who bit Terry do *wrong,* to get put institution?"

"Put *in an* institution," Melinda corrected.

"Okay. *In an.* What did she do?"

"She became a prostitute. That's when you sell your body for money, or other consideration."

"To do what with?"

"It depends."

"Why did she become that?"

"Her father and mother forced her to. So they'll go to jail. She was lucky that Terry was there, to arrest her parents."

Penny looked at me, understandably concerned that cops taking parents away from their children was good luck. I shrugged. Melinda will sail Penny into moral oceans that no nine-year-old can be expected to navigate. Mel believes in treating children as the adults they will become. I believe in treating them like the children they will never be again. This difference of opinion is occasionally hard for us to live with. But because Penelope is not my daughter, I almost always defer to Melinda.

Though I still didn't think a nine-year-old needed to be an expert in the California Penal Code.

My ex-wife believes I never protected my own beautiful son from the "real" world enough, and I agree. I admit that I allowed him to do some of the things he wanted to, foreseeing the hurt he might suffer in the trying. Those tears of his still move me. He was a timid boy in most ways, and I wanted to encourage his confidence. I've changed now, far too late to do him any good. If I had it to do all over again, I would have handled it differently. I truly wish that the living, seven-year-old Matt Naughton was here right now to prove that I had been a good father. Or a bad one; I don't care. Just *here*.

We watched TV for another hour. A little after ten, Melinda told Penny it was time for bed. Penny protested but not very hard, because Melinda is inflexible on household rules, and Penny knows it.

"I want *Terry* to tuck me in," she said.

"Then ask *Terry* to tuck you in," said Mel, and she walked out of the living room and into the kitchen.

An hour later I found Mel in her study. She does a lot of work at home. Since being assigned to the Fraud and Computer Crime detail two years ago, she's gone from being computer illiterate to computer devoted. I keep waiting to catch her playing solitaire, or watching a CD, or browsing consumer products on the Net, but I've never found her doing anything but work on her machine, or sometimes writing letters. For Melinda, work is peace. She is not a person who enjoys many things, but work is one of them. No surprise that in two years she's worked her way to second in command of Fraud and Computer Crime — a twelve-person section.

She looked up at me when I went in, and let her reading glasses dangle on the chain around her neck.

"Tired?" she asked.

"Not really. I'm going to take Moe up the hill. Want to come?"

"I've got work."

She studied me for a moment. She has a clear-eyed, analytical gaze that gathers much more than it gives away. I'd hate to be one of her suspects in an interrogation. In fact, I've seen her work — through the one-way mirrors — and she is extremely effective. But her stare melted into a smile and she nodded her head slightly.

"Nice work today, Terry. Four months to nail that creep. And you ended up doing something decent for the girl. You should feel good about you."

"Thanks, Mel. I do. But I think about the life Chet took away from her."

"You can't be everywhere at once."

I stepped forward and kissed her lips. I didn't hold it long because I knew she had work to do. Those lips are sweet as sugar when she wants them to be. Just six months ago we were to the point of going weeks or more without anything more intimate than a peck on the cheek — if that. Mel was a wreck. Her father had died. And though he had avoided her in childhood like some guilty secret, she had tracked him down and stayed in touch with him in a remote but regular way the last few years of his miserable life. His death hit her hard. And I realized that the end of someone you desperately want to love you but never did can hurt as much as that of someone who treasures you. Maybe it's just one last confirmation of your own unlovability. But Melinda's inner darkness gradually broke, and something of her old self has emerged from the long, black night.

"See you soon," I said.

Our house is on Canyon Edge, the fifth one in from Laguna Canyon Road. It's a ramshackle little place, built in three stages, over three decades, in three "styles" — none of which I can really define. But it was affordable for Mel and me as co-buyers, and the money is worth the quiet canyon life and the beautiful Pacific, which is just a couple of miles away. In the big fire of '93, it was one of only eight houses on Canyon Edge that didn't burn down. Thirty-seven were reduced to nothing but fireplaces and chimneys that day in October.

I let Moe out of the backyard and we headed down Canyon Edge, away from Laguna Canyon Road. The road is crooked and uneven, without streetlights and sidewalks, but it also has almost no traffic because it dead-ends a half mile into the canyon. Once we were past the last rebuilt house I stood for a moment on the scorched foundation of Scotty Barris's place. Scotty didn't rebuild because he wasn't insured. It was an old place, the oldest on the street, built by Scotty's father and uncles back in the early twenties. Now it's just a rectangle of black cement with weeds growing up through it and some twisted rods of rebar bent at odd angles. For sale.

Past the black foundation you pick up a trail in the high weeds and climb a steep embankment. The trail levels off, then meanders back down to the canyon floor and follows a creek bed that is dry except after a rain. Moe led the way. He's a real dog's dog when it comes to the outdoors, always in the brush after birds or critters — true to his Labrador instincts. I've never hunted him. I quit shooting things for sport when Matthew died, just another one of those things I used to love to do and then didn't love anymore. I miss the taste of quail and dove and pheasant. I miss those evenings when I'd take the birds out of the marinade and Ardith would make the salad and rice and

44

Matthew would blunder around in the kitchen with his plastic swords or superhero gear.

We headed up the creek bottom. In the black sky a sliver of moon rocked on its back. The stars looked close. The hills rose up and away in the distance, and their shapes were black like the sky but without stars in them.

Around the first big bend the trail starts uphill again, rimming around the sandstone hill, winding up. It's steep and narrow. It passes through a canopy of scrub oak and lemonadeberry that you have to duck through and walk with your hands in front of you so your face doesn't get scratched. I could feel Lauren's gift on my cheek, and it pulsed hard when I bent my head toward the ground. Then, on the far side of the trees, the trail opens into a nice flat outcropping of sandstone where you can look out to the city to your left, Laguna Canyon Road straight in front, and the dark hills on the right. Below is a long drop. Behind you is a hill face pocked with big and little caves that far-flung families of the Juaneño Indians lived in centuries ago. You wonder if they chose this steep abode for safety or beauty, or both.

The smallest cave on the left holds my hiking provisions — a quart bottle of good Herradura, a coffee cup and a wooden box of Dominican cigars. I keep them in a pillowcase, which is stuffed way back, behind a sleeping bag I bought just for this place. Some months ago, when I first found the caves, I liked to smoke and drink in the big one, way back inside where the Juaneños used to be. I'd listen for their souls brushing against the rock. It was a mess when I found it — all beer cans and trash, an old mattress, skin mags — the usual things adolescents would drag into their den. But after I cleaned it out, no one ever seemed to go there again. Maybe that generation of kids had outgrown the caves and gone on to serious things like colleges or jobs. At any rate, I finally got tired of being inside it, and moved my recreations to the flat outcropping in front, unless it's raining hard.

I'm not exactly sure why I come here. Melinda doesn't mind my tequila, or even cigars, so long as I smoke them outside, which is where I like to smoke them anyway. She's never expressed worry about Penny seeing me do such things, though I have my own concerns about that. In fact, Melinda has come out here with me a few times and matched me drink for drink. No, the reason I come here has more to do with solitude and liberty — the same things that the teenagers used to come here to enjoy. And it has a lot to do with the memory of Matt, which is always more alive up here, more specific and present. When I spend the night here, which I did a lot last summer, I unroll the sleeping bag in the deepest part of the cave and, with Moe curled up beside me, sleep deeply. Often, when I wake up, I won't remember where I am or how I got here or why I didn't just walk home to my companion and bed. I've awakened other places than the cave and had no memory of how I got there either. This is due to somewhat massive tequila intake. Luckily, I have an iron constitution and always wake up before dawn, whether I can see the sun or not, whether I've slept eight hours or forty minutes. And not once in the year I've been doing this has a neighbor seen me stealing back to my home in the accusing dark before sunrise. So far as I know. I drink because it makes me happy and peaceful. Most of the time. God created booze to keep us Irish from taking over the world.

Frankly, I don't sleep out here much anymore. The worst of it was six months back, when Mel was in her own darkness about her dad and I was culminating a year and a half of ardent self-destruction. I have more to live for now. Mel is better. Ardith is going to be all right. Matt won't come back no matter how bad I feel. My work is more important to me than ever. Beginning six months ago, at my lowest point, I began to find a way to love this world again. I'm fine now.

So I sat and smoked and drank a little. Not a lot. I thought of my last day with Matthew, how bright and hot it was, how the water was so blue and calm. The kind of day that seemed like it could last a hundred years and nothing would ever go wrong. I thought about how limp and cool he felt, then how rigid and strong, then how terrifyingly relaxed. You can play things over in your mind a million times, even put different endings on them, but in the long run it won't do you any good. They tell us to imagine the world we want to see, but how can you unimagine something you've already looked at? Matthew was my first real loss in life. My parents are still alive, still married. Up until Matt went away, I still had the vague, youthful notion that nothing bad would happen to me and the people I loved, for a long, long time. In the last two years I've tried to accommodate the facts and the givens. I haven't been very good at it, but I'm getting better.

I thought of Danny's surprise ending and wondered if I should have seen it coming. I tried to weigh the heaviness in my heart for him, but there really wasn't much there. With all the good people in the world who suffer, it's hard to bleed much for the creeps who suffer along with them. Still, you don't see an act like that and not feel something for the suffering animal that carried it out. But feel what?

I looked to the west and imagined The Horridus, out there, waiting, planning. White male, with wavy, "reddish blond" hair. For his second abduction he drove a red van that was seen by the girl's disbelieving mother. He takes them late night or early morning, knows the bedroom, cuts out the screen and a hand-sized hole to unlock the window. Opens it, climbs through and grabs the girl. Then out the door. His first time — the first time we know about, anyway — he was gone with the girl for six hours before her mother even knew what had happened. On the second, the mother heard something, woke up and found her daughter gone, saw a guy get into a red van then pull away from the curb. Both mothers have been single, but we don't know how he knows this ahead of time. I suspect he's ditched the van by now, traded it in on another one. Just a feeling. Both girls have had identical vehicle fibers on them. Late-model Chrysler/Plymouth/Dodge, according to the second mother. The van is where he does what he does, we believe. The clothes he puts on them are thirty years old and in very good condition. We know this from some lengthy product research and the fine work of our crime lab. In addition to the "vintage" clothing, each girl has been outfitted in a white gauzy tunic attached at the neck with a safety pin. It's made out of that netting you'd see in a ballerina's tutu, or a Halloween costume, or a wedding gown. It extends from neck to ankles and gives the victims a floating, angelic look. Each has been found wearing a black velvet hood without eyeholes. The hoods are made by hand, and there are two small holes way down toward the mouth area, probably to help supply air. The first girl, Pamela, was five, and the second, Courtney, six years old. He took them twenty-six days apart. He let them go within five hours of their capture, in remote state park or U.S. forest lands. He seems to know his way around. Other than that we don't have much. We'll get an FBI profile early tomorrow, but profiles, good as they are, are still speculation. When I think of The Horridus my heart beats hard and fast and I feel like all my senses have been stripped back to bare, efficient essentials. I feel like I'm growing fangs. He hasn't raped yet. And he hasn't killed yet, but I suspect that he'll graduate to both. What he hasn't done scares me more than what he has. Criminologists call it an escalating fantasy, though it is not a fantasy for anyone but the dreamer. I've read case histories where the fantasy is played out in different ways, different terms. It always gets worse. Now I'm actually seeing it happen, right here on my watch. I know he won't stop until he gets what he wants. And he won't stop after that, because he'll want it again. And again. And again.

Moe sat beside me for a while, alert, then groaned and lay down and fell asleep. When I started back the moon was gone and there was a damp breeze coming from the west with the smell of the ocean in it. As I picked my way down the trail I wondered what it would be like to tell Melinda I was going to leave her, and if I could do it.

Three

I was at my desk by six-thirty, third cup of
coffee going, rereading the note of thanks from
Donna Mason over at CNB. It was in my
e-mail. I got rid of that one fast — I don't like
my fellows here aware of my doings with the
media. It can be a perilous business and I like
to keep it to myself.

I was waiting for the call from Special Agent
Mike Strickley of the Investigative Support
Unit in Quantico. I'd met him eight years ago
at an FBI "road school" — training sessions
for law enforcement that the then Behavioral
Sciences Unit offered to local law enforcement. He'd told me to call them if I ever
needed them. After the second girl, Courtney,
I knew we had a serial offender and made the
call. I sent him the photographs of both girls,
their statements, videotapes of the release sites
and the forensic evidence we'd culled. That
was eight days ago, and Mike had faxed me
yesterday morning to say he'd be ready today.

I was pondering another angle on how The
Horridus was picking his victims. They were
both fair-skinned, light-haired anglos. One

with blond hair; one with red. They were ages five and six. They both lived with their single mothers except for occasional weekends with their fathers. They both had ground-floor bedrooms with windows not visible from the street. They both lived in Orange County, though he'd taken Pamela in Orange, which is central county, while for Courtney he'd gone south to San Clemente, near the San Diego County line. They were both abducted, held, then released wearing different clothes, with the aforementioned mesh robes and black velvet hoods. No signs of physical abuse other than light bruising on the upper extremities. No penetration, no bruising, no bleeding. No blood, skin or saliva left on them. No semen. They'd both been found with silver 3M duct tape cinched over their mouths. Acetate and wool/rayon blend fibers on the tape suggested that he carried it on his body somewhere, already stripped off, so as not to make any noise rasping it off the roll. He used a different shirt or jacket each time, a new or almost new one, to transfer as little evidence about himself as possible. He named himself for Courtney: written in felt pen on the inside of the tape over her mouth was the word, *Horridus*.

But I hadn't found the link between the girls that he had found. Age. Race. Single-parent households. Ground-floor windows away from the street. How did he know? We had checked, rechecked and checked again for the connection between the girls, the common plane along which he was hunting them. Different cities. Different schools. Different day care. Different friends, parks, pools, shopping places. Different worlds and different lives. But somewhere their lives came together, and it was my job to find that place and be there the next time he hunted it.

Strickley called at six forty-five and apologized for the early hour. I told him I hadn't been sleeping well anyway. We made small talk for about thirty seconds.

"I've looked over the material you sent me, and this is what I think. I'll be faxing this out to you when we're done, so you've got a hard copy, but I'm going to run it by you fast right now."

"I'm ready."

"Let me tell you something, Terry, you've got a genuine problem on your hands. He's intelligent, cautious and he's not going to stop until you take him out. This is a culmination for him, an arrival. He's made the breakthrough, done it twice and he's not turning back. It would be your call, but if you start putting on the pressure in some proactive way — which is what we usually recommend — we think he'll graduate to a rape/kill scenario. Or he'll leave and set up shop somewhere else. This is about control — control over the victims, you, us, everybody. My advice is not to publicize this profile. The more heat he feels, the tougher he's going to get. But it's your call out there, Terry."

"All right."

"Here he is: white male, late twenties to late thirties. The upper end puts him five years out of prime for this kind of pedophile, but the stalking and planning suggest maturity. Average height, slender. Physically presentable, maybe even attractive, this from the fact that he's seen the girls and their mothers and not raised any red flags. And from the wool/rayon fibers and the acetate, which probably come from sport coats. He's carrying the strips of duct tape inside. I'd guess a blazer because of the wool. The acetate is a common liner. I see a good chance he wears glasses. It's just one of those feelings, but he's bright and knows it and wouldn't mind presenting himself in an academic or intellectual light. Glasses have a gentling effect. He might have a physical defect that he hides under clothes — possibly a skin condition like eczema or dramatic birthmarks, herpes, possibly a deformity. That's one of the reasons he can't attach to mature females — he's sensitive about his appearance, but it's something that *doesn't show* in street clothes. That's why he blinds them with the hoods he makes, though the primary reason is to hide his face. Two years of college, maybe more — science and humanities. He had some Latin in school, almost certainly Catholic, that's where he first heard *horridus*. It's Latin for rough, or bristling, and it's used as a designator for animal species, specifically *Moloch horridus*, which is an Asian lizard, and *Crotalus horridus*, which is commonly known as the timber rattler. Look for him to be familiar with reptiles, maybe has a collection, or at least a library. Enjoys the outdoors. Has an extensive collection of pornography, mostly still photos, mostly young girls. He networks on the computer with others like him because he's after validation and free porn. An actual conscience on this one, Terry — the Catholicism, the way he dresses them before he turns them loose, the way he blinds them, the fact he doesn't kill them. He doesn't feel good about himself except when it's happening. Afterward, he spins down into a depressive phase. No military service. Lives alone. Never married. He'll have had many relationships with women, none longer than a few months, no longer in touch with them. He's around women a lot, but not closely — he's an observer, not a mingler. He will have had homosexual experiences while young, possible abuse by a relative or friend, very possibly by a man involved with his mother. He's white collar — clerical or retail. He might have artistic talent — visual, plastic arts — something he can make with his hands and see with his eyes. He makes the hoods and the gauze tunics, and they're done skillfully. He makes good enough money to support himself, drive a late-model van, maybe even own a home, dress well, look successful. His home will be free standing — not a condo type of thing. Probably rather large, fenced and overgrown. Look for a separate guest house or maid's quarters on the grounds. He'll follow you in the media but he's not likely to insinuate himself into the investigation. I doubt you've interviewed him yet. He's taking their clothes as trophies and replacing them with clothes that belong to him — maybe literally, maybe symbolically. Hates his mother because she treated him like a girl, tried to make him behave like one, probably dressed him like one. Rarely saw his father. He's had some precipitating stressor, something that pushed him over the edge. Death of a loved one. Something big."

I was silent for a long moment. Most of what Mike said made sense to me. I'd drawn my own conclusions, made my own speculations, tried to imagine this man from the evidence he had left us, and from the evidence he had not. As usual, the experts at the Bureau had left a flatfoot like me in the dust. I liked the body defect and the description of his house. They gave me something physical to go on.

"Still there, Terry?"

"Thinking."

"Let me say a few things. You have to understand that this guy is a bundle of powerful contradictions. It's a classic escalating fantasy

57

cycle he's in. He has the morality he learned in childhood colliding with hatred of his mother, and of the man or men who abused him when he was small. He has this powerful drive to connect with women, hitting up against his vision of himself as freakish and unlovable. He has heterosexual desire mixed up with his fear of women, and homosexual urges he's still trying to deny, feeding his self-loathing. That's why he goes so young on the girls, Terry — they're a way of punishing his mother for bringing him up in an effeminate way — it's the most forbidden act he can imagine, the most rebellious. But underneath it he's trying to make a statement of his heterosexual desires, though he's terrified of women. So he picks women who aren't women yet — he's going to make the sexual connection without any adult, human interaction at all. His conquests are so small he can tape their mouths and carry them right out of their houses — the pure control he needs to feel, his way of making the world behave the way he wants it to. Right now he's the culmination of probably twenty plus years of inner torment and outer placidity. He won't have any priors. You won't find him in the sex offenders' registry. I made a VICAP run anyway, and it came up dry. But he's made his change. He's consolidated himself, finally, into a more singular personality. And because of that decision, that choice to move from imagination to action, he's thrown himself into even greater stress."

"But you say he consolidated. He's become . . . whole."

"It's killing him. He hates himself even more now, and he's going through radical changes in behavior. I'd guess heavy drinking, or maybe an antidepressant, or both. If he wasn't nocturnal before, he is now. He's probably growing or cutting hair, growing or cutting a beard, maybe dyeing one or both. A change in wardrobe. Sharp changes in personality, to anyone who might notice, but there's a good chance that no one will, because he's alone, absolutely alone in this now. He'll have cut everyone off, except his anonymous, accepting peer group on the Web. Lurk the chat rooms — you might overhear something. Now this is a bit of a leap, but both my people came up with it — it's possible he'll have thought about selling the house. Clearing out. Change of scenery, change of behavior. Maybe he even listed it. If so, he'll be anxiously waiting for a taker. And while he waits, he smolders. So look for the incidence between events to shorten. According to our models he'll start raping, then killing. He won't confess, and if you arrest him he'll look for a way to kill himself. And of course, if there's a way out of it for him, he'll kill you to take it. Exercise extreme caution with this guy, Terry. He's dangerous and he's at the end of whatever tethers you can imagine — even his own. Good luck."

"Thank you."

"And call me when you score. We can help with an interrogation strategy, or we can drink a long-distance toast."

I thanked him again and hung up.

The fax came through ten minutes later, but Ishmael beat me to it. Ishmael is Jordan Ishmael, an administrative lieutenant who oversees all of the Crimes Against Persons units, including mine. He's two years older than me, forty-two, handsome like a panther and smart. He has black hair and green eyes, and teaches a special class in hand-to-hand combat for the Sheriff Academy. He's big in the way that professional baseball players are big — hands, head, legs.

Ishmael is a genuine power broker within the Sheriff-Coroner Division. His desire for the office of sheriff-coroner is no secret, and his rivals are few and meek. He helped me get hired on here when he was just a young deputy himself. He expected fealty, which I offered for a while, then got tired of giving. He has been a friend and champion of Melinda for as long as I've known her. For eight of those years he was her husband. He told me recently, in all seriousness, that if I ever tried to interfere with the welfare of his daughter, Penelope, he would break my neck with his bare hands. I'm slender and wiry and far from powerful, though I believe I could take him if I had to. Maybe that's just my Irish showing. More to the point, I can't stand him anymore, and he can't stand me.

"Here's your psychobabble," he said, dropping the uncut fax transmission onto my desk.

"Nice of you to deliver. What do you think?"

"I just said. Babble."

"Well, here's for your time. Thanks."

I held out a quarter by its edge and waited for Ishmael to react. He left.

If Ishmael wasn't a lieutenant and I wasn't good at busting the creeps who prey on children, the department might have transferred one of us off this floor a long time ago. A year ago to be exact, when I took up cohabitation with Ishmael's ex-wife. The fact that we chose to live together rather than marry probably prevented Personnel from acting — our arrangement is off the record, though well known.

Melinda is relatively free of the continuing vibe, working one floor down, in Fraud and Computer Crime. Ishmael still fawns over her. I doubt his sincerity with her. Inside, I suspect, a part of him must hate her. So far as my proximity goes, Ishmael is actually hamstrung by his own ambition: to lobby for my transfer or removal would make him look even more feudal and conniving than he is. I'm the thorn he can't pull out.

Something else is at work here, too. Namely, I've been talking with Sheriff-Coroner Jim Wade a lot about my future here at the department.

Jim is nearing retirement — another three years and he'll step down and into his well-earned golden years. He's arranging things like a dying man, setting his house in order for a smooth transition. Sheriff-Coroner is a nonpartisan office in Orange County, but it's an elected one, so the deep internal machinery that produces a winning candidate has to engage early to be effective. One of the greatest powers of any sheriff is to actively choose his own successor. Jim hasn't said anything of substance to me, so far. When we talk, it's like golf course talk without the golf. But there is something in the air, and I feel it and it is coming from Jim and his office.

Not that I'd be a likely successor, but I'm still completely floored by the attention.

For one, I'm nonpolitical. I'm not ambitious — at least I wasn't until Jim Wade began to murmur the quiet language of power into my ear.

Second, I'm not only not a family man, but I'm going through the uncommitted motions of family life with one of the department's best detectives, the ex-wife of the department's brightest lieutenant, and their daughter. I'm messy.

Third, I'm head of the division's smallest

and newest unit — Crimes Against Youth — that until recently was accorded neither respect nor recognition. Two years ago, we didn't exist at all. At first there was an attitude toward us, an attitude of snickering jocularity and prurient suspicion. It's the same one that gets aimed at a vice dick who's been on the job too long. People start to wonder why he's spending so much time with prostitutes, pimps, panderers and pornographers. Why doesn't he transfer out? Up? Hit the desk a while? With good reason, maybe: more than a few of them fall to the temptations. I can understand how they do. And I feel compassion for them, but this may be a character flaw in myself, a blurring of the knowledge of good and evil, caused by the death of my son.

But thanks to all the good press I've generated for our little group, things have changed. The other sections and units have grudgingly come to admire, if not our work, then at least the way that the general public has come to know and respect us. I'm considered the media wizard, because I've vigorously lobbied the newspapers and electronic media, cultivated reporters and editors and producers, gotten them on our side, shown them what we do. And they've responded. CAY has been featured on the covers of *Westways* and *Los Angeles* magazines, and the California Law Enforcement Bulletin. (Of the actual CAY players, only Frances has been pictured because we do a lot of undercover stuff. Our media poster boy is actually Jordan Ishmael, who speaks as our supervising lieutenant but has no say in our day-to-day work.) We've gotten lots of positive airtime on the network and local news. *Sixty Minutes* has made some inquiring calls to me and Jim Wade. The *Times* and *The Register* and *OC Weekly* have all covered us favorably. We are proud of that coverage, and the department is proud of us. Other departments in the region have begun to create their versions of our little unit.

Mixed in with the early prejudice against us was something even uglier to me: people secretly believed that kid crime was small time. That, somehow, real cops fight real crime and real crime is crime that matters. Kid porn, so what? Child abuse, so what? Prostitution of minors, hey, it's rare. I have a response to that, but it's long and I might get worked up. I might think of guys like Chet, or The Horridus. The Irish in me again. But that prejudice is changing, thanks to CAY and the number of creeps we've collared, and the media smile we've gotten. I've already proposed a CAY budget twice as big as last year's. If I'm reading the signals from Sheriff Wade correctly, it might even get approved.

Last, I'm not even sober, really. It wasn't until a few months ago that I stopped waking up in places and not knowing how I got there. It wasn't until then that I could go a day without consuming almost a fifth of tequila, plus a few beers (four, max). That was my life before I found a way to love this world after Matthew. But who knows — it might happen again, tonight.

So what gives? I don't know and I don't ask. But I do know that Jim Wade and the people closest to him are looking at me warmly, a warmth subtle and invigorating as the sunshine between storms. And I know this too: not one ray of it is lost on Ishmael.

The morning briefing began as usual: Sheriff Wade, Undersheriffs Woolton and Vega, Captain Burns, Lieutenant Ishmael, the three section leaders and five unit heads.

We commence at eight sharp. Jim Wade presides from the head of a long, cup-stained, wood-veneer table, but he usually lets Vega handle the group. The coffee machine is always going. There are narrow vertical windows in this conference room, and they look out over the parking lot and downtown Santa Ana, the county seat. Except on clear winter days, there isn't much to see. But the mood is usually brisk and optimistic. The purpose of the brief is to get everyone up to speed on the breaking cases, so that each section knows what its neighbor is up to. That, and to float ideas or beefs that can't wait until the weekly meeting of section heads.

Four of the twelve others came over to shake

my hand and offer good words on the Chet bust. Most of them had seen the CNB report and had to mention the comic way that exterminator Louis and dapper Johnny had stood there yapping to each other on camera behind Donna Mason, not realizing they were on.

"You're gonna have to get those guys some media grooming, if you're going to put them on the air so often," said Burns, one of Sheriff Wade's insiders.

"Least they weren't drooling on Donna Mason," said Undersheriff Vega.

"Probably dry by then," said Undersheriff Woolton.

"Naughton takes care of media drool off-screen," said Ishmael. "With Mason, anyway."

"Just part of the job," I said.

"You're a hard worker," he said.

"And look what I get for it," I said, turning my blue-black, bandaged cheek toward him.

"You see Van Exel bump that ref last night?" said Rafter, head of Melinda's unit.

"They'll cook him for that," said Woolton.

"Ten-hut," said Vega. "Ish, why don't you start us off with the CAP news."

"You got it," said Ishmael. "Congrats to Terry's unit for the bust up in Orange. They'll arraign Sharpe and the mommy later this morning over in court three, and I've got Reynolds asking for no bail on either. The Sharpes got Kleo Debelius for counsel —

they'd obviously been saving up their money — and he'll knock it down to half a mil or so. Higher the bail the better — we're figuring the happy couple as a flight risk and hopefully Honorable Ogden will see it our way. Reynolds and I listened to the tapes last night, the ones we got out of Sharpe's house, and they're golden. Between Terry's testimony and the tapes, Reynolds hopes to throw a large net — child abuse, child endangerment, sexual exploitation, pimping and pandering, enticement of minor, keeping or admitting to a house of prostitution — there's plenty of sentence enhancements for under the age of fourteen, so they'll heave the whole book at the Sharpes. We figure Debelius will plea down everything he can, but Reynolds says we'll hold tight. Honorable would probably like to get some mileage out of this one — just like we would — he's on the election block next year. Next, we just got the FBI profile of The Horridus, so —"

"— Excuse me, Jordan," I said, "but what about the girl? Is Reynolds talking charges in juvenile court, or testimony?"

"Both. They'll plead her, then slap her wrist and let her help send Mommy and Daddy up the river."

"We've got some say in that, you know."

Ishmael nodded impatiently. "Well, say it then, Naughton."

"I don't think we should prosecute her. Her

parents made her what she was. She's only ten, for Chrissakes."

"Noble sentiment," said Ishmael, "and I'm sure it would sound real good on CNB, but Reynolds needs some leverage. We can't let her go, then expect her to sink her parents."

"She's not going anywhere but the hall, Jordan. That's enough motivation for her to cooperate, I'd say. You been there lately?"

"She's a prostitute," said Ishmael, "juvenile or not."

"Ish has a point," said Woolton.

"She's also a kid," I said.

"Amen," said Rafter. "Ought to be out playing girls' hoops, but she's cooped up turning tricks for her dad. Give her a break."

"Well," said Sheriff Wade, "is she a *cooperative* kid or not?"

"I'll know this afternoon," I said.

"Table it until then," he said. "Ishmael, ask for a continuance over at Juvenile while we sort this out. See how the girl's going to act. Terry, see me after the interview. Okay. Onward to the wholesome world of The Horridus. Naughton, what do we have?"

I passed out copies of the profile. It was a stripped-down version, without Mike Strickley's opening or closing remarks. The room was quiet, with an occasional sigh or "mmm."

"How do they come up with this stuff?"

68

asked Burns. He's old school, but he's tough and optimistic.

"It's easy for them," said Ishmael. "They just think like creeps."

Sheriff Wade stared down at his page and shook his head. "Naughton? What do we do with all this? How can we use it?"

"There's two basic ways to go, sir," I said. "We can wait, be as ready as we can for number three, and hope to get to her quick. Our physical evidence has been thin, but the sooner we get to the girl the better chance we've got. He'll leave us something, sooner or later."

"Later doesn't sit too well with me," he said.

"Which leads us to option two," I said. "We can try something proactive — draw him out, force his hand."

"Something like what?" said Wade.

"We could edit the profile and release it to the media," I said. "They'd give it good play and he'd feel the pressure."

"The media hound barks again," said Ishmael.

I looked at him sharply. "We could blow up his handwriting sample, Horridus, and put it on billboards, see if anyone recognizes it. It's only one word, but it's fairly distinctive. The Bureau did that once — and it worked."

Ishmael groaned. "*Advertise* for him?"

"That's exactly right," I said. "Or, we can keep the profile to ourselves, just like we have on some of the evidence, and set up something to attract him — I'm just brainstorming now — but, you know . . . get one of the papers to do a piece on fashions for little girls, use five or six models he might like and mention the agency that handles them. Set up a phone number of our own inside the agency, run a trap and trace on the calls that come in. No, this is better, we get the papers to do a story on an *audition* for young girls to star in a commercial, do modeling for clothes . . . something like that. There's a chance he'd show up."

"And if he gets to one of those models, or somebody's girl, we all end up as security guards," said Ishmael.

But Wade seemed interested. "Go on."

"Come on, guys," I said, looking around the table. "Any fool can dance alone."

Woolton was next: "Set up a reptile show."

Vega: "They got those already. Kind of a swap meet. My kid goes."

Burns: "It says he likes reptiles, maybe. We know he likes little girls. So we set up a reptile show for little girls."

All: Laughter.

"Or advertise a kiddies' hour at the show," I said. "Where they get to handle some animals. Use a picture of a girl holding a lizard, to promote it. Right there we've provided him with two temptations. We'd lay in heavy, look for someone who fits the description."

"Kick butt and take names," said Burns.

"He'd change his appearance," said Ishmael.

"Likely," I said. "Plus our description is pretty thin to start with. She saw him at night, a hundred feet away, getting into the van."

"We'll shake down all the guys wearing Groucho glasses," said Woolton.

Ishmael: "And if he finds his next girl there, then what? What if he tracks down the girl with the lizard? That's the trouble with this public stuff — if it backfires it backfires big."

"Noted," I said. "The smaller we keep it, the better we can control it."

"How about a tryout for a girls' basketball league?" asked Rafter, obsessed as always with the game.

The room went quiet, then.

"Naw," Rafter said. "Like Ish said, too many ways to go wrong."

"There's something you all should know," I said. "The Bureau thinks he'll work faster now. They also think he'll start to rape and kill them if we apply pressure and don't get him. They're almost always for proaction, but not for The Horridus."

Sheriff Wade looked at me. "So he's going to speed up if we wait, and he's going to start killing if we move?"

"Great," said Vega.

"The hell does that leave us?" asked Burns.

"It leaves us with quaint methods, such as

old-fashioned police work," said Ishmael.

I nodded and the room went quiet again. "He's right. The first thing I want to do is get my people on the real estate angle. If we figure he's sold his home, or is trying to, we've got a place to start. The detached maid's quarters or guest house is important. It narrows things down considerably. All the offerings are centralized in the multiple listings guide that the realtors use."

"MLS. There you go," said Wade. "Okay."

"Where the hell you going to start?" said Woolton.

"Santa Ana," I said. "It's between Orange and San Clemente, where he took the girls."

"Biggest city in the county," said Vega.

"Should we start with the *smallest* because it's easier to cover?" I snapped.

Vega held up his hands. "Just thinking out loud, Terry."

"Yeah, I know," I said. "This guy's just pissin' me off."

"You and everybody else," said Woolton.

"Look," said Ishmael, turning to the sheriff. "Painful as it is to have Naughton agree with me, I vote to stay basic on this scum. No need to get novelistic right now. If we try something proactive and it flops, we're setting him off. Let him think we're asleep. Work him like we work anybody else, except maybe harder."

"I don't like the idea of him speeding up," said Burns.

"Who could?" said Woolton.

"Terry?" Wade asked. "This is your baby."

"Painful as it is to agree with Ishmael agreeing with me, I do."

Wade studied me. He said, "You've got that bad look on your face, Naughton. Agreeing with Ishmael can't be that awful."

There were the requisite chuckles a leader always gets.

"I wish I knew where he was right now," I said. "What he was doing. Who he is."

"Ishmael? He's right here," said Burns. "Sitting on his ass."

I gave Burns a look that has been described to me as icy, ferocious, drop dead, freezing, withering. Take your pick. To me, it feels like all of them at the same time.

"Terry's getting his panties in a bunch again," someone noted.

"I'm worried about this shitbag."

"Amen," said Rafter.

"What else?" asked Jim Wade.

I filled them in briefly on another high-profile CAY case, that of a dead baby found last week in a storage room file cabinet. The office was out in Buena Park. Nobody knew who the infant was or how she got there. One of the secretaries smelled something and found her. We're working the staff and the cleaning crew and the security company and the vendors and the temp help. A lot of people had keys and could have come in late at night. When something like this happens, the person you're looking for first is the mother. She'll be young, broke, unstable, using drugs and under pressure from a husband or boyfriend. Intolerable as it sounds, that kind of thing happens all the time. Two months ago it was a three-year-old boy who wandered away from home. His parents were distraught. It took us three weeks to find him, and when we did he was at the bottom of a water-district pit less than a half a mile from his house. He'd been dead a week. The parents confessed to dropping him in there because he cried a lot and they couldn't afford to feed him right. That's the kind of stuff we do, day in and day out.

When I was finished with the CAY rundown, Ishmael covered the department's other big CAP (Crimes Against Persons) cases: the former county secretary shot dead in her home by an UNSUB with a crossbow; a postal worker gone nuts and killing three; a young man accused of killing his family then putting them all in a car he then set on fire; rumors of another gang war down in the Santa Ana barrio, less than a mile from where we were sitting.

My mind wandered. It's hard to give serious consideration to cases outside your own, which is one of the reasons we meet like this. I did wonder what kind of cold sonofabitch could shoot a woman in the heart with a crossbow at close range. And I wondered where our man was now, our Horridus, from the Latin *horridus* meaning rough or bristling. As I thought about what he looked like and where he worked and what he saw when he looked in a mirror, the discussion of other crimes swept past my brain: more rumors of blame for the county bankruptcy of '94; political crap going down again in one of our state assembly districts; mobile Asian gangs running strong in central county; white supremacists in Newport Beach; two old women raped in a nursing home in Yorba Linda.

But no matter how I tried to listen, all I could really focus on was The Horridus, how little we knew about him and how sure I was that his escalating fantasy was becoming an escalating nightmare for the rest of us.

Who are you?
Where?

Four

"Nervous?"

"A little."

"That's good. Some nerves make you sharp, but they won't come across on video."

Hypok held open the door for her and smiled as she went in.

"Just have a seat right there and relax, Abby," he said. "I'm going to walk you through a few questions, just so you'll know what's coming. All right?"

"Sounds good," she said. She arranged her purse strap over the back of the chair.

"Abby," he said. "That really is a nice name. You don't hear it much. Abigail?"

"No, just Abby." She smiled. It was the kind of smile Hypok liked — good teeth and healthy lips and not nightclub looking at all, more girl next door. Her hair was light and straight. "Yours was . . . I'm *sorry!*"

"David Lumsden, and don't be. I'm good at remembering names."

He sat across from her and glanced through her biographical information again. He remembered all of it from the night before.

"This is going to be fun," he said. "Skiing,

76

sailing, country western dancing. Cooking, dining out, close friends, a bottle of wine with that someone special . . . yeah . . . this is going to be easy. Do you mind talking about yourself?"

"Well, I've never done it on camera before."

She smiled again. She was pretty, prettier than the still shots that were attached to her application. Nice figure, probably. He liked the way her face opened up when she talked and smiled, the way she seemed to have nothing in the world to hide. She probably didn't. He wondered what she thought of his new hairstyle — short, bleached bright white and brushed up on the sides and front like a surfer in the fifties. Of course, she didn't have the old style to compare it to. He blinked twice.

"Abby, remember one thing — you're talking to me, not to the camera. You and I are having a conversation about you. Talk to me like I'm a friend, and forget everything else. That's all you're going to be doing, talking to a friend."

He smiled as he looked at her through the viewfinder of the video camera. He loosened the tripod-mounting nut and raised the angle of vision just a little. Her image jumped. He started in with his usual spiel, telling her he'd be asking about herself and what she liked to do, what qualities she admired in the opposite gender, a little about her home and work life — just keep things kind of light and general. She nodded along as he talked. She'd worn a red blouse, one of the colors suggested in the Bright Tomorrows kit. Her lipstick was a matching shade, which gave her a kind of overt, forthright sexuality. According to her bio, she was thirty-one and divorced, a secretary for one of the big land development companies in the city of Irvine. She had a five-year-old daughter named Brittany. They lived in Irvine in a ground-floor, end-unit apartment with a tiny fenced backyard that housed a collection of bright plastic toys — a blue and orange slide and ladder, a low-slung pink and violet bike with whitewall tires and training wheels, some big balls in a white basket.

Hypok analyzed the lighting on her. He'd front-light the young, attractive Bright Tomorrows members because it was honest and revealing of beauty, especially in the eyes. The older ones, or the ones with bad skin, that was a different story. You wanted them to look good, but you wanted to present them somewhat honestly, too, so the members who chose them had an idea what they really looked like. In fact, the only complaint that the Bright Tomorrows execs had voiced was that his work was occasionally *too* flattering.

"Abby," he said, "I'm just going to go with the front lighting — it shows you real clearly and you look nice."

"Whatever you think's best."

"I'll back-light some of our more mature members, but you, I don't have to."

"I guess we have to have some truth-in-lending here."

"You'll look good. You're attractive and relaxed. Don't worry. Now, I'm going to start the camera running, then I'll ask you some of those questions and we'll just have a little talk. Feel free to move your hands to make a point, whatever you'd normally do in conversation. Just don't swivel on the chair — that drives the camera crazy and makes you look ill at ease. And remember, we can shoot this ten times if you don't like what we get. The whole idea is to make this little tape something you'll be comfortable with. All right?"

"Okay."

He watched her through the viewfinder.

"Take a deep breath and let it out, Abby. Then we'll start."

He watched her smile, straighten on her inhale, then slowly let it out. Nice top. He hit the record button.

"Hello, Abby."

"Hello."

"Nervous, still?"

"Not so bad now."

She smiled beautifully and blushed just a little. He laughed and so did she.

"So tell me, Abby. I hear you like to sail

and you like to ski. Which do you like the best?"

She said it depended on the weather and where you were. She'd actually only been sailing once or twice, but skiing she did a lot, mostly on the local slopes. Hypok felt that she was already coming off as sort of a ditz, so he steered her onto work. She said a little about her secretarial job, the pressure, the way it satisfied her to put in a good day's work so she felt like she'd earned her free time. A worker bee, he thought: most happy when situated in a hive. He always liked people with a strong sense of purpose. He could see how much this job meant to her.

"Is it true that secretaries do 80 percent of the work and get 20 percent of the credit?" he asked.

"More like ninety-ten!"

"Ninety-ten! I think you're due for a big raise, then. Do you always get something extravagant for Secretary's Day?"

"Well, let's see — that's next week, isn't it? Last year was lunch at El Torito and a really nice watch."

"I thought you got a watch when you retired."

"Here, check it out . . ."

She raised her wrist to the camera and wriggled it. She smiled again — it was a truly beautiful smile and she understood this — and then brought her wrist back to her lap and giggled. It made him think of his own Medic Alert wrist bracelet with the serpent on it. He rubbed it now, lightly, for luck.

"They take pretty good care of me, I have to admit," she said with another goofy but radiant smile.

"Well, Abby, tell our Bright Tomorrows guys just what it means to take good care of you. What qualities do you admire in a man?"

Hypok sat back and looked at her expectantly, thinking: sense of humor, honesty, in touch with his feelings, fit, secure. That was one thing about the women — they always said exactly the same thing.

"I like a man who can make me laugh," said Abby. "That's probably the first thing I . . ."

Hypok nodded along. This sense-of-humor part was something he'd never understood was so important to women until he started the gig with the services. Make me laugh, he thought: do they want a husband or an entertainment center? She would run on now like they all did, just get them started on the qualities they wanted in a guy and you could sit back and think of things you'd like to do. He wondered how much Brittany looked like her mother. He wondered if Abby slept with the windows open when it was warm out, or if she used the air conditioner. She looked like an air conditioner type — neat, safety conscious, convenience oriented.

"Honesty is real important, too. I think that's the basis of . . ."

Hypok studied her through the viewfinder. His brow nudged the rubber eyepiece and he pulled back a little. He still hadn't gotten his depth perception right since getting rid of the glasses. Still bumping into things up close. He cupped his hand over his mouth and smelled his breath. He enjoyed her perfume from here, an outdoorsy, floral bouquet that would undoubtedly be described as "springlike." It was a little bit like that baking soda concoction you dump onto your carpet before you vacuum. He pictured her vacuuming her living room on a Saturday morning — short shorts and tennies with no socks and a T-shirt probably, with her hair up and no makeup on. She'd have Alanis Morissette on the boom box. She'd be singing along. He pictured five-year-old Brittany in the bathtub surrounded by mounds of suds. He imagined running the bar of no-tears kiddy soap over her, his hands sliding on her soft, pliant body. Brittany would smile at him, maybe splash some suds. She'd be happy to be there. Why couldn't a woman be more like a girl — nonverbal, intuitive and appreciative?

". . . how you work through things, make things better."

"What about being in touch with his feelings?" Hypok asked.

"*Definitely*. Women are always more in

touch with their feelings and I think if a man could . . ."

Um-hm. Women *are* more in touch with their feelings, thought Hypok, the operative word being *their*. Watch them drive — they don't pay any attention to things not directly in *their* vision. Watch them shop in a market — they're only aware of *their* purpose, *their* list of items, *their* cart and *their* place in line. They are absolutely self-absorbed, self-serving and self-promoting. *Their, their, their.* And any notion that comes to a woman's mind, no matter how ridiculous or damaging, she's going to put words to it, yap it out loud. Why? Because it's one of *her* feelings. And she's in touch with them.

". . . able to laugh and cry and really feel deeply."

"Hear that guys?" Hypok asked genially. "Get in touch with your feelings or don't even bother with Abby!"

"Does that sound demanding?"

"You can *be* demanding — that's what Bright Tomorrows is all about. Okay now, enough serious stuff. Tell me about your family. You've got a little girl, don't you? What's her name?"

Even through the viewfinder Hypok could see the twinkle that came to Abby's eyes and the wholesome flush of color that washed her cheeks. He just plain had to smile, too. Nothing in the world makes them prouder than *their* children. He brought his hand up to his mouth and smelled his breath again.

"Her name is Brittany. She's five years and two months. She loves butterflies and ice cream. It's a little hard to say, but I think she wants to be a motorcycle racer when she grows up."

"A motorcycle racer!"

Hypok thought that the Websters, his netizen friends, would like to hear this one.

"She's got this little . . ."

Um-hm, pink and violet bike in the backyard with a six-foot grapestake fence I can climb over without a sound.

". . . *all* around the backyard, or in the park."

"So, she must be in kindergarten by now?"

"A private one. They're learning computers already."

Isn't everyone?

"You really sound proud of her, Abby."

"She's my sunshine, all right."

Hypok backed away from the camera and smiled.

"Okay, Abby, here's one that's not in the script. Ready for this?"

"I guess so." Giggles.

"Tell these men, what is a truly romantic evening for you? I mean, the romantic evening to end them all, the romantic evening of *your* dreams."

She blushed just a little and threw back her

hair. "*Well* . . . it would start off with a . . . a full body massage —"

"— Start *off!*"

His exclamation was a little strong: he could smell his deep-down breath in the air in front of him now. Like something crawled down his neck and died. He hoped she wouldn't notice. He dug the breath drops out of his coat pocket and lost his face behind the camera as he squeezed a bunch of it onto his tongue. Cinnamon. It was amazing, he thought, that anything could live in that body of his, considering all the tequila he drank.

"*Start off* with a massage, and maybe a glass of champagne. I mean, *he'd* get one, too. Then, when we were totally limp, we'd get all dressed up and go for dinner at the Ritz-Carlton. Lobster for me, and a bottle of Chardonnay. Then we'd take a long walk on the beach with our shoes off. His tuxedo tie would dangle and my nylons would get damp . . . I mean the *feet* would . . ."

God, what an airhead, Hypok thought, smiling his best. Wait 'til the kiddy netters hear this. Wait 'til the Friendlies get a load of this one. She colored but recovered nicely.

". . . but it wouldn't matter because it would be summer and eighty degrees out and just perfect. *Then,* we'd go back to the hotel . . . have dessert . . . maybe a decaf espresso . . . then . . . well, the rest of it's . . . *confidential* . . ."

She giggled and threw her hair back again.

"As well it should be, Abby! Thanks for talking with us today, and we wish you all the best bright tomorrows."

Hypok turned off the recorder and hit the rewind control. "I think that was real good. Natural. Easy. A good sense of who you are."

"Oh, God, I'm such a spaz. I can't look."

"Well, you really should. We'll play it back and if you don't like it, we'll do it again."

"That would be even worse."

"No, really. Everyone's afraid until they see the tape. I think you'll be pleasantly surprised. You're really very good on camera. Here."

He plugged the camcorder into a monitor on the desk beside them. Abby leaned forward in anticipation, and Hypok leaned back. He always liked to see their reactions, liked to see the way they accepted the inevitable, even if it was just three minutes of video. You could tell a lot about a person by how they accommodated an uncomfortable situation. He blinked a couple of times in rapid succession: the new contact lenses made his eyes dry.

Abby smiled and shook her head and blushed a little, as he knew she would. But she watched very closely, fascinated by *her*self, *her* image, *her* being. Now she'll say how strange it is to —

"— It's really weird to see yourself on TV," she said. "But I don't look as nervous as I felt."

"I told you, some nervousness isn't a bad

thing. I think you handled this romantic evening question real well. I always try to do at least one thing that's spontaneous. Let the reflexive personality show through."

"*Gawd.*"

She was watching herself wriggle out of the damp nylons statement.

"I've got a little one myself," he said. "Ashley. She's four, and I know what you mean about girls and bikes. I wonder if it means they'll like horses someday."

"Isn't four a fun age?"

"They're *all* fun ages, if you ask me. Michael is seven, going on thirteen — a real terror."

"Takes after his dad?"

Hypok blushed. When a woman came right at you, that was the hard pitch to handle. He had to blink again to wet his eyes.

"His mom, to be honest. Look at me, I'm kind of an indoors artsy type, but Michael, all he wants to do is prowl around in the hills and catch lizards and snakes."

"Eeew."

"That's kind of what his mom says, too. When I tell her what we did . . . I mean . . . we're divorced, so we don't talk every day. But it's boy stuff, so I take him out when I can and we rummage around in mother nature, see what she's got to offer."

Abby smiled, but hadn't taken her eyes off the screen. "I'd like to have a little boy someday."

87

"You've come to the right place to find good guys. You'll get chosen a lot — believe me."

"Thanks. I mean, I hope so."

"It's difficult raising them alone, but it has its rewards. How do you work it with your ex, the custody, I mean, do you have a regular schedule?"

"He gets Brittany every other weekend."

"Same as mine. I wish I could see them more, but let's face it, mothers make better mothers."

When the video ended she looked at him.

"What do you think?" he asked.

"It's okay. No, I mean, I really like it. The technical part is just perfect, and you made me look good. It's a keeper."

He smiled. "I thought you'd like it."

"You enjoy this, don't you?"

He nodded but said nothing.

"How long have you been working for Bright Tomorrows?"

He went kind of quiet then, like he always did when they got aggressive, but he told her: about a year now. Just one of my accounts. Kind of a subcontractor with them. Work with some other dating services. Also do weddings. Parties. Events. Whatever. Do some work just for the fun of it.

He mustered up some extra courage and offered her a true personal anecdote, though he resented her for making him do it: "Last year this couple got married in a hot-air balloon and I went up with them. I do almost any kind of video or still photography, really."

If she sensed his uneasiness, or smelled his something-dead-inside breath, she gave no sign of it.

"Fun job," she said.

He signed off on the video request sheet for BTs, then detached her carbon copy and set it on the table by the monitor. She was reaching for it but he didn't hand it to her, didn't want to risk any contact, it would just ruin everything. Get touched, get hurt was what he'd gathered about women. Nice to look at, but keep your skin to yourself. Skin is personal.

"It's been a pleasure, Abby," he said.

She stood and gathered her purse off the chair.

"Thanks . . . oh *gawd*, not again —"

"David Lumsden. You're really very welcome. And good luck with BTs."

She offered her hand but he just opened the door for her and smiled and looked at her eyes, pretending he didn't see it.

Five

I called CAY together right after the morning brief. We meet in a small room without windows or interruptions and we tend to work fast.

We read through the profile and I told them I thought a proactive stance was too risky now. All agreed except for Frances, who was visibly rattled when I told her that Strickley had predicted a quickening of The Horridus's pace, and a likely escalation to rape and murder if he felt we were close to him. Frances is a stocky blonde with a fair Scandinavian complexion that seems to register everything she's thinking. She colored after I spoke my piece.

"We can't wait," she said.

"Nobody's going to wait, Frances," I said. "That's why we're here. What do you have on the fabric he used for the robes?"

Frances did her rundown: it was a material made of nylon, rayon, polyester and/or Lurex, from one of three domestic manufacturers, or one of several offshore. It had various trade names — Wyla, Allure Stretch Mesh, Lacy Sawtooth Galoon, Deco-Mesh, Tuff-Net, Angel's Wing, Gossamesh. They made it in the

U.S., Mexico and China. She could get a maker from the crime lab, but it would take time. The stuff was sold in scores of county yard goods stores, costume supply houses, five-and-dimes — from $1.19 to $7.99 per yard, depending on the design imprinted on the mesh and the quality. Ours was plain white. She had already worked the bigger outlets to see if a man had recently purchased any in quantity — but with our scant physical description it had been a shot in the dark. With Strickley's profile, she'd start all over again.

"And the safety pins are a bust," she added. "They're standard issue — you can get them anywhere."

I assigned her the real estate listings for any homes offered for sale in the past three months that had a detached studio or maid's quarters. I told her he'd be in a hurry to sell, so watch for the bargains. And ignore the mansions — they'd be out of his price range.

"Johnny," I said, "the vehicle."

He'd been working the van — trying to find a late-model red Chrysler/Plymouth/Dodge for sale — and came up with three. One of the sellers was a woman, and one a Vietnamese Baptist priest, but number three was at least a possible: a thirty-two-year-old white male named Gary Cross who said he was tired of spending the money on gas and wanted something smaller.

"It's a red Chrysler Town and Country,"

said Johnny. "Loaded and pampered. Interior is red and the backseats are out. Cross works a day shift at a Lucky's Market up in Anaheim. He's got no priors, his work record is clean, seems to be well liked. I've been watching him after work — he lifts weights and plays racquetball. Has a steady girl. I'm not smelling much."

Johnny leaned back and looked at me with his sharp, almost black eyes. He dresses for a plainclothes assignment whether he's working a case or not: today's garb was chinos, black snakeskin cowboy boots, a crisp white T-shirt with a pocket and a silver chain running from his wallet to a belt loop. Twenty years ago he was down for the barrio on Raitt Street, a kick-ass homeboy known as *Gato* because he was fast and elegant, even as a kid. He's one of the few — the very few — who've managed to pull themselves out of that life and make a real one. He's a good man and he has much to be thankful for now. He's thirty-two years old, with a wife named Gloria — of striking beauty — and three kids. I'd like to dress more like him, but I'm too conventional to pull it off. Johnny's my favorite deputy in the department, not counting Melinda, of course. He's got a quick mind, a big heart, a wicked smile over a sharp goatee and a widow's peak of thick black hair that completes his handsome-as-the-devil look. I trust him with my life.

"Stay on him for another couple of days,"

I said. "In the meantime, check the coroner's files for all deaths of elderly women under suspicious circumstances in the last year. Do the homicides and suicides first. Make that age fifty and up — she might have had him young. Toss out anyone not white or childless."

"Why? What am I looking for?"

"Something Strickley said. It's not in the profile. I just had the thought that the death of his mother would be a wonderful precipitator, especially if he caused it."

"Killed his own mother?" asked Frances.

"You're thinking like these creeps more every day," said Johnny, with a smile.

"That's our leader," said Frances, her color restored.

"Louis — how's the vintage clothing business?"

"I've got twenty-six shops in the county, eight of them have kids' sections, but girls' dresses are pretty rare. The thing is, most of them just fall apart. Jeans and jackets, that's another story. I've gone to six of the stores — two more to go, up in the north county. Nobody remembers selling any little girls' dresses to a guy. The record keeping in these secondhand stores is pretty loose. I'll try our revised physical description on the clerks, but I won't bet on much. My insides, especially after this profile, tell me that the clothes are his. I mean, they used to belong to someone he knew —

sister or cousin or friend. Who knows, maybe his mother dressed him up that way when he was little. Sounds like she could have, from the profile."

"I think you're right," I said. "But do the last two stores. After that, help Frances with the houses for sale — that's a big job."

I also gave Louis the porn shops, to try to isolate a slender, well-dressed, bespectacled white male, late twenties to late thirties, with an interest in little girls. Most pedophiles won't try that angle, because most porn shops make so much money selling adult smut they don't risk the kiddy stuff. But it wouldn't hurt to ask around. Some of the smut sellers owed us.

I took the reptile houses myself, to see if anyone like our suspect had inquired about, or perhaps bought, either *Moloch* or *Crotalus horridus*, whatever in hell they were.

I assigned each of us three more employees of the office complex up in Buena Park — home of Knott's Berry Farm — where the dead girl was found in the file cabinet. None of us believed we'd find the mother that way, but it made sense to clear the workers before we got into the neighborhood. We didn't have a picture of the little girl — she was about eight weeks old — so canvassing was going to be tough.

"Johnny, Louis," I said, "you guys were great on TV last night. You're the talk of the department — again."

"We looked like the Keystone Cops, milling around back there," grumbled Louis. "Man, I came *that* close to picking my nose."

"Any publicity is good publicity," I said.

"Then why don't *you* take some of it, boss?" Johnny asked, with a minor smile.

" 'Cause I don't *want* any of it. Kick butt today," I said. "Tomorrow morning at seven we search the other Sharpe residence. I want you all there."

An hour later I walked into Prehistoric Pets in Fountain Valley. It's a big, well-lit room lined with glass cages. It smells like running water and sawdust and just a hint of something feral and something . . . digested? Excreted? I wasn't sure. On your right, when you walk in, is a big pond with a waterfall and catfish and turtles the kids can feed. A toddler and his mom stood over the water, dropping food pellets.

I went to the big island counter in the middle of the store and asked to talk to the owner. I showed my badge. A moment later a sleepy-looking guy in shorts and a T-shirt that said *Cold Blooded* came from behind a wall of glass terrariums and eyed me without joy. He introduced himself as Steve and led me back the way he had come. Walking past the cages I could see the lizards and snakes prowling their little worlds. The bigger they are the slower they are. A terrarium filled with baby green iguanas had the most action. You could take one home for $10.99. A corner cage held a reticulated python that looked to be eight feet long — $599. It was as big around as my leg. I asked Steve what the python ate.

"Rabbits."

"Can I look around a second?"

There were blood pythons, Burmese pythons, ball pythons, carpet pythons, tree pythons and more reticulated pythons. There were Colombian red-tailed boas, Dumeril's boas, rainbow boas, emerald tree boas and dwarf boas. There were anacondas, cat-eyed snakes, pine snakes, indigo snakes. There were iguanas of all sizes, monitor lizards, water dragons, bearded dragons, *uromastyx*, geckos, skinks and whiptails. Below the glass of the island counter were little white containers like you'd buy deli food in, but with newborn snakes inside them — just inches long and brightly colored. You could get a newborn California king snake for $69.99 or a gaily banded red, white and black Arizona mountain king snake for $139.99.

"What do the little ones eat?"

"Little mice."

The office was small and cluttered with tanks and cages. There was a big gray industrial desk that Steve sat behind, and a folding chair for guests. I asked him what he could tell me about *Moloch horridus* or *Crotalus horridus*.

He looked at me with his sleepy eyes and nodded. He looked to be fortyish. He was lightly built, with thinning black hair, sun-worked skin and a drooping mustache. His voice was slow and pleasant and very clear. He wore glasses.

"Well, the common name for *Moloch horridus* is thorny devil, for reasons pretty obvious when you see one. It's an Old World agamid. The New World counterpart would be the iguanids — they're similar to horned lizards, what some people call horny toads. Small, about eight inches, maybe, brown and orange. Curious little lizards. Live in Australia, in the desert. They eat ants."

I nodded. "Do you sell them here?"

"We buy only captive-breds from licensed dealers."

"I don't really care where you get them."

"Australian reptiles are all protected. When we do get them — the captive-breds, that is — they go for about a hundred. It's fairly easy to get them onto mealworms and they do well in a warm, dry setup."

"Do you sell them often, or just occasionally?"

"Occasionally. They're not popular, maybe because of the price. Plus, the bearded dragons have pretty seriously blown out the agamid market in the last year or so."

"Would you do a special order, if someone wanted one?"

Steve studied me with his calm eyes. He cleared his throat. "Are you asking me to get you one?"

"No."

" 'Special order' is a little upscale for us. Dealers and collectors and breeders can be fairly . . . relaxed when it comes to schedules, or specific animals, or prices."

"So you might put out the word."

"Sure, we could put out the word."

"Has anyone asked you to put out the word lately?"

"No."

"Anyone asked *about* one — care, feeding, maybe?"

"Just you."

Steve stared at me quite frankly, studying my face with his drowsy brown eyes.

"How about *Crotalus horridus?*"

"Horridus horridus or *horridus atricuadatus?"*

"How in hell would I know? Help me here, Steve."

A tiny smile. "Well, *horridus horridus* is the once common timber rattler from the east. Brown and black, dark tail, chocolate brown splotches rimmed in yellow or tan. Handsome. They'll go five feet or so. Heavy bodied. Used to be common, but development, rattlesnake roundups and general fear and ignorance have left them threatened in some states. It came close to being named our national animal, but the bald eagle won out. The 'Don't Tread on

Me' flags showed the timber rattler. They'd always put thirteen buttons on the rattle, for the thirteen colonies. So. *Horridus atricuadatus* is the canebreak rattler, a cousin, if you will. Similar, inhabits lowlands and marshes, occurs further west. We don't deal in venomous reptiles. Never have and never will."

"Anyone ask about a timber rattler, refer to one, lately?"

Steve blinked slowly and sat forward, putting his elbows on the desk. "Yes."

"I like that word, Steve. Expound."

"Kind of. It was about two months ago. I was working the cash register, selling snake food. This guy came in and said he caught a timber rattler in his driveway, wanted to know how much we'd give him for it. Just a kid — fifteen, sixteen. I took a look in the coffee can and he had a little *Crotalus viridis*, which is our common western rattlesnake. I told him what it was and that we didn't buy or sell venomous snakes. He said he looked it up and it was a timber rattler. I said there weren't any timber rattlers in California, unless it was in a collection, or someone let it go. Either way, his was just a western."

"Hmm."

"That's not the interesting part."

Steve rolled back in his chair and folded his arms across his "Cold Blooded" T-shirt. "This is about The Horridus, right?"

I nodded.

It was strange to see the change in him, the way that his proximity to something as aberrant as The Horridus made him different. His eyes gleamed and the muscles in his face tightened. He studied me again, then rolled back to his desk and leaned toward me.

"This is the thing. The guy in line after the kid, he took a look in the coffee can while we were having our little discussion. I remember what he said because most of our customers aren't knowledgeable about reptiles, and even the serious ones aren't generally familiar with the Latin. He looked in the can and said, 'Not *horridus*. It's *viridis*.' "

"Describe him."

His eyes were alive now, sharply focused and intently registering my face. "It was a busy day at the counter and that's not the kind of work I enjoy about this business. I'm not a people person — I'm a reptile person. But I remember him as average height, on the thin side, short brown hair, kind of wavy maybe, coat and tie. He had a beard and mustaches, neat and trimmed. The beard was darker than his hair. Early thirties. Glasses. The overall impression I had was of gentleness. Hesitance. Shyness. Kind of like an academic type. He struck me — but remember this was just a quick impression — as being . . . meek."

My heart was thumping. I felt that wonderful hyperalertness that adrenaline brings. This could be it.

"How well do you remember his face?"

"Not real well. The facial hair hid his features. Plus . . . well, he was just kind of forgettable looking."

"What else?"

"That's all I remember about him."

"What did he buy?"

"Oh, right. He bought rats, mice and rabbits. He wanted them all alive. I don't know how many, but quite a few — over twenty in all. I remember thinking he was feeding a fairly good-sized collection."

"You can buy them dead or alive?"

"We'll fresh-kill them for the customers, if they want. Or we have them frozen."

"What else did he buy?"

"That was all."

"Had you seen him before? Or since?"

Steve shook his head.

"When you remember him, is it a clear picture, one you could describe to a police artist?"

"It's fairly clear. I'm a good observer. But like I said, he was kind of . . . nondescript."

I told him about one of our artists, an extremely talented woman named Amanda Aguilar. Steve said he'd be willing to work with her, but really, he couldn't remember much detail. I told him she could be at Prehistoric Pets at five-thirty, when he got off work. If possible, I like to have witnesses describe suspects to artists in the same setting where they saw them. It helps.

"How did he pay?"

"I don't remember. I can check, but it would take some time."

I leaned forward now, too. "Steve, I don't have any time. He's taken two girls and he'll take more. I need you to find that record for me and I need you to find it now. Can you help?"

"You're damned right I can."

I went outside and used my cell phone to call Amanda Aguilar. She's a freelance artist now, not on staff. After Orange County's notorious bankruptcy of '94, we cut positions to save money, and our full-time artists were lost. Amanda said she would be happy for work. I thought of the fat CAY budget I'd submitted to Jim Wade just weeks ago, and felt a pang of guilt when I realized that hiring back Amanda wasn't a part of it. She agreed to be there at the end of Steve's workday. I told her that Steve's man would have a beard, and that I wanted one sketch with the beard and one without; and one with glasses and another without, also.

"Then we're fishing," she said.

"We are."

When I got back to the Prehistoric Pets office, he had the sales slip. Four rabbits, ten rats, ten mice. Paid in full with cash on the sixteenth of March. Steve was smiling, for the first time since I'd introduced myself.

I pondered the odd purchase, then asked to see where the transaction took place. We went back out to the island counter and Steve took me inside. There were bins that slid under the space below the top. There were long shallow ones for newborn mice, taller ones for mature rats and deeper ones still for the rabbits. There were cardboard boxes for crickets and mealworms. At the counter, a young man ordered three large rats, fresh killed. The clerk pulled out the rat bin, lifted a big white animal and, holding fast to the tail with his left hand, used his right thumb and forefinger to form a collar behind the rat's head, then yanked away from his body, hard. The rodent shrieked — a genuinely disturbing sound — and was dropped into a paper shopping bag. Splat. Then, two more. Steve looked on without apparent emotion.

"Why do some want live ones, and some dead?" I asked.

"It's safer for the reptile if the prey is dead."

"Can't they kill them on their own?"

"Sure. But rats and mice have killed plenty of snakes, too. It's just a precaution."

The next customer wanted fifty small crickets. I watched the clerk fill the bag with crickets, then air from a pump, then tie off the top.

I asked Steve what he could tell me about our mutual friend's collection, based on the food he'd purchased.

He nodded and led me out of the island and

along the back wall of cages. "The rabbits are for big snakes, probably constrictors," he said. "I'd guess seven feet and longer. If you keep a retic or a burmese python long enough, they'll get fifteen, twenty feet long. A snake like that would need a lot of food — say, two rabbits a week, maybe three or four. The rats don't really reveal that much, reptilewise. Most mid-sized snakes will take them. The mice are for smaller reptiles — most of the California native snakes live on mice. The fact that he was feeding his collection back in March means they weren't in brumation —"

"— Brumation?"

"Hibernation. Or 'overwintering.' Basically, just cooling them off. Collectors will do that if they're breeding reptiles. Sometimes they'll do it just to replicate nature's seasons. When the snakes are brumating, they don't eat. So, this guy's animals were eating. They were active."

"What would adult timber rattlers eat?"

"Mice and rats. A big adult might take small rabbits but the rats are more economical."

We arrived at the pond with the catfish and the turtles in it. Steve took a handful of food pellets from the dispenser and gave them to me. I tossed a few in, and watched the fish bend to take them. I tossed a few more toward a turtle that was away from the group, over in the corner alone.

I was thinking. "You've only seen this guy

once. He's got a good-sized collection that's active. He's got to feed them every week or so. That means he's getting food somewhere else, right?"

"Well, it's possible he's only got a few snakes and he's freezing the food when he gets home. For later use. But mostly, a big collection, you either buy fresh once a week or you order frozen by mail — saves money if you buy in bulk. There's other stores that sell food, too. No telling where he's getting it."

"I didn't know a snake would eat frozen things."

"You thaw them out first."

We went back to the counter. I picked up three different reptile magazines and a reptile-show newsletter, but Steve wouldn't let me pay for them. I handed him my card, with my home phone on the back. "If you see him again, call me. If you talk to anybody who mentions him, call me. If you remember anything about him, no matter how small it is or how certain you are, call me. Amanda will be here a little after five."

He gave me one of his cards. It was made of thick yellow card stock and had an embossed green snake across it. We shook hands. His grip was strong and his skin was rough. "How come a collector buys live animals for food, if they can kill his snakes?" I asked.

Steve shrugged. "He probably likes to watch his snakes kill them. Some people enjoy that."

★ ★ ★

From my car I called the name Steven Wicks into Frances, who'd run the CID through Sacramento. Ten minutes later she was back on the line: Wicks was thirty-eight years old, residing in Anaheim, California, with a prior 384a.

I asked her what in hell a 384a was.

"Cutting or destroying shrubs. He took some cactus out of Borrego State Park. He was nineteen at the time. Did ten days and paid a $500 fine. Other than that, he's clean."

I checked three other reptile stores, but no one remembered any customer who had asked about *horridus*. They sold too many rabbits, rats and mice to remember the people who bought them. My physical description wasn't specific enough to be useful yet, but that would change — I hoped — when Steve Wicks met with Amanda Aguilar.

I sat a few minutes with Linda Sharpe late that afternoon in the Juvenile Hall visiting area. It's a hushed and miserable room, where the detainees and visitors — usually parents — have to conduct the sometimes heartbreaking business of familihood with little privacy. There are always deputies present, but the kids and adults aren't separated by glass, as in a prison. Instead, there's a long table and folding chairs, where you can sit face to face and try to keep your conversation away from the

106

people next to you. We got seats at a far end.

She'd been given a pair of loose-fitting jeans, a pair of athletic shoes and a T-shirt. Her pigtails were gone, twisted back into a single ponytail. No makeup, no little girl's dress, no whore's costume. Linda Sharpe, age ten, now actually looked like a ten-year-old.

"Hi," I said.

Her expression was dreamy, surrendered. It's an expression very common to the sexually exploited young. She didn't answer.

"Sorry about what happened yesterday," I said.

"I knew you were a cop."

I shrugged. "I mean I'm sorry about what Danny did. There was no reason you had to see that."

"It didn't really bother me. I didn't like him."

"Well, at least you say what's on your mind."

"Are we done?"

"Is there anything I can get you?"

She shook her head and looked around the room with wide, gathering eyes.

"Out of here would be nice."

I studied her. I'd read through her folder and knew she was at a crossroads now — either an institution or a relocation to be with her nearest relatives, who were way up by Spokane. We had, by Welfare and Institution Code, twenty-one days to keep her until she was placed. A lot of what happened depended on whether we charged her or not. If she went to a Youth Authority facility, her life would be one thing. If she went to live with her mother's sister and husband in Washington, that was another. There's no way to tell which one is going to work out better, or work out at all. The system can't see the future, but it never stops trying.

"I hear you have an aunt up in Washington."

She slouched down low in the chair and glared.

"I hate Washington."

"Been there?"

She looked at me with the mock exasperation young people think is convincing.

"Yeah."

"When?"

"Who cares?"

"I do."

"That's the first thing everybody tries to make you believe. How much they care. There's a word for that, and the word is bullshit."

"I meant it."

"Look, Mr. Cop —"

"— Terry."

"— Cop Terry, I don't have to go to Washington and I don't have to go to jail. I'm a minor. I'm ten and I got all sorts of rights. I got a lawyer and he's twice as smart as you'll ever be. I'm not going to say anything about my mom or my dad. They love me. I do what I want to do and that's the way it is. So, you want to know what you can get me? Get me out of here, get me my house key back and my clothes and the money that was in my purse at home. I want my CDs and my makeup and my friends and my swimming pool. The rest, you can take and shove up your butt."

I nodded and waved over the matron.

"All right," I said. "I'll shove it. And I'll talk to you sometime when you're acting like a human and not a whore. By the way, thanks for the bite. It took six stitches to close it and it hurts like hell. If you test positive, we're both going to die."

She looked at me cheerfully. "Good."

Six

Tonello's is an expensive Italian restaurant in the metro district of Orange County. It's a warm and clubby place, with excellent food and service just formal enough to let you know you're important. It's close to the Performing Arts Center and the South Coast Repertory Theater, two cultural jewels in the county's modest crown. It's a smoky back room without the smoke, given our brutal but sanctimonious times. If you're powerful or ambitious, you want to be known there.

For years it's been the watering hole for the politicians and businesspeople who command their fiefdoms within the county — the supervisors and city pols, the judges and the assemblymen, the developers and real estate magnates, the publishers and editors and media executives, the many lobbyists who represent Wall Street brokerage firms and banks, the philanthropists and the social elite. If your status isn't as high as your ambition, you can still go, so long as you're dressed well, submissive and don't expect a table. Jim Wade is a regular there, along with his heir apparent, Jordan Ishmael. Few others in our Sheriff-

Coroner Department have much reason to patronize the place. We like cop hangouts. But for the last six months or so I've been showing up at Tonello's myself, an unknown in the smiling, boozy world of the Orange County elite. Jim suggested that I might profit from a proximity to these people, though he's never said exactly how. Ishmael, of course, detests my presence. Melinda joins me occasionally. With Linda Sharpe's bitter words still ringing in my ears, I pulled up to the valet line and left my car and a five with Rodrigo. He parked it out of sight, back with the other Fords.

I walked in with a truculent glow, due to my good fortune at Prehistoric Pets. Ishmael was at the bar, and for once I was glad to see him. I delivered to him the line I'd been dying to deliver for the last few hours:

"Where's Wade? I got a sketch of a Horridus suspect coming through in less than an hour."

Ishmael looked at me hard, his green eyes openly suspicious. He motioned behind him with a turn of his head. "With your personal publicist from CNB."

"Perfect," I said, smiling. "Talk to you later, Ish."

I paid, then overtipped the bartender.

"My daughter says she's starting to really like you."

"Everybody in your family likes me, except for you."

"Pride goes before the fall, Naughton."

111

"I always land on my feet."

"When you're not passed out on your face."

"Those days are gone."

"A drunk's a drunk."

I took my Herradura rocks and eased through the crowd to where Sheriff Wade, Donna Mason and a couple of the new county supervisors — Dom Ingardia and Lucille Watrous — were holding down one corner of the lounge. I nodded to my boss and to Donna, clicked glasses with the supervisors.

"Nice work yesterday, Terry," said Lucille. She's an older woman, savvy and tough, who often looks at me with a twinkle in her eyes that makes me feel like a hero, or her son, or perhaps a fatted lamb. "One more offender off the streets. Two more, I guess."

"One more kid in juvie, too," I said.

"Beats turning tricks for Daddy," said Ingardia, who was recently appointed supervisor — the most powerful office in the county — by the governor. He's a real estate salesman, and I don't see how he's going to help guide this county out of the shitswamp of development it's fallen into, but that's another matter.

"Ten years old . . . ," I said.

I turned my attention to Donna Mason. I always feel all alone with her, even in a crowded room. I kind of have to screw up my courage to talk to her in a situation like this. "That was a good segment you did on us," I said.

"You probably don't realize how good," she said. "The phones have been ringing all day. That bite looks bad, Sergeant."

I nodded and smiled at her, rather stupidly, I think. I ran my fingers over the bandage on my face. She looks different than she does on TV, her face is thinner and her smile is quirkier and she seems lighter, less permanent. She's from one of the hollows of West Virginia, born poor but naturally advantaged: she's quite beautiful, extremely smart and knows what she wants. She works long hours, keeps up a demanding social life and still manages to read two or three books a week. I've gathered that much. She was married at twenty-two and divorced two years ago, at twenty-eight. No kids. Her hair is wavy and black and cut short, kind of curls forward around the sides of her face. Her skin is pale and her eyes are brown. She's small, perfectly proportioned, unathletic. The first seconds I spent with her were six months ago in an elevator at a press conference, where we were headed from the briefing room to the seafood buffet. I looked at her, introduced myself and shook her hand. I've been thinking about her ever since, off and on, no matter how hard I try not to.

"It's nice to work together," I said lamely. "You know, law enforcement and the . . . media."

"Oh, can't you just call me the news? Or the press, or a reporter, or even a hyena, vulture, jackal or bloodsucker? I can't get used to being a medium of any kind. It makes me feel so . . . vaporous."

Vaporous, with just a hint of the hollows in the lengthened vowels and the gentle lilt of the "r." You won't hear her talk like that on CNB.

Sheriff Wade smiled down with an avuncular grin. He's labored hard for good press over the years, and I've helped him land an ally in CNB. More accurately, the children I work to protect have helped him into the good graces of the news sellers. Children are hot now. Children — namely the children of the baby boomers, and the bad things that happen to them — sell. CNB is a local news network, but extremely popular here, and getting more so every month. Like other businesses defined by place, CNB's fortunes and the future of Orange County are intertwined.

So, what I did next no cop should do, but I had my reasons.

"Sir," I said to Sheriff Wade, "we're going to be getting an artist's sketch of a Horridus suspect in the next hour. Can I have it sent through to the fax in your car?"

He put his lips together as if to whistle, leveled his gray eyes on me through his glasses and took me by the arm, away from the group.

"Easy, media hound. What's this about?"

We worked our way toward the bar and I told him about the reptile collection angle and my visit to Steve Wicks. Jordan Ishmael eased in our direction, but Wade warned him off in that silent way the powerful have. I glanced over at Donna and the supervisors, then back to the sheriff.

"I thought we were going to let this guy operate," he said.

"For now."

"Comments like that have a way of hitting the news."

"She'll clear it with me. She always has."

He looked across the room at Donna Mason. Wade is over six-three, with the weathered skin and dry pale eyes of a rancher. Then he looked down at me. "What do we know about your guy, besides he likes snakes and knows a little Latin?"

"He matches the physical description on the profile."

"Besides that?"

"Nothing."

"Go easy, Terry. We don't need to be seen swinging at bad pitches. That's best done off-camera."

"I understand."

He nodded. "You and Melinda going to come to the ranch Saturday?"

Sheriff Jim Wade's annual equestrian show and benefit for County Youth Services was set for the weekend. If you're somebody, you go. I'd never been invited until this year, though I know that Jordan and Melinda Ishmael used to attend together.

"Much looking forward to it."

"Go ahead. Call Amanda and use the fax in the Lincoln. Here's the key."

"Thank you."

"You're in charge of CAY, Terry. But I wouldn't go public with that sketch yet, if I were you."

"Understood, sir."

The fax transmission came through the machine in Wade's gold Lincoln about twenty minutes later. It was clear and specific, taunting in its ordinariness. I smoothed it against my lap and studied it. Slender face, wavy hair, the glasses. A high forehead. Mustaches and beard. Smallish ears and a mouth that looked neither cruel nor kind. A look of intelligence, perhaps. I've seen enough artist's sketches derived from witnesses to know how much they can seem to tell you and how little they often do. The next page had him without the facial hair. Same guy, but he looked more ordinary, less individual. Without the glasses he could have been an artist's conception of Everyman. I folded the sheets neatly and put them in the inside pocket of my sport coat.

Back inside I got another drink and made the rounds. I put in a good word for our part of the sheriff's budget with Lucille and Ingardia; they control our purse strings, sort of. I suggested to one of the Disneyland executives that some kind of abused kids' night might be a nice PR stunt for the theme park and the Sheriffs. I felt good. I introduced Ishmael to a *Times* editor I know, with the idea the editor might want to hear about the new Sheriff Department Web site that Ishmael and some of his cohorts are working overtime to establish. Ish silently fumed at my farming out a media source to him, which pleased me. I bought another drink for myself, and one for Peter Stowe, who works for the Irvine Company, which is the county's largest landowner. We talked about this new "developer/environmentalist" agreement that would set aside certain county acreage to preserve endangered species, while opening up other parts of it for houses, industrial parks and what have you. The *Times* and the *Register* — Orange County's two major dailies — had both recently gushed about the sexy way the builders and the environmentalists had jumped into the same bed. Basically, the Orange County press is for developing the county until the last blade of grass is gone, though they publish photo-heavy, love-the-land features that suggest otherwise. To me the new land agreement looked like a good deal for the Irvine Company, and I said so, and Peter Stowe said, smoothly, "Of course it is, or we wouldn't have made it."

I smiled and clicked his glass in a fit of bonhomie I immediately regretted. Truth be told, I kind of hate the Irvine Company and all the development interests who've had carte blanche in this county since the beginning of time. It really was a beautiful, logical, functional place once, and I sorely miss that era. I grew up here and I feel vested in this place: my family is here, my blood and history, my dreams and disappointment, my co-mortgage — shared with Melinda. So I'm a little dour about people like Peter Stowe, and his easy confidence, and the way that people like him and companies like his always, *always* get what they want here.

Orange County has a rural, agrarian history, but it has become a tightly packed grid of suburbs that even now — and I'm not sure why this is — continues to be an in-demand place to live. The traffic is as bad as Los Angeles County, our neighbor to the north, and the air is every bit as contaminated. Crime rates are high. Property is expensive, though not as expensive as it used to be. The developers and county politicians are trying to jam a new international airport — fifth largest in the nation — down the throats of about a million people in south Orange County who voted against it. A few people will make a lot of money from it, though there is a perfectly good airport — just recently opened — about five miles away. More customers, is what it all boils down to. County "business leaders" brought us to this saturation point with earnest vigor, and they have not stopped yet. They're not really leaders; they're opportunists with an eye, always, on the bottom line.

The governing board of supervisors, for instance — of which Ingardia is the newest member — is a drowsy but powerful group of men and women who have been selling off county interests to developers for the better part of a century. The board's names and faces change with the years, but their collective history is a discernible thing. A few years ago they were so enmeshed in their own concerns — like hobnobbing here at Tonello's — that none of them took the time to understand that our near senile tax collector–treasurer was taking insane gambles with public money. Of course, he lost a lot of it — close to $2 billion — and the supervisors quickly denied responsibility for the problem. When they were done braying their innocence, they declared bankruptcy and immediately tried to dump the debt onto the very people whose money they had lost — through a tax hike. Newspapers reported that during those last days before the collapse, one of the supervisors was so distraught with the idea of losing her retirement that all she could talk about while the county sank into bankruptcy was her pension. I think that's a wholly representative anecdote, if it's true. One of the supervisors, in fact, quit his job and returned to be an officer on a local police force, where he had started public service years ago. He was the only one of the lot who earned my respect, though I'm sure my respect had little to do with his decision. When you meet these people face to face, as I have in the last few weeks, it's hard to dislike them personally. But the best thing they and people like them could ever do for this embattled county would be to leave it.

Since Matthew's death, I have not been eager to judge any man, even if I'm tempted to feel superior. But I do tend to get pissed off.

"You guys are slick, Peter," I said.

"Just building communities for people to live in," he said.

"Paying customers," I noted.

"There's nothing wrong with that, Terry."

Maybe. But when I look around at this once serene place and see the cars stalled on the maze of freeways and the surface streets jammed with drivers trying to avoid the freeways and the smog hanging heavily over them all like a mood that can't be willed away, and plans to build an airport large enough to handle a departure or arrival *every minute*, I wonder. I wonder about us and the way we've chosen to live. I wonder what it says about us, and what it will mean to the generations we create and leave behind. I'm not a pessimist, nor certainly apocalyptic, but I can't help but surmise that we've all bought into something so demanding and consuming that we don't even know what it is anymore. The race is frantic but the goal is forgotten. Our energy surges but our conscience has shut down. We are headless horsemen — lost, but making good time. Guys like Peter, they're mainly along for the money, riding out the last few years of manifest destiny in pinstripe suits and loafers with fucking tassels. There at Tonello's I could have gotten worked up about this, but I didn't because my phone rang.

It was Johnny, and he was excited. I made my way outside with the phone to my ear and a sense of self-importance I couldn't help myself from enjoying. The tequila was singing in my brain. I glanced over at Donna again, but she was talking to one of the executives who runs the Anaheim Angels baseball team. I imagined being in one of those private boxes with her, a bottle of champagne going and the Angels pounding Seattle.

Johnny was down in San Clemente, the southernmost city in the county, where The Horridus abducted his second girl. He said the next day's *San Clemente Shopper* was running a for-sale ad for a late-model red Dodge van. Johnny had gotten the *Shopper* editor to let him have a sneak preview of the pages that would go to press that night. He talked to the woman who'd sold the ad — over the counter — to a nicely dressed, thirty-something man with glasses. Johnny made the call, posing as a *Shopper* delivery man who'd seen the ad early, and said he was really interested in the

Dodge. The guy who answered said he could come by at seven tonight if he was serious. He was only taking cash. Johnny made the date.

"Clean shaven or beard?"

"Clean."

"Did you sign up Louis?" I asked.

"Signed and sealed. We'll meet at six-thirty. I hear you found someone for Amanda."

"I've got him in my pocket and he feels good," I said. "Guy was in a reptile house, telling some kid what *Crotalus horridus* was. Fits our description."

"What do you want me to do, Terry, if this van salesman looks right? Rattle him or glide?"

"Get inside his house if you can. Get him talking. Stay cool. Pick his brains about the van. If he feels like talking, let him do it. No pressure, though. If he feels right, glide. If he looks good we'll put a bumper-lock surveillance on him, and get to know him better. If he looks *really* right, make a deposit to hold the van for two or three days — as long as he'll give you. Get his work number."

I clicked off the phone. You're out there somewhere, I thought: selling your house and your van, rubbing your hands over your newly shaven face, feeding your collection of snakes, looking for your next girl. You're out there and I'm right here. But before you know how it happened, I'm going to be straight in your face. And I'm the last guy on earth you want to meet. Bet on it, friend.

I went in and got another drink and talked to a director of the South Coast Repertory Theater, which is one of the county's true world-class institutions. When I try to converse with someone in the arts, I always realize how artless I am, how little I know about the world of creation and performance, the world of themes and ideas.

I ended up kind of glazed, had no idea whatsoever who Wally Shawn was, and let the director pick my brain about The Horridus. He asked me about the name, and trying to sound erudite, I told him it was a Latin designation for two reptiles, *moloch* and *crotalus,* both of which are followed by the species identifier — *horridus*.

"Which, of course, means rough, or bristled," I said. "He wrote it on some evidence associated with his second abduction."

He listened, then he said something interesting.

He said Moloch was a deity to whom the Israelites offered sacrifices of human children. He said that most Bible scholars maintain that Moloch was actually Yahweh himself, the God of the Jewish people, and that only later, shamed by their practice, they changed the name of that bloodthirsty god from Yahweh to Moloch.

"They rewrote history," he said. "Odd to think that our Judeo-Christian tradition featured child sacrifice at one time."

"I guess I would have changed the name of my god, too," I said.

"Or asked him for a more humane program," said the director. "When you catch him, will you castrate him?"

"The State of California frowns on that, but it's been done. A castrated rapist can still rape, you know."

"I didn't know that."

"It's a crime of violence, not sex. At least that's what the current thinking is. When a castrated rapist rapes again, I'd have to agree."

"We live in some very challenging times, don't we, Terry? Can I buy you another drink?"

"Thanks, but I'm just about to leave."

I said my good-byes and looked one last time into the clear brown eyes of Donna Mason. My heart thumped in my chest and my stomach felt like I was going over a highway in a big fast car.

I let myself into the apartment ten minutes later. It's a wonderful place, fifth floor, top level, on the other side of the metro district, just a stone's throw from the nice theaters and expensive restaurants. There's actually a bean field across from one side, a last vestige of our agrarian history. It's also got a man-made stream that flows through the clusters of units — hokey, but pleasant. I opened the windows and a bottle of Cabernet, got out some glasses and wiped them shiny with a paper towel. I looked down over the city and felt inexcusably happy.

Five minutes later Donna Mason slipped in. All I could do was watch her come across the floor and shake my head.

She threw her arms around me and buried her fragrant black curls in my neck. "God, I've missed you," she said.

Seven

Hypok slept until almost midnight. Then he sat up and swung his feet over the bed, straightened his back and breathed deeply. He pulled a burgundy-colored robe over him and let it fall past his waist as he stood and slid his feet into his slippers. He tied the robe sash in a double knot, snug up against his stomach. At the bedroom window he stood erect, each hand in a robe pocket, feet together, head cocked just a little to the right, and stared through the darkness. Same thing he always saw: sycamores dense and high and lit faintly by a neighbor's patio light, the thick black power line sagging upward toward its pole on the street behind his, part of the rooftop belonging to the rose-crazed old jackoff who lived next door, the guest quarters at the far end of his own backyard dark now but the guests inside certainly astir just like he was.

Things start moving early in spring when the moon's down, he thought, like tonight, part of nature's way, what keeps us all fed.

He went to the kitchen and made coffee. Extra strong, to stand up to the milk and kahlua and tequila he added to it — just a wave of each bottle really — to get him off to a firm start. With a big steaming mug in his hand he went into his workroom and turned on the overhead fluorescents. They were arranged on the ceiling in two rows of three long bulbs each, and bathed the room in cool white light. More like moonlight than daylight, he thought.

First, get the mail and check with the Friendlies on the Web. He booted up and keyed to the PlaNet provider software, listened to the modem as it dialed and made contact, saw the standard PlaNet junk fill the screen as he fingered past it to get his e-mail. He leaned his elbows on the desk and lowered his head to his hands for comfort. Odd to feel the new smooth face, he thought, and the new short white hair is odd too. The new me. He read his mail:

Lums —
Things are popping in the Adirondacks: 2 *horridus* already, one male and one female, darker phases, active midday. Westerns out yet? Any six-foot reds?
— S. T. Blevin

Lums —
As you requested, prices for fresh-frozen mice are pinkies, fuzzies and hoppers 40 cents; adults small, medium or large 45 cents. Rats add 20 cents per item. Ship-

ping is by the pound, not bad from Texas unless you're buying by the ton.
— Neiswender

Lums —
Can supply you gossamesh at .89 per yard on orders of 1,000 yards or more. White, black, wine, flesh. Thank you for your interest.
— Brumfield

Lums —
PlaNet has a wonderful new way for you to *save* money on your monthly credit card purchases!

Eat crap, PlaNet. Hypok keyed out of his mailbox and into a private chat room of the Midnight Ramblers, people who shared his interest in youth activities. He got the weekly chat schedule on Mondays from the boring home page for Fawnskin, a resort area up in the mountains of Southern California. First he'd scroll past the weather and fish catches, the precipitation and rental availability, all the way back to the local news items, which contained the coded live chat schedule if you knew where to look for it and how to read it. Then he'd know where and when to lurk the Ramblers. They met three different days of each week, at the changing, prearranged times.

Midnight and the middle of the day were popular. If they weren't careful the server monitors would shut them down, might even call in the cops. Hypok had gotten to know a handful of the Ramblers, and considered them his Friendlies. Talked to them in person, seen them face to face. Let them help him sometimes. Risky but profitable.

He lurked.

E-Rection: True, but that still doesn't explain why so many of us are chatting here, unloved and unoccupied. Isn't there something new and clever we can think of?

O-Ring: Why not finance a set of custom works from some artistic friend? We can pool our resources.

Rod & Real: Too expensive, that's why.

Lancer: I stand by my opinion that the public outdoor shower is the most cost effective way to acquire wood. We lucky enough to live in temperate climes can enjoy the youthful siren song May through October. How to chop it is the problem.

E-Rection: The day of the overcoat is over.

Lancer: Especially in August.

O-Ring: Give me pix any day. Privacy and dignity.

E-Rection: And reusable.

Hypok followed the conversation and drank his coffee. He was tempted to jump in and offer up some custom images, or just some reworkings, but no use sounding eager. He would let them stew, get hotter, drive the value up. For now, the freelance dating service work was paying well and keeping him as busy as he wanted to be. Plus, what went down with Chet and his group was going to spread the heat everywhere. Let it cool. Be cool. Lie low. Create.

He left the computer on so he could lurk later, but he rolled his office chair away from the little desk and positioned himself in front of the work station. The table was a handsome right-angled expanse of two-by-six pine planks held up by sawhorses that took up almost an entire wall of the workroom and part of the adjacent wall. The planks were thick and he'd alternated the grain and inlaid them with strips of dark red cherry and run the dowels in every four inches for strength and planed and sanded the whole thing to the smoothness of a pearl before shellacking then buffing it to a shine not of this world. The wood made him think of the bridge of a great luxury yacht; the technology on top of the wood made him think of the flight deck of a jetliner. He felt great sitting here, important, like the captain of a Spanish galleon or maybe a spaceship. Hypok looked at his powerful 129-meg Mac with the latest Adobe Photoshop, his Pivot 1700 Portrait monitor; his Epsons, his Stylus Pro XL scanner, his 200-meg SyQuest for image storage, his 2000-meg NuDesign backup unit, two film recorders, the video editor, his video and still cameras, his digital cameras, his light table and big desk blotter where he sometimes roughed things out in sketch form the old-fashioned way — with a pencil.

Ah.

He fired up the Mac and told the SyQuest to present the image bank of his latest project: a modernization of some classic Dutch stuff of the early part of the century. It was all black and white and the backgrounds were indistinct, plus the girls themselves had a dated, frankly hokey look to them no matter what they were doing. It was the kind of stuff you could pull off the Web any day of the week, the kind of bread-and-butter images the p'philes started out with, before they got educated in the kinds of things they could get from people like him. He'd spent the last week coloring everything, then brightening up the backgrounds and inserting some modern touches — a digital clock in one, a stereo CD system with bookshelf speakers in another, a personal computer in still another. He'd updated what little clothing the models were wearing. Small things, but they brought the images out of the twenties and thirties and into the nineties very convincingly. Then he had started replacing the girls' faces with those of models in magazines, but none of them really looked right. So today he would start creating his own from scratch, give to each of these little angels a face that today's man would just look at and drool over. Innocent enough, and all just for a buck, Hypok thought: he could sell these as originals by the time he got done with them, and it was one-tenth the work of getting a true original. And about one one-hundredth the risk.

He chose a Photoshop brush of narrow gauge and started sketching. Brain to hand. Eye to brain to hand. Someone young. Someone healthy. Someone innocent of sin but instinctively knowledgeable. The girl next door, the little niece you haven't seen in two years, your best friend's daughter. But something extra about her, something in her that *understands*. Something that desires. Eve as a girl, before God and Adam tamed the fun out of her. Leave it to a snake to find the opening.

When Hypok contemplated an image like this his mind wandered, because every decision he made about her was based somewhere in his own history and it was impossible to separate himself from himself when he was working from scratch, inventing, reaching deep inside to find his own rib. It was such a difficult bone to locate.

So as he began to create this girl from himself, he wondered solemnly at the selfless thing he was, at his many names and many homes and many appearances, at his corelessness, at the nothing that he often seemed to be. By birth: Eugene Earl Vonn, a name given to him by his mother, whom he hated, in keeping with her latest marriage to one Everett Vonn. He came to hate Everett, too, who was stupid enough not only to marry Wanda Grantley (her fourth of five such promises) but to believe the boy born eight months later was his own son.

As he drew the new girl, he thought of the sorry tale of his genesis, told to him years later when he was nine by his real father, one Michael Hypok, former itinerant roughneck, seducer of women, alcoholic and methamphetamine freak who skipped out in a big way — as Eugene feared he would — shortly after young Eugene had finally tracked his father down. It had taken him a month just to find him. But Michael had left him with three things: the truth of Eugene's nativity; a wallet containing two dollars, a driver's license and a tattered Social Security card; and a clot of blood that he blasted onto his son's shirtfront at the moment of his convulsive overdose of a death.

Hypok studied the image taking form before him and ruminated again on the death of his father and the true beginning of himself. Sometimes you had to reiterate the same history to make sure it was still true. And it was still true. The name, money and identification had begun a new life for him. Especially the name. He thought back to when he used the lighter fluid to ignite the damp and reeking sleeping bag in which his father lay, hitchhiking the eleven hours back to the hated Wanda, and never telling a soul about any of it. It was the beginning of his secret self. He was born with the flame. He had changed. He had shed. He was new — a process that thrilled him in a way he had never been thrilled before.

Gene Vonn. Michael Hypok. David Webb. David Lumsden. Who was he, really? Well, it wasn't that simple. His only hard rules were these: he would never be Gene Vonn again because he hated the source of that being; and he would never speak out loud the essential name Michael Hypok because it was his secret name, his secret self, his unspeakable and authentic center. Those rules aside, you just became whoever you needed to be for people you met. Same for the government, DMV, banks, merchants, service providers, neighbors. Everyone. Changeable, obscured, multifaceted, occult. And the documentation if you needed it was a snap for someone who had a valid Social Security number and who could build a young Eve from the marrow of his own secret rib.

Two hours and four stout tequilas later he had a beautiful little creation on the screen before him. Just her face now, disembodied completely from any body, as well as from any rules and laws governing her behavior. A girlish face, with a bit of plumpness around the

134

dimples. The eyes just a little older than the rest of her, and a sense of carnal wisdom in them. Mouth open wide. Somewhat like his older sisters, Collette and Valeen, might have looked not long after he was born. Collie and Valee, his craven mavens. He saved the image and shrunk it down to fit one of the Dutch girls. Using the Blur command under the Filter heading, he gave her just a bit of dreamy distance. Click. He integrated the colors. He used the Sharpen button to strengthen the jaw and lip lines. Click. Then he used Pixilate to even out the grain of the whole image before he enlarged it, Despeckled the pixels just a little, then took it back down to a 5 by 7. Click.

Not bad.

Not bad at all.

Fifty bucks times however many copies he could sell before they got into general circulation on the Web. Fifty, maybe seventy-five. Then, they were worthless.

One down, ten to go.

Time to get cracking on the next Eve, he thought. He stared at the screen and rubbed his fingers over his new, whiskerless cheeks. He felt weary but nervous; spent but eager. Like he always did when a shed was coming on.

Sunrise began. He turned off his machines, then the fluorescent lights and poured a generous tequila as a nightcap. He locked the

135

workroom door and padded in his slippers down the hall, past the kitchen and through the door to the backyard. Under the dark canopy of sycamores unsullied by stars he stood and listened, then let himself into the guest cottage. Incandescent twilight welcomed him. He shut the door and breathed deeply the scent of sawdust and serpent and fresh water. The cages lined two of the walls, each now lit by a UVA black heat bulb that cast a soft lunar glow into the room. Blue, almost silver.

The vipers looked as they always did, stoic and resentful. The cobras moved efficiently. Hard to believe the male *ophiophagus* is eighteen feet long now, Hypok thought. The harmless little *colubrids* were shy as usual, looking at him from beneath water dishes or decorative rocks as he passed their glass like a general inspecting ranks. Cute little soldiers, he thought: jewels. He stepped closer to look at the big *Crotalus horridus horridus* he'd collected in northeastern Texas many springs ago. About this time of year, he thought. What a severe beauty: gold and olive, black and pearl, like old leaves on rich soil, countless epochs of genetic mystery engraved on its skin. Five feet long and bigger around than his arm. *Don't tread on me.*

He stepped back and looked at the whole wall of cages at once, unfocusing his gaze to include them all. What would happen to them if he let them go? He'd thought about it a lot

136

lately, in the last few weeks. Not that he didn't care for them. Not that he didn't admire and even like them. But the idea of releasing them was part of something larger that was growing inside, and Hypok knew that when you grew inside you got bigger on the outside too, and had to shed your skin off to make room for the new, fortified thing you became. And once something started growing inside you it always kept on growing. It might go away for a while, but it always came back. Like . . . well. Once, just last week, he'd packed up all his snakes but one and driven them in his van out to Caspers Wilderness Park to set them free. But he'd just circled the remote parking area, then skedaddled on home, relieved that he could find no convincing reason to go through with it. It would be like letting little parts of your body go free.

But now, as he stood here contemplating all the cages and all the moving bodies within them, he told himself again — just as he had at the park — that to free them would be an act of deepest respect and love, the greatest thing he could ever offer these beautifully made, un-thinking little machines. And every time he added to his collection he imagined the day he would set the new specimen free, didn't he? Yes. Those were the best reasons he could come up with, though they hadn't been good enough at the park and they weren't good enough now. He knew they weren't good enough.

The real reason was that he *had* to. You think it. You feel it. You see yourself doing it. Then you *have* to. To not do it is to deny your nature. Like . . . well, that again.

Then, oddly, he imagined letting them go and it was a pleasant thought — the right thing to do. It scared him, the way his mind could just flip one way and then another, like a switch. It meant a big change was coming on. Again. Take an Item but let the Item go free. Take another Item but let that Item go free. Get Collie to list the house for sale; then get her to unlist it. Drive to the park to let the snakes go; drive home without letting the snakes go. Black hair; brown hair; blond hair. Beard and mustache; smooth. There was no end to it. He reached into his robe pocket and took two nice big gulps off the flat hard bottle. There.

Then he backed away and turned to face the opposite wall. It was one huge tank, made of floor-to-ceiling panels of half-inch glass, built by Hypok's own exacting hands. Moloch dozed in the water basin, his massive girth and weight supported by the liquid. When he inhaled, the water level rose perceptibly on the glass. Blue light, moon-silver shadows, moon-silver eyes. Tongue out. Tongue wavers in lunar glow. Tongue in. Moloch, his pride and joy, the diamond of all the jewels in his crown, his co-conspirator, blood brother, ally, friend and namesake. Something he would *never* let go.

Moloch.

Mike, for short.

Suddenly the silver twilight disappeared, replaced by a bright sunlike shine that cheered the room. The snakes all froze in place, uneasy, threatened by the change that could turn them from hunters into hunted. Hypok stiffened too, pure reflex. He felt suddenly exhausted with the thing growing inside him, with the way he kept changing his mind. Enough now. *Enough!*

He closed his eyes and willed away the pressure, willed away the indecision. For a while his brain was like jazz, just fizzing along without any pattern. Finally it quieted down so he could hear himself think.

Take the things between blinks just one at a time, he thought.

Be happy with what you have. Better. Better now.

Looking around, he was pleased to see his room, his snakes, his cages. Pleased to see his robe. Pleased that the new timer on his cage light circuit was working so well. Yes, pleased to see all of this. He owned it all, every bit of it. Well, Collette's name was on the house but he made the payments to her, so that was just a protective technicality. His idea.

He started to feel better. His things anchored him. What you owned and what you created. He considered the new light that filled the room. Thanks to his timer there would now be twelve hours of artificial full-spectrum sunlight, a time for withdrawal and rest. A time for serpent dreams. In light that he created. In time that he owned.

Better.

He walked into the little rear bedroom and opened the lid of his UV chamber. He'd made it himself, from glass panels and a little wood, to fight the agony of his chronic psoriasis, which had afflicted him since boyhood. It was a medically proven fact that sunbaths were good for his condition, so he had created his own sun chamber to lie in, out of the sight of humans. Lamps along the inside of the lid; lamps left and right of him. Pillows for head and feet. Like a coffin with long rods of UV-emitting lights and heat lamps.

He took off his robe and slippers and the bracelet with the little red serpent on it, flipped the switch, put on his sunglasses and climbed in. Easing down into the chamber he could already feel the heat lamps on his skin, already feel the drying sensation of the UV rays on his sores. Sores, he thought: thank my fucking mother again for those. Amusing, however, that the doctors called the patina that grew over the sores, "scale." I'll show you *scale*, he thought. He lay back, lowered the door and looked up through the glass. Must get more Lidex delivered. So much to think about, and the mind never stops.

He lay still, a festering human in a glass tube filled with light. He relaxed and let the light have him, let the pain of the flesh and the pain of the brain waft up out of him like spirits. He wondered where they went. All he knew for sure was that they never went away.

Half an hour later he padded out of the cottage and locked the door behind him, headed for the main house and his bed, where he could catch a few hours of well-deserved hibernation while the new day dawned.

Eight

Joe Reilly, the director of our Forensic Sciences Lab, had left an e-mail message for me the next morning.

NEW HORRIDUS STUFF. SEE ME ASAP.

I knew that Joe Reilly was a man who took his time to get things right. So I called Johnny at home and told him to start the search of the Sharpe residence without me. I knew that he and Louis and Frances would do better than just a good job — I trusted them completely.

I passed through the doors of the lab five minutes later and found Joe at his desk. It was six o'clock. Reilly is a soft-spoken and thoughtful man in his late fifties, with a head of thinning black hair he combs straight back and a baby's blue eyes. He's Irish American, like me, and I've tried several times to exploit that connection, but Joe is so thoroughly fair and unbiased that my Irish-kin overtures have never worked. Though he was a San Francisco patrolman early in his law enforcement career, it's hard to picture him wearing a gun, let alone pointing it at somebody. Through the department grapevine I've gathered that Joe's off hours are spent studying astronomy and collecting rocks. He has the curiosity and the resourceful mind of a scientist, combined with a cop's shrewdness about the evidence he analyzes.

Our Sheriff's Forensic Sciences Laboratory is one of the best in the nation and operates free of the dictates of law enforcement. Joe Reilly set it up that way. You can't get Joe or his people to slant things in a way that will help you make a case. They are meticulous — sometimes maddeningly so — about their procedures and chain of custody assurance. In Los Angeles County, for instance, the crime lab is run at the beck and call of the PD. Reilly testified at the first Simpson trial about proper methods of collecting, storing and analyzing blood evidence. He helped make the LA crime lab people look like amateurs.

He rose and shook my hand and congratulated me on the Sharpe bust. Joe and his people are wonderfully aloof from most department politics and squabbles, so I knew it was a heartfelt compliment. He led me out of his office and down the hallway to the Hair & Fiber Room, holding open the door for me as I stepped in.

"I think we made some faulty assumptions about the van," he said. "Here."

He took me over to a comparison microscope — actually two microscopes that let you see two different samples at once — and told me to have a look. What I saw on the right side looked like a piece of rope with strands of string peeling off the main shaft. On the left was another piece of rope, but you could see the stalk was relatively clean — no strands or strings attached.

"Hold on now," he said.

He magnified the specimens, which enlarged them to the point that their shape was lost. But it revealed the building blocks of each. The one on the right was made up of ovaloid, asymmetrical cells that looked only loosely coordinated. The sample on the left was packed tightly with perfect rectangles, aligned precisely.

"You can't tell under this magnification and light, but both samples appear red to the naked eye. The one on the left is the acrylic from the van interior. The one on the right looks a lot like it, until you use the scope. We were separating out the fibers collected from Pamela and Courtney, and one of the techs thought she saw a difference. When she ran them through the comparison scope, we found out we were collecting two different red fibers. One was the acrylic from a vehicle interior, but the other isn't acrylic at all. It's good old-fashioned lamb's wool. And there aren't many vehicle manufacturers right now using wool in their interiors. Not on something relatively inexpensive, like a van. The one on your right came from something else."

I asked the obvious question.

"We're not sure. The wool fibers were outnumbered five to one by the vehicle ones. That's why we weren't sure what we had, at first. There were six acrylic and one wool on Pamela, and eight acrylic and three wool on Courtney. Most of them were caught in that robe he put them in, that nylon netting."

"Come on, Joe — cough it. What did the wool come from?"

I straightened up and looked at him. He smiled and nodded patiently. We field cops are always trying to get him to commit to something definitive and absolute, something to answer our many questions. Forensic science, of course, isn't often that easy.

"Could be a wool blanket. Or sweater. We've already got wool/rayon fibers that are probably from some kind of garment — a sport coat. But a red sport coat? Not likely. Plus, the diameter of these are quite a bit thicker than the wool/rayon ones. They're processed for softness. These would make a plush, flexible material, not something strong and tight like a jacket. So — sweater, blanket, bedspread, stadium wrap — something built to be supple and comforting."

"A scarf or muffler?"

"Possibly."

"Socks?"

"Not likely. Too short. Too full. They'd process them for length and tightness for footwear. My guess is they don't come from a garment."

I bent down and took another look. "The fiber didn't come from the van."

"Right."

"Then we might have been wrong assuming the van is where he does what he does to these kids. It might not be the van at all. His rape kit could be anywhere."

"Well, his almost-rape kit. That's right."

I stood up straight and let my thoughts settle. "It makes sense," I said. "He holds them for several hours, from what we can tell. A van is safe, but it's not comfortable and it's not soundproof. He's got them bound and held. There's no bathroom, no space, no way to stand up and move around unless he's got a van conversion. Courtney's mom said it was a regular van, not a conversion with the extended roof. So why not just take them somewhere roomier, more like home? A bed with a nice wool bedspread on it. Or a blanket?"

"That thought crossed my mind, too. Any likely places come to mind?"

"The guest house on his property."

"Oh, the profile."

I looked at Joe and caught the skepticism in his gentle blue eyes. "No," he said, sensing my argument before I made it. "I think the profiling is a good tool. Those guys are right a lot of the time. It's just not physical evidence. This is physical evidence. All I'm saying is, what if The Horridus doesn't have a detached guest house? Then we're heading down the wrong path the whole time. Look at all the man-hours wasted on real estate listings. That's all. That's why I'm the crime lab guy and Strickley is the profile guy. It all helps. They're all just pieces of the same puzzle."

"Well, he's at least got a bedroom or a living room, with something red, made out of wool, in it. And the girls are getting fibers from it on them. And when we find him, we'll be able to match what's in the microscope to something this guy has."

Reilly nodded. "That's all I'm prepared to say right now. Unless, of course —"

"— He gets rid of it."

"Right."

We looked at each other in a silence that grew dreadful.

"What the hell is he doing to these kids for six hours, Terry?"

I couldn't answer so I didn't.

"There's something else you should see."

I began to speculate on how The Horridus might conveniently rid himself of incriminating items. Say he really was undergoing a profound change in behavior, like Strickley had predicted. Say he was selling, or already had sold, his van. Say he was going to sell his house. Why not have a garage sale, too, and shed — just like a snake — not only the skin of who he used to be, but evidence that might damn him? Why not sell the house furnished? Why not burn it down and collect his home-owner's insurance?

I followed Joe to the counter on the other side of the room. He stopped and looked into one of the lab's new scanning electron micro-scopes, then stood back and nodded to me. The magnified object was flat and triangular, with rounded corners. The two sides were just slightly longer than the base. It looked kind of like a guitar pick. Running lengthwise from the middle of the base to the peak was a thin raised ridge. It appeared rough and dusty.

"I spent some time with the netting yester-day," he said. "I knew it was nylon, and thought it might retain some body oils when The Horridus handled it, but you know how tough plastics can be on blood — it just smears the carbon dust. Plus, how can you lift a con-tinuous print off a mesh? I hung Courtney's robe and Super-Glued it, just to see what might show. I was right, the cyanoacrylate hung on the prints. There wasn't anything continuous enough to be useful, but when I was looking at the prints with the glass, I found what you just looked at in the scope. It was folded over once, along the ridge, and caught in one of the squares of the net, like a magazine folded over and put in a mailbox. I thought it was a fish scale, until I remembered Strickley's profile. Then I thought — snake scale. So I went over the net one inch at a time, looking for more. Nothing. I did the same on the first one — Pamela's outfit — and struck out there, too. So I took it over to Gordon Marshall at UCI and he said lizard or snake. It's not an actual scale, it's a shed impression. Marshall said it was a dorsal scale, from the back. The ridge is called a keel, and the scale type is called a keeled mucronate. Snakes and lizards all over the world have keeled mucronates. But the only local reptiles big enough to have a scale like that one are rattlesnakes and gopher snakes — the others are smooth — no ridge. He said this is from a big animal — maybe four or five feet long."

"What about *Crotalus horridus?*"

"Marshall said it could be. There's no way he can identify the species without more of the shed."

"Did The Horridus put that scale in the net?"

"Maybe. Or it could have just wedged itself in when he was making the robe. There's just no way to say."

I thought for a moment.

"When a snake sheds, it comes off in a long, inverted tube, doesn't it? I used to find them in the hills, when I was a kid. It's thin and dry, like paper."

"I think so, yes."

"Then how did one scale get removed?"

Joe's peaceful blue eyes scanned my face and he nodded. "We need to run it through the ALS."

"I think we do."

I could feel the thrill of the hunt as Joe prepared the scale for Alternative Light Source. First, he held it with a pair of fine tweezers and ran an open tube of Super Glue near one side. Super Glue emits cyanoacrylate gas, which reacts to body oils and turns white — a process for finding latent prints that was discovered by accident in a U.S. Army crime lab in Japan. Because the scale was relatively small — about the size of the end of a pencil eraser — we'd need to hit it with the ALS to isolate the print, if there was one. Joe held the scale upright in the tweezers and applied the ALS, adjusting the light wavelengths.

"Nice," he said. "Very nice."

I stuck my head right beside his for a view of the scale. And there, illuminated in the ALS, I could see the white outlines of the friction ridges — part of a fingerprint.

"We've got a bifurcating ridge ending and two minutiae points," he said, his voice hardly more than a whisper now. "The minutiae points are the gold. This is good, Terry. It will help us in court."

"But what about *now?*"

He shook his head slowly. "We can try CAL-ID. But Sacramento won't give us priority because it isn't a homicide. And it's too small to let us do any elimination work with class characteristics. We don't know if we're looking for loop, arch, whorl — just the basic Galton classifiers. Maybe they'll give us a run. Maybe we'll get lucky. Don't count on either. But if we get a suspect, we can match him to these ridge endings."

I looked at the small translucent triangle in Joe Reilly's tweezer tips.

"He cut it off the main shed, didn't he? He put it in the mesh. Stuck it in there like a little postcard."

"He touched it. Somebody touched it. That's all we can say."

"Can you eliminate the staff here, and Courtney, and the people who found her, and the cop who responded, and anybody else who handled that netting for us?"

"We'll have to, or CAL-ID won't even talk to me."

"Can you rush it?"

"Just as soon as you rush out of my lab."

Johnny, Louis and Frances were already at work when I walked into the Sharpe residence at 7:15 A.M. The warrant gave us wide latitude for search, even though the crimes had been committed at a rented house in another part of town. Rick Zant, from the DA's office, was there, building his case against Chet, Caryn, Marlon and, possibly, Linda. They were all working in separate areas, with Zant buzzing from room to room, hovering over my people like a fly.

We scored.

In the master bedroom, Louis found a hand-written ledger that included Marlon, Danny, Arthur Means and ten other names — undoubtedly fictitious — who appeared to be paying customers. The amounts ranged from $750 to $2,000, though Chet had tried to disguise his bookkeeping by calling them "acres."

In the "family room," Johnny found two video cameras on tripods and a collection of tapes featuring Chet's daughter with various partners over the last three years. The earliest footage was of Linda, about age four, and Chet. Johnny said the San Clemente van was a bust — it had a tan/gold interior and the seller was a family man with black hair, no glasses and no record. So much for the advertising saleswoman, he said — it was a wonder she got his phone number right for the ad.

In the den was a collection of pornography that surprised me by its size. I walked in and found Frances with a profoundly sickened expression on her fair face as she listed the confiscated glossies on her evidence log, then slipped the pictures into a cardboard box.

She was sitting at a desk littered with magazines and loose stills. She looked at me when I walked in, then slid some pictures back into a big bright pink envelope and closed the flap.

She seemed unsure of what to do with it, then set it carefully on the stack of photographs in front of her. I can honestly say that I'd never seen such an odd expression on her face before. Sure, there was the disgust you would anticipate, and the revulsion, and plenty of anger. Frances is a tough cop. But along with those predictable emotions there was something else that didn't seem to fit — shock, disbelief, confusion. She looked at me, shook her head as if trying to clear it, then stared at me some more.

"What," I said.

"Nothing," she answered, and her gaze fell to the stacks of obscene pictures before her. "Well, that's obviously not true, is it? Everything, Terry. Everything vulgar and wrong with humanity is what."

I took a stack of glossies and looked at them briefly. Chet's collection went far beyond his own daughter, but his tastes ran to the juvenile, the innocent, the helpless. A lot of it was the old European stuff that used to be legal to make and sell in Holland, Denmark, Germany. When you work sex crimes against youth, you get to know the players. But a lot of it was recent and some of it was even new.

"Swine," I muttered.

"Pigs wouldn't do that," she said sharply.

"Then you think of a word for it."

"There is no word for it, Naughton."

When I dropped the photos back to the desk, Frances was looking at me again with the same baffling expression on her handsome, intelligent face.

"Well, *I* didn't take these damned pictures," I said. "You all right?"

"No," she said, smiling an utterly false smile. "I mean, no. You didn't take them. I'm sorry. I just . . . shit . . . maybe I should just walk these out to the car, get some fresh air. This is hard stuff to take."

I offered her a hand but she tossed the pink envelope in her evidence box and carried it past me. There were tears in her eyes. The tough thing about crimes against youth — especially sex crimes — is that it's difficult to employ the gallows humor that cops use as a way to keep things from getting to you. You just can't say much about a picture of a nine-year-old girl being entered by an adult male. There's nothing humorous in it; there's nothing pathetic in it; there's nothing just or fair in it. There's only damage and sickness and more damage, and there's not much you can say to deflect that sickness and damage away from you. You take it straight, head on, like you would a punch with your arms tied behind your back. Try as you might not to, when you look at pictures of things like that, you become part of the continuing story. You become part conspirator, part victim. It stains your soul. If it doesn't, you are in trouble.

I moved a curtain and looked through the window at Frances as she jammed the box into the trunk of her car, slammed the door shut, then wiped the sleeve of her coat under her eyes. She stood there for a moment, looking at the house — looking back at me, in fact — with a furious confusion on her face. Frances is the mother of two teenage daughters. It was easy to wonder if she might have had enough of crimes against youth. There were plenty of other places in the department that could use a cop like Frances. I let the curtain fall back into place.

I decided to let her work alone with her disgust. Sometimes things are worse when someone else is right there to witness it.

So I helped Johnny go through the garage and tried to keep Zant satisfied that we were getting everything he needed. He's a good prosecutor, but I'd rather he didn't hang around my crime scenes and searches. He's never contaminated anything I know of, but there's a first time for everything. Zant is a young go-getter, and like a lot of young go-getters, he's gotten more crime scene training from movies than from the district attorney's office.

Two hours later we were finished. Frances took me aside while the others walked down the driveway toward their cars.

She still hadn't lost that look of disbelief.

"Frances, are you all right?"

"I'm all right, Terry. Are you?"

She waited, staring at me.

"I believe so."

"Well, good then. I'm going to drop this stuff off in evidence, and take a half day off. You mind?"

"Not at all."

She set her briefcase on the hood of her department sedan and opened it. She handed me a list of names and addresses, computer generated, double spaced, two sheets.

"These people listed houses for sale over the last two months in Orange County. They've all got detached buildings on the lots — granny flats, maid's quarters, studios. I skipped anything over half a million, on the strength of Strickley's profile. We're looking for a working guy, middle class, maybe. Anyhow, there are eighteen of them, but six of the listing parties are women. That leaves twelve. They're the ones with the stars by them. I haven't had time to get ages, or anything else on the owners. The listing agents aren't too keen on giving up that kind of information. Maybe you should give this to Johnny."

I glanced down the list: Alberhill . . . Chavez . . . Fitzgerald . . . Evans . . . Johnson . . . Nguyen . . . Scalfia . . . Tuvell.

"Thanks, Frances."

That damned look again.

"Is there anything I can —"

"— I just need some time to think, Terry."

"Take all you need, Frances. We'll hold the fort for you."

When I got back to the Sheriff building, one of my underclass friends was loitering outside, near the steps. I hadn't seen him for a couple of weeks and had thought of him more than once. His name is Charlie Carter, but a lot of the county employees call him Shopping Carter, because he pushes around a supermarket cart that contains his livelihood. The city of Santa Ana runs off the homeless every once in a while, due to a no-camping ordinance passed not long ago by the city council. They disappear for a few days, then reemerge again, only to be run off again.

Charlie Carter is small and black and worked as a janitor years ago here in Santa Ana until he was shot in the head by a student robber. He's never been "right" since, and though he gets disability pay, no one knows what he does with it. I've wondered if he was pushing his janitor's cart when he got hit, but I've never asked him. I wonder if it might help explain the way he lives now. Charlie pushes his cart in the streets of Santa Ana, weathering storms in whatever shelter or church will have him, plying his trade around the county and city hall buildings downtown. He's always on the move. He vanishes, then he reappears.

His trade is information. There's a tattered pasteboard sign that hangs off one side of his cart, announcing "KNOWLEDGE $1 ($4 Deposit)." Neatly arranged in the cart is a clip file of fairly astonishing depth. Charlie gets most of it from the papers and magazines, which he picks up for free when they're thrown out. He makes the file dividers from cardboard boxes. The last time I talked to him he was saving up for a set of *Encyclopaedia Britannica* so he could add history to his store of Knowledge. Of course, he'd need a separate cart just for those. We once talked about the difficulty of managing two carts instead of one. But he was adamant at the time. "Without history," he said, "information's meaningless."

I shook his dirty hand and studied his dirty face.

"You're looking fit, Charlie."

"I don' fit. Don' want to."

"Still want some encyclopedias?"

"Got a set picked out over at the thrift store on Fourth. Nineteen-eighty-fours, black vinyl, good shape. Comes with the Great Ideas books, all fifty-four volumes. Plato to Freud. Hundred bucks."

"You're going to need a double-decker cart for all that."

"I applied for a vendor's license from the city. They denied it."

"Why?"

"They don' tell you why. Maybe 'cause they think I stole this cart."

"Didn't you?"

158

"Found it abandoned, Naughton. I don' steal things. I'm an educator. How about some *knowledge* today?"

"I need knowledge today," I said, which was true. I often buy knowledge from Shopping Carter. Some of it, I've actually used.

"What's the topic?" he asked.

I thought for a second. Charlie doesn't handle biography, opinion, entertainment reviews or editorials, because he thinks they're all "meaningless." *Meaningless* is one of Shopping Carter's favorite words. And he doesn't handle technology because it changes too fast and his cart's too small to handle it. For some reason, I couldn't get Frances's expression out of my mind, or the image of that bright pink envelope that seemed to disturb her so much.

"I want to know about . . . um . . . burnout. Occupational burnout."

"Law enforcement or other?"

"Law enforcement."

Charlie nodded as he always does, then looked down at his neatly packed cart. "*Time* had a decent piece on that just a few months back."

He ran his dirty hands along the tops of the files, bending them back to read his labels. The late April sunshine bore down on us and I noted his heavy sweaters and filthy pants; his shoes that looked so large; his Angels cap jammed down close to his eyes, touching his sunglasses. I could see the dirt in his hair and smell the odor coming off his clothes. His few personal items were arranged on the bottom level of the cart, where you'd put your case of beer or your economy-size detergent.

He produced the article. It was a photocopied one, which meant that he had sold the original and received in return a clean copy. He likes the copies because they're uniform in size and arrange easier. They don't tear as readily. That's what the $4 deposit is for — when you bring back a fresh copy of your piece, you get your money back, and Charlie gets the good replica. If you don't come back with a copy, you rob Charlie of some Knowledge and yourself of $4. The title was:

Burnout On The Streets
When Cops Can't Take It Anymore

"This looks good," I said.

"It is good." He studied me through his dark, smudged glasses. I got out my wallet, found a five and gave it to him.

"You gettin' close to that Horridus yet?"

I considered before I spoke. "Closer."

"He'll be on the Web, you know. Pedophiles love talking to each other on the Web."

"That's what they say."

"Help each other out. Trade pictures and stories. Get moral support from other people like themselves. Kind of like a self-esteem workshop."

160

"I'd think that was funny if it wasn't so sick," I said.

"Fetishes."

"What's that, Charlie?"

"Fetishes is where it starts for the pervs. In childhood. They get attached to whatever they're lookin' at when their penises feel funny. Then later in life, they're still attached. That's why men dig women's shoes and underwear — see a lot of their mother's shoes and underwear. Because they're small and down low when they're babies, so those things are right in their sight line. Scientific fact, that is. Great piece in *Esquire* a couple of years back."

"I'll take it."

It was an original, tattered and limp with the years of storage in Shopping Carter's portable knowledge bin. I got out my wallet for another five, but Charlie waived the deposit.

"You're good for it," he said.

"Thanks."

I read the callout, blocked out in red in the middle of the page:

A FETISH IS A
STORY
MASQUERADING
AS AN OBJECT —

I felt my breath catch and my eyes get sharp. I thought: a little girl enrobed in white netting.

161

A serpent's scale inserted into the web of the net. The girl. The snake. The web. The net. What is the story here? What is the narrative behind these objects?

I shook Charlie's hand again and started up the stairs with my new knowledge.

At my work station I checked messages on the phone and computer and called Joe Reilly to see how the clearance was going. He said he had three more sets of prints to compare with the print on the snake scale, and still had to print the woman who had originally found Courtney wandering in the wilderness of Caspers Wilderness Park.

I got out Frances's list of home sellers and looked it over. For starters, I'd need ages on all twelve of the male sellers. That meant twelve real estate agents to call and convince to release such information to me. Going in person would up my chances of success, but it would take days instead of hours. I called the agents for the first two listings that Frances had starred — Alberhill and Chavez — but the first agent was out of the office, and the second said she couldn't give out that kind of thing on the phone. Who really would? I thought. Two of the listing agents were from offices close to our building. They were both in, and I made appointments to see them, right away.

But before I left the building I wanted to

know what was inside the pink envelope that Frances had set in her box just before she barged by me and stashed it in the trunk of her car. I wanted to know what had made her look at me that way through the window of the Sharpe house, what had forced her to leave her job for the rest of the day.

I went down to the evidence room and asked the deputy for the case no. 98-1145 boxes, just logged in. I signed for it, then looked through Frances's heavy box of smut, but the pink envelope wasn't there. It wasn't in any of the other boxes we took, either.

I went back upstairs to see if Frances might still be around. She was. I saw her sitting in Sheriff Jim Wade's office, intently leaning toward him as she talked. There was no sense in interrupting. Whatever was eating at Frances wasn't mine to know. There would be some rational explanation for the missing envelope. Besides, I had two listing agents waiting for me, and ten more to go after that.

Shopping Carter was gone when I came down the steps a few minutes later.

Nine

Hypok pulled his van into the last parking area in Caspers Wilderness Park, circled the lot once, then backed the vehicle into a space. He always drove his van rather than his car when he had interesting things to accomplish. There were no other vehicles this deep into the fragrant scrub woods, and there was a nice circle of shade from a big oak tree behind the lot. He turned off the engine and wiped his face with his hand. He pulled the half gallon of generic tequila from under the seat and took a long drink. Then another. The big bottles lasted him two days usually, but the stuff evaporated faster if he was under particular stress. Lots of that lately, he thought. Frankly, this was the last place he imagined he'd be this afternoon, after last week's failed mission. But now he felt great.

He looked in the back of the van at all his jars and pillowcases and burlap bags, filled with snakes again. They were active because it was warm back there, and he could see the bags and pillowcases moving. He wondered again at how easy this was to do now, compared to how hard it was to do last week. Now it felt right again, overwhelmingly right, now was a time for change, for the shedding of skin, for renewal. After all, it was springtime, wasn't it? Look at his own new, clean-shaven face. His freshly cut, bleached and swept-back hair. The new white paint job for his van — an impulse, really, not quite a precaution, just an urge to change its color. Now, letting some of his snakes go. It felt right. He felt giddy about it all, but still right.

He reached back and lifted one of the glass jars. Holding it between his legs he opened the lid and pulled out the nice mountain king snake he'd caught up in the San Bernardinos years ago. It was a beautiful thing, he thought: red and white and black, with a curious little face and the sweetest disposition. He let it explore his arm. He thought about what he was doing. There was some sadness in this, for sure. Still, he was committed now, he was consolidating himself, trimming his past, becoming whole. He felt capable. Capable of this act. Capable of rational things like letting his beloved creatures go free, like changing the way he looked again, things like convincing Collette to take her house — *his* house — off the market, when he had convinced her to sell it in the first place. What a sane, bold stroke the unlisting had been. An example of capability and consolidation, of course correction. He smiled to himself, picturing that listing agent traipsing through his place with her provocative perfume, instructing him on all the things he'd have to do to sell it, *I mean what your sister will have to do in order to sell it*. He'd been quite drunk at the time. He hadn't quite foreseen that people would be allowed to just show up and go through his home. And what about the guest house in back? How could he possibly find a better setup than that? He'd called Collette two days later and all but ordered her to take it off the market. Collette could care less, of course, so long as she either made money on a sale or continued to save taxes and build equity in something she didn't have to pay for.

Solid.

Capable.

Firm.

He had already put the bags and jars in cardboard boxes, and knew it was going to take four trips if he carried one box at a time. They weren't heavy, really, but they were fairly large and wouldn't stack well. Besides, who knew how far he'd have to hike in order to find the perfect spot?

He got out and locked the front doors, then slid open the side and brought out one of the boxes. The pillowcases on top were all moving as he set it on the ground, and the rattlesnakes buzzed in their jars, coiled and looking up at him. He shut and locked the side door, then picked up the box and headed down the trail with it.

Past a stand of live oaks, through the toyon, down a gully rimmed by prickly pear and wild cucumber, then into the meadow. The area looked different than when he was last here, dropping off Item #2, but that was three weeks ago and the season hadn't really turned yet. It was also in another part of the park altogether: no reason to visit it again, really, because the cops, if they're smart, might expect that. Now the purple lupine and yellow mustard smeared their colors on the hills and even the dour oaks were vibrantly green. Bees. Bees everywhere, buzzing, dizzying, hypnotizing bees.

It was surprisingly hot. He could feel the sweat rolling down his sides and the dampness of the box up against his chest. He climbed a hillside and found a very nice outcropping of rocks just over the crest, the kind of place snakes love. He set down the box and looked around. There was a creek about a hundred yards away. It would be dry by summer, but the soil around it was dark now and that meant moisture. To his left the rocks clung to the hillside in a long band. There were rock roses with nice yellow blossoms growing in the cracks. Past the creek the hillside rose steeply, clotted with cactus and more rocks. Perfect, Hypok thought: the whole place is snake heaven.

Though it made him sad, he let the mountain king snake go first. It was a hard one to catch — three years of hiking the mountains in the spring before he'd found one this big and this well marked. He knelt by the rocks and the snake slid off his palm and lay in the brush. Its tongue was working fast and its head was raised just a little: Hypok wondered what it must feel like to spend five years in a cage, then be suddenly released to the vast distances of nature. He watched its sides expand and retract slowly, slightly, as it breathed. The king snake lowered its shiny black head and eased into a crack in the rocks.

"See you, little king snake. Kickie some buttie."

Hypok felt everything swell up inside him then, the sadness and the courage and the urgency and the excitement all boiling together. He waited for them to pass. That was always the way it was. Something had to give. That is nature. And nature is change. The shed had begun again and he would emerge from it soon, fresh and brilliant. Singular and unique. Composed and purposeful. Not stressed by contradiction and not paralyzed by doubt. He would be, finally, his true and actual self.

So he worked quickly, trying to take his mind off of things, trying to focus on just one feeling at a time. He got the box and carried it a few yards before he felt positive about the location. He knelt again. The two red rattlesnakes buzzed lethargically as he opened their jar and held it upright over a large flat rock.

They didn't want to come out. Hypok noted that snakes almost always want to crawl back into confined space rather than explore an open one, and he couldn't blame them for that. The world was full of threat. He pulled them bodily from the jar and tossed them, one at a time, into the grass before they could turn and bite him. Like the mountain king, the rattlers lay in the sun for a moment, stunned by their liberty, before gliding under the big rock. Then the Russell's vipers from Bangladesh; the horned desert vipers from Kuwait; the dwarf adder from Little Namaqualand; the rhombic night adder from Botswana; the yellow eyelash vipers from Costa Rica; the green palm viper from Honduras; the eight-foot bushmaster from Peru; and the fer-de-lance from Mexico.

Hypok stood there for a moment and watched all the tails disappear beneath the rocks and brush. He loved the way snakes traveled silently and effortlessly. They were singular and self-contained. And so beautiful, too. For a moment he was happy. They were free. Then he was sad, when he thought that they would all probably die here, in habitat so different from where they had come. But who knew? They might thrive: reptiles were tough. Hypok was happy again. Then he was concerned that he was upsetting the fragile ecology of a bioregion. But he cheered up again, comparing how little a few snakes could hurt the world when mankind had fucked it up so much already. He thought: wait until the hikers and tree huggers and bird watchers and eco-weenies get a load of these things. Wake them up to the real world. He giggled and watched the huge bushmaster slide down into the brush. He felt a tear form in the corner of his right eye.

One down.

He took the next box closer to the creek. There were only four snakes in this one, but it was heavy. Out came the pale olive nine-foot king cobra from the Philippines; the two yellow gold twelve-footers from The People's Republic of China; and the eighteen-foot dark green one from India — a serpent so big and so deadly that Hypok trembled from twenty yards away as it eased from the burlap bag, reared its head six feet into the air and stared at him, quite literally, eye to eye. Hypok stood still for a full two minutes as the snake stared him down. Finally the majestic thing lowered its shiny, blunt head and slowly nosed its way through the blooming mustard toward the creek. Hypok was smiling while the tears ran down his face.

Then the box of venomous little jewels from across the states, which he carried over the next rise and down into a green swale littered with oak stumps and wild tobacco: the Willard's rattlers and the bright coral snakes from Arizona; the pygmy rattlers from South Carolina; the sidewinders and Mitchell's rattlers from California; the copperheads from Florida. Hypok just opened the jars and tossed the creatures into the air, watching them land all around him. Snake rain. Serpent drops. Yes, he felt happy again.

He saved his favorite snakes for the last. He trotted back to the van and got the box. Holding it to him and making his way back through the woods with them he felt all those rampant emotions vying for attention inside himself again. The box was heavy, filled with timber rattlers from the east, his beloved *Crotalus horridus horridus,* and the thought of setting them free was almost too much for him. But was it too much excitement, or too much sadness, or too much anger? — he couldn't really say. His brain buzzed and his heart felt heavy but fast and his face was sweating but cold. He told himself this liberation was necessary as a part of who he was becoming.

He'd put most of the *horridus* into pillowcases because they were too big for jars, all except for a couple of foot-long yearlings that had been born last summer. In a shaded oak glen not far from the creek he set down the box amid the sharp dry leaves and sighed deeply. Within the pillowcases the big *horridus* were moving, their heads pressed tightly into the corners — Hypok had reinforced those corners himself, by hand, with needle and thread — feeling for a way out. I know how you feel, he thought: change, progress, release.

First he let go the females, four five-footers he'd had since they were hardly more than seven inches long. They buzzed vigorously as he stooped and untied the bags. Hypok then gingerly lifted the bags one at a time by a corner and poured the snakes onto the ground. He watched them coil and face him, rattles high and blurring, heads back and lowered for a strike. He just loved the spirit of the *horridus*.

Strangely, all four of them stopped rattling almost at once, and Hypok could hear the April breeze in the oaks and the dry chatter of the leaves moving against each other at his feet. It was a sad sound and he was smiling.

His heart jumped into the sky when he heard the voice.

"Hello, there! What are you doing?"

He reeled and dropped the two empty cases.

The park ranger was still thirty yards away, but his voice had sounded like he was almost on top of him.

Hypok felt a rapid shudder of nerves down his body and a shortness of breath. The ranger was already making his way across the swale toward him, his arms swinging with certain authority and his head — with that funny Smoky-the-Bear hat — cocked at a stern angle.

Okay, he thought.

Solid.

Capable.

Firm.

Contain yourself. You have rights.

He raised a hand in greeting and smiled.

"Just letting some snakes go, Officer! That's all."

Hypok looked down into his box. Two pillowcases containing the four big male *horridus* and the glass jar with the young ones were all that was left.

The ranger trudged toward him with his head still angled for seriousness. He wore the droop shades you'd see on television cops. He looked heavy and out of place in his stiff tan shirt with the golden badge on it, and green pants. He carried a citation book in his left hand. No gun.

"Good afternoon," said Hypok. He could smell his breath after he spoke, but he thought his voice sounded masculine.

"Afternoon."

His badge said Stefanic. His boots were shiny and his forearms thick. He stopped a few feet away, looking at Hypok, then down into the box.

"What are you doing?"

"Releasing some snakes, sir."

"Those look like rattlesnakes in the jar."

"They are. I discovered a den near my house in Orange. I live by a field. Some boys were crushing them with rocks, so I interceded and saved the last of the juveniles."

The ranger looked at Hypok again. "I'd like to see some ID."

173

"My wallet's back in the car. I'd be happy to get it for you."

Hypok stepped back as if to head toward his van, but Stefanic raised a palm his way, in the manner of a cop directing traffic.

"Not yet."

For a moment the ranger stared into the box. "What's in the pillowcases?"

"Four adult animals."

"What kind of animals?"

"Oh, I'm sorry. Rattlesnakes, also. Western Pacific rattlesnakes I caught out here a few weeks ago."

The ranger tucked his citation book under one arm, then lifted off his shades. He looked at Hypok as he slid them into the breast pocket of his shirt. He tapped the book against one leg.

"What have you set loose out here, so far?"

"Two rattlesnakes."

Oh, Hypok thought, what would Stefanic think when he saw the other three boxes and a dozen bags back in his van?

"That's all?"

"And a small collection of king and gopher snakes."

"How many is small?"

"Six specimens of each. All adults and quite healthy. I've had them for years."

Hypok was suddenly furious with himself for giving up so much information to this idiot. Why couldn't he stay light on his feet, remain glib, move laterally?

"Are you a commercial breeder?"

"Strictly a hobbyist. By trade I'm a photographer and filmmaker."

Stefanic took a step forward, set his citation book over the corner of the box, then lifted out the jar of young timber rattlers. The snakes retracted and looked out at the ranger. One buzzed and coiled to strike.

"These don't look like our westerns or reds. These look like something else."

"I believe they're the common *viridis,* sir, based on the distribution maps I've seen."

"Hmm. Awfully dark. No bands on the tails."

"The juveniles morph considerably, according to Klauber."

"You come here often?"

"Not often. But I love the park. Especially in the spring because all the flowers and reptiles are out. Got to watch for those mountain lions, though."

Tighten up now, Hypok thought: hold your tongue and cut your losses. Stefanic seemed to be considering his mountain lion statement. A girl had been badly mauled here some years ago and every spring there was controversy about whether to open the park, and to whom. You had to be eighteen to be here without parents now, Hypok thought. Something along those lines. He felt a big runner of sweat drip down his back.

"It's illegal to keep venomous reptiles in the State of California," said Stefanic.

"I understand that, sir. It's the reason I'm letting these go. I didn't feel like I had a choice but to collect the small ones, with the boys killing them for no reason."

Hypok entertained a brief vision of the eighteen-foot king cobra appearing now, raising its head six feet off the grass and charging forward to sink its fangs into Stefanic's forehead. That would actually solve a lot of problems.

"Let me see what's in the bags," ordered Stefanic.

"Well, all right."

Hypok knelt down and unknotted one of the pillowcases. He used leather to make the ties. The case had a cream background with little rows of iris across it. One of his mother's, of course. He grasped the corners at the top and lifted the bag, shaking it so the snake wouldn't come flying out at him. Stefanic moved closer and looked in. He took off his hat because the brim was cutting off the light.

"That's a big one."

"Over five feet."

"Where'd you get it?"

"Out here, a couple of seasons back."

"You've been keeping it for two years."

"I have a safe setup and take good care of them. No children or other pets around to cause problems."

"What's it eat?"

"Rats."

Hypok wondered again if anyone in law enforcement would have had the breadth of knowledge to translate his pseudonym into the names of certain animals, then into the names of certain reptiles, then assume that he was a herpetologist, then extrapolate that he must keep a *horridus* as a pet, then recognize a *horridus* when they saw one. He didn't think so when he signed his name to Item #2, and he didn't think so now. But what if they'd gone that far, and asked around at the pet shops handling reptiles? What if an APB had gone out for anyone suspicious who was dealing with snakes? He couldn't imagine that anyone could have found the big scale he'd folded so carefully and inserted into Item #2's shed, although he'd privately wished someone would. But maybe those were some of the subconscious reasons he had for freeing the animals in the first place. Now this Stefanic.

Don't get scared, he thought. *Let those in law enforcement behave stupidly. That's their job. But it would sure be nice if Stefanic got his face a little too close, wouldn't it?*

"That's really something. The size of its head. And what, twelve or thirteen rattles? I've been working out here for two years and I've never seen one this big. Still doesn't look right, though. It looks like the ones we used to find back in the Carolinas when I was a kid. Timber rattlers."

"That's exactly why I kept him," Hypok

177

ad-libbed. His heart was beating fast and light in his ears and his face was hot. Wasn't it just too fucking much to believe, that a slab like Stefanic would know a timber rattler when he saw one? Hypok suddenly hated himself for his arrogance and recklessness. He hated himself for his attempted coyness with the cops, for his mundane decision to taunt them, to get a little publicity. He had led a life of debilitating shyness and caution — he'd be the first to admit that — and now, now that he was emerging consolidated from three decades of simpering gutlessness, he was going overboard and giving himself away. Wouldn't anything ever go right? "Because the coloration and pattern were so unique," he heard himself saying. "Quite a specimen . . ."

Stefanic shook his head in admiration. "Spooky critter."

"I think their reputations are undeserved."

Stefanic set his hat over one of the other corners of the box, and stood. His hair was dented where the headband rested. "What's your name?"

Hypok knew he had about one second to give a convincing reply. Anything but the truth, his instincts told him: say anything but the truth. Sounding calm and a little disappointed, he gave Stefanic his Web name: the name of the creature he became when he was in his workroom with his fingers on the mouse, yakking it up with some of the Friendlies, or the Midnight Ramblers or just any lonely child worshipper spending time in a private chat room.

Hypok smiled and looked down into the bag again. His cheeks were burning hot now and there was a distinct ringing in his ears. *You're carrying your Lumsden license now. Why did you give a different name?* He half expected his mother to run out of the trees and lock him in the basement.

He took a deep breath but kept looking down into the bag so as not to look at the ranger. He knelt and set the pillowcase back in the box and made a show of tying the leather thong over the end, but he left it loose, just draped over itself.

"I'm not going to cite you," Stefanic said.

Hypok still couldn't muster whatever it would take to look at this . . . this unthinking block of stupidity standing over him. He remained kneeling, looking into the box. He felt a little stream of relief try to form inside him and he tried to hold on to it the best he could.

What? Wait — the ranger wasn't going to cite him! He felt the tightness disappear from his chest and he wanted to smile warmly and perhaps clasp the shoulder of this man of the great outdoors, this firm but fair enforcer of natural law and order.

"Well, I really don't feel as if I've done anything wrong."

"Possession of venomous reptiles in the State of —"

179

"— You can understand the circumstances of those boys stoning young animals, *can't* you?"

It came out much sharper than he would have liked. He was just a little out of balance now — his words didn't match his thoughts and his thoughts didn't match his feelings.

"I can understand you were keeping five-foot rattlesnakes as pets, too."

Hypok told himself to just hold on now, just settle down, and everything would be all right. Stefanic would leave, forget his name, forget the encounter. All he was doing was walking in the woods, letting a few snakes go back home. Stefanic was not going to cite him.

"I'll have to write up an incident report, though. That's just to have on file. If I find you out here again, in possession of venomous reptiles, then I *will* have to cite you."

Hypok nodded noncommittally. He felt his heart plummet to the center of earth and come out the other side, somewhere over in fucking China probably. He wondered if the rage showed on his face. In case it did, he looked away to the trees, then down into the box, then at his feet, then finally at Stefanic's nameplate, so he wouldn't have to look the ignorant ball of meat in the face.

"So."

Stefanic took a knee, as if to be familiar, on his victim's level, or at least comfortable while he wrote. He took the citation book off the

180

box and flipped up the black lid. He pulled a silver pen from the pocket of his shirt and looked across at Hypok.

Stefanic spelled out Hypok's Web name letter by letter, looking up at Hypok when he was done.

"Correct?"

"Correct."

Why in the name of Moloch didn't I just tell him my name was Lumsden?

He'll check my license when we're done and see Lumsden.

He'll take the van plate numbers and see Lumsden.

Right then, at that moment, it was impossible for Hypok to tell who he hated more — himself or the crisply starched dipshit kneeling not three feet across from him.

Hypok stood up and expected the ranger to do likewise, but he didn't. The moron was full of surprises.

Stefanic looked up at him. "Age and local address?"

Hypok made them up.

"You know your California driver's license number?"

Hypok made up that, too. He realized that everything was going to be quite all right. He felt good again. Powerful and good. Then, "You know, I hike the parks in Orange County a lot. This is far and away the best one. You guys do a great job."

"We try," said Stefanic, still writing, but not looking up. "We do try."

He was one of those guys, noted Hypok, who took about five minutes to write one letter or number.

"Do you mind if I set the juveniles free?"

"In a minute. Car make and model, year?"

"Oh, it's a Dodge van. Ninety-six. In fact, I waited until last to set these babies loose, because they're such cool, good-looking little animals."

"Trouble, if you step on one."

"That's sure true."

Hypok knelt down again and took up the jar to look at it. "You wonder how many will make it another year. You know, because of how small they are. Have you ever seen one of these eat — I mean, in nature out here?"

Stefanic stopped writing and looked at Hypok. "No. What's your local phone, Ian?"

Hypok stood with the jar in his hands and held it up to the sky. He looked at the little snakes sliding around inside.

"Six-eight-one . . ."

Stefanic lowered his face to write, fifteen minutes to write three numbers, then looked back up at Hypok.

"Four-seven-seven-eight."

Stefanic looked down at his citation page again and Hypok hit him over the head with the jar as hard as he possibly could. It broke into big shards because it was the heavy kind

182

of half-gallon jar made for bulk condiments. Stefanic grunted and his face lowered. The right side of the jar came off in Hypok's right hand so he held fast to the lid and set a big triangle of glass under the ranger's throat and drew up fast and hard with it. He bent his knees for torque. There was this sudden intake on Stefanic's part and a red stream looping in the air. Hypok did it again. The ranger lifted his head to look up and the stream gushed bigger so Stefanic kind of rolled with it, rocking back on his knees and half upright, with both hands at his throat and a bubbling wheeze issuing through his fingers. With his head cocked at an unnatural angle he stared up at Hypok in disbelief. Hypok jumped back and dropped the lid. He reached into the box and felt outside the bag for the big head of the male *horridus* and found it easily because it was nosing its way in the corner of the bag like they usually do, pressing the seams for a way out. He grabbed it firmly through the cotton with one hand and reached in with the other so they almost met and got the head good and firm and dragged the thing out. The other snake he didn't even think about. The big *horridus* was just as strong and heavy as he knew it would be. The rattles hissed like a tire leaking air, but much, much louder. The mouth was open wide from the pressure of Hypok's grip and the fangs stood out when Hypok hit the snake's nose against the box.

Three-quarters of an inch of hollow bone, dripping venom. Stefanic had gotten up. He still had both hands up to his neck and there was blood all over him, but he was up and backpedaling with his head still cranked to one side. He tripped and fell and rolled over. Hypok hustled to his side and pressed the open mouth of the *horridus* against the ranger's calf. The snake bit down like a dog. Stefanic kicked his leg free and seemed to be trying to scream — Hypok was pretty sure — but the sound was a wet hiss that sounded like water against the pebbles of a streambed. Hypok jammed the snake's mouth against the ranger's ass. Stefanic rolled over and struggled upright, but Hypok was beside him and the ranger couldn't see much because his eyes were smeared with blood and he couldn't straighten his head without his neck gaping apart so Hypok drilled the big, white, open mouth of the viper straight into Stefanic's face, right below the cheekbone, pressed it so hard the ranger lost his footing and fell over again. Hypok let go of the snake, but the *horridus* was stuck fast, anchored by those fangs, its upper jaw up by Stefanic's eye and its lower one spread all the way down to the bottom of his chin.

Hypok stood there and looked down.

He'd never seen action like this, not even when he fed his mother to Moloch. If she hadn't been feeble it would have been better. But this was another thing completely. He couldn't stand it. He felt himself excited down there and didn't know what to do. It surprised him to feel that way now. That's what the Items were for, and all the work he went through to collect them. It absolutely shocked him to feel stimulated, and he had the terrifying idea that this might mean he was homosexual. Because of Stefanic.

The ranger was still hissing wetly. But he wasn't strong enough to get up and his chest was heaving, unbelievably fast. It was amazing that much blood could keep coming out. Hypok took a knee and watched, checking the time. It was the oddest thing, but he felt like he had all the time in the world. Compared to Ranger Rick here, he thought, I do. The snake let go and crawled away.

Now what?

Ten

I struck out with both listing agents. Evans was in his seventies and Johnson was a fifty-year-old family man recently diagnosed — the agent told me confidentially — with AIDS. Two of twelve out of the way. I used a pay phone in a mini-mall to call three more of the agents, and set up appointments for the next day. I posed as a potential buyer because tomorrow was Saturday and even agents, hungry as they are for action in a cool market, don't want to give up weekends to answer questions.

But I had a bad feeling about The Horridus investigation, so I went back to the Sheriff headquarters and picked up both the Pamela and Courtney files to study at home. I always have a bad feeling about investigations until they're closed and the creep is in the can. But I felt even worse about this one than the others — something about the "pageantry," the ritual, the threat of escalation and our slender evidence filled me with dread. I looked at Frances's station, wondering if that big pink envelope might be on top, but that was a ridiculous idea, and it wasn't. It's hard not to be suspicious about things when it's part of your job.

On my way home I dropped by two more pet stores that sold reptiles and showed my sketch to the clerks. Never seen him. We sell lots of snake food. Sorry. On the way out of the last one I picked up a *Truck and Van Trader* magazine to see if anyone was offering a late-model red Chrysler van for sale. But because we hadn't released our description of the vehicle, I wondered if this part of the case was a waste of time. If he suspected his van had been seen, why not just garage it for a while? Sell it in Los Angeles or San Diego counties? Or paint it?

By the time I turned off of Laguna Canyon Road and rolled into the narrow driveway on Canyon Edge, I was tired and discouraged. I briefly thought of all the action I was missing at Tonello's — Fridays are a true free-for-all. The liquor flows and the tongues loosen and you never know what you might hear. Maybe Jordan Ishmael would dance in his underwear. I thought of Donna because I always thought of Donna. I was not quite enough of a fool to believe, even for a moment, that the three of us — Melinda, Donna and I — were not headed for some kind of disaster. Someone would get hurt. Maybe we all would. But enough. I was home for a Friday night with people I loved, and I had my files on Pamela and Courtney to ponder late, when the house

187

was quiet and the ghosts were free to roam and offer their opinions.

We took Penny to her tennis class — our standard Friday evening. It's a late one that starts at seven at the high school courts, for the advanced nine- to twelve-year-old girls who love the game. Melinda and I sat on a wooden bench at courtside and watched Penny and the others do their drills. There's something about a youngster who is developing skills that makes me very happy. I watched Penny lean into her two-hand backhands, her head steady and her knees bent, sending the ball high over the net with lots of spin, and deep into her opponents' court. She's an intensely focused player, and quick to pounce on mistakes, much like her mother would be if she played the game. The yellow ball arced back and forth over the clean green court. There was the clomping of tennis shoes and the wonderful pop of strings on felt. The dusk was falling and you could see the Pacific not far away, dark and brooding under the orange-black sky. The light of the sun bounced off the windows of the houses behind us, turning them copper. I turned and looked. Someone was barbecuing up on the hillside. The new palm trees in front of the high school swayed lazily in the breeze and you could already see the first stars and the moon in the sky, even though the sun wasn't down yet. I took Melinda's hand and held it against my leg. She stiffened at first touch, like she almost always did, then relaxed and moved closer to me. She kissed my cheek and I squeezed her fingers with my own. After the hell that Mel went through with her father, and within herself, her new affection was like the sun coming out after a long and bitter night.

We watched Penny, saying little. Something about this time of evening asks you to be quiet. So we sat there close together with our fingers locked and our palms loosely touching and watched the yellow balls go back and forth. I thought about Matt because I always think about Matt when I feel good. When I feel bad I think about him, too. We were snorkeling off of Shaw's Cove here in Laguna when he died. It was a freakish situation that took the doctors several days to explain. I agreed to an autopsy, though the thought of Matthew's perfect little body being torn by the saws was a thought that made me vomit, more than once. I didn't know anything was wrong until I saw him floating on the water. I got to him and stripped the mask off his lolling face and swam for shore with all my might. On the sand I proned him out and slapped his face, listening for his heartbeat. I couldn't hear anything inside him because my ears were roaring and this flock of seagulls had chosen the air right above us to hover and caw and cry. I got him to start breathing. The next thing I did was gather his cool little body in my arms and run. I was a lot faster than a call to 911 and a wait for help. Across the beach, up the steps, and down Coast Highway for about a mile to the little walk-in emergency clinic. It didn't take long, maybe five or six minutes in all, but I held him close the whole way, because to me he was the most precious parcel on earth. I talked to him the whole time. I still remember what I said. I burst into the waiting area and carried Matt past the desk and the nurses, back into one of the examination rooms, where a doctor was talking to a woman. They were both briefly horrified. But the doctor understood almost immediately and he took one look at me and one look at my son, and grabbed Matthew away from me. I told him what happened while he applied the oxygen mask to his face and the nurse attached the cardiac shock pads to his tiny chest. He ordered me to get the extra blanket from the other exam room, which I did, but when I tried to get back in he'd locked me out. A few minutes later, it was over.

Penny's coach told them to take five, so she came over and set her racquet on the bench. She plunked down between us, breathing hard in the way a nine-year-old breathes hard, and you understand that in about fifty seconds they'll be fully recovered and ready to go again. "I'm hitting good, Terry."

"Well. You're hitting well."

I don't know why Penny addresses nearly all her tennis comments to me. She's been playing a lot longer than I've known her. Maybe it's because we come out here and hit sometimes on the weekends. In fact, she's been addressing me instead of her mother, or both of us, for the whole year we've shared the same roof. I've wondered if it's her way of welcoming me to the unit. I'm flattered by it, I suppose, but I sometimes wonder if Melinda is as unfazed by being "second" as she says she is. Not having any children of my own, it's hard for me to say what might hurt a parent's feelings and what might not.

Penny then offered me this very penetrating, unguarded, hopeful look, a look I've never seen her cast on anyone else. Her pupils seem to bore right in, but not in aggression, rather approval. There is a twinkle of humor in her gray irises. I think it means she accepts me as a person, and has unique feelings for me, and that they are good feelings. I've come to think of it as Our Look, because I return it as best I can, though I have no idea what *I* look like, gazing back.

"How's the backhand, Pen?" asked Melinda.

"The usual," she answered absently.

"Well, what's the usual?" asked Melinda.

"You know, *Mom*."

Melinda smiled and pulled Penny's cap down over her eyes.

"Mom, cut it out."

"Boo-hoo," said Melinda.

"Boo-hoo," I said.

Penny bounced off the bench and took up her racquet. She studied us. She tapped her mother on the top of the head with the strings, then me. "You're just sticking up for her, Terry."

"I think she's worth sticking up for," I said.

"And it's nice to be stuck up for, sometimes."

"My boyfriend's going to stick up only for me," said Penny.

"No use hogging all the good feelings," said Melinda. "There's enough of those to go around."

Penny let out that impatient exhale that kids save for the ignorant, then skipped onto the court.

"She sure has gotten to be a smart-ass the last year," Mel said.

"Kinda has."

"She's competitive and jealous."

"Maybe she's going out of her way to make me feel welcome."

Melinda shook her head. "I don't think so. It's not that I don't think she's generous enough for that. Or duplicitous enough to fake it to get what she wants. She genuinely adores you."

I thought about that. Melinda ascribes levels of sophistication — as in sophistry — to Penny that I don't see. I see a lack of guile. It's another example of the difference in the way we see children in general, I suppose.

"Do you really think she'd BS me?"

"Oh, yes. I think it's instinct for some people. Intuitive self-preservation. Smearing a little honey on things. She knows you like her, and that's your weak spot. She's not exploiting it yet, I don't think."

"You make her sound like a Borgia."

"I think she has depths you don't see. Well, *do* you feel welcome with us?"

I thought about that for a moment. The last year had been full of good things for me and full of disappointments, too. "Yes, most of the time. I don't forget that you two are the family and I'm kind of the third wheel, but . . . third wheels are good sometimes. Like on ATVs and trikes and —"

"— No, really, do you feel welcome, or don't you?"

"I have. You've never made me feel like an outsider. And Penny hasn't, either. I think she likes me."

Melinda turned her face to me and studied me hard. She had that interrogator's expression, the placid one that bores in, gathers all and gives up nothing in return. "In fact, she's playing us off against each other a lot more now than she used to. She's using you to leverage her discontents with me."

"I see that. But I wonder where to draw the line."

"You shouldn't cater to her, Terry."

"Do you really think I do?"

"Of course you do. You're a sucker for affection, just like we all are. I don't blame you. I just don't think it's probably good for Penelope, in the long run, if you overdo that kind of thing."

I felt gut punched. I hated even the *idea* of getting between her and her daughter. I wanted harmony, not conflict. Clear lines, no clutter. Who doesn't? Few things in life are more surprising than assuming your partner agrees with you, only to find out she or he vehemently does not. You wonder where you're getting your ideas of who they are.

"I really didn't think I was. But I won't. I'll be real careful about that."

"Do what you think's right, Terry. It's just a phase. It will be over soon."

Melinda turned away and watched the court. "But what I'm saying is, it's a cheap-shit stunt to endear yourself to her if you're not going to stick around."

Wham.

She looked back at me with a cruel little smile. I'd seen a lot of that smile back around the time her father died and we were both in our separate worlds of torment. Not so much, lately.

"I'll always do what's best for *her*, Terry. Always."

"You should. And so far as my sticking

around goes, I'm here. And I'm happy to be here. I adore both of you. You're two of my favorite people in the whole world."

She nodded, still looking back at me. The smile was gone. "So you don't think that I'm just a dried-up old bag who won't give you a family of your own?"

"Not going to answer, Mel. You know what the answer to that is."

And well she did, because this line of inquiry had come up before. So far as being dried up, Melinda has always been squeamish and uncertain about her own sexuality. Not prudish so much as afraid, slightly ashamed. With me, anyway. I have no idea what she was like with Jordan Ishmael. "Dried up" was a phrase she introduced herself, though she has been quite a bit less than dried up on several occasions with me. She's often called herself my "old girl." It's been a term of self-endearment, as well as a way of getting me to acknowledge that her two years of seniority don't bother me in the least. They don't and never have.

So far as not giving me a family, that's a decision she made clear to me from the very moment we even considered moving closer to each other. Long before we decided to share a home. Marriage, maybe, she said: no children. She had been there and done that. I agreed wholeheartedly. I had had Matthew, and he was a perfect human and a perfect memory, and he was enough. I had no desire to bring another child into the world. None of them would ever be him. I believed that I had been blessed once and blessed almost completely. And I believed that only a fool would ask more of life than that.

Melinda has told me a hundred times — the first few in all seriousness, the others as a kind of tossed-off joke — that I'd be better off with a young bimbo who would have my babies and still look good in a two-piece five years from now. But the fact that Melinda is the absolute opposite of a bimbo is exactly what made me love her to begin with. I took to her unadorned qualities like a trout released into a cold mountain brook.

From the beginning there was no ditz or glitz in her; no mindless levity; no primping and preening; no consuming vanity, gyms, StairMasters or step aerobics; no low-calorie, nonfat, high-fiber diets; no weaves or perms or makeovers. In fact, until six months ago, she rarely wore makeup or did more with her hair than wash and comb it. Until six months ago I never saw her bring home clothes from anywhere but the discount warehouses. Until six months ago, when Mel began to pull out of that spiral that began with the death of her indifferent father, she rarely wore lipstick. Since that low point she's shopped upscale two times and made regular attempts to prettify herself. She sometimes wears lipstick and makeup.

I'm not sure what to make of it or how to react to it. If it was a sign of happiness or newfound confidence, I'd be happy, too. But in spite of her noticeable improvement since those dark days, I wouldn't describe Melinda Vickers — she reclaimed her maiden name when she divorced Jordan — as a happy person. There's a sadness in her that I cherished from the start. A sadness that seemed like a perfect mate for my own. And it's still there inside her, just beneath the new outfit from Nordstrom and the occasional lipstick and the neatly trimmed hair. But her sadness is the one thing about Melinda that I loved in the beginning and have become impatient with. I think it's time for her to move beyond it. It's not necessary. But who am I to say what her heart should feel?

I've been no help to her at all. I changed when I met Donna Mason. It actually seemed like something in the air I was breathing in that elevator, and maybe it did have to do with pheromones or some other biological mystery. I was instantly, subtly altered, my polarities tweaked, my point of view adjusted. I was lifted, turned and set down facing a slightly different direction. In that instant I saw myself with different eyes. I saw the world, and Melinda, too, with different eyes. It was like seeing clearly for the first time, or, more realistically, for the first time in a long time. Beginning then, with a four-floor elevator ride, I started to rethink a lot of what I thought I knew. That moment was a beginning and an ending. And since then I've been wondering how to accommodate the changed Terry Naughton with the old one. I've been as cautious as I can, as slow as I can, as self-examined as I can. I've put on the brakes, rationalized the circumstances, had a thousand long talks with myself. I've cursed the change, punished myself for undergoing it just when Melinda needed me most, loathed myself for stepping into that elevator, bludgeoned my own heart for its excitement. But after all of that, the fact remains, untarnished as a ball of solid gold: I am in love with Donna Mason and with the Terry Naughton I become when I think about her. I feel like many good things are possible with her, through her, around her. But I am dazed and suffocated by the Terry Naughton who lives his lying life with Melinda. I feel ready to shed away the old and make room for the new. Bottom line is I've made one gigantic mess of things, and I know this. There will be hell to pay.

I didn't answer her question about being an old bag who wouldn't give me a son or daughter. I sensed the ocean of unsaid things welling up around us, splashing over the sides of our rickety little boat, the sea swells in the distance high and black and frothing at their tops, advancing. I yearned for tequila but I quit carrying the flask two months ago.

After tennis we all went to a bluff-top café on Coast Highway where the food is good and cheap and you can sit on stools overlooking the Pacific. The ocean was flat and shiny as lacquer, but I still kept seeing those waves heaving up toward us.

That night Melinda came to bed in a salmon-colored slip I'd never seen before with lipstick freshly applied and a bit of dizzyingly sensual perfume coming from her. She was assured and eager, even a little greedy.

It was one of those times when you make love without words because you understand that you are either continuing something or ending it, and you don't want to know which.

Eleven

He took his third girl sometime that night or early morning, though we didn't know it until 6:30 A.M.

Her name was Brittany Elder and she was five. Irvine PD called me shortly after the girl's mother had dialed 911. She had gone in to awaken her daughter and found the bed empty. Empty of her daughter, that is. One pane of the bedroom window glass had a hand-sized hole neatly cut in it; the other pane of the slider was open and the screen was down. I requested an all-points alert for any late-model red Chrysler-Plymouth-Dodge van and headed out.

Johnny was the only other CAY deputy at work that early, and we hit the scene twenty minutes later.

Abby Elder, the mother, was still in a blue terry bathrobe when she answered the door. Johnny walked in ahead of me and I saw him eyeing the front doorknob sadly — God knew how many times it had been touched by now. Abby's eyes were red and puffed and her hair was still messed from sleep.

Two Irvine PD officers stood in the bedroom. They looked at me, then down at the bed. I followed their eyes to the thrown-back sheet and covers and the long translucent snakeskin lying lengthwise down the bed. It was papery and wrinkled and its two jaws lay loose and open. It was probably five feet long and four inches wide. I looked at the hideous thing, then back at Abby Elder, who stood with her arms around herself and a big piece of her bottom lip locked under her teeth. Fat clear tears rolled down her cheeks.

"What does he do to them?"

"Nothing, Ms. Elder," I said. "He dresses them and lets them go."

"He should be in prison."

"He will be."

"She's my life. Brittany is my whole life."

"We're going to do everything we can to get her back to you."

I told Johnny to start his crime scene work and took Abby into the living room. I wanted to hear every word she had to say. I told her to take it slowly, tell me the details as she remembered them.

While she talked she looked at me with eyes begging me not to fault or blame her. Parents blame themselves for everything bad that happens to their children. I can vouch from experience. So I interrupted her several times to assure her that this was not her fault in any way, but other than that I kept silent, took notes and let her tell me about the night that was, she said, easily the worst of her life.

"This is every worst nightmare I ever had," she sobbed at one point.

"People wake up from nightmares," I said. "You're going to. So is Brittany."

At the mention of her daughter's name, a fresh river of tears poured down Abby Elder's face. I said nothing. Instead, I looked at the pictures hanging on the living room wall. They were school portraits of Brittany — a pretty, dark-haired girl with brown eyes and a mischievous grin. There was a pink ribbon in her hair. In another photograph she was posed with her mother. They both looked happy and healthy, like they had nothing but good things to do that day. I wondered again at the courage and energy it must take for a mother to raise a child alone. Or a father. A single parent, I thought. Like Pamela's mother. Like Courtney's. I realized something then, but I couldn't quite grasp what it was. So I listened.

Her story was actually quite brief and clear: she had awakened at 6 A.M. as she always did on workdays, to her alarm. She liked waking up to a reggae station. She put on her robe, got a cup of coffee — the machine timer had it brewed up by five-thirty because she loved the smell of coffee in the morning. She poured in some milk and took the cup with her to peek in on Brittany. Usually, she said, Brittany would sleep until Abby was done with showering and dressing, around seven. But Abby always checked on her, first thing, or almost first thing, after she had that first cup of coffee going.

"And," she said, blinking and looking down at the carpet. She took a deep breath but didn't look at me. "And when I opened the door and looked . . . she wasn't there. She just . . . *wasn't there*. Instead, that . . . *thing* was in her bed. Where she was supposed to be."

The room was still fairly dark and it felt different, she said, so she turned on the light and overrode her shock a little, thinking that Brittany might be way under the covers, down by the foot of the bed, as she sometimes was. She wasn't. Abby had pulled the bed away from the wall and looked under it. She'd flung open the closet, then run to the child's bathroom. When she went back into the bedroom she felt the breeze and saw the window slid open and realized the screen was gone. She had screamed. Then she had raced to the kitchen and dialed 911.

"The room felt different because the window was open?" I asked.

"Yes. The wind coming through? I didn't register it until I came back in."

"Did it feel different for any other reason?"

She brought her red-laced eyes to me. "It felt like a room that something bad had happened in."

I made a note of that. Abby said she'd looked through Brittany's room again after calling 911. Then she looked on the patio and in her own bathroom, and, for reasons not rational, under the big cream sofa in the living room. She looked in the garage. She looked in the washer and dryer. She said she was standing in the living room crying when the Irvine officers arrived, and when she answered the door she was too distraught to even speak. Her gaze shifted to the floor again and I knew that Abby Elder was punishing herself for what had happened. She shook her head and buried her face in her hands.

I could see down the short hallway toward Brittany's room where Johnny was photographing the bed with the shed skin in it. He'd already set his crime scene ribbon across the beginning of the hall, and stationed the Irvine cops on the other side of it. They stood there side by side, one looking back at Johnny and the other looking forward at me. They both looked spent: graveyard patrolmen on their last hour of the shift.

"When was the last time you checked on her?" I asked.

"Before I turned out my lights. It was eleven-twenty."

Abby Elder's words sounded detached and dreamlike now, as if delivered on her behalf by someone next to her.

I asked her if she had any relatives in the area.

She said her mother, up in Fullerton, maybe half an hour away.

"Why don't you call her? See if she'll come over and be here with you."

"I . . . I think that's a really good idea. Now?"

"Sure. We're almost finished with this."

I asked for a cup of that coffee, both because I wanted it and because I wanted to get Abby focused away from herself a little. For the next twenty minutes we talked about her life, job, habits, haunts, friends, acquaintances, routines, activities. Her family, her ex, her neighborhood. I was trying to find the intersection with Pamela and Courtney. I saw little Pamela in Orange — which was north of here; and I saw little Courtney down in San Clemente — to the south. Brittany was in the middle. None of their tangents crossed in any way that I could find. Until I looked at Brittany's picture on the wall and began to understand what I'd almost understood just a few minutes ago. This was it: Pamela, Courtney and Brittany looked nothing alike. A blonde, a redhead and a brunette. Their mothers — Jennifer, Bridget and Abby — *looked very much alike.*

He's not picking the girls, I thought: he's picking the mothers. That's why we haven't connected the girls. It's not they who catch his eye. It's *Mommy.* That's where we'll find the plane of intersection.

"Abby," I said. "Would you name for me, right off the top of your head, every group you've belonged to recently — church group,

205

parents' group, classes, workshops, seminars, social groups, clubs, unions, affiliations, anything? *Everything?* Please? Just take off and start naming."

I'd asked Jennifer Clark and Bridget Simenon the same question, and I had their answers carefully recorded in the case files of Pamela and Courtney. But I knew I had been focusing on affiliations where the girls would be present. Now I knew that the girls came second. The mothers came first, to his eyes. It was a small candle in our room of darkness, but its light was warm and promising.

None of the three women were particularly active, either socially or professionally. They basically did their jobs and went home to take care of their daughters. Abby said she went to church occasionally, but usually not to the same one. It made her uncomfortable to be introduced as a guest, so she tended just to read her Bible sometimes for inspiration. She belonged to no professional associations except a credit union through work. She was an Automobile Club member, but she assumed that didn't count. She took a junior college class in astronomy seven years ago, when her marriage was on the rocks, before Brittany was born. She said she didn't belong to any of the "anonymous" programs because she didn't have an addictive personality.

"I . . . well . . . no, that wouldn't —"

"— Go ahead," I said.

"Well . . . I joined a singles club. A dating service? Just recently. Last week."

I imagined a membership of young men with access to Abby, and my heart sped up.

She gave me the name of the place.

"I mean, it was just three days ago I went on their active membership. I haven't had a single date or even sent anyone a card. Or gotten one. That's how it works — you look at pictures and send the person a card that says you're interested? I would think that who-ever did this would have . . ." Two big tears ran down her face and she looked at the carpet again. ". . . Would have known about me and Brittany before that."

"Maybe not. Do the men who look at your pictures get your address or phone number or full name?"

She shook her head and looked down again. "It's supposed to be confidential. They prom-ise you that. Not until later, you give the guy that information if you want to."

"You have a nickname, then, or a number so they can send you the card?"

"It's first names and then a membership number."

"I want yours."

She went into her bedroom and came back a moment later. She told me the number and sat back down.

"They always say it's someone you know, don't they?"

"It isn't, Abby. It could be someone you met yesterday. Have any of the Bright Tomorrows members talked to you? Even casually, at the service?"

She shook her head. "I haven't spent a single minute there, as a member. That's what I'm saying."

I considered. "I want you to think back — I know it's hard, but try — think back to every new male you've met in the last month, who's between twenty and forty years old. In any circumstance, any occasion. Any one you talked to, were introduced to, had a conversation or encounter with. No matter how minor it might seem."

"Oh, God. How can I —"

"— Just try. You'll remember what's important if you just relax."

"You mean clerks and salesmen and — ?"

"— All of them. Go ahead. Don't edit. Just recall."

She didn't do real well. Her heart was heavy for Brittany and herself, and her mind was jammed with worry. She couldn't recall names, her descriptions were hazy, her sense of time uncertain at best.

So I took out copies of Amanda's sketches of the reptile fancier who had known so much about rattlesnakes.

"Have you seen a man who looks like this? Even slightly?"

The bearded version was a definite no. So

was the unbearded. So was the glasses version, and the one without glasses. I watched her eyes as she studied the sketches, and I could tell that at least half of her mind was elsewhere. How couldn't it be?

"I'm sorry," she said. "I mean, he looks kind of familiar. But it's like . . . he looks like . . . everybody else? I'm sorry."

It was true. Amanda hadn't been able to pry from Steven Wicks's memory the details of an image that wasn't there. And even if it had been there, I knew that The Horridus was changing, shedding, "consolidating," as Strickley had said. The old skin in Brittany's bed said the same thing. I understood it. It was exactly what I would have done if I were him. The old was passing and the new was taking form. He was hatching out — egg to serpent. The only thing we could assume was that he probably didn't look anything like these pictures.

When her mother arrived a few minutes later Abby Elder collapsed into a fit of sobs, and her usefulness was temporarily over. The last thing I got from her were the name and telephone numbers of her ex-husband, and a surprisingly hostile stare from her mother. I got a recording at the ex's home and a recording at his work. I called Bright Tomorrows, too, and still another canned message telling me they didn't open until ten. It was that time of morning — seven-fifty — when everyone is on his way somewhere, but nobody's there yet. When everyone is changing from who they are at home to who they become at work. Hatching out. Old to new. Egg to serpent.

I went outside and sketched the layout of the condo, trying to see what The Horridus had seen, what might have helped him decide. I stood there in the cool April morning and felt the old thing coming toward me. It's a feeling I've gotten since I was a kid, and it comes at unexpected times. After all these years, I've learned to pay attention to it. It's a feeling of change — rapid, dramatic, unalterable change. The kind of change that leaves you breathless, looking back at the way things were and will never be again. It's the foreknowledge that a freight train of events from which you cannot get away will soon and suddenly be bearing down on you. I felt it coming, just a few days before Matthew. I felt it in the elevator with Donna Mason. And I felt it now as the neighbors peeked through their windows at me and the joggers huffed by askance and a jet left a thin contrail high in the blue spring sky.

Johnny found plenty of prints from Brittany's room, but most of them were small, and the others came from places her mother would likely have touched. He lifted a partial from the aluminum window frame and another from one corner of the window glass. The screen yielded nothing. He rolled the shed skin lengthwise in newspaper, hoping that the ALS or bench laser in the Crime Lab might illuminate a latent print.

"He's slick as shit," Johnny said to me quietly, glancing toward the hallway. "I'll glass this whole room and where he was standing outside. I'll get down on my hands and knees. I'll pick up every bit of sand, hair or fiber I can find outside this window and let Reilly figure out where it came from. But you know what, man? He's careful, he knows what he's doing and he's not giving us one goddamned thing."

"He'll make a mistake."

He sighed and looked at the hole cut out of the glass. I pictured a snake crawling through that hole. "That's what I want. I want to find a guy who's got that piece of glass stashed in his van. Or his garage. Or his guest house. He's not that careless, though. He'll take it into a parking lot, step on it and kick the pieces everywhere. And even Johnny Escobedo won't be able to put them together again."

"Work it, Johnny. That's all you can do."

"We got to do something more, man. We can't just wait on him. I'm sitting here playing with fingerprint tape and he's got her out in the woods somewhere. Is that woman in there ever going to see her girl alive again?"

I knew he was right. The Horridus had waited twenty-six days between Pamela and

Courtney. Now he was down to fifteen.

"There's a miracle in here, Johnny. Somewhere. Find it."

Johnny ran his hand past his widow's peak and through his thick black hair. "We got to make a miracle of our own, man. He's not going to do it for us."

I called Louis and told him to drop the vintage clothing stores for now and triple up with me and Frances on the homes-for-sale listings. We were down to ten sellers who might be our man.

"Ish told me Frances isn't coming in today."

"Why not?"

"Still upset about yesterday, I guess."

"We're all upset, goddamnit."

"Yeah, but no telling what kind of pictures she found in Chet's *den*."

"Then it's just you and me on the listings, Louis."

I read off the next five names and agents to him, complete with phone numbers and the real estate office addresses.

"Double time, Louis. This guy's brave and getting braver."

Before ringing off I got Jennifer Clark's and Bridget Simenon's numbers from Louis. I had to wonder if either of them might have been looking for "bright tomorrows." Who wasn't?

I called Melinda. She answered in her investigator's voice.

"It's just me," I said. "He took another one."

"I heard. How old?"

"Five. He left a snakeskin in her bed. I . . . I just called to say things are going to be okay. They have to be okay."

"What things? What do you mean?"

"I don't know."

She was silent for a moment. "Well, Terry," she said. "When you do, you can fill me in."

"I just . . . Penny get off to school okay?"

"Of course she did. Why?"

"All right, Mel. Okay."

"Okay."

"Last night was really good."

"Yes. It was."

I hung up and called Donna. Her secretary knows me only as Skip, and to always put me through. She did.

"I wanted to hear your voice," I said.

"And I yours. You don't sound too good."

"He took another one. A five-year-old."

Donna's intake of breath caught in her throat. For a woman who made her living on mostly bad news, Donna Mason could also choke — almost literally — at times of great emotion.

"I'm with you," she said.

"I wish you were. I've got these bad feelings all around and I'm trying not to let them get in."

"Where are you?"

I told her.

Twelve

He hefted Item #3 over his shoulder and backed out of the side door of the van. The automatic opener had already shut the door behind him and the garage was lit only by a bare bulb, but it was enough to see by. The blinds on the window were down. He steadied his load as he straightened and walked toward the door to the guest house. The Item kicked and made noises, but its mouth and hands and ankles were taped and it was in the thick duffel and couldn't move very well. When he was inside the bedroom he set it on the bed and opened the top of the bag wide.

He tried not to look directly at its face while he tied the little black velvet hood over its head. He'd made the hood himself, with small holes at the bottom so they could breathe but couldn't see. During the brief time it took to fit the hood over its head he got a brief look at it — a lot like the mother — slender and pretty. But dark hair. Its eyes were brown, and wide with unutterable terror. The tape around its head was still tight over its mouth. With its eyes bugging out like this it looked like a rat being constricted by a snake, like his mother

214

had looked when Moloch was wrapped around her. He snugged the drawstrings firmly and knotted them. Then he dug the Hiker's Headlight out of the duffel, where he'd put it after stripping it off his head once he was back inside the van.

He didn't worry that it would be able to describe him later because he was hidden behind the oversized, wraparound angler's sunglasses — polarized to cut glare and reveal trout underwater — the baseball cap pulled down right on top of the frames and the bandanna over his nose and mouth like a bandit. His breath smelled extra terrible, trapped up close to his nose like this. When he had the hood secured over Item #3 he stripped off the hat and shades, pulled the bandanna down around his neck and dropped some cinnamon breath drops onto his tongue.

Stop crying and don't worry, he said amiably, screwing the top back onto the little bottle. Fresh. *You're going to be just fine.*

He set up the three tall tripods and affixed his cameras to them — one video and two digital stills. He used a stool to get them aimed down at the bed where Item #3 lay and get the still cameras focused right. Then he climbed down and took the extra long remote exposure cables and set them on the floor just under the bed where he could reach them easily.

Brittany lay on her side, breathing fast, her

215

heart pounding. She felt her ankles wrapped tight together and her arms tied behind her back. Not being able to move was the worst feeling in the world. Her nightie was all twisted up and half choking her. She had thought just minutes ago, when she was inside the heavy bag, that she might faint from the lack of air. She just couldn't draw enough in with her mouth taped shut and the bag all around her. And she could hardly move. They were in a white van then, she knew that. He hadn't put her in the bag until they were inside and the door was shut.

Now she was on a bed and there was some kind of opening near her nose and she was getting deep breaths that didn't smell like canvas tennis shoes. Instead, she smelled someone else's smells, like when she stayed at her grandmother's house. These odors were kind of similar — bed smells, blanket smells — sweet and personal. Then they would go away and she would smell something sticky and industrial that she understood was the tape beneath her nose.

The hood he had just put over her was already damp on the side from her tears. She had only gotten that one quick look at him in the sudden light. Sunglasses. Cap. And a scarf around his face. He could be anybody, but she named him Dead Gopher Man because his breath was awful. She'd first noticed it when he carried her from her room to the front door of her house, the way he held her head right under his chin. At first she thought he was Daddy, but she realized quick he wasn't. Daddy wasn't that rough, that much in a hurry, and his breath didn't smell like the dead gopher they'd found in the corner of the playground at school. Daddy wouldn't wake her from sleep by wrapping a piece of tape around her face. Daddy didn't have one giant bright eye shining at her from his forehead.

She opened her eyes inside the hood but saw only darkness. She closed them and the darkness got darker. She could hear him across the room, talking quietly to someone.

Like it? I thought you would. See, I can get them to like me any time I want. They see me like Collie and Valee saw me. Like you never did. Oh, fuck you, bitch, and stay where you belong.

Brittany decided again that this was just a bad dream. And, like any other bad dream, she could get out of it by shaking her head real fast, squishing her eyes shut real hard and screaming real loud. And when you screamed you shook your whole body as hard as you could and that's how you broke out of a bad dream. When you opened your eyes again, you were out of it. It worked. It worked when Finger Man was chasing her and she couldn't run. It worked when Slow Man came up at her from under the bed. It worked when she was falling. She called it Dream Busting. You just closed your eyes and shook hard, and when you opened your eyes again you had busted out.

She took a deep breath through her nose.

She closed her eyes as hard as she could.

She screamed against the tape, but the scream stayed inside her throat and sounded against the inside of her ears.

She shook her whole body as hard as she could.

She shook it some more.

What are you doing, you little idiot?

She shook it even more than that.

It's having a fit. What shall we do about that, Mom?

His *mom* is here?

Brittany gave her body one last supreme shake — head to toe and everything in between. Then she opened her eyes.

She saw only the darkness and felt the stifling closeness of the hood.

Her sobs pulsed down in her neck and she could hear them with the inside of her ears instead of the outside. She could feel the wet part of the hood higher on her cheek now because it had moved when she shook. The open spot that let in the air was still down by her nose, but she could see a little light now. She could feel the new tears running down toward the tape. When she cranked her eyeballs all the way down she could see through a real small slit in the open part: a red bedspread.

Don't go full convulsive. Everything's cool. Just lie there and get used to your habitat.

His voice was kind of high, like it was coming through his nose. It was a dull voice. It sounded like he was talking to someone he didn't believe was there, or maybe talking in a dream.

Better now?

She lay still and listened to the hiss of breath coming in and out of her nose. She strained her eyeballs down and saw the sliver of red bedspread. She smelled the bed she was lying on — someone else's, an old person's bed — and she closed her eyes again.

Somehow, Brittany thought, if you saved up and concentrated real hard and did it just right, the Dream Busting might work — *even if you weren't dreaming.* You could just burst your way out of one place and into another. I'm going to do that, soon as I stop crying. Soon as I stop crying. Soon as I stop crying.

He opened a can of ravioli, dumped it into a pan and turned the gas up high. He filled a tumbler with ice and poured it three-quarters full of tequila, the rest with water. Predation made him hungry and thirsty. He was in the little guest house kitchen, but he could look through the doorway to the cage room and see the bed and Item #3 upon it and the tripods with his gear attached, aimed down. It was a feisty one. The way it would shake and try to scream, then stop and lie still, as if it were trying to break out of a nightmare. Maybe it was, he thought. He thought about what he might describe to the Midnight Ramblers in the chat room. You had to be careful, but you also wanted to let them know what a good thing you'd had.

When the ravioli was hot he got a spoon and picked up the pan by the handle and went back into the living room with it. He brought the highball, too. He sat in the overstuffed chair — the old floral thing with his mother's matching arm protectors still on it — and looked at Item #3 on the bed, then past the bed to Mike's huge glass tank.

He admired the tank and its construction. Twenty-seven feet long, seven high and seven deep. It intruded well into the room. Hypok could walk around in it, no problem, so long as he stayed alert. Full-spectrum light and heat lamps ran behind the bars on top, and underneath the gravel stratum on the cage floor were electric heat elements. The left one-third of it was a deep pool with a running waterfall. In the middle was a pile of big flat rocks overhung by the trunk and branches of a big orange tree he'd trimmed to fit. The right section of the cage was taken up by a child's playhouse. Hypok sometimes thought of the tank as a separate world, with its own air, light and water, its own shelter — all created by him.

The playhouse looked something like a Victorian dollhouse, with a gabled roof and shingles and even a spire. It was a remarkably sturdy little house, strong enough for kids to climb in and out of the door and windows. It was purchased for Hypok's sisters when he was five, and they had loved the thing. His mother had forced him to play with them in it — not as "Father," which he'd wanted to be, or even "Brother," but "Baby" or "Jeannie" like the girl's name, or sometimes "Little Sister #3." It had stayed behind when his sisters outgrew it, and Hypok had brought it here — to stately old-town Tustin — when he moved himself and his mother into more appropriate quarters.

Moloch was piled high inside the playhouse, with his head — about the length and width of a phone book — poking out near the top of the door. Moloch got curious when Hypok was in the room because it usually meant food. You wouldn't really see him move inside the house, unless you were watching hard. That's the way it was with big snakes — they didn't locomote so much as simply adjust. One second you'd look through the playhouse door and see two huge inert green coils lying atop each other, still as mossy logs, then the next time you looked his head would be there and he'd be eyeing you. Like now. Hypok could see his big silver eye with the black vertical slash of a pupil through it, and the heavy black tongue going patiently in and out of his closed mouth. Moloch — *Eunectes murinus* — his beloved anaconda from Paraguay, was close to thirty feet long now, and Hypok guessed his weight at a rather obese five hundred pounds. Realistically, though, how do you weigh such a thing?

Item #3 burst into another fit on the bed but Hypok ignored it. Was it epileptic? Whatever. He drank down the tequila — still warm — then went back to the kitchen for another couple of inches and some fresh ice.

When he came back to his chair he was reflecting upon, for the thousandth time, what a miracle it was that the snake was even alive. Yes, his own mother had tried to kill it when it was just a newborn, hardly twenty-four inches long, by spraying it every morning with bug killer. He was eleven when he bought the reptile, from a friend. He had long been sleeping in the "den" of the house, a miserable, windowless little room that Wanda locked him in during the night. This, due to some curious explorations on the part of Collette and Valeen, starting when he was four. The snake's cage was in his "room," and his mother would slide the outside deadbolt early, come in, check to see if Genie — her nickname for Gene — was asleep. And if she was convinced he was — he was great at faking it and lifting one eyelid from the depths of his pillow — she'd produce from the big pocket of her housecoat a red can of roach killer, slide open the cage top and shoot the poor thing right in the face with it. This went on for almost a week, until Hypok had gotten a small padlock and hidden the key. Moloch — he was named Mike, back then — had quit eating, lost his skin in little patches and generally grown depressed. Hypok's own skin had started turning bad about that time, and he attributed both of their sufferings to the roach spray, but he was more worried about the snake than about himself. He thought the little anaconda would die. But slowly Mike got strong again, then he started growing extra fast. Hypok believed then, and still did now, that the roach killer had actually boosted Mike's growth rate. A short two years later he was four feet long and taking large rats. Now he was high twenties, at least! The Brooklyn Zoo had just acquired a reticulated python that measured twenty-*three,* and that had made the news. So much for Mom and her stupid fucking hateful ideas on things. Even twenty-two years ago, as Hypok faked sleep and watched his tiny, wretched, perpetually drunken mother spray his snake, he had imagined how great it would be if Mike could just get big enough to eat her someday. Any woman who tried to turn her boy into a girl, then treated him like a criminal when it didn't work, deserved what she got, in Hypok's opinion. And the more he thought about it, the angrier he got.

Three Dream Busts later, Brittany was dispirited and exhausted. She'd almost fallen off the bed during the last one. She was certain that Dead Gopher Man would come over and hit her, or at least drag her back to the middle of the mattress, but he didn't. She could hear him across the room, eating something right from the pan, muttering to someone she was now convinced was not there. So she scrunched herself back onto the bed using the side of her head and feet as pivots, raising the middle of her body like a big inchworm, wriggling backward, her ankles aching against each other and the black hood riding up so far onto her head that she could now see through the airholes if she moved her eyeballs down a little.

She lay on her side. Dead Gopher Man was somewhere in the room behind her. When she tilted back her head and looked down through the breathing hole, she saw a big window with a naked tree, a pond and a playhouse behind it. There were walls inside at both ends. It was lit from above and looked clean. Was it a cage? A playroom for a toddler? Where were the toys?

Soundlessly, Dead Gopher Man came into her view. He had his back to her and he was looking through the glass. He looked neither tall nor short; neither fat nor skinny. He wore a jacket like Daddy did sometimes when he picked her up after his work. With his cap and bandanna gone she could see his short, white, brushed-back hair. It wasn't a hairstyle you saw a lot. When he turned to the side, his face looked kind of tight and mean. He was holding something in one hand that looked like a little girl's dress — pink with white trim, like you'd wear to church. In the other hand was some kind of white lacy thing. He was looking at the playhouse behind the glass.

Then he turned all the way and looked at her. She closed her eyes. But she did see his face first — a regular face, maybe a little thin, with brown eyes. It was a serious face, one that you wouldn't want to talk to if your mouth was full of food. That was a big thing with her dad. Dead Gopher Man looked like he would spank you for anything. She started sobbing again, thinking of her dad, and the way he was big and strong and would beat the crap out of this guy if he was here. He was never there when you wanted him to be. Maybe just one more big giant Dream Bust would work and she'd open her eyes to find all of this gone.

She opened her eyes again and looked down toward the breathing hole and she didn't see the glass cage at all, but instead, a face up close and looking in at her. Then she smelled his breath again. She tried to keep her body from shaking as she scrunched her eyes shut hard and sobbed, but it didn't do any good at all.

Hypok rearranged the hood over its head, just to make sure it was getting breath and not looking out. Then he took out the big scissors and cut the nightgown from neck to hem, then the sleeves, then he peeled it away like a skin. It shivered and pressed its hooded head into one of the pillows. Its skin was pale and perfect, its panties white. He wanted to see and maybe touch what was under those. Hypok put one of Valeen's old dresses on Item #3, touching it as little as possible but consuming every inch of it with his eyes. When it was arranged, he stood and looked down at it, pleased.

He went into the bedroom and got his good skin from a drawer in the old dresser. He took off his clothes and stepped through the leg openings. He didn't look in the mirror because he'd seen himself enough times in all these years to have the image branded in his memory: the raw pink stretchy patches that invaded all of him except his face and neck and hands, the lesions, the rock-hard scars left by two-plus decades of chronic psoriasis that no amount of Lidex or UVA baths could control let alone cure, the vanishing wilderness of his original skin, his birth skin, his good skin, the way God had intended him to be before his mother got to him with the spray. No, he didn't even look. One worked with what one had. The cards one is dealt. He slipped his legs into the thin cotton suit, pulled it up snugly to his waist, then over his shoulders, then put his hands through the armholes and stretched them out straight to bring the thing taut against his back. He reached down to his crotch and zipped himself all the way up to his chin and in.

Now he looked in the mirror. And there he was, newly hatched in a skein of overlapping bright silver blue metallic scales that housed him in a supple, holographic shimmer. He gave a turn. The polyester scales picked up the dim light and gathered it into a rainbow of reflected color. Next, the booties and gloves. And a lingering final assessment in the glass: yes, reptilian and celestial all at once, he thought, essential and ideal, yet tactile and present. The best he could be. Hypok transcendent. Touchable.

His heart was beating slow and smooth as he went back to the living room. He finished the tequila and poured more. He felt capable with the good skin on him. His shoulders were relaxed, loose and low, and his neck was strong but flexible. He walked, feeling himself. His head was quick on a neck this powerful, and it was pleasurable to feel it swiveling left, straight ahead, then hard right, as he took the measure of his environment. He felt like he could smoothly glide around any obstacle — rock or brick or branches. He felt as if he could enter a swamp, slowly and noiselessly, and account himself well in the mysteries of dark water. Item #3 was behaving now, curled into itself atop the old red blanket he and his sisters had slept under all those years ago, its hooded face toward the tank. Moloch stared at him from the depth of the pool. Hypok reached up and turned on the video recorder.

He gulped the tequila, set the glass on the chair arm, then guided himself down beside the Item, lying between it and the glass. His scales slid without resistance against the wool. He basked for a moment. For a while he watched the unmoving head of Moloch and sensed the breathing behind him. To his heightened sense of smell, the old blanket smelled like it did three decades ago — of thickly fatted mammal and juvenile human females. But thirty years ago was right now. And right now was the past, too — all the way back to the black sloughs where life begins — and whatever future he chose to take. He reached down to the floor and got the two remote exposure controls. These he transferred to his left hand. Without looking he reached behind himself with his right arm and set his brightly scaled hand on the small of the Item's back. It began sobbing.

Shhhhh.

Hypok closed his eyes and inhaled the smells — the girl, the blanket, the faint fecal aroma of Moloch. He pressed the cable controls: shoot, shoot, shoot. The Item had a soapier smell than Collette and Valeen, though Valeen's old clothes undercut that freshness with the dank richness of time. This

228

is close to how it was back then: the scent of the available female, the dark liquid power of his instincts, the punishing reality of the maternal nearby, overhead, perhaps, like a bird of prey:

Collette: Let's inspect Genie again.
Valeen: Genie, are you asleep yet?
Gene: (groans as if in sleep, turning onto his back)
Collette: Everybody be real quiet now.
Oooooooh . . .

All the nascent power returns to him in the memory, along with all the power of his subsequent years. The past has crawled forward to swallow the present, and together, this thirty-year span of desire resides in Hypok with all the sharpness and immediacy of a spark. He feels present in the past and present in the moment because it is all just one huge thing, a chain of hours linked to make a life. He begins to undulate in his good skin. He peers out at Moloch and groans as if in sleep: *here you are, you hateful bitch if you can see me.* Then he closes his eyes again and knows that she'll never beat him with the belt for what his sisters loved to do, will never lock him away in the small cold room with the loaf of bread and the jug of water, will never humiliate him for his shyness, punish him for his breath, ridicule him for his skin or pound him for his desires again. Moloch has blessed him with that. So he undulates in his beautiful skin, the power of the years gathering. He feels beneath his scaled hand the body he has always needed. He doesn't even need to see it. There it is: the object of all desire. He will never be that body. It will always be another. To possess it would mean to inject it with his life, and offer it to Moloch. This is the direction of his years, the shape of his destiny. He has been here before and he has lost his courage. He has been here before and not lost it. He wonders if he is truly ready to attain the summit again. He opens his eyes. Moloch stares at him from the tree. Shoot, shoot, shoot.

Brittany could still see through the airhole she was meant to breathe through. Dead Gopher Man was covered in silver scales like a fish and lying just a few feet away from her. His back was to her and his whole body was moving, slowly and rhythmically, like he was swimming in slow motion. He made noises every few seconds, but nothing she could understand. It was kind of moaning, kind of talking. She heard this funny sound above her every once in a while — kind of a short click with a rattle after it. Two or three times. Then it stopped. His hand was still on her back and she could see his arm extending back toward her, covered in the shimmering scales. She could see just a tiny bit of the dress he had put on her and she knew it wasn't one of hers.

Beyond Dead Gopher Man this slow dark shape moved through a tree. Dead Gopher Man kept moving, faster now but still evenly — what was he doing?

Brittany closed her eyes as hard as she could and tried to scream and shook herself into a Dream Bust. She shook so hard she thought her bones would come undone. But the scream wouldn't get out past the tape and she realized why the Dream Bust had failed her today: because the scream was the most important part; it frightened away everything else in the dream, but she couldn't do it because of the tape.

Suddenly she was on her back and she felt two strong hands on her arms pinning her down and she couldn't see past the hood but when he spoke she knew he was just inches from her face. His voice was a quick, foul hiss:

Stop it! Mother's watching!

Thirteen

Marcine Browne ushered me into her office at Bright Tomorrows. It was 9:55 A.M. She was mid-thirties, dressed and made up with pride, red haired and quite attractive. She flicked on the lights and pointed to a chair in front of a desk.

"Can I get you some coffee?"

"I'd rather not waste your time," I said.

"Can I get *me* some coffee?"

She was back in five minutes with two cups. They were white mugs with BRIGHT TOMOR-ROWS emblazoned across them in optimistic red script. She looked at the bandage on my face as she offered me the coffee.

"Thank you," I said. "Ms. Browne, I'm the lead investigator for the Sheriff's Crimes Against Youth unit. We're small, we work hard and we believe that children in our society need protection."

I waited a beat. I like to let the importance of what we do sink in.

"All right."

"Can I speak frankly with you?"

"Please do."

"Have you heard of The Horridus?"

"Yes."

"He took his third girl from a condo in Irvine, about four hours ago. The condo is three miles from here. The girl is missing, her mother is ready to break down and I've failed them. She's five years old, and somewhere out in this county of 2.6 million souls, he's got her."

She said nothing. I liked her face.

"The Horridus named himself. It's the Latin root for rough. He's living through what the FBI calls an escalating fantasy. That means he's got a vision, a goal in his imagination. It isn't something he can just go out and start doing. It's something he has to work up to. That's what the abductions are — practice runs for the real thing. Who knows, maybe this time, it will be the real thing. Rough."

I paused but she said nothing. I was reassured by the intelligence in her face, though I knew my chances of getting what I wanted from Marcine Browne were somewhere between slim and none.

I was pleased that she was finally unable to resist the bait.

"I think this is absolutely terrible," she said. "I feel awful. I'm not a mother myself, but I can imagine how it would feel, to have that happen to your daughter. What would the 'real thing' be?"

"You really want to know?"

"Yes."

"He'll rape and kill them. Probably in that

order. It's a matter of time. Right now, it might be a matter of minutes."

I let this sink in. She looked at me with her lovely green eyes. "Investigator Naughton, why are you here?"

"I need your help."

"How?"

One of Marcine Browne's co-workers stuck her head in the door and said good morning. She smiled brightly at me, no doubt the lure-the-new-male-membership smile. Marcine asked her to shut the door, please.

The quiet in the office was just what I wanted. What Marcine did in the next few minutes would be between herself and her soul, and the soul is best heard in silence.

"We know, very generally, what he looks like. We have some general indications as to his age, what he drives, what kind of a house he lives in and what kind of a past he has. We have some suspicions — founded on the opinions of people who profile unknown subjects for a living — about what kind of work he does, how he behaves socially, what his interests are."

"That sounds like a lot."

"Until you realize it isn't. Until you realize we don't know his name. And that people can change their appearance pretty easily. That there are five thousand other vehicles like his on the roads out there. And over two and a half million people in this county alone. Plenty more in Los Angeles and down in San Diego. Until you realize he just kidnapped a five-year-old while we were all asleep. While her own mother was asleep fifteen feet away. When you realize all that, you understand how little you've really got."

She looked at me again. I could see the confusion on her face. She sighed, sat back, then sat forward again. "Mr. Naughton, maybe I watch too much TV, but this isn't like anything I ever saw a cop do. You're telling me all this stuff, but you're not asking me any questions. May I see your ID again?"

I showed it to her again.

"I'm sorry. But what is it that you want?"

"Let me tell you just a little something more. I talked to the mother of the second girl. That's part of my job. The girl was named Courtney and she was six. I was trying to put things together. I'm glad I did. Her mother was a member of Dawn Christie and Associates."

Marcine looked at me with a hard, uncomprehending stare. "Well, they're another service. They have a different philosophy than we do. Our competitors, but . . . so what?"

"The mother of the girl who was taken four hours ago was a member here. A new member, Abby Elder."

"Oh, God," she said quietly. "I was afraid that's why you were here."

I waited. I knew she'd make a mental run

for it, and my only chance was to keep her right here in front of me, where decisions could be made.

"You'll have to talk to James Rudker — he's the founder-owner."

"I don't have time to talk to Mr. Rudker. There's a member of Bright Tomorrows I need to see, Ms. Browne. He's a member of Dawn Christie, too. And the only way I can find him is by comparing your membership list with theirs."

"I simply can't give it to you. It's impossible. Look, I signed an *oath* as an employee to follow the rules. Furnishing our members' names to anyone goes against those rules. And it breaks all the promises of confidentiality we make to our members. We'd have been out of business years ago if we did that. You're asking me to give up my job."

"No. The list goes from you to me. I put it in my pocket and it stays there until I get to my office. There, I compare the names against Dawn Christie's list, and —"

"— *She* gave you *hers?*"

I said nothing as I lifted from my pocket the sheet of real estate listings that Frances had given me, and held it up.

Marcine shook her head. "That's really hard to believe. I mean, I've met Dawn and she's not exactly . . . a pushover."

"She's tough as nails. And she's bright. That's why she knows she can trust me. When

I finish the comparison, the list goes back to you. This list goes back to her. If I get the match, I'll take it from there. No one but us will know that this guy was a member here. That's a promise. I'll put it in writing and sign it, just like you did your employment agreement, if you want me to."

"You'll have to talk to Mr. Rudker."

"We think he takes them to his house."

"*What?*"

"We think The Horridus takes the girls to his house to do his thing. If we're right, and I think we are, that's where he is right now. At home. With an abducted five-year-old girl who may or may not come out of this alive. I can make a match in ten minutes, Marcine. With your list. I can get cops to his residence in about another five, maybe less. Without the list, I may as well cruise the Caribbean. There's a window open now, and it's going to slam shut fast. Do you understand what I'm saying to you?"

"Call Mr. Rudker. Please. I'll write down his number for you. Oh . . . oh . . . *shit*. He's . . . he's actually *in* the Caribbean. We're opening an office in Miami and he's . . . vacationing."

"I see," I said quietly. I let the reverberations of owner-founder James Rudker's Caribbean vacation sound their irony into Marcine Browne's heart. She looked at me angrily, then down at her desk.

"Ms. Browne, I can make this easy for you. Or, you can do it the hard way. You can look into yourself and ask yourself what the right thing is. Then do it."

"Go ahead. Get a court order," she snapped. "Why didn't you just get it before you came here?"

"No court order. That's not what I mean."

"Then what?"

"Mr. Rudker doesn't want it known that Bright Tomorrows may have cooperated in a kidnapping investigation involving one of its members. That's understandable. But how would he like it being known that Bright Tomorrows *refused* to cooperate in a kidnapping investigation involving one of its members? And what if that refusal came at a time when this . . . animal . . . could have been identified and arrested, and his third victim set free?"

She nodded. "That would be a shitty thing to do to us, mister."

"I'll do it."

She glared at me. "I absolutely detest being manipulated by someone."

"Maybe you'll thank me someday."

She looked at me with a final beam of resentment in her eyes, but I watched it dissolve into absolute capitulation. "Abby Elder's girl?"

"Abby Elder's girl."

"I signed her up myself. Oh . . . *damn*."

"Go get the list."

She shook her head and stared down at her desk again. "I could strangle y—"

"— *Go!*"

I pulled the same stunt on Dawn Christie and it worked. She still had a baleful stare as I left her office and jogged to my car. I threw open the sheets and started looking. There were 486 names on the Bright Tomorrows sheets, and 293 on Dawn Christie's. They were both in alphabetical order. My eyes swam. The first thing I did was check the ten qualifying home sellers against both lists. Nothing. I looked for Steven Wicks, the reptile dealer. Not there. I tried Gary Cross, who was selling his red Chrysler van because it used too much gas. Nothing. The next thing I did was turn on the air conditioner and aim the vents straight at my face.

Aarhaus, Blake . . .

No.

Aaron, Richard . . .

No.

Aaron, Steven . . .

No.

Too slow. Too slow!

I set the light up on the hood and slammed the car into gear. I needed help and if I drove like a demon I knew I could make the twenty-minute drive in fifteen.

I did.

I ran past Shopping Carter without stop-

239

ping, took the concrete steps two at a time and used the stairs instead of the elevator. I got Louis by the sleeve of his coat and almost yanked him off his chair. I sat him down at my desk with the Christie list and explained the drill. Twenty minutes later we had our answer.

I didn't like it so we ran through it again. Every friggin' name, one at a time. And the answer came up the same: Nothing.

"So he's using another name," said Louis.

I didn't answer. I just saw that faint outline of red on everything I looked at. It's like looking through red lenses for a second. I kicked the lower drawer of my file cabinet, a sheet of metal already crumpled by dents. I mean big dents, authentically pissed-off, hard-as-you-can-kick-the-bastard dents. The thing won't lock or even close right anymore.

"Why don't you call CNB, get it on TV?" someone piped from over the room divider.

"Go piss up a rope," I said.

"Love you, too, Terry."

I put my hand on Louis's shoulder. He was unbothered by my outburst, having seen enough of them to know how routine and fleeting they are. He just looked at the file cabinet, shook his head and stared down again at the list.

"I wouldn't join two services and use the same name," he said. "Especially if I joined them for the reason we think. No way. I'd want to be at least two different guys. I'd want to be as many guys as I could be."

I knew he was right.

"This doesn't mean we're on the wrong track, Terry. I'm smelling the same thing you are. It just means we gotta dig him out."

Ishmael walked into our area and gave me an utterly disdainful look. Pathos, with an undercurrent of triumph, and his usual dose of loathing. The look I gave him back was probably full of the same. He looked at my wreck of a file cabinet, then at me.

"A hiker found the girl off the Ortega Highway, way out in the sticks," he said. "She's with deputies at the Capo substation. She's alive. Unharmed, they think. But definitely alive. Somehow, she saw through the hood. Claims she did. Says she knows what he looks like."

Fourteen

An hour later — almost one o'clock — I got to talk to Brittany Elder at the substation. Her mother was already there. In a back office Brittany slumped liked a creature without bones into Abby's lap. The girl's eyes were dull and unfocused and there was a wide pink strip of inflamed skin across her mouth and cheeks where the tape had been. She hardly moved. Two dark eyes looked at the present but saw only the past. She had dirt on her dress and scuffs on her knees. On a desk in one corner of the office sat a white net robe and a black velvet hood, each bagged as evidence. I smiled at Abby Elder and she looked at me like I was an insane stranger.

I wrote on a notepad:

CAN I ASK HER SOME QUESTIONS NOW? YOU CAN STAY RIGHT WHERE YOU ARE. THE SOONER SHE TALKS THE BETTER SHE'LL BE. DON'T ANSWER. JUST NOD IF IT'S OKAY TO TRY.

I walked over and angled the notepad up so Abby could see it but Brittany wouldn't.

Abby nodded.

I cheerfully asked Louis, Johnny and the other deputies to leave the room. Johnny shut the door with perfect pitch: slowly, firmly, quietly.

"Well, Brittany," I said, "I'm glad you're doing all right. Your mom was just about sick with worry. I was, too. When my son was your age all I did was worry about him."

Abby cocked an eye up at me. She was petting Brittany's hair. I'd never mentioned my son to her, and I must have struck her as the childless type. I don't know. She looked a little surprised.

"My name's Terry, by the way. Your mom called me when she couldn't find you. It's my job to look for lost people sometimes. So, well . . . I'm just really glad you're here. You did my job for me. You made me look good. So thanks."

She stared into space, unblinking, her fists balled up by her chin, her mother's arms around her.

"Brittany, you want a Coke or something?"

She shook her head.

Contact.

"Abby?"

"No, thank you."

"Are you sure?"

I lifted my eyebrows and nodded encouragingly.

"You know, I really would love a Coke."

"Me too," I said. "So, one for you, and I guess I'll have one. That's two."

I stood there and watched the wall clock for a few seconds. I looked through the window blinds to the stucco wall that ran behind the substation. Then I started walking toward the door.

"Me too," Brittany mumbled into her fists. She wanted what the big people wanted.

Just like Matthew, I thought. He'd have followed me off a building.

Or into the sea.

Abby looked at me and she was smiling with tears running down her face. Brittany breathed in deeply, then out again.

"Coming up," I said.

I left the room and scrambled across the parking lot to a liquor store to make the purchase. I got some candy and snacks, too, just in case. When I came back, Brittany was still sitting on her mother's lap, but she now had both arms around her mother's neck. They both looked at me as I walked toward them, and for the first time since six that morning I believed that somehow, some way, sometime not too long from then, Abby and Brittany Elder were going to be okay.

And that's why I work this job.

Here is what she told me over the next twenty minutes:

She woke up when someone lifted her out

of bed. She thought it was her daddy, but then she knew it wasn't. She tried to call her mother, but her mouth was taped shut. She was jammed hard up against a man's chest, with her head pushed to his chin, and he moved real fast and his breath was awful. She never saw him real good because it was dark and he had a bright light coming off his head that blinded her. He put her in a white van, and it was a big one because he was standing up with her. He put her in a bag that smelled like tennis shoes. It was tight at the top and she couldn't get out. She cried for a long time while the car moved. He didn't say anything. The radio had the news. Then the car stopped and he carried her into a room and put her on a bed. He let her out of the bag and put a dark thing over her head. She saw him for a second then. He had on a baseball hat and big sunglasses and something over his face. The hood had an opening for her to breathe through, but after she shook and moved around, she could see through it, just a little. The bedspread was red. It smelled like old people. They were in a room. There was a big glass wall with a snake in it and the snake was as big around as a telephone pole and about that long. It might not have been a real snake. The man stood and watched the snake for a while, and she saw him through the opening. He had a sharp, mean face and his hair was white and short. He wasn't big or small or fat or thin.

He went away and came back later dressed in something that was scaly. The scales were shiny, like a fish. Silver and gold and blue. He lay down on the bed beside her, with his back to her and he watched the snake. He moved funny. It was like he was crawling on his belly but not going anywhere. He had a hand on her while he did this. There was something up in the air behind her that made clicking noises every once in a while. She tried to scream and shake herself away from him, then he got over her and grabbed her arms and told her to be quiet because his mother was listening. He held real still then. Then he picked her up and carried her over to the glass. He put her up close to it and stood beside her. She couldn't see anymore because the breathing hole went back down when he stood her up. He said, *next time* to the snake, or maybe to his mother. After a while he put her back in the bag. Then they drove in his car again and it stopped and he carried her inside the bag for a few minutes. He took her out of the bag and put something over her that he tied at the neck. It was a thing that rustled and felt dry when it brushed against her arms and legs. He cut the tape off her ankles but not her hands or mouth. Then she heard his footsteps on dried leaves and the footsteps got further away. After a long time she started walking. Then this lady came up and asked her if she was okay. Oh, and his eyes were brown.

And that was all.

Brittany fell asleep.

"We should go," Abby whispered.

"Yes, you should. The deputies outside will take you to the Medical Center, where doctors can examine Brittany. They're good and they'll treat her well. Starting tonight, spend a few nights away from home. It's going to be a while before she thinks of her bed as a friend. Please let me know where you are. Something that she's forgotten for now could break this case. I'd like her to meet with our sketch artist as soon as possible. Tomorrow morning would be ideal for us."

"Okay," she said tentatively.

"It's going to be all right. I've seen things turn out a lot . . . not as well as this."

Abby pursed her lips. "I'm just renting. Should we move?"

"Yes."

"How far?"

"I think around the corner would be far enough. It's for Brittany. Not because of the guy who did this."

She nodded and stood. Brittany draped over her shoulder like a big doll.

"The press will want to talk to you," I said. "You can control their access, to a point. Don't let them talk to Brittany. And don't tell them Brittany saw him. Whatever you say, don't say that."

"Don't worry. I won't."

"I know a reporter over at CNB who would handle this story professionally, and with respect for your privacy and your feelings. She knows what information to give out and what not to. She likes our unit and what we do. She'd spread the word, and it might help this not happen to someone else."

"Is there more danger to us, if I talk?"

"That's extremely unlikely. But there's more danger to everyone else, if you don't."

She stood in front of me and managed to offer me her hand. I shook it with both of mine.

"I'll talk to CNB on my own terms."

"I'll make that clear."

I wrote my home phone on a card and slipped it into her purse.

"Call me tonight," I said. "I want to know how you're both doing, and I want to know what time you can meet with our artist tomorrow. I can't tell you how important a good sketch can turn out to be. She'll be real good to your girl."

"I will. Thank you, Mr. Naughton."

I held open the door for her and watched Brittany's sleeping face slide past me. I thought of Ardith and the way she'd bring Matthew to our bed in the morning when he was just an infant, and how small his head looked against her. Odd how some things hurt so much to remember, but you won't part with them for anything in the world.

★ ★ ★

I called Donna on my way back to the station. I left a Skip message and she called me back just as I was pulling into the Sheriff Department employees' lot. I told her the girl was all right. Abducted, terrified and numb, but basically all right. I told her she had a scoop on the story — all she had to do was be good to a young mother and love me forever and without condition. I could tell she was at her desk.

"Be easier if *I could see you once in a while*," she whispered.

"This evening, after work."

"I'll be talking to Abby Elder then, if you're kind enough to give me her number."

I did.

"Call her soon. You can be done with it by the time I leave here."

"After Tonello's, then?" she asked.

"Let's skip that part."

"Skipped, Skip. See you soon."

"I look forward."

"So do I, dear man. By the way, your best friend Jordan Ishmael called. He said there was about to be some big news coming out of the department. He said he'd be happy to keep me informed."

"What in hell is that supposed to mean?"

"I was wondering if you might tell me. He tries to emit mystery, but comes off a glum bureaucrat."

I wondered if he was trying to create a buzz over his Sheriff Department page on the Web, or something else related to his relentless, slow-motion pursuit of the department's highest position. Maybe he was going to strip off his shirt, oil up his muscles and demonstrate his silent kill moves for the CNB cameras. Maybe he had secret video footage of my banged-up file cabinet.

"I'll keep my eyes open," I said.

"I hope to see them looking my way, in about three hours."

Those next three hours at the station were interesting. First of all, I had a fax from Mike Strickley at the Bureau:

Terry — Something remote came up, but I'm passing it along anyway. We're putting together a national index for sex crimes against juveniles, per President Clinton. We hope to have it up and running late this year. It's going to put some more teeth in Megan's law. Right now, we're collecting everything we can get our hands on. I'd discussed The Horridus with one of our people who's working on the index. Yesterday, she came across this, from Wichita Falls, Texas. Seems they had a guy two years ago, he was driving around in a van and offering free clothes to girls on their way home from school. The clothes weren't new. He'd let them use the van to change out of their old ones. Two changed, one just took her booty home with her. White male, late twenties to early thirties, medium build, beard and glasses. Three complaints from citizens and that was the end of it. Wichita Falls cops never found a suspect. They hit the child molesters' registry and came up with nothing. One month later a six-year-old disappeared between school and home. She's still missing — maybe a connection with the van man, maybe not. Those were the only incidents. Nothing since then and no leads — several subjects questioned and released. But the van, the clothes, the ages of the girls fit your man. If he's abducting now to make them wear what he likes, it's a classic escalation. Maybe he split and landed in your backyard. Maybe he wanted more girls to choose from. Maybe he got scared. Maybe he scared himself. Use it if you can. The guy to talk to in Wichita Falls is Captain Sam Welborn. Good guy. Good luck.

The air in the station that afternoon was strange, though it had nothing to do with my compatriots in CAY. Louis stayed in the field to interview the listing agents about the sellers of homes with second units. We were down to eight now — the two Louis had investigated that morning came up clean. One was black and the other was too old. Frances was at home, allegedly, still sick. I called twice to see how she was doing, but got only her message and no return call. Johnny was down in the lab, hovering over Joe Reilly while he processed the

251

evidence from the Brittany Elder abduction.

The strange thing was the brass — under-sheriffs Woolton and Vega, Captain Burns and Lieutenant Ishmael — and even Jim Wade himself. They seemed to linger around the station, looking at me. Wade from behind the glass of his office. Ishmael during strolls past my work station. Woolton and Vega from a coffee machine that lies at a diagonal from my desk, to and from which there is a clear sight line. Burns peeked at me once over the top of my divider and said he was looking for Frances, but everybody knew she wasn't in. How couldn't he?

It was Friday afternoon, and like a lot of other workplaces on Friday afternoon, the department usually went through a communal exhale. Nobody was exhaling. No talk of weekend plans, none of the usual goofy pleasantries that mark the end of the workweek for most of us. Instead there was a rigid silence in the air, and a feeling of anticipation. It was especially odd, also, because Wade's swanky annual equestrian show and benefit for County Youth Services — called simply the Orange Classic — was set for Sunday. This weekend, the last in April, was always a high time for Jim and the whole Sheriff Department. In fact, I wondered what he was doing still in his office, looking gray and grim as a shark, with all the work he had to do to get his ranch ready for the fling.

I stuck my head in his door.

"What gives?"

He looked at me and shook his head, but said nothing. So I beat it. Kick some furniture and people start to think you're dangerous. I wasn't worried. I had more important things to do than worry about why the Sheriff Department heavies were all treating me like I had toilet paper stuck to my shoe.

Fridays I usually leave work an hour early and visit Matt. He's up in Newport Beach, on a bluff that overlooks the Pacific. It's between the department and Laguna, right on my way home.

Ardith is often there, too, as she was on this unsettling Friday, already standing on the grass by the grave when I pulled up and parked along the curb.

It's blustery and cool up the bluff, on almost any day of the year. That Friday the breeze was quite stiff coming off the ocean toward us. Out on the sea the triangles of sails cut slowly through the whitecaps. The water was dark gray and the end of the earth was just a thin black line with the blue of an April sky above it. Catalina Island lay offshore, clearly revealed by the wind.

Ardith had her long black coat on, and her curly blond hair was tangled by the breeze. The dark solidity of her shape and the lightness of her hair stood out against the green of the cemetery grass. She wore jeans under the coat and little black boots that laced to just above her ankles, and a red scarf around her neck. When she looked at me I was struck by the sun-browned color of her skin, but I always am. Ardith has a face of summer: bronze skin and straw-yellow hair and eyes blue as desert sky. She is a California girl. Grew up here, like I did. She works for a ritzy hotel now, group bookings. Her lips are slender and pretty and they turn downward at the edges, giving her a look of etched sadness. A spray of wrinkles beside each of her striking eyes echoes the turn of her mouth and reminds me that Ardith and the world and I are all growing older by the second.

"Hi," I said.

She looked at me and smiled faintly.

"Hi, Terry."

I stood across the headstone from her. It's a flat stone, flush with the ground, because the upright style isn't allowed here. We picked a red granite one, on the theory that red was cheerful and youthful. The letters are a cursive script rather than the more formal blocked ones; again, we were trying for something more upbeat than conventional. It's hard to say if it worked. I guess that depends on your mood. The red is red, all right, but the sun seems to have dulled it more than its neighbors of slate gray and black. No matter how many times I spray and wipe it with the glass cleaner and paper towels I keep in my trunk, it maintains a dull barrier instead of the glistening red patina I'd envisioned when we ordered it. I've doubted in my more somber hours that the concept of an upbeat headstone is a sound one.

I knelt, sprayed off the stone and wiped it with one paper towel, then another. Opaque streaks formed in the heat of the rock, then shrunk away. *Matthew Paul Naughton.* I picked off the dead grass that always jumps onto the stone when you nudge the paper towel against the edges of the lawn as you wipe. It's the springy Bermuda grass that has lots of dry dead blades in it.

I stood and looked down. It wasn't very good, but no matter how many times you wipe that granite, it looks the same. I can imagine the shape and size and condition of what lies beneath that headstone, but only vaguely, and not for long. I don't mean to be morbid, it just happens. I always blot out that kind of thinking with memories of my beautiful robust son, alive in the world. I go from the horrible to the beautiful in just a beat of the heart, then travel back to the here and now. The trouble is the here and now has a big empty space in it. You don't want that space to be empty. So you try to fill it with something. Imagination is a poor substitute for living flesh and flowing blood, for the sound of voice and the thrill of touch. You do what you can.

"That granite just won't come clean," I said.
"It's all right, Terry."

I monitor Ardith's voice for every nuance and subtlety, every shading and slant. It's a sweet, low, calm voice — she used to read radio commercials years ago — but it sends a buzz of nerves through my body like it came from a wall socket. We were married ten years and ten years is a long time. It was a good marriage. When Matthew died it collapsed, like a building with dynamite in the foundation. We were the walls. She fell toward me and I fell toward her and we missed. If we hadn't, maybe the building would have stayed up somehow. She held me solely and fully responsible for what happened to Matt. I did, too, but for different reasons. You don't continue to live with a person under those conditions. You have to get away. At least I did.

We had different ideas on how to raise our son. It was always something like this —

If we went to the mountains Ardith would worry about the bears eating Matthew.

I'd say, *The bears won't eat Matt. He's too bony.*

If we went to Mexico Ardith would worry about him being stolen and sold as a blue-eyed gringo.

I'd say, *Maybe they'll pay for his college.*

If we went to the desert she'd worry about rattlesnakes.

I'd say, *Don't worry, he's too big to eat.*

If we went to the beach she'd worry about the sharks.

I'd say, *That kid could outswim any shark.*

She thought he was doomed for tragedy and I thought he was invincible. Now I guess I agree with her.

So fuck me, and fuck the way I was.

"Work go okay this week?" I asked.

"Um-hm," she said. "The world still loves Southern California. I don't know why."

"How'd the Mitsubishi guys go?"

"All they wanted to do was play golf."

"I guess that was easy to arrange."

"Oh, yes. You?"

"That guy took another girl. We got her back today, more or less okay."

"I've been seeing the news. Made me wish you'd catch up with him and shoot him about a hundred times."

"I've had that pleasant daydream, too."

"All the things that can happen to children in this world, and there's somebody out there, doing that. I just don't understand."

"They're different than the rest of us."

She didn't say it — she never would — but I knew what she was thinking: *and you feel just a little bit sorry for them, don't you, Terry?*

I took the spray bottle and paper towels back to the car. I got out the big old beach towel and walked back to the grave with it, unfolded and spread it out on the grass. It's a faded blue one, with seahorses and starfish and little holes. The thing about this cemetery is, to sit on the grass next to your loved one, you have to sit on someone else. You'd have to stay directly in front of the stone to observe the property lines. But then you'd be sitting on Matthew's chest, I guess. Anyway, we always sit at opposite ends of the towel. The red stone is in front of us, then the smooth green grass sloping away, dotted with flower arrangements. Beyond the grass you can see the city reservoir of still gray water mirrored with clouds, then the proud towers of Newport Center — expensive stores, corporate this and that — then the ocean, way out to the sky. It's a good place to think about living and dying.

Ardith and I meet here almost every week. Some Fridays she'll miss and some I will. It didn't start out that way. About six months after Matt was buried — three months after I moved out of the house — we just happened to be here at the same time. It was excruciatingly difficult to be around her then. Independently, we'd decided that Friday afternoons would be our time to visit, and neither one of us would back down. Sticking to our guns, no matter how vague or even destructive they might be, is something we've both always been good at. And through our stubbornness came an accommodation that seems to be necessary for both of us, though necessary for reasons I only partially understand. For me, seeing Ardith reminds me, fully and honestly, of what I did to her son. One of the things I come here for is an outside shot at her forgiveness. For her, I can't say exactly why she comes, but I think it has something to do with wanting to forgive me, which she can't. She can't because to do it, she'd have to admit that she blames me for Matthew. She's never admitted that, but she believes it. I will and I do. But we still show up, most Fridays, knowing full well who's on the guest list.

A lot of it is just small talk.

I remarked about the weather.

She told me about her car.

I asked if her homeowners' insurance had paid out.

Our home — now Ardith's home — was burglarized a few months ago and she's had problems collecting. They took some costume jewelry and a clock radio, and that was about it.

The insurance had finally paid up.

I asked about her photography, which is one of Ardith's loves from college years, and she said she hadn't shot much lately. She takes great pictures, lots of mood and emotion in them.

"I get out the old albums sometimes," she said. "All that stuff of you and Matt. Some of it's quite beautiful. But all of it makes me cry."

Those pictures — Matt and I wrestling on the floor, Matt and I goofing at the beach, Matt and I doing you name it — would have made me cry, too. Ardith seemed to follow us around with her camera for every one of those five short years.

Small talk has a way of getting bigger when you've been through the things that Ardith and I have been through. This time, she changed the subject.

"Did you see the notice this mortuary ran in the paper?"

"Yeah. I called. They said they were computerizing their list of 'property owners.' Said not to worry."

"Well, they told me the same thing, so I worried. I thought about that cemetery up in L.A. County, where they just dug up the old ones and cremated them, then sold the plots to new people."

"I don't think they'll try that here," I said.

"Why wouldn't they?"

"Because if they do, we'll see the earth has been disturbed and I'll personally throw each and every one of them in jail."

"You tell them that on the phone?"

"In fact, I did."

"Good."

I reached into my jacket pocket and brought out the flask of Herradura I keep in the trunk of the car, along with the spray bottle, paper and beach towel. Jordan Ishmael looked into the trunk one day and saw the box and what was in it, and because it's a county sedan, he had to say something about lugging around personal stuff. I told him the towel was for my son and the tequila was for his ex-wife and that shut him up. As I took a pull on the liquor I thought back to the bizarre expression on Ishmael's face at the station just a few hours ago. I thought of the look on Frances's face, too, the day before. Same look, I thought: confused and pissed off and frightened and utterly bloodthirsty. You'd think I'd have better things to remember with the remains of my son just a few feet away.

I offered her the flask and she took a sip.

"Still blacking out on this stuff?"

"No. I've cut back a lot."

"Those were some scary times."

"Dumb."

She handed back the flask. "You're not built for booze. It just takes too much to put you down where you like to be."

"I really don't want to be there anymore. I nip maybe a half pint a night now, usually less. Maybe a beer or two."

"That's still an awful lot of booze."

"A little less every week. I'm going to be okay with it, Ardith."

"You're not going to be young forever."

"I'm not even young now."

"You still go to that cave? Drink and smoke and sleep it off?"

"I still like it out there. No pass-out nights, recently."

"That you can remember."

"No, really. I'm over the worst of it."

I looked down the slope to where a fresh grave was being dug. Gravediggers don't use shovels now; they use CAT backhoes. They carry the lining vaults around in little trailers attached to little tractors. The ones here all go about their work with an indifference that makes me wince sometimes. It's just a business, really, just a living. You can't expect them to stare off toward the Pacific and think of the boy they buried almost two years ago.

"Kenneth doing well?"

She nodded.

"I'm glad you're happy."

"Thanks."

In fact, I'm not glad she's happy. I'm not a capacious enough man to wish her supreme happiness with a new husband, when she never really had it with her old one. She married Kenneth not long after I moved out. At first it surprised me, because she never told me she was even dating. Then I realized how naked and unsupported Ardith felt — and had been feeling — for some time. Kenneth is a retired commercial pilot, a big, heavy-handshaking, wide-smiling block of a guy who has the personality of a sunny eight-year-old. He's financially solid, and according to Ardith, a kind and caring man. I've spent as little time as possible around him, but it's easy to see he adores her. She's a trophy. And he's a rock for her.

"I'm glad it's working out for you two," I said.

"Why?"

"Because I'd like to see you have a family again someday."

I truly would like to see that. Ardith is only thirty-five years old, but time goes by fast. It would kill something inside me, but maybe some things inside me would be better off dead.

"No. Kenneth won't do that. He's got four grown."

"Things can change."

"I've never yet seen a human being grow younger."

Well.

"How are you and Melinda?"

"Okay."

"Okay sounds not so good."

"I think . . . well, it could be argued that we didn't really make a good decision."

"It was too soon, Terry. You knew that."

"Everybody knew it. We did it anyway."

"People aren't overly bright."

"I'm not."

"That's not what I meant. I just mean all of us, in general."

"I know what you meant."

"Hang in there. There's another chance for you, Terry. But you have to take care of yourself. You got to be standing up for it."

Ardith has a kind and loving heart. It was

one of the many things I loved about her and still do. But she was always, always, always, first and foremost, before and after everything else, afraid. She was always afraid. And that is the part of Matthew's death I blame on her.

"I still love and care about you a lot, Ardith. Just for what it's worth."

"I love and care about you, too."

"We had a lot of bad luck."

"Lots of that."

The gravediggers worked and the clouds slid across the reservoir and Catalina Island sat in the ocean like a black stump.

We sat a few more minutes. Ardith reached over and hugged me, then stood and walked off to her car. I stayed a while longer, drank some tequila and lay down on the beach towel to look up at the passing clouds.

Fifteen

I was proud to walk onto Sheriff Jim Wade's sprawling ranch property for the Orange Classic. It was a sunny cool morning and the aroma of the hillside sage mixed with the smell of horses and hay and leather. Penny skipped along between Melinda and me, holding our hands, in her pink dress and white straw hat with the pink ribbon. I felt patriarchal.

I was also temporarily content at what we'd been able to do for Brittany and Abby Elder. The Horridus had made his move, but he hadn't done what I feared the most, and we'd been there fast to get the physical evidence and, most importantly, the physical description we needed so badly. I checked my watch. Right now, as we rode the tram toward the Wade Ranch, I knew that Amanda Aguilar and Brittany were conspiring to give a face to our monster. I felt luck in the air and luck in my blood and I knew that Amanda was going to get from Brittany what she hadn't been able to get from Steven Wicks. We were going to get him, soon.

I also felt happy to have truly arrived in high society. They were all there, sitting in the bleachers and sauntering over the grounds — the politicians and captains of industry, the judges and the big attorneys, the publishers and entertainers, the philanthropists and civic leaders, the owners and chairmen and chief executives, the builders, the movers and the shakers. The Tonello's crowd — but more of them. Even the governor of California was expected to arrive by helicopter for a brief visit around noon. Orange County had voted strong for him in the last gubernatorial race. Not that I really knew many of these people, or really believed that their world was mine. This was merely the beginning of my association with them. But few men — especially those of us in law enforcement — are immune to the attractions of power. I'm not.

Best of all, I felt like a Sheriff Department insider, one of the handful of ambassadors that Jim Wade had picked to represent us to the top echelon of our county. To the people there at the Orange Classic, on any other day of the year, sheriffs are mainly just cops. But on the last Sunday of April we are the best of the best, the ones who can put away our guns and use our energies to nurture the culture's finest aspirations — like providing for needy kids — through this splendid, ostentatious, lucrative event. Cops feel like outsiders, of course, not really a part of the society they serve and sometimes die for. That's an old story. But here at Jim Wade's ranch they are momentary insiders, powerful players within the system. They're *the* insiders, the very core responsible for this extravagant event. Some are chosen. And I was one of them.

So when the tram dropped us off and we walked under the wooden J. WADE RANCH sign that hung between two massive redwood stanchions at the entrance of his property, my head was big and my heart was full. I'd bought a light-colored suit for the occasion, and Penny's outfit was new, too. Even Melinda, so reluctant to buy clothes for herself, had found a department store dress on sale — a summery floral print — and bought it for today. We looked like subjects for an impressionist.

Jim and his wife, Annette, met us as we approached the big ranch-style house. He looked distracted, as I knew he would be, looking over my shoulder to see who might require more personal attention than one of his loyal deputies. He studied me for a split second when he shook my hand, then turned his attention to Melinda. Before we moved past him he leaned up close to my ear and said he'd see me in his study in an hour. I couldn't tell by his expression what might be afoot. But a little shudder of excitement went through me as I nodded, then gathered my little instant family together and moved on toward the arenas.

We talked to Burns and Vega, both of whom seemed glum, considering the occasion. It's always a little hard to see co-workers socially, hard to know which version of themselves they're trying to be.

I tugged gently on Melinda's arm and we eased away. We walked past one of the arenas to where the food and beverage tables were set up. We got drinks, then followed another family down one of the many trails of the Wade Ranch and into a meadow of wildflowers. There were orange poppy and red lupine and purple penstemon all in bloom, an eye-shivering carpet of color. Big oak trees stood in solitary distance around the meadow, casting black shadows. And all of us humans in our Sunday best, outfitted like flowers, too, roaming through the tall grass.

We took our seats in the grandstand about a half hour later, to watch the hunters and jumpers. I saw Ishmael walk in front of the stand, with a pretty dark-haired woman I'd never seen. If there was anything tense in Melinda's reaction, I didn't feel it. Penny jumped down and ran to them and Ish lifted her up for a kiss and held her for a moment against his big athletic body. He looked up and nodded at us.

Just then Donna Mason came up the pathway in front of the stand and stopped to talk to Ishmael. She wore a simple white dress and a hat with flowers on it, and she looked to me like something from a very good dream. Her camera crew lagged behind. I could see Ish introducing Penny and his companion to her.

"There's your PR department," said Melinda.

"And she's not even on the payroll."

Melinda poked me in the ribs playfully.

Donna's interview with Abby Elder had made the nine o'clock news on CNB. Another good story on the Orange County Sheriff Department Crimes Against Youth unit. I was a little disappointed that Jim hadn't remarked on it when we came in. Frances had again been our spokesperson. I'd been surprised that Donna had tracked her down so easily for an interview when Frances was sick and hadn't even returned my calls to her home. I'd watched it with Melinda. But my thoughts were still back in my little apartment in the metro district, and my heart still very much in the embrace of Donna, just as my body had been a few hours earlier. I had watched the segment with Melinda, hating myself.

"Penny seems to grow an inch a month," I said.

"I'm glad she doesn't resent her father."

"I am too."

"It's real important that they stay close."

Donna looked up into the stands toward us, holding on to her hat with one hand as she squinted into the sun. I don't know if she saw me or not. She was talking to her director and camera guy.

I sat back and felt the sunshine on my hair

and neck. March was cold and wet, and April's warmth felt like the creation of the world. I wondered about my meeting with Jim Wade in a few minutes. Or was it a meeting? Neither Burns nor Vega had said anything. Melinda wasn't asked to attend. Ishmael hardly looked to be on his way to the ranch house.

Then I had a thought.

I saw a way to understand Frances's strange looks of two days ago. And Jim Wade's odd expression the day before. And Ishmael's haughty, fearful grimace just yesterday afternoon. And all the silent attention focused on me by the department brass.

It was so simple and so clear.

And it hit me with a wave of pleasure: *Jim was going to move me up.*

To where, I had no idea, yet. But I realized as I sat there in the renewing spring sunshine that all of our seemingly casual private talk in his office of late, all his encouragement of me to turn out at Tonello's, all the subliminal approval from his inner circle was going to be explained in just a few minutes. I closed my eyes and wondered if this might be the day Jim Wade chose the line of succession to his office. It seemed suddenly very possible that he was going to set me forward as a knight in the new court. I even toyed with the idea of being offered his position, remote as the chances were. I would be so perfect in some ways, and so bad in others. But no matter what was offered, I realized, I was being called into the inner, *inner* sanctum.

So much had happened. Matt. Ardith. My ill-advised decision with Melinda. The self-destruction and self-hatred of Terry Naughton.

But for the moment I allowed myself to think of Donna. I let myself think of us as husband and wife. I imagined children, hers and mine. And for just that brief moment I could actually feel what it would be like to be happy again.

I took a deep breath and opened my eyes and looked out at the bright red jump poles in the arena. I put my hand on Melinda's knee and felt her unmistakable low-voltage recoil at my touch.

Jim's office was a rustic room with exposed timber ceilings, a collection of handsome saddles on the wood-paneled walls and Indian blankets carefully exhibited to show the beauty of their workmanship. Electric lanterns cast an orange light. There was a big stone fireplace with some old Winchester Repeaters over it. The room was large and dusky, given to shadows despite the lanterns. Jim sat behind a burnished oak desk and motioned me to sit across from him.

The county attorney, Laird Hawlsey, was already seated when we came in. He shook my hand and smiled wanly. On my right was assistant DA Rick Zant. Hawlsey had a notepad open on his lap, but no writing on it. Zant slumped down with his legs crossed and his argyle socks showing. I wondered at this odd arrangement of the county's defender and the county's prosecutor teamed up in the same place. Lots of power right there, in those two men. Not to mention the sheriff-coroner himself.

"I like this room," I said.

"Thank you," Jim said.

He sighed and shook his head. He looked at me with an oddly objective, analytical expression.

"I'm not sure what to do," he said. "All the years and all the things I've seen. And here I am, not sure what to do."

I let the silence stretch.

"I'll help if I can," I offered.

"Terry, I'm going to take you up on that."

He reached into the top drawer and took out a large pink envelope. Frances's discovery in Chet's den of obscenity, I thought, whatever it was that had made her ill enough to miss a day and a half of work. He handed it to me and said, "Take a look."

The envelope contained three 5-by-7 color photographs. The top one was of a very young girl — prepubescent — fondling an older man. I stared at it for a long time. During that time I felt my heart pounding in my ears like a big drum, accompanied by a whine as loud as a siren. The second photograph showed the same girl and man, in coitus. The last was an oral act on his part. They were partially clothed. The light was dim and carnal. The camera was above them and seemed to maintain the same angle for all three shots, like it was on a tripod. The lens angle was wide enough to get some of the backdrop. You could see the thin line of a cord lying on the sleeping bag in one of the pictures. In the other two, the guy had the end of it in his hand. The photographs were unmistakably taken in the Laguna Canyon cave I used to drink in some nights. I'd never seen the girl before.

I was the guy.

My hands were trembling, but I looked straight into Jim Wade's unhappy eyes.

"Cute party gag," I said.

He nodded. All three of them were silent.

"You guys can't believe they're real."

No. They could not.

Wade just stared at me, then down at his desk.

"Sonofabitch," I said.

"What am I supposed to make of these?" he asked.

"Do you think I'd do something like that?"

"Someone with your face did."

"Ah, shit, Jim."

Again, the long stare.

"Just run them past Reilly," I said. "A fake is a fake, and you can tell."

Wade nodded again. Hawlsey stared down

at his empty notepad. I heard Zant adjust himself in his seat, but didn't look at him.

"Reilly analyzed them for me," said Jim. "He's not one of the forensic scientists at the FBI in Washington, but Reilly is pretty good. He says he isn't sure. Says they might be retouched, fabricated somehow, like the tabloids do. If they are, he can't see it. He says they might be real. Real pictures of a real event. He can't see any signs of tampering at all."

My guts had twisted around themselves and the terrible ringing in my ears got louder. "What's Chet say about them?"

Zant looked at me. "He says he's never seen them before."

"Which is what he says about all that other shit we found in his house."

"Yes, basically."

"He mocked them up," I said.

"He didn't have the equipment to do that."

More silence. I still wasn't willing to believe that my peers even *considered* that I might really have been with that girl.

"Sheriff Wade," I said. Then, turning first to Laird, then to Zant, "Counselor Hawlsey and Counselor Zant. I am going to tell you one thing now that's the truth. There was no real event. This didn't happen. And it pisses me off to no end that you're sitting there thinking it did. Just for the record — fuck all of you."

I stood up. In the second or two that passed next I could easily have attacked any of them.

In fact, only their number deterred me: I couldn't decide which one to throttle first.

The pictures and envelope hit the floor. The chair fell over behind me. My legs wobbled. My ears rang. I went to the window and looked through the curtains at the pure April sunshine beaming down on the riding arenas, the people in their colorful clothes, the tawny flanks of a jumper clearing the fence.

"Do you know the girl?" Zant asked.

"Of course I don't, Rick."

"I have to ask you these things. Have you seen her before?"

"I've never seen her, period."

"Do you recognize the scene?" asked Hawlsey.

"It's a cave out in Laguna Canyon. I slept in it a few times. Without girls."

Jim Wade's sigh hit me with gale force. I could hear one of the lawyers collecting the pictures off the floor.

"I'll take you there. You can go through it," I said. "You won't find —"

"We have," said Jim. "Hairs like the girl's. Hair like yours. Fibers. Girl's underwear. The mattress that's in the pictures. The sleeping bag."

My mind was burning itself alive, trying to keep up with the information.

"I took these pictures of myself?"

Silence again.

"Come on."

"They're convincing, Terry," said Zant. "You look at them and they look real. And once presented with them, we have to do something. We can't just toss them out because you work with us. You understand that, don't you?"

"Who knows about this?"

No response. They were going to make me work.

"Melinda?" I asked.

"She doesn't know," said Jim. "I talked to her but she doesn't know. I got the location of the cave from her. Some other things. She doesn't know it all. I thought . . . well. That part of it is between you and Melinda, Terry."

"That's really kind of you," I managed. "Ishmael?"

"Ishmael, Vega and Woolton," said Jim. "Hawlsey and Zant. Johnny and Louis. That was my decision. Nobody else."

"Don't forget Frances," I said.

"It killed her to bring these things to me, Terry."

"It hasn't done a lot for my mood, either," I said quietly. Outside another sun-blanched horse glided through the sky over the poles. The applause came muffled through the glass. I saw a helicopter descending from the blue — the governor, no doubt, arriving in time to watch my execution.

"So, what are you going to do, Sheriff?"

"Just take a week of special duty, at home.

It will give us the time we need. It will keep you paid. It will keep things quiet for a while."

"The Horridus."

"CAY can work The Horridus."

"While I sit on my butt for eight hours a day?"

"I thought of a leave of absence, due to the stress of watching your friend blow out his brains in Chet's backyard. A suspension would be good insurance, but bad faith. An arrest wasn't out of the question, based on what you're holding in your hand there and the way we found them. I'd be happy if I were you. I'm going to move carefully. Those are copies. I've sent the originals to the FBI. Reilly is processing what we found in the cave. If a case arises against you, Terry, we're going to prosecute it. If it doesn't, we're going to owe you a rather huge apology."

"For what it's worth," said Zant, "I hope it's the latter."

Somehow, my nerves had repaired themselves and the ringing had left my ears. I felt blanched and drained, but in control of my own parts.

"What about the press?" I asked.

"They don't need to know."

"They'll find out."

"Not from us, they won't," said Wade. "You're on special duty. That's all it is right now, Terry."

There was a heavy silence in the dark room,

undercut with the cheers from outside. Hawlsey was still buried in his blank notepad. Zant sat forward like a fan at a boxing match.

Sheriff Wade was rigid in his chair, with his arms on the desk and his head cocked just slightly as he looked at me. "Naughton, stay low. I hope this doesn't turn out to be what it looks like. That's for your sake as well as my own."

"It already isn't what it looks like," I said.

"Noted."

I set up the chair I'd knocked over. "You think I did it? Jim? Rick? Laird?"

The question hung in the air like the silence after a scream. No one spoke.

"I'll tell you something," I said. "You gloomy chickenshit bureaucrats are all going to regret this. A lot. I promise. Not quite as much as the sonofabitch who did it, maybe, but a lot."

"Naughton," said Wade, "give us the same respect we're trying to give you. You're a good investigator and a decent-seeming guy, when you're not sinking your teeth into somebody's ankle. You are also not in possession of photographs picturing *me* with underage girls. I have those, of you. That means I could roll your head and wash my hands right now, and save a big gamble. The CAY unit leader doesn't show up in photographs with girls. It stinks up my entire department. If the media finds out, and I'm not doing something, my head rolls right alongside yours, down the ramp and into the basket. So I'm doing something. I'm gathering the facts. Lay low. Let the facts come in. If you're scared of what we'll find, then sell your house and get the best lawyers you can afford. If you're not, you might actually think about cooperating. In the meantime, stay out of my sight. And when the Classic is over, get off my property."

I told Melinda right after dinner. Penny was at the neighbors' house, playing with a friend. Mel set the plate she was rinsing into the sink. For the longest time she just stood there, arms still in the rinse water, the faucet running, her back to me. When she turned her face to me it was a classic translation of the mask of tragedy.

"Terry?"

"You know I wouldn't do that. You do, don't you?"

"Pictures?"

"Somehow, they've been mocked up. I'm not sure how you do it, but I know you can. Reilly says they look genuine, but he's wrong."

Her mouth was open and her head was shaking very slightly, very quickly, side to side.

"Joe says they're real?"

"They're going out to the FBI, Mel. They've got more sophisticated ways of analyzing them. I know . . . I'm absolutely positive we'll find out they're doctored, staged, mocked up, whatever you call it."

I went to her and turned her around. "Please, have some faith in me," I said.

Her face was pale and I thought for a moment she might cry. Her prying eyes moved quickly back and forth, searching my face. Tears welled up in the corners, but Melinda let not a drop fall down her cheek.

"I need to sit down," she said.

I held her arm as we walked across the scuffed hardwood floor to the sofa. I sat beside her. I could feel her recoil, the proximity of her jangling nerves.

"What's Wade going to do?"

"I'm on special duty. House arrest for my usual shift, eight hours a day. Full pay. That's funny, isn't it? While he collects evidence to charge me. Hawlsey and Zant are leading the charge."

"Good God."

It was just us and the silence of the house for a long while.

"I'd like a minute to just sit here," she said. "Alone."

"I'll walk Moe up the hill. When I come back, I'll do whatever you've decided is best."

I had no idea I could get that far into the wilder recesses of Laguna Canyon so quickly. I wondered what the neighbors must have thought as I ran along the road with Moe on his leash. Then I thought, who cared? When

I passed the burned foundation of Scotty Barris's old home I cut off through the brush and onto the trail.

Moe was dragging by the time I made the cave, but I felt fresh and alert. The first thing I checked was my little cache of vices, near the cave. My sleeping bag was gone. My cigars, tequila and pillowcase were gone. Booked into evidence?

Inside, it was obvious that someone had been there. I couldn't itemize all my furnishings from memory, but I noticed my old foam egg-crate pad, a GI surplus wool blanket and my propane lantern were all missing. I could tell that the fire ring had been used because the rocks were arranged in a neat circle that I'd never bothered to maintain, and because of the pile of blackened ashes in its center. I could smell the recent fire. Even the uncertain light was enough to show me that there were footprints everywhere. With some dread I shone a flashlight on the cave belly and saw the gray carbon fingerprint dust still on the harder surfaces of the rock.

I shuddered. If you've ever had a guilty secret, you know the naked shame you feel when you are exposed to the merciless light of day. And it's all the more shocking when you realize you never really felt guilty about it until someone *knows*.

I stood there and wondered who I had told about the cave. Melinda and Penny. Donna.

Johnny and Louis, I think. Ardith. Frances? I couldn't be sure. Mel and Penny were the only ones I'd actually brought here. It was amazing to me how lax I'd been in talking about the place. I'd never considered the cave, or what I did in it, as something to hide. Not that I mentioned the blackouts, or the mornings when I'd awaken somewhere else altogether. But those were a thing of the past, right? Now all I could see as I stood there inside it was a blond-headed girl of maybe eight, engaging my own hungry, lascivious body.

And as I saw that horrible image in my mind, suddenly I had a thought that made all of this even worse. Considerably worse. I had to brace my hands on the cave wall to keep myself up, and lower my head for air. I breathed deeply to purge my mind of the image, but I couldn't. Because the girl in the photographs looked familiar. I couldn't say where or when, but I believed I had seen her before. I *knew* I had. But where? Somehow, my presence in the cave triggered the memory, a memory that wouldn't come to me as I sat in Jim Wade's ranch-house office, confronted with false evidence of my own criminal pathology.

I turned and looked around me, trying to picture her here. I tried to picture myself here. It was easy to do. But were the images in my mind's eye scenes of what had happened, or scenes appropriated from doctored photographs by my desperate memory?

I stared blankly into the dead ashes in the fire ring. I stared hard while my chest ached and my stomach tightened into an even tighter knot. When I finally blinked, I could see clearly again. I could see clearly enough to understand that the first forty years of my life had just tapered to this tremulous point, then vanished. I was a man bisected, a man whose history had not prepared him for his future. And I knew that nothing to come would be anything like what had gone before. I was over. And I was just beginning. I stared into the dead fire, a new man with new eyes. How badly I wanted to be the old one.

Terry Naughton, I thought, champion of the little people, always on the case. Film at eleven. Donna.

My head felt light and my breathing was short and shallow as I walked back outside to the gathering dusk.

The image of Lauren Sharpe came to my mind. With her face next to mine and her teeth sunk into my cheek. No, it wasn't Lauren in those pictures. But it was *someone* I'd seen.

I didn't do that, I told myself. I didn't do that. I didn't.

Ishmael was leaning against the big pepper tree in our front yard when I walked up the driveway. I hardly noticed him at first, in the faltering light. He had one foot resting against the trunk, and his arms crossed over his chest. I noted that Melinda's car was gone. He looked at me with his green panther's eyes.

"Now that things are out in the open, I just wanted to tell you how sorry I am," he said. His tone was jocular, amused.

"You're a feeling human being, Ish."

"And that if I ever see you in the general vicinity of Penelope again, I'll kill you."

"Whatever blows your hair back."

"It'd make me happy, you little bagga shit."

With this, he straightened off the tree and, watching me like a mailman watches a dog, walked across the yard, hopped the little fence in one graceful motion and moved toward his car.

I watched him drive off before letting myself into the house.

Melinda's note was taped to the hardwood floor just inside our front door:

Dear Terry,

I'm looking for a way to believe in you. Maybe I'll find one, because I love and respect you. I don't see any way that your being here would be good for any of us. I have Penny to consider. Take whatever you'll need and go. I'll be here for you. I'll be there for you. If you're the man I think you are maybe we'll laugh about this someday, after we sue the shit out of somebody. If you're not, you must get the help you need. I'll explain this to Penelope as best I can. God be with you, with all of us.

Mel

I packed a few things. Then I went to the liquor store, drove to the little apartment in the metro district, let myself in, opened the windows. I sat at a table in the dining nook and looked out. The Performing Arts Center was lit up like a shrine. The bean field was an empty black rectangle. Beyond it flowed a river of headlights, and the big hotels rose into the night and the palm trees stood erect and motionless. The dark glass of the business towers caught the lesser lights below, wearing them like medals. Tonello's glowed with self-importance, and I could see the valets standing just under the awning in their red vests and bow ties.

I got out a notepad and made a list of the people I thought might have the opportunity to do this to me. Included were Jordan Ishmael, Jim Wade, Frances White, Johnny Escobedo and Louis Briar. I added Ardith Naughton, Melinda Vickers and Donna Mason. I added Burns, Woolton and Vega. But who knew about the cave, or could have found out about it? I hadn't told Wade, Ish or either of the undersheriffs directly, but any one of them could conceivably have learned about it, located it and salted it. Right? I added three fat question marks, for the people who might have been told about the cave by the people *I* had told. They could be anybody. Then I put the names together in various combinations, like cards in a poker hand. Even with knowledge of the cave, who had the opportunity to slip the falsified photos into Chet's den? That eliminated Ardith and Donna. And even with knowledge and opportunity, who had the technical skill to create such documents? That eliminated only Melinda, positively, because I truly didn't know what secret skills my co-workers might possess. Anything was possible. But even with knowledge, opportunity and technical capacity, who had a motive to see my career, my relationships — perhaps my life — destroyed? I could only write down one name for certain: Ishmael.

Strange, I thought, the way that name comes off the tongue: *Ishmael.*

I drank swiftly and earnestly.

I remember a cab ride through the metro district. I remember standing amid the fragrant furrowed earth of the bean field to behold the quarter moon. I remember part of a movie, a long hot shower that didn't slow the cold shivers of my body, the tequila and beer vanishing, a late-night taxi stop to get more, words with two men as I got back into the cab, the way the floor of the apartment seemed to pivot steeply in alternate directions as I navigated my way across it. I remember fast-food wrappers flying out the window of a car I wasn't driving. I remember a phone booth. I remember vivid dreams — I can only assume they were dreams — of caves and girls and women and various methods of execution, my body always on the verge of something either deadly or pleasureful, neither of which was consummated, and swirling planes of bright stars in a blue night, and smells. I remember the smells of damp stone, blood and sagebrush, female sweat. I remember dreaming that Donna crawled into bed with me and held my naked, clammy form and tried to reassure me. That morning when I awoke she was in fact there, splendidly fresh and dressed for work, running her fingers through my damp hair.

I felt like I'd returned from death itself. But I didn't know how to feel about it.

I looked up at her.

"You said some crazy things last night," she said. Her expression was more interested than accusatory.

"Bad. Dreams."

"No. You were awake still. Lots of talk about the pictures. What pictures?"

"Hm?" There was a riot of pain, an insurrection of agony led by my soul.

"The pictures. Don't you remember anything you said?"

"Uh-uh."

"You kept saying the pictures had followed you. The pictures had caught you. Someone was trying to get you. What were you talking about?"

"Beats me," I managed.

She brought me a cup of coffee, sat on the bed beside me and put her cool hand on my head. I closed my eyes. I could tell by the turn of her wrist that she looked at her watch.

"You and Melinda had a fight. You did tell me that much. I'm sorry for that. It brought us together for a night, but I'm still sorry."

I looked at her. "No. I am. Sorry. About last night. About everything."

"You don't have to be, Terry. But you really ought to come clean with me. I can live with half of you for now, but that half's got to be all there."

"Yeah. I'm trying."

"What's happening?"

"Not sure yet. Special duty. I really can't tell you about it. You know — regulations."

She looked down at me with frank suspicion. Even through the throbbing fog in my brain I could tell she was vetting my stories. I was dully aware that that's what she did for a living. She looked at her watch again. She leaned down and wrapped my head in her arms and whispered in my ear, *Terry, I got to be at the newsroom in thirty-five minutes. It's a half-hour drive this time of morning. That leaves five minutes to spare and I'm going to use that time to tell you something you might not understand.*

288

I watched her make some adjustments in her underthings, then climb over me. She looked like she might on TV, the upper half of her a thing of beauty and intelligence, the lower half of her unseen. But that lower half was connected to me in a way that made me want to stay right there with her forever. It was like being plugged straight into heaven. Like a live feed from an angel. She closed her eyes. Her bangs dangled and cast moving shadows on her forehead. I heard the bathroom water running. Before she left she kissed me on the lips, then cheek, then stood there looking down at me.

She touched my face with her fingers. "I hate mysteries. I hate all the things you don't tell me, all the mysteries you hold back. I like the truth. And I like things I can see and touch and hold — things that prove the truth. I love you, too, Terry Naughton. But you sure don't make it easy."

Sixteen

Darien Aftergood was an old acquaintance of mine from high school. We were both second-string guards for the freshman basketball team, the Laguna Artists, and we went 3-14 that year. I couldn't really handle the ball and he couldn't really shoot, but we had the boundless hustle of second stringers everywhere. We were skinny kids who rarely had our heads in the game. We left the hoops after that first year. He started running with the art-theater crowd and I spent my afternoon surfing Brooks Street. Darien must have taken our mascot name literally. Now he's an artist and gallery owner in Laguna, with a studio/gallery/apartment downtown on Ocean Avenue. Darien is plugged into the art world at a hundred different sockets. He guest-curates for the Orange County Art Museum; he organizes shows at his own space; he is a critic for two national magazines and his work has been collected and shown around the world. He's a photographer who manipulates his images in the lab. The results are images that sometimes look like photographs, but aren't photographs at all.

He tried to explain to me, through the painful haze of my hangover, how he manages to create pictures that look so real but aren't.

"We have to define 'reality' if we're going to get anywhere, Terry. The reality of the image is what you see. It doesn't exist until the artist creates it. To say it isn't real misses a large part of the whole point. For instance, how can you say that this image isn't a reality?"

I looked at the picture on the wall in front of us. We were standing in the main room of his little gallery. The art was done by a New York compatriot of Darien's, and it depicted a huge can of tuna fish, upright on its side in the middle of an expansive American prairie. Two photographically "real" people stood in the foreground and looked upward at the can. The photographically "real" tuna fish can was about sixty feet tall.

"But that scene never took place," I said. "It might be a real image, but it's based on a false event."

"No, not really, Terry. It's not based on an event at all. The event *is* the image. The event doesn't take place until the artist brings it into being."

"But there's no reality there."

"Literal visual truth — as you're referring to it — died decades ago. We photographers killed it. Even *National Geographic* was reworking its photographs for the magazine, I mean taking some pretty big liberties by the standards of journalism. Look at any supermarket tabloid. You can see the splices quite easily. But on a work like this, you can't. It's a matter of degree."

"How did he do it?"

Darien explained the process: a combination of digital imaging and an Iris printer, which uses continual ink-jet technology to apply colored ink to paper or canvas; photographs altered with painted passages, combined with monoprints of video footage of computer-generated images; enlarged Polaroid prints; and images drawn from a digital file. You just scan in an image, he said, then go to work on it with the Adobe Photoshop program on your computer and hurl 129 megabytes of power at it.

"I've been working on some traditional, labor-intensive processes too," he said. "That involves producing photographic prints using pigment transfer and platinum printing. The pigment transfer is suspending the pigment in gelatin or gum Arabic, then building up layers of the color. The interesting thing about the older process is that the color will be stable on the paper for five hundred years. It's time consuming and expensive."

I nodded. The price tag for the giant tuna can was $1,400.

"Is it one of a kind?"

"It is now, but we can pull prints. It's up to the artist, how many copies he wants out there."

I thought. "What about . . . what if . . . what if the artist had certain images to begin with? Say, photographs. Pictures of a background, and pictures of a subject. Could he manipulate those to create an image that looked like this certain person was doing something in this certain place?"

Darien smiled and glanced at the work on the wall. "The guy on the left there, that's me. And I guarantee you I never stood on a Nebraska prairie and stared up at a monster can of tuna fish."

"Then it's easy."

"No. It's complicated. There are new tools now. That's what all this technology is — it's just tools. They're powerful tools and you have to know how to use them. They're expensive. No, it's not easy, but a lot of things are possible now that used to be impossible. Most of these artists might tell you that making it look easy is part of the art. Others, well, they like to let the technology show. Two different aesthetics, really."

"If I showed that tuna fish picture to an expert in photography at the FBI, would he be able to tell it's fake?"

"Wouldn't take the FBI to see that it's fake, Terry! In the way you mean 'fake,' that is."

"Okay. Say it was just a can of tuna fish on a table. And the tools behind the image were digital processing and the Iris printer. Then, could that expert tell by examining the picture that it was done without a real can of tuna fish?"

"It *was* done with a real can of tuna fish. The real can of tuna fish was reproduced and stored by the digital file. It's as 'real' a can of tuna fish in the file as it is in a picture. You know?"

"But a photograph is supposed to capture an image."

"Wrong. A photograph *creates* an image. That's the difference now. That's where it's all changing. Madison Avenue has been working on it for decades. But right now, the explosion in tools has made things possible that weren't possible just three years ago. Three years from now . . . who knows?"

We toured the gallery and looked at other works. Some were obviously "created" — like the tuna can; others — like a portrait of a woman with her cat — were absolutely convincing as plain old photographs.

"Why's that one so special?" I asked. "There's millions of cats like that."

"The cat's real. The woman doesn't exist. She was created on a computer."

I stepped up close to look at the lines on her face, the singular expression in her eyes, the details of her hands. You could see the wrinkles in her skin, the underlying veins, the blemishes and hairs.

"You can make anything," I said.

"Almost."

"What can't you make?"

Darien crossed his arms and raised a hand to his face. He set his chin into the little cradle of thumb and curled forefinger. "I'm not sure. But why don't you tell me what you *want*. And I'll tell you if it's makeable."

"All right. I want five-by-seven photographs of a woman bathing her son. I want the woman to be a real woman, and I've got photographs of her face you can work with. The boy is real, and I can give you pictures of his face, also. But he's never actually been bathed by this woman. They've never actually seen each other. And I want the bathroom to be a certain bathroom, and I've got pictures of that to give you, too. And when you've created an image of this woman bathing a kid she's never seen in a genuine bathtub, I'm going to send the thing off to the FBI's best scientists and I don't want them to be able to say it was staged, retouched, enhanced, created, digitally manufactured or Iris ink-jet printed. I want them to say, yeah, that's a picture of a woman giving a boy a bath. It's real. It's genuine. It happened. It's evidence."

"Color or black and white?"

"Color."

"What's your budget?"

"Whatever it takes."

"Consider it done. There will be some limitations on it. If the image required visual information that wasn't in the photographs you supplied, it would have to be generated by computer, by an artist who could extrapolate, who could imagine what was missing. Say he needed the inside of her left hand, but you didn't have it on film. He'd have to create it."

"Then the FBI guys would see a fake hand?"

"They'd have to compare it to the real one for that. There'd be no way — just based on the image — for them to know that it was created, *if* it was created skillfully. And Terry, that document he'd create, that picture you'd finally show the FBI, it would be totally, 100 percent *genuine*. It would be — or could be — finally, after all the work was done, just a simple, authentic photograph."

"Even though the event depicted never happened."

"It didn't happen until the artist created it."

"It never *happened*, Darien. What you *see* in the *picture* did not fucking *happen*. Did it? The woman never gave the kid a bath. Did she?"

"Okay. It never happened."

"Good Christ, no wonder we could never run a simple pick and roll."

Silence for a moment, my anger waning.

"We were bad basketball players, weren't we?" he asked.

"Didn't you get ten against Newport Harbor?"

"Eight. I never got double digits my whole career."

"Me neither."

We sat in his office for a while and talked about the old days, the new days, some of the days in between. Then the conversation got thin.

"What are you working on, Terry? Can I ask?"

I considered my reply for a moment. "Darien, there's a mudbath pending for a very close friend of mine. We're talking about somebody getting royally screwed by pictures of something he didn't do."

"That's bad."

"It's worse than bad. It's a career, a life, maybe a prison term. This guy didn't do what they say he did. What the pictures say he did."

"They'd have to have more than just pictures, wouldn't they?"

"For a court of law, maybe. For everything else, the pictures will do quite nicely. They'll ruin him."

"Blackmail?"

"No. The cops are sending the pictures to the FBI and the alleged perp is trying to save his ass."

Darien sat back, fiddling with a pencil on his desktop. "The anomaly would have to be in the image, then — not in the medium."

"Yeah?"

"Yeah. I mean, if portions of the image are unique, the way a person is unique, a fingerprint is unique, then anything digitally created could be shown to be inaccurate."

"But you'd need the real thing to prove it."

"Right. You'd need the mother, or the boy, or the bathroom."

I thought about this. Me. The cave. The girl.

Who has pictures of me?

Ardith, the enthused amateur: many. Melinda, an occasional snapshooter: a few. Louis, Johnny and Frances, from our frequent socializing: maybe. Donna, via file footage: some.

And everyone else at the Sheriff's Department, through my personnel file: left side, right side, straight on.

I got Johnny by phone just before lunch. I shamed him into faxing me a copy of Amanda's sketch of The Horridus, as described by Brittany Elder. I had to go to a pharmacy in Laguna with a fax service to receive the thing, banished as I was from my home. I asked about the real estate listings and Johnny said they were down to three male sellers of detached-unit homes.

"If the male sellers don't pan out, try the women," I said.

He was quiet for a moment. It was my first whiff of actual day-to-day banishment, and it weighed my heart like a death in the family. I was putting Johnny Escobedo in an impossible jam.

"Shit, Johnny, I'm sorry," I said.

"I understand, man. I really do."

He didn't rush to hang up on me, for which I loved him dearly.

"The worst part, Johnny, is I'm out. The Horridus is planning number four, we've got kids in ditches, infants in file cabinets and pervs all over the place and I'm sitting here with my thumb up my ass."

"If it didn't happen it didn't happen. I know it didn't happen."

A desperate heart is a soft one. Mine practically melted. "I love you, man. And I don't even want your beer. Though I could use one right now."

"I should go."

"What's Reilly got on the Elder scene?"

"Still working. Nothing yet. The news here is the park ranger out at Caspers."

He told me about a ranger named Bret Stefanic who was found murdered the evening before.

"Way out in the woods off the Ortega," said Johnny. "Guy cut his throat wide open. Didn't really grab my interest until the ME said he'd been bitten three times by a venomous snake — probably a rattlesnake."

I thought a moment.

"It looked like Stefanic stopped somebody out there. His citation book was out, found it in the weeds. The last three tickets were ripped out of the book. We think the perp was written up, surprised him somehow. Reilly said he died from the slashing. The snake bites were premortem. Very strange, uh . . . Frank."

Reduced to Frank. It was what I had left.

"Crotalus horridus?"

"We're sending out some of Stefanic's blood to a toxicologist over at Irvine and a herpetologist in Chicago. They both told me already there'd be no way to differentiate one rattlesnake venom from another, once it's in the blood. That's if the bites even *were* from a rattler. The ME said venomous snake. There's lots of those."

"Well, not around here there aren't, Johnny."

"That's what I mean. The only poisonous ones found here in the wild are the rattlers. But what if it's a cobra, or a water moccasin or something?"

I was silent for a moment, as I tried to imagine The Horridus out in the far reaches of a wilderness. It fit. He let his victims go in places like that. In fact, he'd let Courtney go in the Caspers Wilderness Park. He liked the outdoors. It made sense, but not a lot.

"Where were the bites?"

"Buttocks, leg, face."

"Bitten while he was alive."

"Correct. And the ME said he was bitten just before he died. The venom hadn't been assimilated very far into the tissue. He died not long after the bites."

I just couldn't put it together. "So this inquiring ranger tries to cite a guy for something, gets his throat cut, then falls down and a rattlesnake that just happens to be in the grass bites him once on the ass, once on the leg, then finished with a bite to his face? Johnny, there's a whole lot of something wrong with that picture."

"I know. Let me ask you something, Terry. If we strike out on the male sellers, why try the women?"

"Mother. Wife, girlfriend, sister."

"That's out of profile, isn't it?"

"You know me, Johnny — I throw the net wide as I can."

Another silence while Johnny vetted my methods. I've long been known at the department as the guy who goes the extra mile when he doesn't have to. Maybe checking the women was just a waste of time. Apparently, Johnny Escobedo thought so.

"Hey, I should go."

"Johnny, one more thing. I got this fax from Strickley at the Bureau. He found a weird thread that leads back to Texas. I think it's worth —"

"— I already laid it on Ish. No dice."

"Ishmael?"

"He's acting head of CAY."

"Ah, holy shit —"

"— And he said we're better off looking here than looking in Texas, considering we don't work in Texas. I'm trying to get them to send us a file. Slow going — the whole thing's cool by now."

My balls frosted with the news of Ishmael as acting head of my unit. It was all I could do to keep my mind halfway on track. "It's worth it for one of us — one of you — to spend a couple of days back there. Who'd you talk to? Welborn?"

"Yeah. He's . . . hey, Frank, I gotta go."

"Listen, Johnny, there's one more thing. I know I keep saying that. But we got to try the two dating services again."

"None of the names matched."

"But those were members. What about employees, service people who have both accounts, subcontractors and vendors?"

There was a pause. "That's right, uh, Frank. I hadn't thought of that. All right, man. Over and out."

"Check the women sellers if the men —"
Click.

I got the fax and walked down to the beach. I sat on a green bench. The bench had a plaque on it, dedicated to Edward Kilfoy — 1967–73. Six years old. What happened to him? I watched the people walk by. Some kids chased the retreating remnants of a wave, stopped with their skinny legs bent, then screamed and ran back in ahead of the next one. Good, cold, April, Pacific Ocean brine, I thought. I opened the folded fax. There he was: short hair cut in a flattop, swept back,

302

and a tight, narrow face. High cheekbones and a small mouth. Sleepy eyes, brown, according to the description. Medium everything. A sport coat, collared shirt, tan trousers. No glasses. I thought of Brittany telling me how bad his breath was. Should we have put that in the description? I recalled Steven Wicks's version. They weren't really close. Similarities, yes, but only general ones. What I wouldn't give for a picture of him as good as the ones they had of me, to turn into billboards for freeways all over the county. I wondered if this rendition would be good enough to get results. I had to think not. But it was another piece, another tool.

I drove out Laguna Canyon Road to my street — former street — and passed it. What a sad-strange feeling, to pass a place that used to have your home on it. I U-turned, headed back, U-turned again and made a right onto Canyon Edge.

There was no reason for the house to look different than it had less than a day earlier, but it did. The pepper tree outside was bigger, lazier, sadder. The little house seemed to have missed me. I pulled into the driveway and sat there for a while. Moe *had* missed me, and I saw the proof. He stood on his hind legs with his paws up on the fence, barking and wagging his tail. I rolled down the window. The pepper tree dropped a cluster of dried-out pinkish balls to the hood. The cluster skidded across the paint in the breeze. How on earth, I thought, have you managed to mess everything up so bad? Mel would be at work; Penny at school. I doubted she'd changed the locks this fast. After taking a deep breath I swung open the car door and got out. Moe mugged me inside the gate and I got down on my knees and grabbed the thick fur and skin around his neck. He plopped over and I scratched his yellow soft belly. I knelt there for a moment, petting my dog, trying to look integral. No one would know I wasn't. Right?

But my heart was thumping as I tried my key. It worked. I let myself in as I'd done a thousand times before, and closed the door behind me. My heart was still pounding. The smell of the place got me: the old wood and varnish of the floors, the faint aroma of food cooked recently, the fresh femininity of Melinda and Penny, all hovering nicely above the scent of Moe's dogness.

So, having burgled my way onto private property, I went to Melinda's study. Moe clicked along beside me. I caught Melinda's smell in here too, but stronger. I tried to ignore it. The drapes were pulled shut and the room was cool. I turned on her computer and booted it up. It's a fast, strong machine, supplied by the department for Melinda's Fraud and Computer Crime work at home. I got onto the Web and got myself to a site I'd been to many times before.

http: \ \ www. fawnskin.com

After the usual delays and waiting, I got myself to the Web site. *Fawnskin*. Interesting word, isn't it? For one, it's the name of a mountain community in Southern California. You think of snow and slopes and cabins. Beyond that, it suggests something sensually engaging, something tactile and pleasant. It suggests youth and the touching of youth. After a few hours on the sex net — and I had spent many there as part of my job — you start to learn the vernacular. The home page was boring enough, with a slow graphic of a snowy mountain with a ski run going up the side, and big letters at the top, announcing LOCAL SNOW! Below the title was the home page synopsis for the site:

http: \ \ www. fawnskin.com — Nothing beats the local mountains for quick and fun skiing, camping, fishing and hiking. Find your trail through us.

I scrolled forward to the list of realtors who handled rentals. Fine. The site had that dull, legitimate face of business. But to me it felt like the jacket for something else entirely, which is how the illegal networkers hide their faces from innocent browsers. The last realtor listed had a different Web site, so I clicked there and waited. It isn't a realtor's home page at all — it's a coded chat room schedule for men whose sexual preference is for children. A chat "room" is comprised of Internet Relay Chat, IRC for short. Providers sell access to private and public IRC as part of their service — anybody can use a room, as long as they can find it. At any rate, I was looking for some men who call themselves the Midnight Ramblers. I know the individual who updates this changing chat room schedule, and he knows me. He was in federal lockup between 1986 and 1989 for distributing child pornography across state lines. I was the one who busted him, long before our CAY unit was established. I allow him to operate here because his roving band of Web perverts are open to my lurking, so long as I don't shut them down. They don't know that Mal — my Web name — is Terry Naughton, the same way that I'm not supposed to know who they really are. Some I do; most I don't. I knew the chat room site, and I was pretty certain the pervs would be talking. But I checked the schedule to make sure. It was just a matter of reading the *Farmer's Almanac* quote at the end of the page. It was always followed by a series of random-looking numbers that appear to be a mistake or a code in the posting. They just run them together for the next date and times, backward.

May 2, noon to 3 P.M., and May 3, 1 A.M. to 3 A.M.

Easy. From years of experience I knew that noon was one of their usual times to yak it up through IRC. The Midnight Ramblers were currently in session.

I wound my way through the search engine and found the private room. The name Mal was my admission.

Mal: contented with day-to-day. Seeks counsel of like brethren in soul chit-chat and bets on the come line . . . seeks info only sexperts might possess.

This is sex-net talk. You learn it after a few hours on the computer, networking with sick fucks who don't have a whole lot better to do, apparently. Sex talk is legal. Even sex talk between pedophiles is legal, to a point. But it's esoteric, cryptic and circuitous. It's exclusive. And I was lucky right then, because at least one other twisted soul out there in our strange huge world was lurking the chat room:

Lancer: I remember you, Mal-content, Mal-adjusted, Mal-ady.

There it was. Right off the bat I was remembered. Nice. I hadn't been on-line with the Ramblers for three or four months.

Mal: Nice to be back. I'm searching.

307

Lancer: Praytell for what, Mal-approp?
Mal: Image is everything.
O-Ring: Amen to that. Praise the lewd. New or used?
Mal: Newly minted.
Lancer: Semen-proof and very pricey.
O-Ring: See I. R. Shroud.
E-Rection: Go see Shroud! He's your mail-man, male-man — delivers the goods. Why not go again?

I sat there for a moment in Melinda's study, surprised by E-Rection's assumption that I had already dealt with one I. R. Shroud, the man who "delivers the goods."

My scalp tightened and my hands felt cold. I had *not* dealt with I. R. Shroud. So someone else had used my name — Mal — on the kid porn web.

I couldn't wait too long, or my embarrassment might be inferred.

Mal: I'm fully intending to, but can't find my old friend. Have you seen him? Did he take an extended Thai holiday?

The Thai holiday, of course, refers to the places in Thailand where children can be bought for sex. It's every perv's dream to stay at Pattaya — the country's leading sex resort — and have intercourse with children to their heart's content.

O-Ring: Shroud comes and Shroud goes. There's other ways to acquire pix of qualitee-hee-hee.

E-Rection: I. R. is still the best. Cream of the cream.

Lancer: Mal-odorous, were you happy with what you acquired from the Shroud-man?

Careful, I thought: you can miss a beat here, and the chat room will empty like a theater on fire. What I needed was the approved way to contact Shroud — more than likely his e-mail box — but I couldn't just ask without blowing the whole ruse. I had to stay cool, state my interest and get off the lot, like working a car salesman for a better deal.

Mal: I just need more, more, more.
Lancer: Don't we all?
O-Ring: Why not post your treasures?
E-Rection: Share and share alike.
Mal: I intend to. There will be a time for that.
Lancer: Once you squee-gee them off, Mal-e-dick-shun.
Mal: I may require I. R. again.
O-Ring: I'm sure you will.
Mal: See you next time through Fawnskin.
E-Rection: Bugger off!

Good enough — O-Ring would pass the word. They were gone and I was alone again in Melinda's study. It's such a strange thing to slide into the Web like that, connect down to the underbelly. It feels like you're geezing into a vein of pure wickedness. And it's always there, always around and always invisible. It's like a stream made out of nothing but vapors, evil and endless, and it runs through everything.

The guys were probably happy to have Mal back, another p-phile out there, another pedofreak, a man like themselves, a guy who considers himself a gourmet, an artist, an aesthetician of the world's daintiest delicacies. They love to riddle and pun. They love anagrams, symbols, innuendo, code. What the hell kind of name is I. R. Shroud, anyway, besides fabricated? IRS? Internal Revenue Cover? I Am Death? It goes on and on. They love word games that make them look bright. They'll tell you the art and practice of "loving children" goes back to ancient Greece, or the Romans, or to the Egyptians or the Bible. They've even got an organization — the North American Man-Boy Love Association (NAMBLA), which has a newsletter and a lobby in Washington. Really, that's no lie. Everything they do — from the children to the verbiage to the little games — is a way of trying to mask their inadequacies. And they're about as inadequate as men can get. That's why they're despised, even in prison — the cons will turn them into bleeding punchcards in no time at all. The cons hate child molesters even more than they hate cops. A child-molester cop? He wouldn't last long in the big house. I didn't want to try, though the idea crossed my mind that I might have to.

This guy, I. R. Shroud, had porn for sale. Maybe he was a buyer, too. Maybe a collector. He might even create it himself. Which was an interesting thought, considering my circumstances.

I always get off the kid porn Web feeling like I should take a long bath in acid, or have my skin peeled and replaced. You touch your finger to that invisible stream, and it'll try to suck you in. It goes right for your soul.

I shut down the computer and wandered the house for a while. I stood for a moment in Melinda's bedroom — my bedroom until last night — and registered its presence. The furniture was all hers, as was most of the furniture in the house. I'd left "ours" with Ardith; Jordan had left "theirs" with Mel. I'd never fully acclimated to putting my ass onto the same couch that had cushioned Jordan Ishmael's. It was odd, though. With me gone, the room didn't seem very different than it did with me in it. The whole house didn't seem very different. I remembered our brief contentions over what came into the new home and what stayed in storage (mostly my stuff), how things were to be arranged, how the household would be organized. She was particular about what went where — furnishings, electronics, pictures, knickknacks. Melinda had her way on almost every point, and to be truthful, that was fine with me. I've got no eye for design. But it was strange to see how little I'd influenced my own home. Take out Terry, his clothes, personal effects and dog, and there wasn't much left to prove he'd ever lived here. I felt leased.

I drove to the nearest computer store and got a slick new machine set up with a fast modem and plenty of memory to get me into the Net. It was a portable one and quite expensive, about the price of my first new car, a 1975 VW. I paid cash. I considered it a sound investment in reclaiming my life from whoever was trying to take it. I might have bought a powerful automatic handgun too, and learned how to use it, but I already had one and already did.

I really wanted to get to know this I. R. Shroud. Though the other kid-rapers on the Net thought we had dealt with each other before, we hadn't. I'd know, wouldn't I? Even during my months of blackout drinking, I'd remember purchasing pornography from one I. R. Shroud. Correct? But somebody on the Web had used my name to get to the Ramblers, and that person had gotten product from Shroud. E-Rection had told me so.

I was walking out of the computer store when an idea hit me. Just one of those little blips of thought that race in from nowhere and slide away forever if you don't slow them down and make them feel welcome. I wondered if this pretending Mal might have requested images of a certain guy. They're called customs, where the customer wants his own body in the image. Naturally, the ultimate pornography features yourself. But in this case, Mal had ordered images of someone else — me. Interesting. I locked the new machine in the trunk with a corollary thought: no one except a few of my cohorts at the department knew that I was Mal, or that the name would get him into the Ramblers' chat room. In fact, I couldn't think of anyone I worked with outside of CAY who knew my handle. Johnny, Louis and Frances. Oh, and of course, supervising lieutenant Jordan Ishmael.

I got my stitches removed at a walk-in clinic in Laguna — not the one where I took my son, because that one has since gone out of business. Fun. The puncture wounds were ugly and the scars would be small but definite.

Then I stopped by a travel agency and booked a little two-day vacation. I needed it. American Airlines to Dallas/Ft. Worth, Alamo Rental Car. Holiday Inn in Wichita Falls. Just the kind of place where there's enough to keep you busy, and the rest of the time you can forget the world you left behind, and hope it forgets you.

Seventeen

Wichita Falls is in north central Texas, way up by the Oklahoma border, about a two-and-a-half-hour drive from D/FW International Airport. Those are Texas hours, by the way — quite a bit longer than the ones we have in California. The city lies in the Red River Valley, also the name of a tune that is difficult to get out of your head once you hear it. I heard it on the radio. It didn't matter, because I've always liked it. I clipped along in the rental Olds at the speed limit, which — I remember from the stories of friends once stationed out at Sheppard Air Force Base — is strictly enforced.

The land is green in April, and always flat. You can see oil rigs and water towers far out in the distance against the vast sky, and have little idea of how far away they really are. Oil goes boom and bust out there, and right now, it's mostly bust. There's some ranching and farming — cattle and cotton. It was a big cattle center for a while. I always thought the Texans were smart to exploit their land for beef and oil, two staples this country will always need.

The locals are quick to point out two things

of interest. First is that Larry McMurtry lives near here, and he is just a regular guy. You see him all the time. Second is that Wichita Falls sits in "Tornado Alley," as mentioned by a convenience store employee, the Holiday Inn desk clerk and a desk officer at the WFPD, who answered my arrival call to his captain. The desk clerk told me the big one of '64 flattened her parents' house and threw a heavy steel mascot steer that once adorned a local butcher shop some eight hundred yards into a cotton field. It was found there, upright, the next day. It also blew blades of straw into a soft-drink bottle that her dad discovered, unopened and perfectly intact, after the twister passed. She said she's seen the bottle and it's true — he still has it on his fireplace in the new house they built.

Police Captain Sam Welborn had a friendly, green-eyed face with a smile that seemed half for me and half for himself. He seemed amused. He was tall and big boned, with thinning black hair and an air of congeniality. He was the kind of big friendly cop you wouldn't want to get riled up. He handed me file 199591, then rolled back on his chair and spit a brown tobacco blast into a plastic cup. I could smell the wintergreen.

"She was a real sweet girl, they say. Good student, minded her parents real good. It was a pretty big deal here, when she went missin'."

I opened the folder. "We've got a guy who's

315

taken three in less than two months. Hasn't raped them yet. Hasn't killed them yet. He dresses them up in old clothes, these lacy robes and hoods, then cuts them loose out in the woods. We think he's escalating."

"This one here had a thing about clothes. Trying to get young girls to put them on."

"That's what got our attention."

"FBI?"

"Yeah."

"Those boys can be pushy sometimes, but they're pretty sharp, too."

I scanned through the missing persons' report on Mary Lou Kidder. She left school a little late after talking to a teacher, never came home. A woman who lived on Mary Lou's route home from school said she saw a white van parked on her street that she hadn't seen before and never saw again. She didn't notice who was driving it, and she didn't see anybody get in or out. Mary Lou Kidder had been gone now for two years, one month and three days. There was a picture of her from school — a round-faced, happy-looking girl with bangs and a bow in her hair.

"We couldn't connect the clothes guy with Mary Lou," said the captain. "But we still think he took her."

"I'd think that, too."

In line with that assumption, the WFPD had included in Mary Lou's file the incident reports, witness and subject interviews on the

UNSUB Male who'd been trying to outfit school girls in free clothes that weren't new. The physical description was somewhat similar to our early Horridus: white male, early thirties, medium build, eyeglasses, beard and mustaches. The cops had even put together a composite sketch of the suspect. I took a copy of our first Horridus attempt from my briefcase and compared the two. He looked not unlike Amanda's version from Steven Wicks, with the facial hair and glasses. The Texas version was fuller in the face, and his hair was longer. The glasses were shaped differently. Both sketches were frustratingly vague. I handed our sketch, and the file, over the desk to Welborn.

"Hmm. Eyes look the same. He's got that . . . intellectual look. Like a guy who went to college, maybe. But these sketches — seems they're either right there or way off."

"I know."

"I'll tell ya, we passed that picture out to everybody in town, twice. We had it on the TV and all the papers. We thought we'd probably run him out, then the girl went missing. Man, it was bad. Just breaks your heart when something like that happens on your watch."

"I know that, too, Captain."

He studied me with his clear green eyes. I could see the lump of dip stuck up under his cheek, and smell the wintergreen flavoring.

"My personal belief is that he wasn't from

317

this town," Welborn said. "Now, I can't sub-
stantiate that with anything concrete, but I
believe it. See, we get to know our people here
pretty well. We only got about a hundred
thousand in Wichita, and we get to know 'em.
You got your black element on the other side
of Flood Street, then you got your Mexicans
mostly grouped up in the north end, around
Scotland Park and the river. This fella was
Caucasian. Preying on his own type. And that
group is pretty well connected up. They recognize each other, mostly. We recognize them.
Know what I mean?"

I nodded.

"I think he lived somewhere close by. Not
here, though. It's just a theory."

I took back the file and scanned through.
"If I wanted to check real estate listings for
the time period after Mary Lou Kidder disappeared, who would you recommend?"

"Katie Butler, over at Coldwell Banker.
Happy to make a call for you. What's the idea
behind that?"

"If you smoked him out of town and he
owned a home, he'd sell. The Bureau has a
strong hunch that our guy lives in a place that
has a detached second unit. If your guy is our
guy, maybe he lived in one here, too."

"Well, the big mansions in Country Club
all have servants' quarters. Rent them out
now, mostly."

"We wouldn't anticipate him coming from

that kind of wealth. We're thinking middle class. A house with a granny flat or maybe even a detached garage he could convert."

Welborn's green eyes settled on me again. "Convert into what?"

"A place to take them. His victims."

"You got evidence of that?"

"Some."

"The Feds do up one of those profiles for you?"

"They did."

He shook his head. "I always thought that was voodoo, myself. But that's just me. I hope you catch your guy. I hope he's our guy, too. We can execute him once in each state."

"If you'd be willing to call Ms. Butler, I'd much appreciate it."

He set his dip cup on the desk and dialed out. "Katie, this is Sam. How ya *doin'* over there, sweetheart?"

Katie Butler was stout and wide faced, with a swirl of red hair done up stiff. She smiled like she'd known me all her life. She welcomed me to Wichita — the locals all seemed to drop the Falls — and said if I ever wanted to move here, it was a buyers' market, great deals all over, get three times the house I could have in California, for less money.

"A course, we've got our tornadoes here," she said. "You just have to include acts of God as part of life. But you got your quakes and all, so you know what natural disaster is like. They're usually not so bad as everybody likes to make out."

"Most of our earthquakes aren't so bad, either. You don't even know they're happening."

"Well, we do get champion-sized twisters here, I'll tell you. In '72 the steer blew off the butcher and landed in Archer County, standing up in a pasture like the real cows. That's a five-hundred-pound, decorative steel steer. Funny things like that happen all the time."

She set me up with the multiple listings for March through June of two years back. My window was kind of big, but that might make it easier to crawl through. She led me to a private little room and brought me a big cup of coffee.

"Sam says you're looking into the Mary Lou thing?"

"That's right."

"My niece went to school with her. They were friends. She was a cute little girl. I remember her smile, because it was so happy looking, and funny, too, because her two front teeth fell out and left a gap. She was a real doll, a real angel."

I nodded, but didn't say anything. Her warm blue eyes were gray now, and I could not mistake the ferocity in them.

"Think she's alive?" she asked.

"I really can't say, Ms. Butler."

Her face turned accusing, then askance, then judgmental, then resigned. And, finally, for reasons I would never know, forgiving. "Ya'll let me know what else I can get you. 'Kay?"

An hour later I'd found all the listings for homes with detached units. Four were in a moderate price range, and three of them were sold by men. None of their names matched the sellers in Orange County, the ones that Johnny was just about finished checking out. I got that funny, embarrassing feeling in my guts that told me I'd been following a trail that was about to disappear into nothing.

Katie Butler read each one that I'd marked.

"Now, I knew this fella — Al Jeeter — and he sold because he wanted to move back to Virginia, where he grew up."

"How old was he?"

"Oh my . . . late sixties, I'd say."

"What about the next one?"

"Lindy Dillard? Don't know him, but I do know we sold the house. I can get the paperwork if you want. Sometimes, escrow documents have the age of the seller and buyer. Here, let me just get them all for you."

"Forget Wanda Grantley," I said.

"Pretty easy to do," said Katie.

"Why's that?"

"Not my kind of people, those two. Be right back."

I waited in the lobby while she went through

her files. I could see her hard red hair past the counter when she knelt at a file cabinet. I drank another cup of coffee and thought about Donna and how surprised she was that I was leaving. She was suspicious, but she held her questions. I thought of Melinda and Penny. I thought of the pictures that Wade had of me, and the trail that led to I. R. Shroud. I thought of the ranger, Stefanic, and wondered if our boy had been there. I thought of The Horridus, waiting, watching, planning. Would Johnny work the dating services again, try to find a common point? Or would he let Ishmael run the show now, forget about me and my big ideas? I sighed. Here I was, a million miles away, working a case that was no longer mine, escaping one miserable swamp of problems for another. I suddenly felt tired and stupid, tracking down obscure leads for a department that didn't want me around in the first place.

"Okay," said Katie, sitting on a chair beside me. "Jeeter was sixty-eight, about like I guessed. Lindy Dillard was fifty-two. If I remember right, it was a relocation for him. I'm really not sure. This last one, Bevaro, the escrow papers say he was forty-six."

I wrote down the ages of each seller in my notepad, as my mind drifted off to other times and places: my honeymoon with Ardith on Grand Cayman; Matthew and me chasing blue lizards over white dunes on vacation in New Mexico — *don't worry, Ardith, the sun isn't going to kill him;* Donna Mason astride me just one morning ago and her faintly southern voice filling that little dawn-filled apartment with something I hope is love. It's amazing how a man — no matter what he's done — still wants love, and can convince himself that he deserves it.

Nice as Katie Butler was, nice as Sam Welborn and the rest of Wichita Falls seemed to be, I wanted out of there. I wanted to be back home where I could scream.

"Forget Wanda, then?" Katie asked.

"Umm?"

"Wanda Grantley, the other seller. That listing was out in Hopkin, anyway. Two towns over. Widow. Says here late fifties, but she looked eighty."

I felt eighty. "You said she was married."

"I most certainly did not, Mr. Naughton."

"You said 'those two' weren't your kind of people."

"I know I shouldn't be so quick to judge."

"What two people, though, if she was a widow?"

"Her son."

I did the math. I woke from my reverie, a little excited. Finally, a nibble. "He'd be in his late twenties, early thirties."

"Full grown, anyway. Probably somewhere that age. Living with her."

"In the second unit?"

"Oh, I don't know. Hardly ever saw either

of them out and about. She had some older daughters, used to come around. Trashy women, if I have to say so. The mother — Wanda — tiny little thing, about as friendly as a rattlesnake. Now I *heard,* and this might not be true, but I was told she married something like six or seven times. I can't say for sure, though. They all could have been decent folks, I guess. But you hear things. I just know they were real private people. Didn't talk to the neighbors, kept to themselves. Had some money, but lived kind of low. Got no idea where they went to. You know, that place of theirs didn't sell until last year. They were asking too much. Then, the man who bought it, it was for his daughter so she'd be on her own, well she got married anyway and moved out of state. So now it's for sale again. Slow market. Buyers' market, like I was saying."

"So nobody's lived there since the Grantleys?"

"No, not unless some freeloaders broke in and squatted it. We put a lock box on it, but that happens sometimes."

"Here, let me take down that address, and the month of sale."

"You already did, Mr. Naughton. You all right?"

"Yeah. Tell me how to get there, will you? And how about the key to that lock box?"

Hopkin was about twenty miles southwest,

off of Highway 277. Birchwood was two turns off the main route, to the north, then west again. It was a long straight road with mailboxes every hundred yards or so. The asphalt was gray and the gravel on the shoulders almost white, and the sumac growing down to the shoulders was dark green in the spring light. The houses sat well back from the street, under canopies of trees and hedges and sagging power lines. The houses had porches and the porches had swings. Nice houses once, I thought, but sliding downhill now, neglected and alone as old people.

The Grantley place had a rusted mailbox with the metal flag up to signal outgoing parcels. The weeds had grown up around the stanchion and the house was hardly visible through the trees. I passed it once, then doubled back and eased into the driveway. I lowered the window, killed the engine and sat there. The house was clearly vacant. I could see through the glass of one of the windows, straight to a blank interior wall. The other front window had a shade drawn down most of the way. Nothing on the patio. The "For Sale" sign leaned back like an outfielder watching a home run. The lawn was dead except for the green on the sides, where a fresh crop of weeds had grown. The weeds climbed over a pink crenelated divider and spilled onto the walkway. The house was painted gray and the paint was starting to peel. Cicadas trilled from the black recesses of a huge elm tree and a mockingbird sang an insane melody to himself.

I got the house key from the lock box on the garage door. Through a chain-link fence I could see the second unit in the back, overhung by a big walnut tree. Back on the porch, the screen door creaked as I held it open and worked a rusty key into a rusty lock.

The first thing I smelled inside was bacon. Then dust, mildew and old carpet. The living room was the first thing you walked into. It was small and square, with a doorway leading to the kitchen and another to a hall. The fireplace was brick, with a mantelpiece of painted wood. There were three bedrooms, all small and dark in the eternal shade of the big trees outside. The wall-to-wall carpet was a pale blue. The kitchen had a little cheer to it — yellow tiles on the counter and yellow linoleum with white flecks in it. The wallpaper was yellow and white. The flooring was dark and warped up where the refrigerator had stood. The only furnishing in the whole place was a small end table with a phone on it. I picked up the earpiece and got nothing but silence and the muted cicadas and mockingbird, still at it in the trees outside.

When you stood in the backyard you couldn't see the neighbors or the street. Just the back side of the house and the front of the second unit, which was a small, rectangular version of the main house. It had a little porch and a screen door. I stood there in the middle of the dead lawn and kicked the hulls of the walnuts, which lay thick and cracked over the tan grass. There was a birdbath tilted and empty, the dish stained black. When I looked up, it was all foliage and power lines with a swatch of light blue sky in the middle. The day was warm but the yard was cool, and I had the feeling that I could have done just about anything I wanted here, and nobody would see.

I went through the lock-box routine for the second unit and let myself in. The feeling inside was altogether different. The first smell I got was faint and fecal, but it wasn't a human smell, or a canine one. Different. The floor was hardwood and dusty. The walls were paneled in dark wood, there were still shelves up everywhere, the kind you attached with L brackets to set the planks on. There was a fireplace, but it was just a facade painted black in the middle to give it the illusion of depth. The kitchenette was off to the left. Nothing much remained: two cardboard salt-and-pepper shakers, a filthy tumbler, an empty plastic half gallon of generic tequila on the floor in the corner. Beside it was a brown pasteboard box, with partitions inside to protect bottles in shipping. I pulled up the empty bottles one at a time: more generic tequila. A fellow cactus addict, I thought. Something beside the box caught my eye, though, so I picked it up: a little triangle of white net material, just a scrap, no bigger than a stamp. Like the girls were made to wear. Robes. Nets. Wings. Webs.

My heart jumped.

You got to the back room through the kitchen. I opened a door with a loose glass knob and pushed through.

The fecal smell was stronger, but I still couldn't identify it. Maybe it wasn't fecal after all, but it had a meaty, digested, though not foul aroma. A smell like you might think coyote shit would have, all that fur and bone processed by the body for the little muscle it contained. It was almost rodentlike, maybe. Old.

But there in this back room, you could actually see. Muted rays came in through a skylight panel on the roof. There was a bathroom off to the right. To my left was another wall filled with empty shelves. The far wall, though, that was the weird thing — one long pane of glass from floor to ceiling. Behind the glass I could see what looked like a place for tropical plants, or an animal, or birds perhaps. The floor was built up a couple of feet with rough cement that was shaped to look like rock. There was an empty pool at one end. It looked like the deceased version of one of those vivarium displays you might see in a store — a store that carried tropical plants, or birds, or fish . . . or snakes. I felt the hair on my neck quiver and a cold little tingle break out on the skin of my back.

I got behind the glass through a full-sized door at the right end. There were four heavy-duty slide locks on it — top, bottom and two on the side. I wondered what kind of wildlife required four locks to keep in. Not canaries, bromeliads or chameleons.

I stood within the cage and looked out. The room became oddly interesting when viewed from inside the glass, like it might be a representative model of *Homo sapiens*-environment, late twentieth century. I felt covert. It was the same feeling I got behind the one-way mirror of one of our interview rooms at the station. The ceiling above me was plywood, and I could tell from the spacing of the screws — about one inch — that it was built to last. The outlines of fixtures were visible every four feet or so, but the fixtures were gone and only the screw holes remained. Lights? Heating or cooling elements? The sides were not glass at all, but a continuation of the rock-look concrete. It must have been molded over a wire-and-wood mold. Same with the back. The old rodent smell was stronger inside. I walked over to the pool and saw the drain at the bottom. Kneeling, I swept my fingertips over the drain grate and brought up a dry smear of what looked like sand. In the far corner of the tank, behind the pool, was a gray football-sized mound of what looked like dried tar laced with milk, or some kind of industrial glue, or, perhaps, some kind of excrement. I leaned into the corner and took a tentative whiff. The smell was stronger. Looking down on the thing, I could see tufts of fur and the outline of a thin bone. It looked like something you'd see in the La Brea tar pits, but dehydrated, like a snack food. Crap. Eagle crap? Maybe, if the eagle was the size of a Shetland pony. Snake shit? Maybe, if the snake was as long as a football field.

Grantley was starting to amuse me.

I went back outside and stood on the dead grass. I walked around the back of the guest unit. The lot was a big one, with a grapestake fence running along each side and all but vanishing in a thick berry patch. Over the berries I could see the back fence erect in the shade. The neighbor's trees rose up around the property, deepening the sense of permanent dusk. Against the left fence sat an old lawn mower, a bike with flat tires and a barbecue. On the right side, garden tools hung by nails. Beyond the tools was a hutch built off the ground. It was made of wire mesh and two-bys, the kind of thing you could raise chickens in, or rabbits. The ground, up to the tangled patch of berries, was tan and dry and littered with broken, overripe walnuts. And there were more of the black mounds like I'd found in the corner of the cage. More fur, more bones, a pair of curved, side-by-side incisor teeth that either came from a big rat or a small rabbit. I could see that still more of the stuff had been thrown into the berry bushes. A shovel lying against the fence by the patch suggested how it got there. The smell was all around me in the spring warmth — old, rodentine, dank. I stood on my toes to see over the berries, but they were high and thick, and all I could make out was the back fence. I squeezed past the thorny patch by climbing along the bottom support beam of the fence. The area behind the berries was damp and cool. Weeds. Big piles of the black-furry-bony stuff, like they were built up over time. The smell. There were flies and meat bees everywhere, lazy and sated. Against the back fence the shit was knee high. I picked my way through the grim obstacles and climbed up on the support beam again, to see over. It was the back end of another lot, covered with leaves and a junked car up on cinder blocks.

I was looking down to find a clear place for my foot when I saw the pale thing protruding — just slightly — from the heap of dung against the fence. I jumped onto a decent spot. With my pen in hand, I leaned over the pile and touched what appeared to be a white plate. It was hard, locked solid in the dung. I scraped around it, and the black mulch came off easily, but the white thing didn't pop out, it just got bigger. Finally, I hooked an opening and lifted. There was a muffled crack and the thing got lighter. It dangled there before me, unbalanced, rocking on my pen. More or less round. Bigger than a softball, smaller than a soccer ball. The bigger, rounded end canted down and to my left, the smaller one settled upward and to the right. My pen was through the upper of two large holes. I lowered my head to see clearly around my hand and the extended pen. There were fragments of blackened material still attached in places, but basically, it was stripped clean. The teeth were still there, except for the front two. I studied it, a child's death head with a gap-toothed grin. I lowered it to the top of the pile, adjusted it for balance, then moved away and knelt down.

The body freezes at a time like this, but the spirit soars because it wants to get away. He was all around me. His ground, his air, his smell, his shade. I'd never been this close to the essence of him — not even in Brittany Elder's bedroom — and I wasn't prepared for it. He wasn't like anything. I had nothing to compare him to. But I could feel all the power of his need, and all the secret, cunning efficiency of his will.

He wasn't escalating. He'd already been where he was going. At least once. Right here.

Grantley had moved half a continent away, and found The Horridus waiting.

An hour later, I was pretty sure I had the Grantley son's first name: Gene. The neighbors weren't positive. And they were even less sure of his last name because Wanda had married "a bunch." Some said Webb, or Webster, one of those. Some said Vonn. Some said Grantley. Most said they had no idea. But none of the surnames matched my lists from Bright Tomorrows or Dawn Christie; none had listed homes with detached units for sale in Orange County; none of them connected with any names we'd come up with in the Horridus investigation so far.

But the Hopkin neighbors agreed in their assessment of him: late twenties, maybe early thirties; long hair and beard, but neatly trimmed; a well-groomed fella; very quiet; didn't seem to have a steady job; kept to himself. Ever notice how neighbors always say the same thing about these shitbaskets? They said his mother, Wanda, was small, tense and unfriendly. The young man had a van. Wanda had an older model Lincoln Town Car and the neighbors had often seen her peering under the curve of the steering wheel as she made her occasional low-speed runs through town.

One of them said the sketch from Steven Wicks's memory was "kinda like him, all right." The one from Brittany Elder "ain't him."

I found a pay phone outside a liquor store

and called Johnny. Just his message tape. I tried Louis — same thing. But I got Frances at her desk.

"Frances, this is Terry."

Her catch of breath reminded me of all the hideous suspicion now clinging to my own name, in my own department.

"I need you to listen to me for a minute —"

"— I —"

"Goddamnit Frances, listen to me!"

I told her to track the names Gene Vonn, Webb, Webster and Grantley through all our sources — county and state criminal files, DMV, TRW, the assessor's office, tax rolls, voters' lists, even the phone books if she had to. Triple-check it against the treasurer's property tax rolls and the realtors' multiple listings. I wanted his ass covered and I wanted it covered now.

"This guy killed a girl in Texas," I said. "And I'm betting my badge he's our man."

There was a moment of hesitation as the ludicrousness of my statement hit us both.

"You know what I mean, Frances."

She was silent for a moment. "You're not where you're supposed to be."

"I couldn't watch soaps all day, Frances. Look . . . go ahead and think what you have to think. Believe what you have to believe. But also know that those pictures were doctored, and I didn't do what they show. You can hate me or fear me or loathe me, Frances, but I want you to know the truth. Don't hate me so much we can't work together when I get back in there where I belong. We're still going to need you on the team. I guess I'm sounding, at this point, fairly ridiculous, aren't I?"

"You went to Wichita Falls."

"I shouldn't say, Frances. You don't need to know that. But you do need to know that this Gene creep abducted a six-year-old girl and killed her. Amanda's first sketch, with the beard and glasses, got positive reviews from the neighbors. I think he's our guy. Go find him, will you? Arrest The Horridus, will you?"

She was silent for a moment. "Johnny finished the multiple listings yesterday. None of them worked out. There wasn't a Gene on it, either."

"Then get on the women."

"Oh, for Chrissakes, Terry. There's no Webb, Vonn or Grantley on the list, I can tell you that right now."

"What about Webster?"

"*No.*"

I thought of Gene's older "trashy" sisters.

"What if he's living in a house owned by —"

"— Terry? *Terry? You are not* my boss right now. And, just for the record, I want you to know how absolutely disgusted I am by what I saw. Disgusted, betrayed. And basically really goddamned pissed off at you."

"Fine. Now, what's the latest on Stefanic, he's the park ranger who —"

"— *Goddamn you, Naughton, get a lawyer!*"
she whispered, and hung up.

I tried Louis and Johnny again, but they
were still gone. I left Johnny the names Gene
Vonn, Webb, Webster and Grantley. I left
them for Louis, too.

Then I called Jim Wade and told his secretary who I was. A moment later he was on the
line.

"You've violated our agreement," he said.

"I'm sorry, sir. But I've got the gold."

I told him what I'd found and where I'd
found it. I begged him to assign some more
deputies to CAY and scour the county for
Gene Vonn/Webb/Webster/Grantley and
Wanda Grantley. He actually listened to what
I was saying, and I heard his pencil scratching
on paper.

"Is that actually possible? For a snake to eat
a human?"

"I'll be talking to —"

"— No, you won't, Terry. This is what
you're going to do. You're going to board the
first plane back to Orange County that you
can get. And you're going to be in my office
thirty minutes after that plane lands. Clear?"

"Sir — there's so much work to —"

"— I can have an arrest warrant issued by
phone in about ten minutes. I'll do it."

I watched the treetops swaying and thought
of Mary Lou Kidder's end in a heap of dung
in Gene Somebody's backyard. I couldn't help

but see those pictures of myself again; they were following me wherever I went, unshakable and determined as bloodhounds. I wanted a drink quite badly. And I realized something about myself in that moment: I was willing to sacrifice almost anything to get The Horridus. At least, that's what I was doing. I felt so *close*. But how could Frances and Wade feel it? They hadn't seen what I'd seen. They hadn't smelled the smell and felt the feel.

"Let me work the rest of the day here," I said. "I'll take the first flight out tomorrow morning."

"Isn't there one tonight?"

"No, sir," I lied.

"Where are you staying?"

"I'd rather not, uh . . . well . . . the Holiday Inn in Wichita Falls."

"Call me when you get back there. And *stay* there until you leave in the morning. Those are direct orders."

I told him I believed it was time to go public with the Brittany Elder description and the drawing by Amanda. I thought we should bring the water under him up to a boil. But Sheriff Wade must have had bigger things to think about, because he hung up.

Next I called Sam Welborn. I told him to get out to the old Grantley place in Hopkin, and gave him the address. "You're going to need someone for prints and photos and video," I said. "You're going to need the coroner, sooner or later. I'll be waiting for you."

"Be damned," he said quietly. " 'Mon my way."

It was easy to get the reptile expert at the Fort Worth Zoo. The zoo receptionist was quite pleasant and she put me right through. His name was Joseph Dee and I identified myself as an Orange County Sheriff investigator working a kidnapping and sexual assault case that had led me to Texas. I asked him if it was possible for a very large snake to eat a small person. He said nothing for a moment, then:

"Well, yes — it's possible."

He went on to explain that folklore and anecdotal literature were filled with unsubstantiated reports of snakes taking humans for food. But some of them were "reasonably authenticated" enough to be considered true. Three snakes — the anaconda of South America, the reticulated python and the African rock python — were the three most popular culprits. One report, he said, from Borneo, was documented well enough by local authorities to qualify as factual. There, a twenty-two-foot reticulated python had eaten a thirteen-year-old boy down by a stream. He said that the many reports of the African rock python predating humans were unlikely but possible, and usually involved children. He said that most of the incidents took place in remote villages and were all but impossible to authenticate. He added that lots of things happen in small villages that we in our cities rarely hear about, let alone believe.

"I examined an African python — dead, unfortunately — that contained a small leopard," he said. "The specimen was thirteen feet long. If you doubled that length, which is possible in an older adult, you could conceive of it eating a small human. Entirely possible. But you have to understand that such instances would be aberrant. Humans are not their usual prey."

"How, exactly, would they do it?"

"Like they eat anything else," said Dee. "Surprise the prey. The teeth of big snakes can be quite long — maybe half an inch, and they hook backward, like some fish teeth. They're quite sharp and they hold well. Their jaws are fairly strong. They kill by constriction — not by crushing bones, as people believe. Constrictors are immensely strong. The coils tighten and the victim can't draw breath. It can happen quickly. Even the twelve-to-eighteen foot specimens we have here can require two or three men to handle them safely."

"How big is the biggest snake you've got?"

"We have a twenty-two-foot retic from Indonesia. It takes four of us to handle it, if we have to."

"What's it eat?"

"Rabbits, ducks and pigs."

I drove back to the Grantley house to wait for Sam Welborn.

Eighteen

I sat in room 21 of the Holiday Inn and stared for a while out the window. The sky had gone deep indigo and the breeze was still up. It was seven. Sam had invited me to the stock car races and I'd accepted, recklessly aware that I was disobeying still another order from my commander in chief. I figured, if they didn't want me to go out and watch cars go around in circles, tough. Plus I'd had a nip or two from my bottle of tequila — I'd bought the second smallest one at the store, a pint — and its courage had begun to set in.

I called Donna but she was on assignment. I left a message from Skip on her voice mail. I called Melinda at home, and when Penny answered we talked very briefly. We were just getting past the hello, how are you stuff when Melinda cut in, asked me not to call the house like that and hung up. I still hadn't thought of a way to tell Penny the truth without confusing and hurting her, so maybe it was just as well that Melinda cut us off. I resented Melinda for taking sides against me, but I respected what she had to do for Penny — maybe I would have done the same. I left another message for Johnny about the Gene Webb/Webster/Vonn/Grantley or Wanda Grantley home — told him to take the title search into Los Angeles and San Diego counties just to be safe. I blathered on about the Grantley house, Welborn, the great flat state of Texas. I was lonely. Johnny's machine ran out of tape before I finished, so I had to call back to make sure he had it all, and to wish him good luck. I told him again that I thought they should release the drawing based on Brittany Elder's description — the "sharp mean face" and the short white hair. After seeing the remains of Mary Lou Kidder, I was in favor of all the proaction we could muster: smoke him out, make him flinch, rattle his cage. I knew the risks, but I thought they were worth taking. I left the same information with Louis, just to double-cover. I did all this in the name of Frank. It made me mad to have to slink around the world as different people. It was demeaning and it implied guilt. That was one thing I wasn't ready to shoulder, not on the scale that I was being asked to by . . . Ishmael? A Wade-Vega-Woolton cabal? I. R. Shroud?

Sam picked me up at seven-thirty and we rode out to the track in his sedan.

We sat in the grandstand and watched the cars go by. Sam waved to a half-dozen people on our way up the steps. We had hot dogs and giant beers and the captain had an extra cup for his dip. He had a friend driving in the third race.

"These things'll get up to ninety-five on the straights," he said, staring straight ahead as the cars spun past. He hadn't said much on the way here and I knew why: the sight of Mary Lou Kidder had damaged him.

"You a family man, Terry?"

"Divorced. Had a son but he died when he was five."

Sam turned and looked at me with his wide, quizzical face. "I'm awful sorry to hear that. Don't mean to be pryin'."

"It's all right."

The stock cars roared under the lights. I liked the reverberations in my chest and the whining of rpms in my ears. Three cars almost piled up on turn three but they veered out of it in a chaos of white smoke. The Copenhagen Smokeless Tobacco car — irony noted — came out ahead of the Budweiser and Marlboro cars and banked low and fast into the straight to build a two-length lead.

"That's one of the reasons I started up the Crimes Against Youth unit," I said. "For my son. Kind of like a tribute to him, or a memorial."

Sam nodded.

I don't know why I say things like that sometimes, usually to friendly strangers, bartenders, people I might like a little but don't really know. It just comes out. Sometimes I say

343

things just to see if I believe them or not.

"Was he a victim, your boy?"

"An embolism while he was swimming," I lied. "It was an accident."

"Shame, Terry."

"You keep them alive inside, somehow."

"I got three girls, and they're the best things in my life. Them and their mother. Don't know what I'd do if something happened to one of them."

"I know exactly how you feel."

"You see that Ford out there, the blue one? The guy that built those engines is a buddy of mine. Buck. He's been workin' on cars since he was about four. Think he could rebuild a Ford motor blindfolded if he had to."

The blue Mustang was running fourth now, right up behind the Marlboro Camaro.

I offered Sam the tequila but he shook his head. "Don't like the hard stuff anymore."

I nipped and tucked.

"You mind telling me how a guy could feed a six-year-old *girl* to a snake? I just don't get it, Terry."

"I don't either. Criminal scientists would say that he's living out his fantasies."

"Who's got a fantasy like that?"

"I don't know."

"What's that really mean, though? Living out a fantasy?"

"In basic terms — it means getting off."

He turned and looked at me again, then

shook his head. "Sex?"

"Yeah."

"Ah, man. Does he have sex with them first?"

"We'll probably never know on Mary Lou, but I'd guess he did. In Orange County, he isn't. He isn't killing them, either. He takes them for a few hours, then lets them go out where there's no people. He dresses them in old clothes, girls' clothes — that's what led us to Wichita Falls in the first place. And he puts these . . . well, these lacy kind of . . . *robes* on them. And he puts hoods on them. I suspect he photographs or tape-records them. Then he lets them go. And they wander around until someone finds them."

He looked at me again. It isn't often you see a look of such affronted disgust on a peace officer. "Doesn't rape them?"

"Not yet. I think he has before. I think he'll start again."

"Now why do you think that, Terry?"

"It's about sex. Sex in his head. Sex in his memory, in his past. You know how strong it can be. We think about it. Talk about it. Dream about it. Sooner or later, we try our damnedest to make it real. That's what he's doing — making it real. And once you start, well, you can call yourself off if you've got enough willpower, maybe. But not forever. Not once you know you can get what you need. He's working himself up to the act again.

345

That's my take on it."

"Little lacy robes, like they were angels?"

I thought about that. I hadn't really figured out the robes — if they even *were* figurable. I had assumed they were some kind of symbolic skin. Something akin to the shed he'd left in Brittany Elder's bed. A way of saying that he was about to . . . change the girls, hatch them into something else. But Sam's word connected to something I'd thought before, namely, that The Horridus wasn't — in his mind — taking the girls as captives, he was *freeing* them. So, maybe they were angels' robes, or angels' wings. He was taking them as mortals and releasing them as angels. After what I'd seen today in Wanda Grantley's backyard, I would have believed almost anything about him.

"Angels, hatchlings — I don't know."

"Hatchlings?"

"It's just a . . . notion, Sam. Tied in with his snake totem and his fantasy. He calls himself The Horridus. Horridus is Latin for a kind of rattlesnake."

"If I saw him, I'd shoot him like a rattlesnake. And that's about how bad I'd feel after. I got no tolerance for people like that. None a' tall."

"Get me all of Wanda Grantley's married names, if you can."

He looked at me but said nothing.

After the second race we went down to the

pits and found his friend, Buck. He was a wiry little guy with a red jumpsuit on and an STP cap tilted way up on his head. Big smile, a drawl. The hood of his Ford was up and Sam leaned in with him for a look at the works. They talked for a minute about the supercharger and how to cool it. I stood back and looked at them, wishing I knew something about cars, wishing I had a friend I'd known for thirty years who I could just be with. Like Sam was just being with Buck — casually interested in the same things, tacitly pulling for each other, relaxed, undefended, whole. The big dark Texas sky seemed to make everybody look smaller to me, to reduce them to a heavenly perspective. It made me feel real small, like I was just one guy out of many millions, walking on feet, breathing through lungs, seeing through eyes and doing the best he can with his seventy years, or whatever I'd get. And that's a good thing, I think: people behave better when they know they're not the center of the universe. Where I'm from, in California, a lot of them never realize that.

We walked through the pits, Sam spitting into his cup, his free hand jammed into his windbreaker.

"Be a good thing for you to leave in the morning," he said. He didn't look at me, but I noted the hard-pressed expression of his face as he looked over the lip of the cup. It was the face of the Sam Welborn you wouldn't want to mess with.

"You met my team," I noted quietly.

"I don't know what you're into back there, Terry. Don't want to know. But I'm not supposed to discuss this case with you anymore. I told them you'd be back on that plane first thing tomorrow, and I don't want you makin' a liar outta me."

"Who called you?"

"Don't ask."

"I was planning to go, anyway."

"Puts me in a tough position, you know, because I got nothin' against you. Fact, I like ya. You helped me out with Mary Lou. You solved a crime I'd been working on for two years and getting nowhere."

"There's some politics going on back home. That's all it is."

We rounded the pits and stood up by the entryway fence to watch Buck's Ford rumble past. On the ground like this, the cars were even more impressive — you could feel their power rattling your guts and bones when they were just idling. Buck, lost in a red helmet, waved at us from behind his meshed side window.

There wasn't much more Sam and I could say to each other. His suspicion, and my implied guilt, hung over us like a black, oppressive sky. I was furious, but had no target for my anger, no vent for my bile.

Buck won and we clapped. After that Sam

gave me a ride back to the Holiday Inn.

Twelve hours later I got off the plane at John Wayne Airport, greeted by Jordan Ishmael and two deputies I barely knew.

"Guys," I said.

"Terry."

"Nice to see some friendly faces."

I thought of running for it, but I know a dumb idea when I get one. Most of the time.

They fell in around me and we headed away from the crowd of people awaiting the passengers. Ishmael leaned in close, like he was telling me a secret.

"You're under arrest, Terry. Unlawful sexual intercourse, lewd act on a child, oral cop. I can waive the cuffs for now but not the Miranda. Let's head over to that corner there, get it taken care of without causing some big hairy scene, okay? Unless you want me to call Donna Mason for the story."

Ishmael's powerful, controlling grip on my arm was the single greatest insult I have ever known.

Nineteen

If you're a regular guy, they march you to the Intake-Release Center, which sits next to the jail. Then they take away everything you've got, search you, take off your cuffs, make you sign some forms, try to figure how much of a hazard you are to others and yourself, finger-print you, photograph you, spray your body for lice — making you bend over naked to get a solid dose between your cheeks — let you rinse in a cold shower, then give you an orange jumpsuit with Orange County Jail stenciled on the back. Then they let you make your calls. Then you go to your tank and the fun really starts.

If you're a cop accused of sex with children, it's all the same, but they put you in a small cell alone instead of a general population tank because general population inmates are known to murder men like you. It's called protective custody, and it's reserved, generally, for child molesters, those accused of heinous crimes, cops and celebrities. I felt like I was the first three, with a good shot at becoming the fourth.

I made my two phone calls from the Intake-Release Center, from a phone bank built into the dreary wall. It was a little room with a smoke-stained acoustic ceiling and a table with a bunch of phone books strewn across it. Other accused were making calls, some whispering, some whimpering, some shouting, some just standing silent with the receivers to their ears, as if being pumped with some numbing drug through the cord. I hunkered up close to the wall and called Donna. I was surprised and crestfallen that she answered. I didn't even try to ease into the subject — it can't be done — and just blurted out that I'd been arrested, and why. I said I was innocent. I said I was being framed. I said there were photographs that had been altered or tampered with and that the FBI would establish this to be true. My heart sank even lower as I said this, realizing that the FBI had likely done just the opposite, and my arrest had been the result.

All I heard for the longest time was the in and out of Donna's breath, followed by the silence during which I could see her clearly: slender face and sad brown southern eyes, her dark hair curling forward over her pale skin, the swatches of blush on her cheeks, her red and knowing lips. I told her I was innocent. I told her I wanted her to learn about this from me, first. I told her I was innocent again. I told her I wasn't sure what I'd do — try to make bail and lie low until my defense experts could disqualify the evidence. I told her, matter-of-factly, that I loved her, and, again, that I was innocent.

Finally she spoke. "You want me to cover this for CNB, or let someone else?"

"It's yours if you want it."

"That would be, ah . . . extremely perilous."

"I'm a good story. Think of it as another exclusive. Stick with me. You'll get all the firsts."

"Terry," she whispered. *"Terry. I can't stick with you very far. You may be innocent, but we'll crucify you first and cut you down later. It's the way we do it."*

I took a deep breath and felt the walls moving closer around me, felt the acoustic ceiling — stained by years of whispered alibis and desperate lies — lowering onto my head like a lid onto a coffin.

"I love you, Donna."

I hung up and called the law office of Loren Runnels, an old friend of mine, a deputy DA turned to private practice. Luckily, he was listed in one of the phone books.

When I explained to Loren what had happened, I got one of those surprises you should see coming but never do. I discovered that in spite of being the star of my personal, purgatorial pageant, I would have to wait.

"I'm due in court in twenty minutes," he said. "I'll see you after lunch. Anybody wants to know anything, you tell them to talk to me. Hang in there, Terry."

They put me in a protective cell, in a small block reserved for people so bad even other prisoners hate them. Module J, to be specific. I kept my head up and my eyes level as I looked into the other cells on the way by. The eyes that followed me were curious, resigned, amused, blank. My cell smelled faintly of urine and disinfectant, but the lice spray on my skin followed me in and cut down on the stink. It mixed with the smell of my own nervous sweat. When I heard the door slam shut behind me and echo down the long hallway, a part of my soul withered, broke off and blew away. Those echoes are the harmonics of hell.

At 1:25 P.M. I was led into a booth in the Attorney-Bonds Visiting Room and told to *sit*.

The deputy who led me in was four inches taller than me and probably outweighed me by forty pounds. You look at these young guys — I was one of them once — and you wonder at the predictable relish they take in their power, in the tiny cruelties that help them set the "us" apart from the "them." You wonder at the absolute authority when one man can order another to sit, like he'd order a dog, and the man in fact sits, just like a dog would.

I shook my head, smiled and sat. Of course, he just couldn't let it go. The same way I wouldn't have let it go twenty years ago when I worked this loud, stinking, overcrowded jail my first two years as a Sheriff deputy.

"Is there some problem you've got with that?"

"None at all, Deputy."

"You look like that Chet guy we had in here last week."

"I arrested him, and we don't look alike at all."

"The kids you both screw look alike?"

"Yeah. We like them young, dumb and blond. Like you."

"How would you like your ass kicked?"

"Whatever fries your eggs, kid."

The booths offer a reasonable amount of privacy. There's a glassed guard station behind where the prisoners sit, and the deputy can see everything in the room, but can't hear much. There's a table in front of you, separated from another table by a low partition. I watched Loren Runnels come through a door on the other side of the room. He lugged his briefcase toward me and sat. He studied me through silver wire-rimmed glasses that matched perfectly his thinning silver hair. The bald patch on the top of his head was a deeper tan than I had had in years. He had thin lips and bright white teeth he rarely showed.

"You all right?"

"I'm absolutely not fucking all right, Loren. They've got pictures but —"

He sat back and looked around in an exaggerated manner, shaking his head.

I looked away from him and felt the anger

in my guts and the sadness and humiliation in my heart. How many times had I heard some guy say just about the same thing to me? And how many times had I assumed he was human sludge, a loser, a liar, a creep? I swallowed my pride a thousand times in that one brief moment. Then swallowed it a thousand more.

And I let my attorney lead.

"I've seen the complaint," he said. "The arraignment is set for eleven tomorrow morning. It looks like Zant will be in court tomorrow. He'll probably ask two hundred bail, as a flight risk. I'll ask you be O-R'd as a deputy with an impeccable record. The judge can do anything in between, but unless we draw Honorable Ogden, I'd guess it'll be more like fifty grand. Can you raise fifteen plus collateral for bond?"

I hadn't thought about the cost of my nightmare before this. Nothing is free, not even hell. I had about eighty bucks in my wallet — which was in the possession of the county. I had four hundred in a checking account, eighteen hundred in a savings account and ten grand in an IRA I couldn't use without penalties. I had a Ford, eight years old, worth maybe nine grand on the market. I'd put thirty thousand toward the down payment on the Canyon Edge place, to match Melinda's thirty. It was all the savings I had at the time.

"I can get it."

"The sooner the better, Terry. I'll send Alex

from County-Wide over — you two work it out. I'm going to need five to get us through the arraignment. After that, we can talk. I'm not cheap but I am good. If you can afford someone you think is better, hire him."

"I called you because I want you."

"I'm proud to represent you, then."

"When do you want the dough?"

"Tomorrow."

"I'll have it."

He nodded and looked at me. It was a long, thoughtful gaze, his pale blue eyes trying to sap something out of me, but I wasn't sure what it was. "We'll get you out of here, sooner than later. With luck, and without Ogden, we'll have you O-R'd and out before lunch. Until then, stay cool."

I nodded but I didn't say anything. It was strange, very strange, to have a friend. In fact, I'd never been so grateful to have a friend in all my life.

"Loren, I'm being framed."

"That's pretty obvious. We're going to have to find out by whom. Listen, I don't want you to say any names yet. Not here. Not now. But I do want you to tell me one thing: do you think you know who it is?"

I held his stare, then shook my head.

"All right."

"When can I talk to the press?"

He looked at me quizzically. "Don't, Terry. It's going to be tough sledding, when they get hold of this one."

"I want a conference."

"No. And I'll tell you why. The reporters will murder us whether you talk to them or not — and if you do, *anything* you say can be used against you by the media and, possibly, by the DA. There's no confidentiality if you start making statements in public. Some defendants can get sympathy through the press, but it won't work for us with these charges. I don't have to tell you why. The more you show your face the more you make yourself a target. You think you can handle all the dirt they'll dig?"

"I didn't do it, Loren." I never, never thought I'd see the day when I reminded myself of the sniveling men I'd arrested so many times. I looked at him, then down at the table in front of me. I could feel my mind begin to fog up, then to haze over into a stupor. I felt like a vessel taking on water. I tried to fight it off. I was not sure, for just a moment, that this was actually happening. Loren Runnels's hard-eyed stare assured me that it was.

"Look, they're going to dig and dig hard. Whatever privacy you think you had, you can forget. They'll go back to your schooling. Back to your training. Your marriage, your divorce, your relationships. They'll go back to what happened to your son. They'll turn every stone and turn it again. You want to answer for everything you've ever done? We can't look good, doing that. We can't look good to anybody at this point, Terry, we can only look bad. You're on the defensive. When we get you out of here we go on the offensive. That's why you've got me. Use me. I'll tell the media what they need to know, when they need to know it. Right now, you're going to have to endure all the assumptions people might make. That's your part of our deal here. It's hard and I know it's hard. But fuck 'em for now, Terry. That's how you've got to think. I've got a good team of investigators and we can get you out of this. I know a photographic examiner who can analyze those photos — Will Fortune — he's ex-FBI and he's the best there is. I've talked to him. He'll cost you a hundred and fifty an hour, plus a hundred an hour to travel. Your time will come. Be patient."

"I have to say *something*."

"You are. Tomorrow you're going to tell the world you're not guilty."

I was arraigned in Superior Court 8, the Honorable Lewis Sewell presiding. Sewell is generally considered to be an old-time conservative, tough on crime, efficient in his courtroom. I had testified before him several times, and always liked the economy of his proceedings. He was a prosecutor's judge. Now I dreaded him.

The county courtrooms are large, modern and somewhat sterile. They hint of bureaucratic dispatch rather than the halls-of-justice drama you find in older, more seasoned ones. The room was jammed. The back part was irate citizens, all eager to see with their own eyes the cunning pervert once entrusted with the protection of their children. There was a bristling phalanx of reporters in the front rows, at least four sketch artists set up to capture me for their newspapers and networks. I immediately realized the wisdom of Loren's refusing to let me talk to the media right then. Those people were there to crucify me, pure and simple, just like Donna had said. There were no cameras in Sewell's court, for which I was profoundly grateful. I recognized people from the *Times* and *Register*, *OC Weekly*, KFWB and KNX radio and a rather beautiful reporter for CNB, Donna Mason. She looked up from the ranks as I was led in. Her pencil was poised over a reporter's notebook and the look on her face was unrevealing. She looked at me without any visible trace of personal interest, which sent my guts into a free fall. But, under the circumstances, what else could she do?

I sat beside Loren in my street clothes, which he was kind enough to have sent in earlier that morning. He explained that the street clothes were a risky move: he wanted the court to see me at my nominal best, but he didn't want Sewell to think I assumed I'd be walking into the late April sunshine of Orange County in a matter of minutes. I had shaved and combed my hair, which was still wet from the dribble of water from my protective custody faucet.

He slipped the *Times* and *Register* morning editions onto the table before me and I scanned the headlines, both quite large:

Sheriff Deputy Named In Sex-With-Minors Charge

and

Crimes Against Children Cop To Be Charged As Molester

"This is hard to look at," I whispered to Loren.

"That's just the breeze," he said. "Here's the wind."

He slid the papers back into his briefcase, then set down our copy of the complaint. I read through the list of witnesses to be called against me:

Joe Reilly, Director, Orange County Sheriff Department Forensic Laboratory

Karl Neelson, Deputy Director, Orange County Sheriff Department Forensic Laboratory

Margo Fixx, Assistant Director, Orange County Sheriff Department Forensic Laboratory

Lieutenant Jordan Ishmael, Orange County Sheriff Department

Deputy Alonzo Arriaga
Deputy Edward Reston
Deputy Frances White
Timothy Monaghan, Special Agent F.B.I.,
Washington, D.C.
Laurie Mize, Special Agent F.B.I., Washing-
ton, D.C.
Alton Allen Sharpe
Caryn Lynn Sharpe
Linda Elizabeth Sharpe
Melinda Ellen Vickers
Penelope Anne Ishmael

I think my breath was short by then.

I know it was by the time I read the items listed in search warrants for my home and workplace:

Hair specimen
Fiber specimen, clothing, carpet
Soils specimen
Floorboard fiber specimen, vehicle(s)
Shirt, plaid flannel
Shirt, plaid cotton (blue)
Shirt, white cotton T
Pants, cotton twill (beige)
Pants, cotton denim (blue)
Socks, blend (navy)
Socks, cotton (white)
Shoes, leather chukka (suede)

I entered the haze again. Still within it, I

looked behind me to see Donna Mason — and a million other faces — sizing my neck for the guillotine. Jordan Ishmael stood beside her with a fawning smile on his *GQ* face. Rick Zant was chatting with the KFWB and KNX reporters. Inside my ears there was a roar, then a silence, then the roar again.

I looked back down at the complaint.

The voice of the docket clerk rang out as Judge Sewell entered his courtroom and took his seat behind the bench. I stood on invisible legs and watched with fogged, uncertain eyes.

A moment later the clerk spoke again: "Criminal Case 97-1103."

I walked to the podium, Loren on my right. I was dimly aware of our path converging with that of Rick Zant and Victoria Espinoza, a young deputy prosecutor. We met, loosely, in front of the bench. When I looked up at the Honorable Lewis Sewell, he was already looking down at me, with an oddly dispassionate expression. He nodded and said hello, Terry. I said hello, Your Honor, back. When I looked over at Zant, he caught my gaze with a piercingly anonymous stare, then smiled up at the judge.

"Counsel," said Sewell, "please identify yourselves for the record."

Zant took a half step to the side and said, in his sonorous courtroom voice, "Your Honor, Richard Zant for the People of the

State. With me is Victoria Espinoza, deputy district attorney."

Loren said, rather quietly, "Loren Runnels for the defendant, Terry Naughton, Your Honor. We request leave, Your Honor, to file our appearance."

Sewell allowed the motion, which legally confirmed Loren as my counsel.

Loren took a small step forward and away from me. I felt like I'd been left in a dumpster by my mother.

His voice was a little louder, then, with a suggestion of controlled authority in it.

"Your Honor, the defendant is before you now. We acknowledge receipt of a copy of the complaint, and waive a formal reading at this time. On behalf of Mr. Naughton, Your Honor, we ask you to enter a plea of not guilty to the charges."

"Plea of not guilty entered to the charges," said Sewell. He glanced at me, then at Zant.

Zant asked that bail be set at half a million dollars, citing my danger as a flight risk and my danger to the public of this fine county.

"That's absurd, Your Honor," said Loren. "The defendant has obligations here he intends to honor. He has a long and distinguished record — a record unblemished until now — of public service. He intends to clear that record by vigorously defending himself from these charges. He is, may I remind Mr. Zant, a public employee on a public employee's salary. Half a million dollars' bail is punitive and unnecessary."

A low grumble rose from the crowd behind me. It stopped when Sewell peered back at them.

Zant cited my recent, unannounced, unapproved and against orders trip to "someplace in Texas" as an example of my state of mind and my proclivity for flight.

"Your Honor, the defendant took a leave on personal time to attend to personal business in Texas. No complaint had been filed at that time and we —"

"— Mr. Zant, the accused's travel itinerary prior to this proceeding could not interest this court less. What are you asking me to do, Mr. Runnels?"

"Your Honor, we ask that the defendant be released on his own recognizance, to report as ordered for trial. He is neither a flight risk nor a danger in any way to any person."

Victoria Espinoza's voice cut through the air. "Your Honor, if I may — this defendant is a risk to every child he might come in contact with. He is precisely the kind of accused for which bail can act both as a guarantor of appearance and a protection for the People."

An approving buzz issued from behind me. Sewell slammed his gavel down hard and the sharp report silenced the mob.

"Mr. Runnels?"

"Your Honor, we are simply asking the

court to extend to Mr. Naughton the same respect and responsibilities the People were so willing to entrust to him before these allegations were created. He is, I'd like to remind Ms. Espinoza, innocent of all charges until proven otherwise. This piece of paper, Your Honor — the complaint — no more abrogates his twenty years of exemplary performance than it establishes him as a menace to society."

Sewell glanced out at the crowd, the reporters, then down at me, and over at Zant and Victoria.

The room was nearly silent, but I could still hear a deeper hush descending upon it.

"I'm going to set bail at one hundred thousand dollars, securable to this court by a signature bond only. Mr. Naughton, I don't see you in flight or in commission of crimes while you behave yourself in my county. If you do, I'll see that you pay for it in more ways than one."

"Thank you, Your Honor," I managed.

Yeah, we'll shoot him dead! someone piped from behind.

We've got Megan's law!

Castrate him!

Sewell's bailiff moved toward the seats, and the catcalls stopped.

"Any more cracks from back there and I'll throw you all out of my court," said Sewell. "Every last one of you."

The silence was begrudged and tentative.

Loren asked for a preliminary hearing, which was granted, date to be set by whichever judge ended up with the case for trial.

Loren bickered about the witness list being too wide in scope, but Sewell overrode him.

The gavel hit wood. Loren tugged me gently toward the door that would lead us back to jail, where I would be processed and released. I followed him easily, lightly — as frail and unresisting as a ghost.

I looked back to see Donna Mason watching me, with a small smile on her face. But how small that lovely perfect face was in the mob of citizens staring at me with absolute hatred in their eyes. I could hear the drone of their malice just beneath the shuffling of feet and opening of doors. It scared me.

Once out of the courtroom I shook Loren's hand. I was trembling. I would have done almost anything in the world for him then. I was still uncertain that I was not in a dream, but this part of the dream was, by comparison, a lot better than what had gone on before.

"Call me when you land," he said. "We've got some work to do. I'll send Wilkers to help get you out with minimal circus atmosphere."

"Thank you. But explain one thing to me now. How come they listed seven photographs on the evidence list? There were only three."

Loren shook his head. "They got four more the morning you left for Texas. Another batch they found at Sharpe's house. Allegedly, it took them that long to sift through his collection. And they found the negatives, too, for all of them."

I looked at him, literally tongue-tied.

"What do the new ones show?" I finally managed.

"Same kind of stuff, Terry. Same place. Different girl."

Twenty

I made it from the courthouse to the inmate transport bus without the press getting to me — they are kept behind a fence several hundred feet away from the prisoner loading zone. You can make it from the building to the bus in just six quick steps. I settled into my caged compartment at the back of the bus, the same ignominious chamber that had held me — for my own protection — during the short ride from jail to courthouse. But the photographers and professional shooters of video know their way around the county landscape, and at least a dozen of them were standing at the corner of Civic Center Drive and Fifth, where my bus was forced to stop for a light, and the caged compartment housing the animal Terry Naughton was duly photographed. I slunk down out of sight and felt the handcuffs biting into my wrists. There have probably been lower moments in my self-regard, but I can't remember one, and that is saying a lot.

Through the good graces of Loren, I managed to get from the jail to the parking lot disguised as a custodian. Loren's kindly assistant — Rex Wilkers — met me at the Intake-

Release Center with a short-sleeved blue shirt that said "Allen" over the pocket, a matching blue cap and a stick-on mustache that matched my hair color not at all. I wondered if it was some wry joke on Loren's part — the name *Allen* — then decided it was just something they had handy. But it worked. We embedded ourselves behind a pair of young Latino men who spilled into freedom and the waiting arms and kisses of a small crowd of relatives and friends. We cut across a sidewalk and used a relaxed but forceful stride to disappear into the parking lot. Wilkers had parked up close, and we were enclosed in the semisecurity of his dark-windowed Porsche before anyone was the wiser. He dropped me off at the airport, and a few minutes later I paid my way through the long-term parking gate and rolled toward the Interstate.

The afternoon was breezy and warm and the hillsides of south Orange County were still green from the winter rains. The wild artichokes sprinkled the hills between the on-ramps with their thorny purple blooms. A flock of ravens pestered a red-shouldered hawk that was perched on the power line over an auto mall, but the old bird looked too tired to fly; he just hunched within his insolent feathers and ignored the cackling multitude around him. Hang in there, buddy, I thought: from a chickenhawk to a red-shouldered one.

I was driving toward home — Melinda's,

now — without any real idea of why. I was quite a bit less than unwelcome there. Maybe I would arrive as the search warrant was being carried out. And the friendly little hamlet of Laguna Beach was the last place I wanted my face to be seen. But still I headed south on the 405 until I realized the senselessness of it. Then I got off at a big retail complex and went to the movies. I sat in the middle of the dark and nearly empty theater, watching a Hollywood star solve a crime by cloning the memory of a dead victim via frozen seminal fluid implanted in a rat. The rat had electrodes attached to its tiny conical head, which then translated its thoughts into 35 mm, Surround-Sound images that advanced the plot, complete with music. What effects. I concluded idly that I was, and always had been, in the wrong business.

The haze descended again. I walked from theater to theater, trying to find a movie that might keep it away. No way. I watched the films through a filter I couldn't take off, through the darkly clouded lens of my predicament. For a while I pretended that this was all over; I had been exonerated and offered back my job as head of CAY. I imagined walking into the department building for the first time, seeing my new work station — surely, the old one would have been turned over to someone else by then; I imagined looking into the faces of the deputies I worked with, and the secretaries and the support staff and the cafeteria workers and even Shopping Carter, and I wondered how on earth they would ever believe, ever *really, truly, 100 percent believe* that I was not just an innocent man, but a good one. It was hard to imagine. The Irish in me said to fight, hold up my head and walk proudly into whatever wrath awaited me in the coming days, and, later, when I was proven innocent, to do likewise with every person I encountered. I told myself that I would evolve to that, I would rise to the occasion. But for now I was defeated and I wanted little more than a dark room, a large bottle of Herradura and my laptop computer, through which I might contact I. R. Shroud and arrange through him to obtain certain images — just as someone before me, I had reason to hope, had already done.

I thought of Matthew, as I often do when I'm miserable. Good memories can help offset a bad present, but they can also make it worse. It's always hard to remember the living, vibrant Matt, and not remember the cold, bluing boy who died in my arms as I ran up Coast Highway toward the walk-in clinic that hot summer day. In fact, the parts of that past always come together in my memory, to form a complete, contradictory whole. Matthew's life becomes Matthew's death. It is not a remembrance that heals the heart or comforts the soul. It is not a remembrance I can happily live with, but I can hardly conceive of living without it. A drowning man clings to small branches.

As I sat in the theater I thought of one of the last movies Matt and Ardith and I had really enjoyed together, which was *The Lion King*. I thought of all the merchandise that we bought for him, with pictures of the characters on it. Lion King coloring books. Lion King sing-along tapes. Lion King bedsheets. An aerosol can of Lion King shave cream and a wooden Lion King razor. I remembered bringing a chair into the bathroom for Matt to stand on as we looked into the same mirror and he mimicked my shaving procedure, remembered the way he got more of the stuff in his hair and ears than on his cheeks, remembered Ardith's proud exclamations of smoothness as she ran her hand over his face when her men were finished. For a moment I could even smell the faint scent of the cream. I remembered the way that, even then, Matthew's competitive spirit had shown itself: if I shaved one time, he would shave twice; if I shaved twice, he would shave three times; when Ardith judged our shaves as having the same closeness — she only did this once — Matt shaved again to come in first.

And, as I knew it would, thinking about my living son led me unwaveringly to his death. He was expired by the time we lay him on the doctor's table and I was cleverly locked out of the examination room. I know that now. For five days Ardith and I waited with desperate anticipation for the autopsy results. We believed that the why of his death would free us from a mystery too heavy to bear. *Why? Why Matthew? Why us? Why me?* It didn't. The facts of his death, when they were known, only filled us with a sense of lucklessness so profound we could hardly look at each other after we knew them. I'm always saddened when I read of crime victims who believe that an arrest of the perpetrator, guilty verdict, a stiff sentence, a death penalty will bring "closure" to their agony. People want the mystery solved, the criminal put to death, the amends made. They think they'll feel better, that it will put an end to their pain as they know it. For me, all the autopsy report brought was an unbearable acknowledgment of the permanency of Matt's absence. I got fucking closure, all right. Final, absolute and irreversible. But this was not how I wanted to feel at all. I didn't want closure, or anything like it. I didn't want his memory to end on a table in a walk-in medical clinic. No. I wanted continuity. And not only a continuation of Matthew's life — though I knew that was impossible — but a continuation of the life around me, of Ardith and me as husband and wife, of the pulse of our little household, of the paperboy in the morning and the mockingbirds in the evening and the long silences during which we would let our fingers touch across the dinner table and wonder. But we got closure to that, too, and plenty of it. We lost our way. The wind died. The compass fogged. Landfall vanished and the paddles were too small to get us very far. Where were we trying to go, anyway?

Be careful what you wish for.

What I saw most clearly about his death is what I always see: the top of his wet blond-brown head pressed into the crook of my neck, nearly out of eyesight, my big hand behind it, holding him close for warmth and safety and with the conviction that somehow my beating heart would connect to his beating heart if they were just held close enough — it *was* still beating, wasn't it? Why are his arms suddenly loose and dangling? And I saw the fractured, up-and-down images along Pacific Coast Highway — the pink homes and white stores, the red oleander and the deep green pine trees, the bright cars and gawking walkers — as they wavered, laboring past us, saw me raising my knees high and digging my bare toes into the sidewalk and stretching my stride longer and longer and holding on to Matt for dear life as I gasped closer to the walk-in clinic. It seemed to get further and further away.

This is what I come back to when I think of him and this is why he is the most heart-breaking and beautiful memory in my life.

It was dusk when I drove past my apartment

in the metro district. I had circled the complex twice, and the parking area twice, to see if I was being followed. There was no practical way that a reporter could find out about this place so quickly, but I also knew that some straightforward prying into my bank accounts — and the transfers wired to the management company here — would eventually blow my cover. A radio talk show was taking call-ins about me, and the thrust of the opinion was for life imprisonment, castration or execution. Everyone felt betrayed. The host was calling me "Naughty Naughton." I couldn't take much. Satisfied that my apartment wasn't surrounded by a lynch mob, I parked and made my way in, hunched over like a tired Allen returning from his day on the job. I had a bag of fast food and a bag of Herradura.

Donna sat at the little dinette by the window. She gave a start when she saw my cap and shirt, and the ill-matched but successful mustaches.

She stood and we looked at each other for a long beat. Her dark eyes, simultaneously inquiring and restrained, were glassy and rimmed in red.

" 'Lo, Al."

"Hi, Donna," I said, uncertainly. "Check the oil and tires?"

"They're in good shape."

"Long day at the pumps."

"I can imagine. Here . . ."

She walked across the room to me, lifted off my cap and gently pulled away the gummy mustaches.

"You looked petrified in court today," she said.

"I was."

"Runnels seems capable."

"I think he is."

"If you don't know he is, get another lawyer."

"I think he is, Donna, or I wouldn't goddamned hire him, now would I?"

"I'm sorry. Settle down."

"Settling down is not possible."

"I know that . . . um . . . hey, I put some beer in the freezer."

"Let's quickly crack a couple."

She put the mustaches inside the cap and set the cap on the kitchen counter. She put my fast food in the oven and my tequila in the refrigerator. I looked out the window while she got the beer. I was still looking out it when she handed me a bottle.

"I didn't do it."

"I know you didn't."

"I absolutely did not do it. I know I sound like fucking O. J., but I *didn't*. I didn't do anything they say I did. The FBI will prove it. I'm getting my own examiner."

She said nothing for a moment, but she let her eyes walk my face and pry my soul.

"I want you to know," she said, "that if you

feel a deep need to reassure me that you're not a child molester then I'll walk out of this apartment and out of your life, forever. I believe you and I'm in this with you. We have to get that part straight right now."

I pondered this. "I needed to say it to you."

"Said. Closed. Done."

I felt a river of gratitude and love rush from my heart and charge into the channels of my body. I was shaking and there was a high-pitched whine arcing inside my head from ear to ear.

"Sit down, Terry. Drink your beer."

I sat.

I turned on the TV and watched the local news. There was a brief report about me — no pictures except a personnel shot that I'm sure Ishmael leaked — and a video shot by Channel 4 that showed my transport bus. I watched it like it was a story about another human, wholly unconnected to myself. My heart raced and my head got light.

So I switched to the Angels' *Baseball Warmup Show*. Jim Edmonds talked about how he played the outfield, how if you weren't willing to sacrifice your body out there, you'd never be a good fielder. He said he didn't think about it, really, it was just part of his personality. They showed some clips of him picking fly balls off of wall tops, snatching hard line drives midrun, tumbling forever across a green field to finally rise with his arm stretched skyward and a white ball in his glove. He was so beautiful I wanted to cry. In fact, I did.

I was aware of Donna looking at me, then going into the bedroom. I heard the bathwater running. Then she came back past me and into the kitchen and shuffled in a drawer and walked past me again — past my riveted, teary-eyed adoration of Jim Edmonds making a perfect peg from center field to the plate — and into the bedroom once more.

A few minutes later she came out, took my hand and helped me up. I was boneless. I wiped my face and looked at her briefly, then down.

"Come with me, Terry."

She took my hand and I followed her into the bedroom. There I stopped, startled. The bed was moved away from the far wall and in its place was a stool. The painting that hung above the bed was removed, as was the hook that held it. To my left was a tall tripod topped by a heavy-duty, commercial video camera that was pointing toward the stool. Next to the tripod was a big light setup that was aimed at the now blank wall.

"What?" I managed. *"What?"*

"You know what," she said very gently, almost sweetly. "I was going to explain it first, but there's something we need to do. Please, come with me, Terry."

She led me into the bathroom and shut the door. It was dark, but there was a warm orange light around us. The tub was full. A layer of suds floated a few inches from the top and steam wafted up through the suds. There was a candle in the soap dish and another two floating down in the bubbles. I started crying harder then, with the big chest shakes and that distorted mask of woe we all wear from time to time. I must have looked beyond pathetic. But just the fact that Donna had gone to this trouble for me — for *me* — made the tears pour out faster. She must *really believe me.* She helped me out of my clothes and into the water. I sat there like a kid at first, feeling the hot liquid under the feathery suds. She rubbed my neck and shoulders with her strong hands. I melted down through the bubbles to my chin and looked blearily across the downy white plain to the orange nest of light bobbing down by my upraised knees. It looked like a town at the foot of steep mountains, a hundred miles away. I listened to the break of tiny bubbles. I could see the outline of Donna's shoulders and head just beyond.

"Something need saying, Terry?"

"I love you."

"Umm."

Pleased but not satisfied, this was Donna Mason's polite way of both accepting and rejecting.

"When this is all over . . ."

But I never finished. I just watched the light of the distant village under the big peaks and wondered what the tiny people who lived there were doing. Did they know that one shift of the giant's thighs would send their whole stinking civilization down to the bottom? So I was careful when I got out a long while later, careful not to sink them. Donna helped me dry off, then she took me into the bedroom/soundstage and guided me past the camera and lights to our bed, now pushed against the far wall under a window from which you could see the bean field and the freeway. We lay down together. She turned me on my front and smoothed some sweet-smelling oil over me, working it in with her palms and fingers: neck, shoulders, arms and hands, back, butt, thighs and calves, ankles and feet, then back up to the butt again. I was gorged with desire by then — the desire of desperation — and I felt myself working against the mattress in a slow circular motion. She turned me over and I looked down to watch her head moving slowly up and down on me. On *me*. Sometime later she was above, with a fragrant arm resting on either side of my head. Then she straightened and looked up to the ceiling while we found a rhythm and kept it. She smoothed her hands over my face and combed her fingernails through my damp hair and brushed my eyelids closed with her fingertips.

After a short nap I woke up to find myself bundled safely in Donna's arms. Her breasts smelled like perfume and warm skin. I said it was time for a large amount of Herradura over ice.

"I'd wait," she said matter-of-factly.

"Why?"

"Because you've got to get dressed real sharp and comb your hair back. I'd shave, too, if I were you. I'd also use the eyedrops in the cabinet in there. Then you're going on air, Terry Naughton. And you're going to answer my questions. And you're going to tell our CNB viewers what you did and didn't do. I'd think about your answers to the cave question while you get ready. It's an odd thing, if a grown man sleeps in a cave some summer nights, when he's got a soft bed less than a mile away. You need to tell it and I need to hear it. Truth first. Tequila later."

"Don't ask me about Matt."

She stared at me a long moment. "Agreed."

I will never forget that interview.

Donna: Your name and occupation?

Me: Terry Naughton. I'm unemployed. I was a sergeant with the Orange County Sheriff.

Donna: What area of law enforcement did you work in?

Me: CAY. That's Crimes Against Youth. I'm — I was — head of the unit.

Donna: What happened?

Me: They've charged me with a crime I didn't

commit. More than one crime. So, currently I'm on unpaid leave until the matter is resolved.

Donna: What are the crimes?

Me: Sex with minors. Girls. I didn't do it.

Donna: Do they have evidence against you?

Me: No. They have falsified documents that appear to be photographs. But they're not real.

Donna: The documents are not real?

Me: Well, they're real documents. You can hold them in your hand. I have. But what they depict is not real. What they show never happened.

Donna: How can these documents portray something that didn't happen?

Me: I'm not sure of the technicalities, yet, but basically, the same way Hollywood can show you space invaders blowing up New York City. If I could explain the exact process, I would. It has something to do with digital data banks and image manipulation. I think a thing called an Iris printer may be used, too.

Donna: Who created this evidence you say is false?

Me: I don't know.

Donna: How did you learn of it?

Me: It was found during a search.

Donna: You're saying you were framed?

Me: I was framed.

Donna: The images show you in what setting?

Me: A cave.

Donna: Cave?

Me: It was a place I used to go sometimes to think in private, to get away from things.

Donna: So, you have actually been to the place the photographs show?

Me: Yes. But never in the company of a woman, or . . . girl. Well, I mean, I did take my step . . . ah . . . the daughter of a good friend of mine, there. But she isn't the girl in the fake photographs.

Donna: You never had sex in the cave?

Me: No.

Donna: Did you ever have sex with the girl in the picture of you two, having sex?

Me: No.

Donna: Do you know who this girl is?

I suddenly broke into a cold, miserable sweat. My eyeballs felt like they were on wires. The lights burned. Something truly horrible had just broken loose in my memory, like a calf sliding off from an iceberg, and now came floating out into my ocean of despair. The girl in the cave.

I'd seen her!

Donna: Do you know who the girl in the picture is? Have you seen her before?

Me: No. Never.

There it was, my first on-camera lie. I knew how obvious it would have to be, with the sweat shining on my face and the sudden rigid dilation of my pupils. I glanced at Donna's shocked and frightened expression. Anybody who saw this video was going to demand that I be crucified. Because I *had* seen this girl before, and there was no way I could hide it.

Donna: Mr. Naughton . . . you must realize that a great many people aren't going to believe what you just told me. They're going to assume the worst about you.
Me: Damn every one of them.
Donna: Is there something you're not telling me?
Me: Turn off the camera, Donna.
Donna: Mr. Naughton?
Me: Donna, turn off the camera.
Donna: Mr. Naugh—
*Me: — Turn off the fucking *camera* goddamnit!*

I was off the stool and across the room before I even knew it. What I saw next was Donna up against the wall, flat as a shadow, and the camera, tripods and lights scattered on the floor in front of her. The recorder's little red indicator light was still on. There was a big dent in the plaster above it. And we were surrounded by the abrupt quiet that often follows violence.

"Did I throw you there?"

"I got here under my own power. Who is she, Terry?"

"I don't know. Come off that wall, please."

"You've seen her before, haven't you?"

"Yes. I didn't push you, did I?"

"I'm fine, Terry. Now explain her to me."

"I can't. I just . . . know I've seen her. Somehow and somewhere. But Donna, I swear, that's not the worst of it. I mean . . ."

She didn't even bother to speak.

"Will you *please* come off that wall?"

She stepped away from the wall, toeing her way past the splayed equipment, her dark West Virginian eyes not leaving my face, not even for a second.

"Say it, Terry."

"I've seen *myself* there before, too."

"In the cave, with her?"

"No, not the cave, not *there*, but *doing* that . . . I don't know. I can't say where. Just that I've seen myself from that angle before. I've been in that . . . posture. Some other time. I've *seen* me like that. Like . . . in a dream maybe. Like in a movie about myself."

"In another picture?"

Then I understood. A simple, logical question like that, and I knew.

"It was one that Ardith took, years ago. I haven't looked at any of those since Matt . . . you know . . ."

"I know."

"Right, well, that's . . . where I saw me. That's where I was doing . . . that's what I was . . . I mean, that's where I was. With Matt."

"In the cave?"

"No! I didn't know about the cave back then."

"You're not making full sense, Terry. What about the girl?"

I stared at her a moment, then backed off and looked down at the tangled mass of video gear. The girl's image flickered in from my memory, like a speeding dove in a vast blue sky. But my memory was not of the pictures. It was of something else. Something similar, but different.

"Then who's the girl?"

"I don't know, but I've seen her before."

"Another picture, then?"

"I can't say."

"I hope you *can* say pretty soon, Terry. Because until you do, all you've got is a greased skid straight to some hellhole of a prison."

I tried to read her expression. Doubtful. Hopeful. Askance. Willing to believe. Believe what?

"You think that's where I belong?"

"I told you I wouldn't answer that again. I won't. You're going to have to clean and jerk your own conscience, Terry. I can't do that for you. What I can do is go make myself useful now. I'm going to edit that interview we just had."

She knelt down and unscrewed the video camera from its tripod plate. She stood up, holding the big thing by the handle, like a suitcase.

"Don't forget to turn it off," I said.

She blushed. It was the first time that I'd caught Donna Mason in a dishonesty, or at least the first I knew of.

"The red light's still going," I said. "You knew it was on."

"Well . . . yes, I did."

Donna was still red faced and flustered. She said nothing, but she looked down at the camera and turned it off. I heard the traffic out on the freeway. I smelled my own fear.

"Now what?" I asked.

She looked very tired, suddenly, and she spoke quietly, with a trace of the south in her voice. "Go back to the studio and edit. After that, I got a late flight out to Dallas. My bags are packed and waiting in the car."

"Mary Lou Kidder?"

"Yeah. It's our Texas connection to The Horridus. Nobody has that angle but me. Thanks to you."

Donna: ambition, guts, energy.

"I'm trusting you," I said.

"You should. Thanks for the trust. Thanks for the exclusive, too."

She nodded at me and lugged her camera out of the room. I heard the front door open, then slam shut.

I spent the evening drinking and thinking. I checked the user-group bulletin board where I'd left my messages, but I. R. Shroud had left nothing for me. I composed another note to reiterate my interest in obtaining pictures of a young girl engaged in sexual activity. I now had a young girl in mind, one I somehow remembered but couldn't say from when or where — and I wondered if this Shroud could help me find her image, and then her. Of course, I couched my request in the kind of bright, vague language that wouldn't be decipherable to the layperson.

Asking for such a thing, even for a man who is hoping to do some good with it, brings a stain to the soul that no tequila can bleach out.

Twenty-one

The next morning I crept back into Laguna with all the dignity of a lab rat. The girl who had served me coffee and a donut five times a week for nearly a year looked at me with frank disbelief. The teller at my bank adopted a stiff formality, asked for two forms of ID and double-snapped the new twenties toward me without looking me in the eye. The gas station attendant smiled mercifully as he took one of the new bills, then huddled with a co-worker at the register and they burst out laughing as I walked toward my car. My favorite checker at the market said nothing as she rang up my newspaper and orange juice.

I sat in my car and spread the paper open against the wheel: there I was, above the fold, a Sheriff Department personnel shot that, like a lot of personnel shots, made me look exactly like the criminal I was assumed to be.

Accused Deputy Had Troubled Life
Son's Death Led to Alcohol Abuse
CNB airs interview tonight

A sheriff deputy accused of sixteen

counts of sex with children was suffering stress over the death of his son.

Deputy Terry Naughton, 40, of Laguna Beach, was apparently despondent over the drowning of his five-year-old son two years ago. The incident that claimed the life of Matthew Naughton led the distraught deputy to alcohol abuse and depression, according to sources within the sheriff's office.

Files obtained by the *Journal* state that Deputy Naughton was "profoundly shaken" by the death of his son, Matthew, in a swimming accident off of Shaw's Cove in Laguna Beach.

The files also suggested that the deputy may have used alcohol to cope with his son's death. Sources within the Sheriff Department who wished not to be named said . . .

I scanned through the rest of the article for information about the cause of Matthew's death. There was no mention of medical particulars. Or lack of them. Yet.

My fury was whole. Sources within. *Sources within. Files obtained.* Jordan Ishmael? At that moment I could have successfully strangled him, hand-to-hand combat skills or not. Frances? Wade himself? What did it really matter?

Didn't anyone even care that a monster

called The Horridus was out there, watching all of us while I sat in jail? How could they splash my picture all over the paper, but not publish the composite that Amanda had based on Brittany Elder's eyewitness account? I noted the time for Donna's interview — 7 P.M. — and hurled the paper into the backseat, spilling orange juice over my lap. I stopped by the hardware store to get batteries for my flashlights, and the pretty young clerk, who had always cheerfully talked with me, gave me nothing but a malignant stare, then sighed as she waited for me to get the plastic bag off her counter. She glanced at my wet pants and thought God knows what.

I drove slowly down to Ardith's place.

She was waiting for me, as she said she would be. When she opened the door I looked away from her, unwilling to absorb whatever feelings she was having toward me. I had already done more than my share in life to make hers miserable. I knew it; she knew it. I studied her entryway tiles like they were treasures from King Tut's tomb.

"I'd like to look at the pictures," I said.

She reached out and brought up my chin so I'd have to look her in the eye.

"All right."

Haunted is the man who sets foot in a house that used to be his, to face a woman who no longer is. Same furniture — the big things, anyway. Same defined spaces. Same invisible rhythms, same small atmospheres room by room, same ambient sound. And because of that sameness, you feel as if you've changed in a million ways you never intended to. You have.

She led me upstairs. There was a small room at the top, with a pillowed bench for reading set below dormer windows that gathered up the mild May sun. Down the short hall to our left was the room that used to be our "office," although neither of us did much work in it. To the right was Matt's room.

"Mind if I —"

"— It hasn't changed."

I pushed open the door and felt the musty onrush of my son's habitat. I stepped to the center of the room. There was the smell of plastic and rubber — all those toys and balls. And the smell of clean sheets. There was the sweet, pillowy smell of stuffed animals, and the greenish smell of a bundle of dried twigs and flowers he'd collected with his mother. Then there was the smell of Matthew himself, a low-lying human scent of boy so faint I doubted anyone in the world except me, and certainly Ardith, could even detect it. Lion King poster. Batman poster. Pictures of baseball players cut from sports pages and stuck to the wall with tape slowly whitening in the wake of the years. Pictures, a piggy bank, a peanut butter jar filled with lucky feathers he'd found.

"I can't do it," I said, turning.

"Neither can I."

In the office, Ardith pulled open a sliding closet door and stood before a wall of boxes. Typical of Ardith's passion for order, the boxes were identical in size and labeled on the tops and on two adjacent corners, so their contents would be discernible from almost any likely angle.

"Which ones, Terry?"

"Matt and me. Say . . . age four."

Ardith uncrossed her arms and stepped toward the pasteboard wall. I looked at her. My wife. Once. My one and only. The mother of my vanquished son. I wished all memory would just go away. Every bit of it. Why not a past that is cleaned and polished to a clinical shine? Like an aluminum table in a doctor's office, a new .45 cartridge, a spaceship?

She spotted the appropriate box and looked back at me. It was shoulder high, so I stepped in and lifted the one above it while she worried it out. She moved back past me and swung it onto the desk.

"It's been almost six months since I looked at any of this," she said.

"I'll go through it alone, if you want."

"I'd like to be here, if it's all right with you."

"Of course it is, Ardith. You know . . ."

"What?"

"I want to get something real straight between us."

I saw the fear manifest in the depths of her eyes. With Ardith there was always fear.

"I didn't do any of the things they're talking about on the news."

The fear transformed into something like relief. She nodded and put her hand on my arm. "I know that."

"If they start crawling all over you —"

"— They already tried. I haven't said one thing about you or me or Matt. I won't."

"Thank you."

What a strange look came back from her.

The clear tape that sealed the box was already cut. I folded open the four sides and pressed them down. Ardith's photo books were all the same size and design — pure Ardith, she bought thirty of them all at once because she liked them so much — maybe fourteen inches square, with a floral cloth cover that had a little inset plaque that said *Family Photos*.

"These are early in his fourth year, Terry. Do you know what image you're looking for?"

"It's me and Matt, wrestling, maybe. Or maybe I'm hugging him. I'm not sure. But I know that I'm kind of bent over, on top of him, with my weight on one arm, and the other around his neck — maybe cradling his head. I don't know exactly."

"I think those were taken earlier."

"I don't think so."

"Well, then go through and see what you find."

I started with the first book. But I didn't find the shot that I *knew* I had seen before, the shot that looked so much like the one of me joining a very young girl in sexual congress. I moved through the pages quickly, because they were painful to look at. Matt. Ardith. Me. There were three or four pictures on most pages; two enlargements on others; and some held only one large blowup of a particularly fine photograph. All were held neatly in place by gummed sheets and clear plastic overlays.

There were seven books in the box and I looked through all of them.

"That was the time period," I said. "Maybe a little more recent."

"I know you're going the wrong direction, Terry."

"Then you go back and I'll go forward. All right?"

We wrestled out two more boxes. I methodically started at the beginning. Ardith put hers on the floor and sat down beside it, leaning her back against the wall.

I flipped the pages fast, then faster. Matt and me at the beach. Ardith and Matt walking the shoreline — slightly out of focus, poorly centered, my handiwork. Matt taking cuts at the T-ball. Matt hefting a ball toward the bright yellow backboard of a kid's basketball setup. Ardith getting dressed for a dinner date, standing in front of the mirror with her little black dress on and her hair curled up, fastening a string of pearls around her elegant neck. That was quite a night.

"Oh," she said.

I put away the book and took out the next: first bike with training wheels, me and a new fishing rod I'd just bought, shots of Matt and me in a little rented boat on Irvine Lake. I was whipping the pages. Too much memory, too much past.

"Terry?"

"What."

Flip, flip, flip.

"It's not here."

"Then look in the next one."

Flip, flip, flip.

"I mean, they're gone. The whole series — all of them."

Flip, flip, flip.

"Gone where?"

"Don't snap at me. I'm not your wife anymore. Get your butt over here and look for yourself."

I set my book into the box and moved across the room to look down at Ardith's. The open pages were blank. She flipped backward to show me two more empty pages, then forward. Six pages, nothing but adhesive and clear overlay.

"They were shots of you and Matt in bed. Remember? It was that morning back four winters ago when it was raining so hard the roads were closed? You called in stranded and we all got in bed and listened to the rain come down? Then we wrestled around like alligators? Remember? I got the camera and shot you and Matt goofing off. Matt had on his pajamas with the —"

"— And I had on my boxers. No top."

"That's right. Really nice shots of you guys thrashing around, pulling the bedsheets over your heads. I blew one up to nine by twelve — you on your knees in bed, holding Matt under your right arm and bracing yourself with your left. It was just before you crashed down on top of him, you know, made that growling alligator noise. He was on your forearm, on his back, giggling like crazy and looking up at you and in the picture your faces are so close it looks like you're about to kiss. And your eyes were shut — remember that shot?"

"Perfectly."

"Well, somebody stole it. And all the others of that morning. The whole series is gone."

As would any cop, any doubter, any ex, I studied Ardith's face for falsehood. There was none.

"Terry . . . what did you want that picture *for?*"

"I'm not sure."

"For Melinda?"

"No. It . . . I was reminded of it when, well . . ."

So I explained it to Ardith. She looked at me a little unbelievingly, at first; then I could see she understood.

There were other photographs missing, too. We spent the next three hours going through each book. Eight more pages were blank. Gone was a series of pictures of me lying on a towel in the sun, and a series of me hamming it up on the living room carpet one hot summer evening, jeans on, shirt off, doing muscleman poses. As Ardith described the pictures to me, I remembered them. And I remembered that she had used certain filters and had dimmed the living room lights to produce shots that were forthrightly, harmlessly erotic.

"They were all of *you*, Terry. They took the ones that showed your body."

When we were finished, we stood amid the stacks of boxes and piles of photo albums. I picked my way across to the window and slid it open. The warm breeze wafted in.

"Ardith, when was the break-in here? The burglary?"

"February the twenty-eighth. It was a Wednesday. Do you think that's when . . . this happened?"

"It never did make sense, the way you described it. They break into a house that's unoccupied, and steal some costume jewelry and clock radio? But they leave the TV, VCR, stereo and the pearls sitting out on the dresser? What the hell kind of burglary is that? Any thirteen-year-old kid would have enough sense to take some of the good stuff. It wasn't burglars looking for loot. It was somebody looking for those photographs. So they could use them."

"But who could possibly know that I had them? Know exactly where they were?"

I looked at her for a moment, then out the window. My old neighborhood stretched out before me, a huge tract of duplicate two-story town homes vanishing over a distant hilltop. Tan stucco. Red tile roofs. Then I turned back and looked at Ardith.

"Nobody knew, except you and me," I said.

"Well, I didn't steal my own pictures, Terry. Get that look off your face."

"I know."

"But who else knew?"

I shook my head. "They didn't know until they found them. They bet on a hunch and the hunch was right. They stole a few trinkets to throw you off the trail. It worked."

I was three steps outside Ardith's front door when the figure in the bushes sped past me, stopped, knelt and hit the autodrive on his 35 millimeter. The lens protruded insultingly. You know how I can get. The film was still chattering forward when my toe sent the camera into a quick flight that reversed itself at the end of the strap. The heavy thing slammed back down into the photographer's head. He yelped. Then he tilted onto his butt. I put my foot on his chest and pushed him the rest of the way over. He spread out his arms and opened his hands, like he was trying to assure me of his innocence.

I knelt down beside him. "How do you do?"

"Not so good. I was trying to do my job."

"No more hot pix today, friend. I've had enough of those to last a lifetime." I picked up his camera.

"Dick March, the *Journal*. That's a six-hundred-dollar Nikon, Mr. Naughton."

"What a time to run out of film."

I popped the roll and stripped out the film, dropping it to the lawn. Then I stood up and offered Dick a hand, which he reluctantly took. I yanked him up, then got into my car. Pulling away from the curb, I could see him fumbling to get another canister into his camera, but it was too late: I stood on the pedal and screeched around the bend.

Twenty-two

Loren Runnels's secretary showed me into his rather swank Newport Beach office an hour later. Loren sat behind his desk with his feet up and his arms locked behind his head. Two men sat across from him. One was Rex Wilkers, the PI who had sprung me so anonymously from the jail just days before. I shook his hand and thanked him again. Next to him, and already standing as I turned to offer my hand, was Will Fortune. We shook and I sat between them. I looked briefly at the card he gave me before sliding it into my pocket:

Fortune Forensic Sciences
William L. Fortune
Examiner of Questioned Documents

Fortune looked about my age, with a big frame and a big face that reminded me of pictures of young Hemingway. He had a mustache, and a pleasing combination of boyishness and manliness about him. His smile was cheerful and without irony, but his eyes were very direct and acquisitive.

Loren was his usual self: slender and silver

haired, with the air of a man whose purpose in life was to live well and who was accomplishing it.

Wilkers, a stocky blond who looked like a California surfer and probably was, crossed his legs and snugged his white socks up from his athletic shoes.

"Will got in from Boise yesterday morning," said Loren. "He's seen the photo evidence. Rick Zant and the rest of his office were polite and helpful."

He scooted back his chair so we could see each other more comfortably. Will Fortune did not mince words.

"I couldn't tell much from those prints. The negatives haven't been altered — there was no interruption of the silver halide/gelatin structure."

I wanted more dramatic exoneration than silver halide/gelatin structure, whatever in hell that was. I was getting worked up, quickly. "Does this reek of a frame or am I just stupid? What do I have to do, Loren, prove I couldn't have been in the cave at that precise *hour* before somebody sees how goddamned false and orchestrated this all is?"

"In fact, that's one of the things we'll try to determine," said Fortune. "There's just enough light in the cave for me to try a shadow analysis. I say *try*. It'll be tough."

My anger subsided just enough to wonder what this man — who got $100 of my money per hour just to sit on a plane — was talking about. "Shadow analysis?"

He nodded. "Shadows move with the sun. So there's only two days a year when the same object in the same place will cast the same shadow. If you were somewhere else on those days, and can prove it — this evidence falls apart."

"Well, I'm liking the sound of that," I said.

"It will depend on the light in the cave," he said. "I need to be there and see it, make some control photographs of my own."

I sighed, shook my head and looked at him. "Then I take it you couldn't tell just by looking at them that they were fake."

"Nobody could."

The dismal implication hung in the air. For whatever it was worth, in that moment I forgave Joe Reilly, fellow Irishman, for being unable to declare my innocence with his naked eye.

Fortune again: "And the fact that they come in a sequence on a film roll means that whoever made them didn't arrange things for one grand-slam image that's supposed to send you upriver for life. So, the first two things I look for if the images are visually convincing — existence of a negative and the sequential pattern from a film roll — are against us."

"Then I'd like to hear about things three through ten you look for," I said bitterly.

Will Fortune looked at Loren.

"Shoot," said my lawyer.

"Physical anomalies," said Fortune. "I'll need my own photographs of you to find those. Optical anomalies — light source, color, focus and perspective. There wasn't anything obvious, but that's what my lab is for. Edge marks on the negatives — you need the camera that took the photos for that. I'll certainly want to examine yours, and it's our good fortune that it wasn't on the evidence list. You've got one, I take it?"

"In some closet somewhere."

"Well, it may give us what we're looking for. I'll need it as soon as you can get it to me. Next, we can look at the models and do some photogrammetry to see how they fit the setting. The models in this case would be you and/or the girl. Photogrammetry is a way of measuring the size of objects in an image. If the physical parameters of the cave tell us, for instance, that you, Terry Naughton, stand seven feet ten inches in height, we know we have an altered image."

"No, I'm about three foot four, right now."
Chuckles.

Loren leaned forward. "We can go into this later, but Rex can try to locate the girl. Expensive and not likely to succeed, to be honest with you. Anyway — back to you, Will."

I didn't mention that I was tracking that delightful little girl on my own, through the Midnight Ramblers chat rooms and one I. R.

Shroud. It wasn't exactly happening quickly. Something told me to keep it to myself.

"I examined those prints for sharpness irregularities — none I could argue in court because the images are all kind of hazy. Just hazy enough to hide inconsistencies. Same with the matrix of the print grain — it's smooth enough to suggest credibility of the film. I'll have a closer look at that later in my lab."

There was a silence then, during which all my hope and optimism funneled down to the person of William L. Fortune, examiner of questioned documents.

"Look," he said with that full-cheeked boy's grin. "We can sit here at one-fifty an hour, or you can take me to the cave and we can get on it."

I drove. We parked on Canyon Edge, a few houses up from my former home. I got Moe out of the yard and let him come with us up the trail.

Big as Will Fortune was, he made the uphill climb easily. Moe flushed a brace of valley quail from a cactus patch near the path, and Will stopped to watch the birds zoom off low across the brush tops and vanish with a quick braking of wings.

"You hunt him?"

"No. I quit shooting things when my son died."

Will said nothing.

"Long story," I said.

"I've got a couple of German shorthairs back home. We spend about every spare second we have after pheasant and chukar and quail."

"It's a good thing to be doing," I said earnestly, if absently.

We made the cave in good time. Moe plopped into the shade of a lemonadeberry tree while Will set down his bag of equipment, looked at the cave mouth, then up at the sun.

"They used a secondary light source for the shoot," he said. "But there's enough natural sunlight in those images to work a shadow analysis. I hope whoever made those things didn't rearrange the cave walls just to throw us off."

"Will, nothing would much surprise me."

"That was supposed to be a joke."

"I don't get jokes."

"I understand."

He brought out a tape recorder and announced the date and time and location. Inside, he stood in the middle of the little rock room, turning slowly, saying nothing. He looked at the walls up close, knelt and felt the bottom. "All right," he said, with something of the coach sending his team onto the field of play.

For the next hour he photographed the cave from every possible angle: outside, inside, with

406

the camera at ground level and the camera raised on a telescoping tripod to just under seven feet. He shot black and white and color, prints and slides. He used six different cameras, including an ESP camera, which he explained stood for electronic still photography.

"The finished images were photographic in nature," he said. "Taken on film with a standard 35 millimeter camera. But that doesn't mean they started out that way. You can begin with a digitized image, like this camera takes, and turn it back into an analogue, filmic one. All you need is a film recorder. It's important for two reasons. First, you can manipulate digital images quite easily on a good computer with Adobe software and the right Photoshop programs. If those shots of you were created from scratch — well, almost scratch — that's how it was done. Second, DA Zant has edge marks on those negatives, and he doesn't know it yet, but edge marks on film are like tool marks on bullets. Every gun leaves a different pattern. Well, every camera does, too. I don't know what those edge marks tell us yet, and I won't until I get back to my lab. But he let me see some magnifications of the negs, and I got photographic copies of the blowups. All right, it's time for some shots of you in here, Terry. We can do a few with clothes, but after that I want you naked as Moe. Fair enough?"

"Naked?"

"Naked."

"This is a sad moment. But shoot away, William L. What do I have to lose?"

I can't accurately describe what it's like to be photographed naked in a cave by an examiner of questioned documents who reminds you of Hemingway. Humiliating. Infuriating. Mystifying. Dreamlike. Hilarious. Demeaning. Chilly. At one point he asked me to hold out my penis for various angles, and I realized from that moment on, my life would simply have to improve. The penis in the evidence pictures was partially obscured by shadow, but who was I to say what a picture of a dick proved or didn't prove? Finally I put my clothes on and stepped out to the afternoon sunshine feeling no emotion that I had ever felt before in my life.

Fortune already had his bag packed. He was squatting down, petting Moe.

"I'll need those photographs of your wife's that you told me about on the way here," he said.

"They were stolen, like I told you."

"I'll need the others."

"I'll send them to you."

"Immediately if not sooner?"

"That's right."

"I want your camera, too."

We walked back down to my ex-home and I put Moe back in the yard. I let myself into the house and tried to act like it was still my home, like I was still welcome there. Curiosity got the better of me and I stole briefly into my old room to see if my suede chukka boots had been confiscated, per the search warrant. They had. I came out a moment later feeling invaded, assaulted, raped. What had Mel felt, as they pillaged her home? If Will Fortune suspected my feelings he didn't show it. I found my old Yashica 35 millimeter in the hallway closet, its case covered with dust, and I put it in a paper grocery bag and gave it to him.

Outside I patted Moe's head and dug my fingers into his thick neck fur. I knew my hand would smell like him until I washed it — something I've always found sort of pleasant. He whimpered as I walked away. I drove Fortune back to his car at Loren's office and we watched the dark blue Pacific churning away below Coast Highway.

"You live in a real nice place," said Will.

"I feel lucky sometimes."

"You weren't lucky with those photos. They're good, Terry. They're damned good."

"I didn't hire you to tell me how good they are."

"I contracted with you to deliver the truth and nothing more. There are examiners out there more eager to please their clients. They're even cheaper than me. Loren could have got you one if he thought you needed it. If you're that worried, hire one. I don't think you are."

I watched a bicycler labor up the PCH grade. His feet rotated on the pedals at about one rpm and the bike was wobbling so bad it looked ready to fall over. I wondered why people did things that were difficult simply because they were difficult.

"The thing is, Will, I already *know* the truth you promised me. I'm waiting for you to catch up. And the world is looking at me like I'm something stuck to the bottom of a shoe. I'm already sick of it and it's going to get worse before it gets better."

"Then let me tell you something. The images are good. But good, and good enough to fool me, are two different things. I'm a modest man, more or less. I like to hunt birds and spend time with my family and do my work. I quit the Bureau pretty young in life, because I didn't like working for someone else. Not that I didn't like the Bureau, or my bosses there. It just wasn't what I wanted. But the FBI will still tell you I'm the best examiner in the country. The American Academy of Forensic Sciences will tell you the same thing. The American Board of Forensic Document Examiners will tell you that, too. Same with the American Society of Photogrammetry and Remote Sensing, and the Association of Federal Photographers. Last of all, *I'll* tell you that. I'm the best. There isn't an artist, craftsman, creep or criminal out there who can fool me. And I'll tell you just as soon as I can whether or not those pictures will stand in a court of law."

I drove awhile, thinking.

"Thanks, Will."

"I look forward to helping. Get me those pictures your wife took as soon as you can. Get some rest. Maybe get that dog of yours out for some birds someday. He's just crying to hunt."

"Yes, he is. How long is it going to take — your examination?"

"Three days, tops."

"That's a long wait."

"Hang in there. Do something good for yourself."

"Listen, Will. There's a thing calling itself The Horridus out here. He's going to do some awful things to some young people if we don't stop him. That's the worst of it. I'm getting my dick photographed in a cave while this animal is out there planning his massacre."

"I didn't realize he's killing."

"He will. And you can massacre a person without killing them. You ruin a life or you take it — they're both first-degree mortal sins if you ask me."

Will was quiet for a while.

"Stay on him, Terry. Just because your badge is gone doesn't mean you can't stay on him."

I thought about that and I realized — strange how it can take you so long to see the obvious — that Will Fortune was right.

Twenty-three

That afternoon I stood in the meadow at Caspers Wilderness Park, where Ranger Bret Stefanic had met his bloody end just five days before. I could see a grassy swale, a ring of big oak trees and the bed of a stream that flowed only in winter. There was still a long fragment of crime scene ribbon tape staked up, lilting in the breeze like a yellow kite tail. I had a copy of the arriving deputy's report, which I'd filed in my briefcase before my arrest so I could work at home. I was doing something good for myself, as ordered by the best examiner of questioned documents in the world.

The early May afternoon was warm. The sky was light blue, with a circle of black vultures turning far overhead. The locusts buzzed on and off in short bursts that sounded like signals. I could smell the damp richness of the grass and trees surrounding me, and feel the winter's rain evaporating with spring. Another six weeks, I thought, and everything here but the oaks will be tan, dry and hot.

I knelt by the tape stake and looked out at the grass. According to the deputy's drawing, Stefanic was lying about ten yards from me, on his back, head east and feet west. The deputy had duly noted an area of matted, bloodied grass, about twenty feet from the body. Blood turns black in the sun, of course. I watched the grass blades tilt in the breeze. I'd brought my yellow shooting glasses from the car and slipped them on. They concentrate the light and enhance contrast when you're outdoors, which is why hunters like them, especially early in the morning or at dusk. It took my eyes a moment to adjust to the fresh onslaught of sunlight, but when they did, I could easily see what I was looking for. The yellowing grass caked in black jumped out at me. The clotted blades didn't tilt in unison with the others because they were heavier, and some of them had been choked dead by the fluid. I could see the big patches where the CSIs had collected specimens. I looked at their report to remind myself of what else they'd taken: citation book, park ranger's (1); hat, park ranger's, size 7¼ (1); sunglasses, Ray-Ban aviator style, green lens and cable temples (1 pr.); pen, aluminum ballpoint, black ink, Scripto brand.

When I looked back out from the CSI report I thought I saw a huge green snake looking at me from a bush about fifty feet away. It was up off the ground, head maybe four or five feet high, swaying in the breeze. I'd seen enough *National Geographic* specials to recognize a king cobra when I saw one, but I knew they weren't out here. I blinked and it was gone. Just an optical illusion, something imagined. I stared at the bush for a moment, knowing how eyes play tricks. The trunk looked like a snake, a green one, in fact, though I must have supplied the swaying head on my own. I got that same giddy, sinking feeling I'd had in Wanda Grantley's guest quarters in Hopkin, Texas.

I turned back to the report and flipped back a few pages for more detail on the citation book. The CSI had said that the top page was numbered 068. It was a ticket for an illegal campfire, written four days before Stefanic's death. He'd gone almost four whole days without citing anyone? But the book was found twenty-two feet from the body. He'd had it out, then, unless it fell from his belt in a struggle. Say he was ready to issue. Say he'd already taken down some information. Say the citation was the inciting incident. Good. Then what does the killer do when he's finished? He rips out the ticket about to be issued to him. He probably grabs more than just the top one — he takes four days' worth of citations and wads them into a ball. Then what? Well, if he's scared and careless, he throws it into the bushes. If he's stupid, he takes it with him. If he's not too much of either, maybe he hides it someplace he thinks is safe.

Betting on the first, I beat the bushes. I started where the citation book was recovered and worked a slow circle outward. I thought I saw the cobra spying on me again from a

414

clump of manzanita, but it was just the man-zanita. I knelt and pried down into the trunks of the thick shrubs, wondering if the ball of tickets might have been stuffed into a secure nook. I found dried blood. Lots of it. Near the initial attack there was one patch of ground that was a foot square and just drenched in it. I found an old cigarette pack and two screw-tops. I found a penny. I put them in the pocket of my coat, resigned to their irrelevance. No citations. My circle ended fifty yards from where the attack had begun. I looked back over the distance I'd covered, then at my watch. A forty-minute loop. The sweat had run off my forehead and formed rivulets on the yellow lenses of my shooting glasses. When I took them off to wipe them I could have sworn I saw the cobra looking at me over the tall grass, but when I put the glasses back on I couldn't see anything but swaying blades. I wondered if I was really seeing what I was telling myself I couldn't be seeing. The Horridus is chang-ing. The Horridus is consolidating. He changes his appearance. He sells his house. He lets his pets go in the wild, and that's what he was doing when the park ranger found him. Why not? Then the cobra could be real.

I walked back to the parking area. It was almost two hundred yards from where Stefanic had been found. I checked the map I'd been given at the Ranger Station to see where else — if anywhere — our slaughterer might have left his vehicle. No, he would have parked here, I thought: the next lot was half a mile to the east.

You parked here.

You walked out from here.

What were you doing?

Why did you choose to kill?

How did you get a viper to do to Stefanic what a viper wouldn't do on its own?

At the far end of the parking area, in the shade of a stout old oak, stood a cinder-block outhouse. Women right; Men left. There was a drinking fountain with yellow jackets buzzing over the faucet, and a big steel-mesh garbage container with a lid on it. A chain ran from the lid to the mesh.

I scanned the CSI's report to make sure they'd gone through the contents for evidence. Surely they'd done the math on the ticket book and drawn the same conclusion I had. But there was no mention of the book — other than its description — and no mention of the garbage container. Great.

I sighed, walked over to it and lifted the lid.

Half an hour later I'd gone through every item inside, from the ketchup-and-ant-caked french fry box to the plastic Big Slurp cup to the empty peach can and the reeking cantaloupe rinds. There was newspaper, tissue paper and even a swatch of gift wrap, but no tickets once issued by a conscientious and now very dead Bret Stefanic. There's no way, I thought, that a rattlesnake stole up and bit him on the calf, then the butt, then jumped up and bit him on the face while someone cut his throat.

Gene, do I smell you again?

I threw the trash back into the container and went into the bathroom to wash my hands. I dried them off on a roll of that crisp brown paper that decomposes the second it touches moisture. I tossed the soggy ball into the wall bin, but it hit all the other paper stuffed in there and plopped to the cement floor. More trash to go through, I thought. So I went through it.

Nothing.

I went back into the shady warmth of the parking area again and had an idea: if our guy was going to stash something in a bathroom, why not use the women's side? A weekday in a remote wilderness park. No crowds. Maybe not even any other cars in the lot. Why not?

So I went into the ladies' room and reached down into the wall bin. It was almost full. I used both hands to shovel the stuff into the sink beside me. It was mostly wadded brown paper. When I got down near the bottom there was a funny hissing sound, like one of the grasshoppers outside had found its way into the trash. It must have gotten scared because it stopped buzzing. I reached in for the last load and brought it out. The buzzing started up again. When I dropped that last batch into the sink I saw the cloth bag — it looked like a pillowcase — knotted at the top, mixed in with the other rubbish. Inside, something was moving. When I picked it up — by the knot — the buzz commenced. It felt like the bag was empty, but I knew I'd seen movement inside. I untied the cloth and opened up the end and looked in. Down at the very bottom, in one corner, curled into a circle no larger than a coaster was a small dark rattlesnake. His little tail was held up and the end of it was a blur. He tracked me with a small triangular head. In the opposite corner was a wadded ball of pink and white paper. I closed the end, took the bag firmly in my hand, swung it over my head and down to the floor, hard. The buzzing stopped. When I looked inside again the serpent was stretched along the bottom and kinked up kind of funny, bleeding from its mouth.

I got the paper out and flattened it against the floor.

CALIFORNIA DEPARTMENT
OF FISH AND GAME
DAY: 26 MONTH: 04 YEAR: 98
RECIPIENT NAME: IAN RICHARD SHROUD
DOB: 12 26 67
STREET/NUMBER: 18181 FOREST
CITY/ZIP: ORANGE 92867 STATE: CA
DRIVER LICENSE/STATE: E0460644
PHONE: (714) 681-4778
CITATION #

RANGER NAME/ID #
VIOLATION #
DESCRIPTION OF VIOLATION:

COMMENTS

CITING RANGER SIGNATURE:
RECIPIENT SIGNATURE:

I knelt there for a moment and read the information twice. I studied the final slash of Ranger Bret Stefanic's pen. I studied the big stain of blood that had splashed against the paper. Then I read the name again, Ian Richard Shroud, and I felt that odd combination of vertigo and illumination happening at the same time. I fell through bright light, and there he was.

My man.

My man I. R. Shroud, The Horridus.

I. R. Shroud = Horridus. Another game.

You were so close to where I am now, I thought.

On my way out of the park I called the number Shroud had given Stefanic. It was a supermarket. I called Johnny next, who confirmed there was no I. R. Shroud listed or unlisted anywhere in Orange County.

Less than an hour later I was sitting in Steven Wicks's office at Prehistoric Pets, watching him count the mouth scales of the rattlesnake on his desk. The animal was still moving, slowly and without progress, like in a dream. Wicks shook his head very slowly, which I took as a criticism of my specimen collection technique. He had a book on rattlesnakes open in front of him. When he was done he looked up at me.

"*Crotalus horridus*," he said. "Timber rattler."

Back at the apartment I checked my computer, suspecting that The Horridus wouldn't have contacted me again either. Right again. After all, he'd been busy. Abducting girls. Supplying evidence that damned the very cop who was after him the hardest.

Question: did he know who Mal was? How? If so, was he playing a game with me, or did he believe that Terry Naughton was a bad cop with a bad habit?

Either way, I had to get him to answer me. He was my savior. So I left a plaintive note for him on the bulletin board:

I. R. — Need some real-time chatter to get to the heart of this matter. Free adult seeking to exercise constitutional rights. Need directions to dream girl. Need to go to live feed. Aforementioned budget generous within reason. Reconsider loyal Mal.

"Going live" or "going to live feed" is pedo

parlance for "acquiring" the object of desire in the flesh. Not the picture. Not the video. Not the film.

The actual live girl. It's risky and expensive. And I'd never done it before.

Half an hour later I met Johnny Escobedo at Fontana, a restaurant down in the Santa Ana barrio, not far from the county buildings. He had tried to turn me down, but I was all over him. I told him I had new evidence on The Horridus and Stefanic — and that was enough. That's one of the things I love about Johnny: he'll do almost anything on earth to bust a creep.

He slipped through the screen door and into the booth, looking more like a cartel enforcer than a cop: his usual jeans and white T-shirt, cowboy boots and silk windbreaker. The windbreaker had shrunken skulls embroidered across the shoulders. He stared at me from behind his sunglasses for a silent moment, then took them off and smiled.

"You're looking good, boss."

"If I was really your boss, you'd be wearing a coat and tie. You're working crimes against youth, you know. You're supposed to look squeaky and square, like a cop you could trust."

"Well then, I guess you never really were my boss, boss."

"I'll tell you, Johnny, I intend to be again someday."

"Ishmael's so slow about everything, it's a wonder he gets his teeth brushed before work. You gotta run each and every thing past him before he'll cut you loose. He watches us like we're children. He doesn't have any urgency, no speed at all. Like working for a turtle."

We ordered two coffees, a basket of chips and salsa.

"Where are you on Grantley, Vonn and Webb and Webster?" I demanded.

He eyed me. "I thought *I* was getting the dope here."

"You're getting the dope." I pulled the pillowcase from my jacket pocket and set it on the table. Johnny looked at the little bloodstain on it, then at me. "But I need some first."

"Grantley's a bust so far — no homes with guest units bought, sold or leased by a Grantley in the last two years, in any of the three counties. There's two Eugene Vonns in Orange County — father-son, both clean. Junior is twelve. No Eugene or Gene Grantley anywhere. There are eighteen Eugene Webbs in the three counties, and we've checked out all but four. We've got seven Eugene Websters and two Gene Websters. Haven't had time to touch them yet. Welborn called from Texas with Wanda's married names — total of five. Haven't had time for them, yet, either. If all that doesn't pay, we're back to where we started."

"Then where the hell is he, Johnny? You

run through the state files, DMV, tax rolls, voter regis—"

"— I just told you, boss."

Creeps who go off the grid are tough. You'd be surprised how many people aren't who you think they are. You don't know who you're looking for, and all the standard locators don't work. I was quiet a second as the frustration built. But, as with most frustration, there was nowhere for it to go. "What about subcontractors and custodial people for Bright Tomorrows and —"

"— Dawn Christie helped, but Marcine Browne won't even talk to me."

"How could she resist you, Johnny?"

Escobedo leaned in close. I saw the quick anger in his eyes. "Because she didn't resist *you*, man. She got her pretty face fired for talking with you. Her boss gets back from St. John or someplace and one of her assistants tells him she's been talking to you about members. Rats her out completely. Guess who the new manager is now? I talked to one of their legal department. They're not releasing shit to us without a subpoena or a warrant. Period. They're just not talking, man. Of course I got Marcine's home number and tried that. She hung up."

It hit me hard that I'd gotten a helpful young woman fired. I added that to the frustration, too. Johnny could see the look on my face and he knew what it meant. A pissed-off Irishman and a pissed-off Mexican boil down to about the same thing.

"Then get the warrant," I said.

"We're working on it."

I sighed and sat back. It was either that or throw a chair through the plate-glass window. Or throw myself. "What about the female-owned houses?"

Johnny sat forward, speaking quietly: "Look, boss. We're way past this FBI profile. Forget the houses and guest houses and listings. Forget all the names we don't have for this guy. He's off the grid — a lot of people are off it. But we've got a good composite out of Brittany Elder and we need to work it the best we can. There might be something at Bright Tomorrows, but that's going to take a little time. I've requested a subpoena but the judges are busy. It's the usual stuff, Terry. Hours. Days. Time."

"No. There's the women. The women who listed houses with guest quarters. He could have a wife, a sister, you never know who holds the paper on a place and who really lives there."

Now he sat back, shaking his head sadly. "Ishmael nixed that this morning. I agreed."

What can you say when your unit revolts against you? "I'll see what *I* can do," I said, all fake bravura.

The words must have sounded stupidly brave to Johnny, because he arched his dark brows and stared hard at me again. But for all his cool and street smarts, Johnny's as straight as a cop can be. I could almost read his thoughts: *you start prowling around as a charged felon repping yourself as a cop and you're going to take a long hard fall. I can't help you there. I'm taking a chance on you, man.*

"All right, Johnny," I said. "Thank you. Thanks for helping me. I mean that."

Then he looked at me with undisguised regret. I knew it wasn't giving me information that he regretted, but the fact that I was still working the case. That I was still there, getting in deeper, trying to make it mine while the County built its case against me for a morals rap. I saw myself as a little bit crazy in Johnny Escobedo's eyes. He saw me tying a rope around my own neck, but he still had a job to do. He was the system and I wasn't. I was pure poison.

"This is for you, John — The Horridus has another handle. I. R. Shroud."

"How do you know that?" he asked quietly, still askance at Terry Naughton, former head of CAY, former champion of the little people.

I took a napkin out of the plastic holder and the pen out of my pocket. I wrote:

HORRIDUS = I. R. SHROUD

He looked at the words for a long moment. "It's an anagram. Same letters. I'll be damned.

But where'd you get the name?"

I told him about the killing field at Caspers Wilderness Park, the bathroom, the bag, citation and guardian serpent.

Then I slid the bundled pillowcase over to him and told him it was all his.

"Don't worry," I said. "The snake's dead. Get Reilly to laser the ticket for prints."

The anger flashed in his eyes again. "How am I going to book this? We can't take it to court. I shouldn't even touch it. It's not evidence, coming from you. What it is, is useless, amigo."

"Go discover it yourself."

He shook his head. "That's my career, if it ever gets out. And The Horridus walks, if it comes out in court. Look, Terry, I can work this I. R. Shroud angle until —"

"— But you won't find anything."

His face asked the question before his voice did. "Why not?"

"It's just a name," I said. "Not a person."

"On Stefanic's citation?"

"It's also a user name on the Web. He's one of the kind of networkers we like to mingle with sometimes. One of the kiddy touchers, the pervs. One of the bloodsucking ticks we deal with."

"The Horridus is on-line? You mean we've talked to him?"

"Somebody has."

Johnny looked confused more than anything else. "Who?"

"I don't know."

"What do you *mean*, man! What the hell are you talking riddles to me for?"

"I think somebody at the department has, and I don't think he wants anybody to know. He talked to I. R. Shroud on the Web. They made some arrangements. Maybe he didn't make the connect to The Horridus. Maybe he did."

He continued to eye me, dark and sullen.

He shook his head and leaned back. "I'm not getting you, man. You're telling me that one of the CAY people has talked to The Horridus on the Web, but never said anything to you about it?"

"Somebody at the department. Not necessarily CAY. And they talked to I. R. Shroud. Like I said, it's *possible* he didn't get the joke."

"But it wasn't me and it wasn't you."

"Correct."

"Well, why in hell would somebody at the department mail Shroud but not tell CAY? Not tell *you?*"

"Pictures."

His dark eyebrows rose again, and he groaned. "So, what are you saying?"

"Whoever framed me had to be inside. They'd have to know me, hate me, have a way into the porn networks, and a reason to burn my ass."

"You're saying it was Ishmael."

I nodded.

Johnny said nothing.

But he intuited my request, as I knew he would.

"Oh, man," he said quietly. "You god-damned Irish *pendejo*. I'm starting to think CAY's better off without you. *No*."

I shrugged. "It's just a matter of checking his log-ons and his IRC receptors. They're on the printouts —"

"— No, man. It's a matter of getting my ass thrown off the department forever, is what it is."

"Then don't do it."

"Hey, friend, there's no way on earth I can do that."

"I had to ask."

"No. No. *No*."

"Understood."

He shook his head and pushed his empty coffee cup away. Johnny hated me in that moment, for forcing him to betray his department or disappoint his friend. Those dark eyes of his flashed across my face with both fury and sadness in them.

"I wouldn't be here if I didn't think you were stand-up, Terry. I'm with you, man. You know that."

"I know."

"But don't bleed me unless you have to."

"All right."

He picked up the bag and looked down inside.

"Thing's still moving in there."

"They take forever to die."

"Yeah. I cut one's head off and skinned it out when I was a kid. Tacked the skin to a board and salted it. Left the guts beside it for the hornets to eat. I stood there with my brother and watched the heart beat. It was this little tiny heart. Four hours later we come back out and it was still beating. Wouldn't quit for nothin'. Just like you."

Then the very long, agonizing silence while Escobedo tried to weigh his friendship with me against his loyalty to the department, my power as a pariah against Ishmael's as a lieutenant in good standing.

"You been talking to The Horridus on-line, boss?"

"I'm trying. I used our Ramblers' chat room to get a line on a good kiddy pornographer. Someone who has the new stuff. Maybe he actually makes the stuff. A producer. Someone who can do a custom."

"And you got Shroud?"

"That's exactly who I got. I didn't see the connection until I found Stefanic's ticket."

Silence again.

"You really think Ishmael ordered up customs of you?"

"I know he did."

Johnny turned and leaned his arm over the back of the booth. He looked back through the window, to the barrio outside. I guessed it was just a little vacation, a break from all the crap that he had to do all day long. He spoke without turning.

"You know, it's Frances who spends the most computer time in CAY. She's got a stable full of freaks on the Web."

"Frances isn't going to sit down over chips and coffee with me."

"And then there's the obvious." He turned back to me, closing the bag and wrapping the end back into a knot. "You know, Terry, you might have already thought of this, but Melinda's the one who has *all* the computer crooks in her machine. We've been sharing every CAY computer contact with her for a year now. So does every other section and unit — if there's a crime and a computer involved, Melinda knows about it. Remember, Wade ordered us all to copy Fraud and Computer Crime if there was a computer involved? You remember that directive from Wade, don't you?"

"Yeah, I remember it."

"Well, anyway, she's got all the computer creeps, somewhere in her files. Maybe she could line out Ishmael's logs for you."

"In order to help me."

"Yeah, uh-huh. In order to help you."

It seemed like the first time in days I'd actually laughed. It just jumped out of me — the idea of Melinda helping me — and I had to choke down a little coffee to keep it from coming out. I just broke down and *laughed,* like you do when you're a kid and rarely do later.

Escobedo looked at me and laughed, too. It was one of those desperate, semiwicked connections between people willing to admit that something ugly is also very funny. Johnny looked like a gleeful devil for a second there, with his goatee and his hair slicked back from the widow's peak and his straight white teeth and shrunken skulls.

So, we had our comic relief.

"She's a good person," I said.

"Yeah, she's all of that. She also gets the monthly log-ons because she's a section head. She knows who's been talking to who on those damned computers."

"That's true, too."

"I mean, well . . . I don't know what it means."

"I don't, either, Johnny."

Johnny stood and reached for his wallet, but I already had it covered.

"One more thing, Terry," he said. "We're going public with the Brittany drawing. Press conference this afternoon at five. We'll be handing out copies to everybody who wants them."

"It's about time," I said. "Ishmael gave in?"

"Naw. He acted like it was his idea — ordered us to go ahead with it. He's Mr. Proaction now. He's also taking your idea about the freeway billboard. We're having the thing blown up to thirty feet across and hanging it all over the county."

I had to smile. "John, I'll get those log-ons some other way. Forget it."

"What log-ons?"

"Would you sit back down for just a second and talk to me, friend?"

He sat back down and he let it out. "Terry, if someone inside the department has been talking to The Horridus, and not said anything? That's not done, man. That's the kind of thing nobody's going to condone. You prove Ishmael's been *cutting deals* with that scum, deals to set you up for a fall like the one you took? Ishmael's head is going to roll right alongside yours, real quick. It's gonna be a bloodbath for us."

"I know."

"You better be goddamned careful what you do."

I nodded. "Johnny, I got to ask you something."

"Then ask it, man."

"What *do* I do? You were me, what would *you* do? Can I trust Wade with this?"

He looked at the tabletop for a long moment: yellow Formica with brown flecks and plenty of scratches from the flatware, old circular stains from warming beer glasses stacked up onto each other; cigarette burns; dings.

"I don't think you can say anything. Until

you know for sure, you know it all, and you know you can prove it. Until then, I think it's your solemn duty to keep your mouth shut. It's also what's best for you. What if you're wrong?"

I nodded and watched the clock hand move for exactly twenty-three seconds.

"Thanks."

"Can you get him, through the Net?"

"I'm trying. I'd love to lure him out, but he's real shy."

"What about the other way?"

"Vinson? You know where he stands on helping us."

He patted my hand, then gently slapped my face. "Know something, boss?"

"You'll have to tell me."

"I don't ever want to be you. I want to be a regular guy with no big problems, raise a family, do thirty with the Sheriffs and retire up in Havasu. Fish all day, maybe get a boat. Speed over to Laughlin once a week to gamble and drink. Teach a grandson how to play blackjack, kick a football. Doesn't that sound better than being you?"

"Quite a goddamned bit!"

He slapped my shoulder on his way out.

Vinson Clay is a lean, tanned, curly-haired man, quick to smile, slow to act. He's like a dam, all roaring activity on one side, while behind him piles up a large tonnage of silent power. He was with the Sheriffs for twenty years, and all that time we wondered if he was slow or just congenial and content. When he left us five years ago to attend law school we began to see the arc of his ambition, and when he signed on with PlaNet legal department as corporate security director — for a rumored salary of $200,000 — we sort of gulped and rewrote our opinions of him. At the Sheriffs he'd worked computer crime and PR, so our paths didn't directly cross all that much. I remembered him as cheerful but kind of remote, too, never the type to fraternize after work or drink with the other deputies. You got his hours and you got his easy good humor, then he was gone, vanished to a home life that no one knew about, and to a career path that no one was aware of. You had to respect him.

It wasn't easy to get my call through that afternoon. I had to plead with his secretary just to get him on the line, and when I finally did I begged even harder for twenty minutes of his time. I felt like Moe. But it worked.

"I surmise this has to do with you and the charges against you," he said.

"Vinson," I said, "it's got to do with The Horridus."

"And I'm talking to you as a deputy or a citizen?"

"Just a citizen."

"Twenty minutes is about all I've got, Terry."

The PlaNet offices were located on a shady Pasadena street, halfway between downtown and the Jet Propulsion Lab. Pasadena is where the money used to live, back when Los Angeles was a young town. The building was on the outskirts of a neighborhood of tree-shaded, million-dollar homes. I was ten minutes early. His secretary escorted me in ten minutes late. Vinson and I shook hands and sat across from each other, with his prodigious curving acrylic desk between us like some kind of crystal clear river.

He was still all smiles, his crooked teeth giving him a hick, friendly look. But Vinson's suit was of the two-thousand-dollar variety and his nails were either professionally manicured or he spent more time on them than any man I know. I started out by asking how he liked L.A., and he said the best thing was the Dodgers being close by. "I catch all the home games I can," he said with a smile. "Well, Terry, how are you holding up?"

"I've been framed. Framed by someone very good at manipulating images. The FBI has the alleged evidence against me, and I'm certain they'll find out that it was created."

His grin was half there now, like something he'd forgotten to close all the way.

"This is the deal, Vinson: I think it was an inside job — inside the Sheriffs, I mean. I've been using the Net to talk with the pedophiles and pornographers. That's my area anyway,

435

and I've made good progress. I've got the guy who either procured those pictures of me, or maybe even produced them. He goes by I. R. Shroud in the Fawnskin chat room."

"That's just a handle, right, not his user name?"

"He wouldn't be dumb enough to put his user name or his e-mail address out there."

"So, you're buying from this guy?"

I nodded.

"You said something about The Horridus."

"The Horridus is I. R. Shroud. It's an anagram."

He ran a hand through his curly golden hair and stared down.

"Is this a joke?"

"Definitely not. The FBI profile says The Horridus will be a networker, a porn collector. Why not a supplier, too? There's money in it. Thrills."

"What browser are you using to talk to him?"

I told him.

He nodded and looked down at the paper again. "Is he talking business?"

"Not yet. I hope he will be, and soon."

"No monitor interruptions from us?"

"Not one. I've been lurking these guys for a year and a half, Vinson."

Monitoring computer conversations, of course, is the way the software industry tries to keep crime off the Web. They always talk a hard game about listening in on transactions, making sure no one is breaking the law. The trouble is, talking about anything is basically legal — short of conspiring to commit a crime — and talking about sex is legal, too. There's a fine line between talking about sex and conducting business around sex, and the pervs have come up with their own language to sound less suspicious. Guys like Vinson — and me — are always a step behind them. And guys like Vinson don't want their networks to get reputations as being insecure or risky in any way. They say it's a matter of First Amendment rights, and it partially is. But the bottom line in business is business, and no Net supplier wants to be known as the one with the big ears. So, tough monitoring is bad for business. Vinson knew this, and so did I.

"Have you completed a business transaction with him, using PlaNet?"

"No."

"You haven't exchanged any kind of payment or goods for any product or service, as of this date?"

"Not yet."

He looked at me now, his smile gone, his suit throwing off a swank reflection of the recessed lights above the desk. "I can shut him down, Terry. I can shut down anybody I want to."

"That would kill me, Vinson. I need him

working. I need *him*."

"Then you're in a peck of trouble."

"I know. If you shut him down, I might not ever hear from him again. You have to remember, he's not just making dirty pictures of guys like me. He's abducting children and doing things unimaginable to them. Let me give you an example. This hasn't gone outside my department, Vinson, so it's just your ears, all right?"

The way to win a confidence is to offer one. So I told him about Mary Lou Kidder in Wichita Falls, Texas, and what The Horridus had done to her. I speculated that before she died, young Mary Lou was probably subjected to a massive sexual assault. I took pains to describe the pile of reptile feces in which I found the skull of a once vibrant, much loved and beautiful little human girl.

"What if Shroud is punning on Horridus? Different guys all along?"

"Shroud called himself that before Horridus was even known. They're the same man, Vinson. If I doubted that, I wouldn't be here. I know you've got everybody's constitutional rights to protect here, and I don't mean to demean that. But you've got a monster loose on your Net, and I'm asking you to give him to me."

Vinson sat back and crossed his hands on his lap. I could see them under the acrylic table, clear as trout in a mountain stream.

"You are an accused sexual predator, Terry."

"I need Shroud, Vinson."

He nodded and continued to look at me.

I did my best to close him: "Look, Vinson. I know the drill here. You take the information to the law department, you balance the risks and the gains, you go to committee. It takes time. Maybe you land on a user, maybe you don't. I'm asking you to go off road with this one. Give him to me. You don't talk to the law department. You don't talk to the sheriff. You don't talk to law enforcement. You just listen in when I tell you we're going to be on, and you trace his number in your user directory. You give me his name and address and I'm never heard from again. You pop an animal and I get my record cleared up. It's just us and it's right."

He waved in irritation and sat forward.

"I'll think about it."

I ignored my obvious cue to get up and leave. I looked across the clear sweeping desk to him. "Let me just say one more thing, Vinson. I'd still be sitting here talking to you if none of this had happened to me. It's not about me. It's not about the Constitution. It's about The Horridus."

"You make a good case, Counselor."

It was pure Vinson Clay — friendly and vague, affirming and noncommittal. The crooked smile was back as he stood to offer his manicured hand across the desk.

I rose and shook it and walked out. And I knew I'd never hear from him.

Twenty-four

On my way home I stopped by the first four female-owned homes that were listed for sale on the MLS. Time is cheap to the unemployed. More than that, though, it was either follow through or desperation — take your pick. The Nicols residence in Anaheim, not far from the stadium, had closed escrow two weeks earlier and the old owner gone to Hawaii. The Parlett home in the Fullerton hills was a horse property owned by an elderly woman who lived alone — no tenants in the guest cottage down by the stable. She looked at me with gray lonely eyes as we talked. The Haun residence in Orange had a for sale sign and a lock box on the front door. The sheet told me it was built in 1976, with a nonconforming "second unit" bootlegged in the back in 1980. It was in a decent neighborhood, one of those streets with lots of nice flat lawns but not a lot of trees. The block felt kind of open and exposed. The fact that the home was empty would have deterred some investigators, but I slipped into the backyard and approached the second unit for a first-hand look. It was locked, too. I peered through a side window at the hardwood floors, the freshly painted walls, the little kitchen with chipper pink tile around a white sink.

Next was Tustin, roughly on the way to my place in the metro district. Collette Loach's house had been listed for $225,000. It was a three bedroom with a detached guest unit and "mature landscaping." It was built in 1948 and it was small — 1,300 square feet for the main and another 600 for the guest house. I vaguely remembered the street — Wytton — for two reasons. First, I had played in the nearby Tustin Tiller gymnasium just a few blocks away as a guard on the Laguna freshman basketball team (Darien Aftergood was on that team, and it was one of the few games we won that year, I believe). Second, I'd once arrested a terrified kid who had played a Fourth of July prank on his best friend and set three Wytton Street houses on fire with a smoke bomb. It was a nice old block, not far from the high school, small on crime and big on quiet.

The house was hidden by old sycamore trees that cast the roof in shade, and by a rock wall that came out almost to the sidewalk. The wall was six feet high. It was one of several houses on the street with walls, and they all looked just a little funny sitting there amid the frank and unguarded others, saying, it seemed: stay out, stay clear, stay away. There was a wrought-iron gate across the driveway opening in the wall, and a buzzer box was fastened to the stones beside it. Under the box was the mail slot.

I got out and went up to the buzzer and pressed it. I have no idea where or if it rang. There was no movement from the house. So I walked along the wall, turned and followed it back until I was stopped by the next-door neighbor's grapestake fence. It was cool in the shade there and when I looked up through the canopy of fresh May sycamore all I saw of the lowering sun were slivers slanting in from the west.

I backtracked around to the front and tried the other side. There was a very narrow pathway between the neighbor's rose garden and the rock wall. The rose garden was the most lovingly tended patch of dirt I'd ever seen, weedless and rich brown, with dark green bushes heaving scores of color-drenched flowers into the air. An old man stood in the middle of the garden looking at me. He had baggy tan trousers and a green cardigan sweater and a pair of clippers in one hand. His face and head were brilliantly pale, almost blue white.

I said good afternoon and he nodded.

"I'm interested in the house," I said, only then realizing there was no for sale sign in the yard.

The old man's voice was faint. "I lost three Mr. Lincolns last week. Lost two Snowfires, two Deep Purples and a Blue Girl. Did you take them?"

"No, sir. I'm not a thief."

"How do you do?"

"Fine, thank you."

"You could be one," he said, but his voice was full of deliberation, not accusation. "Peg can tell a thief from a pilot."

I shrugged and smiled stupidly. "Have you seen Collette recently? Ms. Loach, the owner?"

"I can't really see you."

"She lives here, I think. She listed the house for sale, but I didn't see a sign."

"Pangloss. My wife said I'm a Pangloss. She died."

"I'm sorry."

"Her sons live there. Two of them. Nice young men — a minister and a salesman."

"Do you mean Mrs. Loach's sons?"

"Yes. Here, take this. The body of Christ."

He held out a brilliant white rose with eight inches of stem. I took it and thanked him.

I looked at the wall beside me. Over the top I could see the roof of the house, and the dense sycamore. A power pole stood just behind the trees and you could see where the line curved upward to the pole top and where the utility company had trimmed the foliage back for safety.

"What are the sons' names?"

"I don't know."

"Can you describe them to me?"

"I don't see them often. I only see up close. They look like sons to me."

"Maybe I'll just knock on the door," I said.

"Thank you," he said.

I went around to the front and tried the gate. Locked. So I walked around to the other side and climbed over the wall.

The house was wood, stained dark brown. The trim was white. The front yard was grass, healthy and trimmed along the cement drive that led to the garage. No flowers, hedges or shrubs. There was a long porch running along the front. No patio furniture. No flower pots. No birdbath or naked cherub or St. Francis or painted deer. A busy guy's place, I thought: neat, efficient, low maintenance. Two guys, like the old man said? There were two windows facing the front, both with blinds drawn shut tight. I knocked on the door and nothing happened. I waited and knocked again. Then I went around to the guest quarters behind. It looked closed up to me. The porch was littered with leaves and the windows were blocked off by thick curtains I couldn't see through or around. I tried some windows on the side of the little cottage, but couldn't see inside so much as an inch. The garage was connected: door locked, window blinds down.

I talked to three more neighbors but gathered little. Suburbs can be the most private places on earth, which is why places like Orange County can harbor some of the worst people in the world. Like Chet. Like The Horridus. One of the neighbors said he thought two young men lived there; the others said it was just one. They all agreed that the occupant(s) came and went in a white Saturn four-door.

Looking back at the place in the rearview I was reminded of the Grantley place in Hopkin. But then, I wanted to be.

On my way home I called the listing agent for the Loach house, to find out anything I could about Collette and the property. What I found out was that the owner had retracted the listing just after the MLS sheet went to print. My spirits sank and I cursed my luck. Then they began to rise. What would be a better reflection of an unstable, changing character than listing and unlisting a home in less than one week? The agent told me that Collette Loach had personal reasons for changing her mind. I asked for her phone number, but the agent said she was under strict orders from Loach not to give it out to anyone — a common practice for busy, private individuals, she informed me. All inquiries were to be handled by the realtor. I begged, pleaded and got nowhere with her. I toyed with the idea of telling her that I was not really an interested buyer, but worried that she might have read the papers or seen the news.

I toyed with the idea of impersonating another deputy, say, Johnny Escobedo, but I remembered the look of warning on his face at the café. Plus, believe it or not, I know the difference between a moral act and an immoral one, not that I haven't in my life chosen the latter. But I did call a friend of mine at the phone company in L.A. He was kind enough to check their statewide for me, only to confirm what I had feared: no Collette Loach with a telephone number in California.

Halfway home it was my turn to get a call. Will Fortune from Idaho, with an edge to his voice.

"Good news, bad news, and maybe news," he said.

"Bad first."

"The photographs were partially made by your old Yashica."

My heart fell and my mouth went dry as sand.

"The good news is, I don't think the final images were taken *exclusively* from photographs at all. They're mainly digitized composites done by someone with a lot of patience, a lot of skill and some pretty good materials to start with — pictures of you and pictures of the girl and pictures of that cave. Our artist shot the final digitized images with a film recorder, thus a photograph. But he was careless. The edge marks from the original photos of the cave — taken with your camera — were still on the negs, just inside the edge marks the film recorder left. It's a slick piece of work, but he was off by fractions of a millimeter. That fraction was big enough for me to drive a truck through."

"If the photographs came from my camera, I'm sunk."

"No. The final image was *made up* from photographs taken with your camera and photographs that may not have been. It's image manipulation, pure and simple, and I will testify to that. But it gets better . . . maybe."

"Give me the maybe better."

"The shadow analysis worked beautifully. Those cave shots were taken on January the eleventh of this year. That was a Friday. If you can put yourself somewhere else, it means someone else took them. If someone else took them, you've been set up. I'll testify to that, too. The DA can argue with me all he wants, but he can't argue with the sun."

It's such a strange feeling, to have your heart shooting around inside your body like a balloon with the air escaping.

"You'll be the first to know."

"I'd reserve that privilege for Loren if I were you. Good luck."

Few dates stay in the memory that long, unless they're special. January the eleventh was all of that: I was with Donna. Newport Marriott Hotel, room 317. Our third time consummating the powerful desire that had

448

grown since those first moments alone to-gether in a county elevator two months before. I'd told Ishmael I was leaving the office, claim-ing an interview with a suspected child mo-lester, up in Anaheim. It seemed like a small thing at the time: so little risked and so much gained. I did the actual interview the next Monday and dated the notes three days earlier. The suspected child molester was the man who became our turncoat, Professor Christo-pher Muhlberger, aka Danny, who blew out his brains in despair by the pool in Chet Al-ton's rented Orange house.

It was an easy date to remember, too, be-cause it was my fortieth birthday, and Melinda and Penny had awakened me that morning with a cake bearing a single candle that, when you lit it, whistled "Happy Birthday" over and over, until you blew it out.

Danny wouldn't be contesting our interview time and date, though Danny's calendar might. University professors keep pretty tight schedules, but he wouldn't have stated his true reason for being away from his professional duties — ratting out friends so he'd get a lesser sex-with-minors pop — would he?

Ishmael might not "remember" my leaving at all. Why should he?

If need be, I could call Donna Mason to the stand and humiliate her in front of each and every one of her CNB viewers. And she could tell the truth about Terry Naughton, champion of the little people, where he was and what he was really doing that day. Maybe if I gave her the white rose sitting on the seat beside me, she'd be willing. Here, take this.

Twenty-five

By late evening I was back in my apartment, with the windows open and the TV turned to CNB. What a program lineup that night: Sheriff Department press conference on The Horridus, followed by an exclusive interview with accused child molester Terry Naughton. Must-see TV.

I checked my e-mail again: no word from I. R. Shroud. I was almost certain he'd blown me off. Cautious. Scared. The acid test was tonight, though: what would he do if he saw me — as I had to assume he would — plastered all over CNB, or one of their sister stations around the country, or in any of thousands of newspapers the next day? Would he think Mal was a profoundly disturbed cop who had ordered up customs of himself for his personal needs? Would he assume the pictures he sold were used against me, or would he assume there was more evidence than just those? Might he speculate that Naughton had been framed by Mal? Worst of all, would he wonder if Mal's fall was all part of some elaborate covert plan to locate him, The Horridus?

How should I play it? That was the only

question I really had an answer to.

I listened to a long message from Donna, who sounded exhausted. She said she'd gotten some dramatic film for the Texas connection story; Welborn was a great guy; the sight of Mary Lou Kidder's skull had made her cry on camera and she'd never once done that in her life. She said Gene was a monster, and her guts told her that he was our guy. She said she hoped the interview this evening would help somehow. She said she loved me and she'd be home late, but she'd be home. She left her number at the Holiday Inn, but told me she'd only go back there to shower, pack and head out.

I called Johnny, Louis and Frances and explained to each that there was a house on Wytton Street in Tustin that needed checking out. Johnny said a house listed by a woman — then *un*listed — was not a priority in any way he could see. I told him to lean on the listing agent for Loach's phone number, but I could tell he wasn't going to put it on the fast track. I could tell he was barely hearing this new request, because he was still burdened by my last one. I'd overstepped the bounds of friendship with him, and I knew it. Louis treated me like a senile relative. Frances hung up.

I got an idea and called Sam Welborn in Wichita Falls. He had gone home already, but I talked to a desk sergeant. I told him I was working a case with Welborn and needed the married names, addresses and phone numbers of Wanda Grantley's sisters and daughters. He said he couldn't help me just this second. He said every reporter in the state of Texas needed something about the guy out in Hopkin that fed Mary Lou Kidder to his python. I asked him how he knew it was a python and he said a big snake's a big snake. "Everybody's got their knickers in a twist," he said slowly. He took down the information, said he'd give it to Welborn, and that was that.

Half an hour later the press conference started, featuring Jim Wade and Jordan Ishmael, with supporting roles for Frances and Louis. Wade went on first, covering the basics of the search for The Horridus, the department's frustrations, the almost celestial good fortune for everyone that this "cunning monster" had chosen to "torment" his young victims rather than commit even "greater evil" upon them. He was matter-of-fact, as Jim Wade always was. He was credible because he was calm. He'd done conferences like this a hundred times, and he knew his lines. He was also old and tired. Tired enough to have been fooled by one of his own underlings. I could tell from the expression and posture of Ishmael, sitting to Wade's right, that he believed he had been chosen. Ish now considered himself the elect. I was certain, too, that he'd be the insiders' candidate to become the next sheriff-coroner of Orange County.

Yes, there he was, Ishmael, large and feline and relaxed and anointed. When he took the podium to say his piece, I couldn't help but admit what a presence he had on camera, the way his handsome, green-eyed face so easily commanded: *trust me, obey me, join me.* He had the allure of a star, the ego of a celebrity and the charisma of a politician. I felt small and venal compared to him. One thing about the Irish, though: we never quit. I pictured Jordan Ishmael going through the photo albums in Ardith's study. I pictured him surfing through the porn network, searching out a supplier, a purveyor, and finally, a creator. Landing on I. R. Shroud. Question: did Ish know who he was dealing with? I didn't want to believe it. In spite of my disgust for him, I didn't want to believe a cop would knowingly use The Horridus to frame up another cop. I would have to ruin him, however. I wouldn't rest until I ruined him. I knew it, and Ishmael must have known it, too. I needed a record of his log-ons and IRC receptors — his real-time chat destinations. I needed Johnny to come through.

I wondered if there was another way to get what I needed: might Melinda be willing to help me?

What a joke, I thought.

What a sad, bad joke. So funny I'd laughed out loud about it in the café with Johnny.

Maybe it was my growing sense of urgency that made it seem at least possible.

"Lieutenant Jordan Ishmael," he intoned on-screen, "Sheriff-Coroner Department, Orange County. We've had a break in our investigation of a suspect calling himself The Horridus. As you just heard from Sheriff Wade, he is wanted for the abduction of three juvenile females in the last two months. We believe that he is partaking in what we call an escalating fantasy and that he will graduate to more serious acts that could logically end in homicide. We are prepared to do anything within our power to see that this does not occur. We understand the fears and anxieties in our communities. We are part of those communities and we share these concerns. This man is preying on young children. Our children are our most precious members, and our future. This is why, beginning two years ago, the Orange County Sheriff Department created a new Crimes Against Youth unit, dedicated to protecting our minors. Some of our best people joined that unit. Since the first Horridus abduction, CAY has been dedicated to apprehending this individual. CAY has been joined by other personnel from other sections of the force. As head of the unit, I can assure you that we are doing everything we can to find this monster and bring him to justice."

Ishmael turned away from the camera and took a sip of water.

Some of our best people. Head of the unit.
He'd even taken my job.

I felt that kind of blind anger you can't do anything about. At least nothing immediately. I had to sit there, along with two and a half million other countyans, and take it on the chin from Ishmael, head of CAY, by his own admission one of the department's best and brightest crimebusters.

"Now, modern law enforcement has two methods of apprehending suspects. The traditional method is to gather evidence, locate the subject and proceed to interview and perhaps arrest. The other method, which has been gaining favor lately in more sophisticated departments, is one of proaction. In proaction, you take steps that will increase your chances of finding a suspect *before* he commits another crime. Proaction can be seen as a drawing out of the suspect. Neighborhood policing, neighborhood watch, fugitive publicity and even the holding of press conferences such as this, can all be parts of an effective, proactive campaign. To this end, we now present a composite drawing of the unidentified white male subject who calls himself The Horridus. Louis?"

Condescending prick, I thought.

The screen filled with a poster enlargement of Amanda Aguilar's drawing. It looked much more human than the photocopy I had smuggled out of my work station, because I was seeing it in color for the first time. The Horridus looked back at me, with his slender face and tall forehead, his short white hair up like the bristles of a brush, his unrevealing eyes, his thin, unhappy mouth. He didn't look evil. He didn't even look suspicious. He looked "above average," whatever that is — intelligent, kempt, unthreatening. Which is one of the reasons he had been able to do what he had done.

I could hear Ishmael's voice-over: ". . . white male, late twenties to early thirties, average height and weight, slender build. Brown eyes. Clean shaven. The suspect was last seen wearing a dark blue sport coat and tan trousers. The suspect drives a late model white van. The suspect has a pronounced case of halitosis. We should also add that the subject has been known to wear facial hair at times, and to change the appearance and style of his hair. *If you see someone who answers this description we want you to call the dedicated Sheriff-CAY-Horridus number, one-eight hundred, six-four-seven-S-A-V-E. We ask you not to use nine-one-one. Now, in conjunction with the release of this drawing, we . . .*"

Ishmael went on to describe the new billboards that were being set up along Interstate 5, the 405, the 91, the 57 and on eight heavy-use surface streets in the county. He said the Sheriff Department number would be visible on each, just beneath the drawing.

Ishmael, I thought. Ishmael, who knew I left

the office on January 11, the day the cave pictures were shot. But did you leave, too?

With a tight, desperate flutter in my chest I picked up the phone and dialed Melinda at her office. I was surprised, almost chagrined, that she picked up.

"How are you, Mel?"

"Oh, Terry. A little pissed off, I guess."

"At me." Not a question.

"Yes."

"How's Penny?"

"Ditto the above."

There was a silence.

"How come you're not at the conference?"

"I've got work to do."

"He took my job."

"That's got to be the least of your troubles."

"It ranks a lot higher than you might know."

"What do you want, Terry?"

"I want the IRC log-on records for Ishmael's computer, and his phone-out sheet. I need to know who he's networked with, and who he's talked to. And I want to know if he left the building on January eleventh, and for how long."

She was quiet for a moment. "Ridiculous."

"I need that stuff worse than I can tell you."

She hesitated again. "Why?"

"I think he set me up."

"Oh, *Terry*."

"Melinda, have you networked with I. R. Shroud?"

"No."

"Are you absolutely certain?"

"Yes. Absolutely."

"Is that name in your network file? It would have come in through CAY. He's a pedophile."

"That's your world."

I caught the condemning irony in her voice.

"I didn't mean it that way," she said quickly.

"All right. But you're copied every time we open a link. And you review the log-on printouts every month. You know that."

"Okay, I'll look. But I'll tell you what the answer is."

More silence, then she was back.

"No. I told you."

"Melinda, do you have a pencil and paper handy? Good. Now write out the initials and name, I. R. Shroud."

She sighed, but I could hear her shuffling, and the distant crack of a sheet of paper.

"So what?"

"See what else those letters spell."

More time went by. I could hear her breathing.

"I'm no good at games like this."

"It spells Horridus."

One of those loaded hushes.

"Oh. Jesus Christ — it does."

"I need to know who's been networking with him."

"But . . . how do you know *anyone* has?"

"It's a hunch. The Horridus gave Shroud's

name to Stefanic on the citation, before he killed him."

"I never heard about a citation."

"You won't. I found it in the ladies' room out at Caspers. I've been . . . well, staying busy."

A brief second while Mel processed.

"But what's it prove?"

"Nothing, goddamnit, until you check Ish's log-ons."

"Terry."

"Look, Melinda, you think I did that stuff with the girls? Come on now, you know me better than just about anyone. You've seen me through the booze and the hate and the coming back out. You helped me get both feet on the ground, and you've seen my worst, woman — I know it, and so do you. So is that what you're saying? That you spent a year of your life living with a child molester? That you left your only daughter alone with me a million —"

"— I don't believe that. I never said I did. And that isn't what this is about."

"This is about the rest of my life. So put your money where your mouth is, Mel. Get Ishmael's log-ons and IRC parties. See if I. R. Shroud is on them. *He's in the conference, so do it now. The master logs are in that binder right on his desk. He sees everybody else's, so why can't you look at his?*"

"You're out of your mind, Terry."

"Go see, Mel. It will take you five minutes. All the heavies are at the courthouse. You're the computer crime expert — so go see who Jordan's computer has been talking to. It's your *job*, Melinda."

"I'll call you back."

I gave her the number.

"Where are you?"

"It doesn't matter. Do the right thing, Melinda. If I'm wrong, you haven't hurt a soul."

"Except mine."

Ten minutes later she called.

"Shroud is one of his log-ons. I. R. Shroud."

"When?"

"There are, well . . . thirty-two of them over the last sixty days. I went back two months."

I smiled a bitter inward smile.

"But you know, Terry, it still doesn't prove anything."

"It proves he talked to The Horridus, for God's sake."

"No, Terry. That's one of the rules we live by in Computer Crime. All it means is that *somebody* used that machine."

"Okay, it was Jim Wade, then. It was one of the late-night janitors. It was Elvis."

"Be careful what you infer, Terry."

"It was Jordan, Mel. What more is there to say? He used the pedophile network to get a job done. The job was to make those pictures of me. I'm due in court to defend myself on sixteen counts of sex with children, and he's out running my unit, acting like he can catch The Horridus."

Silence. I loved every revealing, damning second of it. I knew that Melinda could only embrace the good and detest the wicked. It's her character. She's always on the side of right. She knows no grays. That is the binary nature of her mind, and it is one of the things that drew me to her in the beginning. It was what made her a good woman and an excellent cop. It also made her a difficult, judgmental person to live with, for anyone less than perfect. And that's why I called on her.

"I checked the sign-out sheet for January eleventh. He was meeting with Ingardia in the afternoon."

I thought about that, wondering if Dom Ingardia's secretary would say the same thing.

"I've got to go," she said. It was almost a whisper.

"Thank you."

"We need to talk, Terry. Soon, face to face and for real."

"Name the time and place."

She did, and I wrote them down. Then she hung up.

You haven't fully lived until you've watched yourself on the TV news, denying that you are a sexual predator of children. I sat there with my mouth open, watching this cop firmly proclaiming his innocence. He gave it his all. And

I couldn't help but note that the interviewer was not hostile; she seemed evenhanded, truth seeking, unprejudiced.

She did, however, heavily edit what I had said to her that evening. My bumbling and self-mystification were gone. The bizarre last third of the interview while the camera showed only ceiling was gone. She deleted my attack from the stool. There was nothing of my confession to "recognizing" the girl in the pictures with me but not being able to remember from where or when. Likewise, my confession to "recognizing" myself but not remembering from where or when was blessedly dropped. Donna also edited out the passage about Ardith's pictures of my son and me. All in all, Donna Mason had edited in my favor. And her intro and close were subtly, reassuringly, pro Terry. I wondered if her producers at CNB ever got to see the original, and realized that they hadn't.

It was late that night when I. R. Shroud finally responded to my postings. His message came in sometime between 8:45 and 11:30 P.M.

Hello, Mal. We have much to talk about. I. R. Shroud. Meet at Midnight Ramblers and we'll go from there.

A few minutes later I was on with him, chatting live in the privacy of the Ramblers' room. He cut straight to the chase.

I. R. Shroud: Quite an interview tonight. RU TN of CNB fame?

I took the plunge.

Mal: I am he.
Lancer: You are who?
I. R. Shroud: Lancer, be gone. I'll cut you off and cut your throat. Out, out damned snot. All of you or you'll never see Shroud's treasures again. Be gone!
Mal: Thank you for the wrap.
I. R. Shroud: Cop with needs or cop framed as claimed?
Mal: Mal's needs predate Mal's work.
I. R. Shroud: How did product land you in predicament?
Mal: Betrayed by a kiss. Domestic partner. Product is my only consolation on these cold, revealed nights. That is why more requested.
I. R. Shroud: Why ingest more of what has poisoned you?
Mal: The need no man dares speak.

There was a long wait then, while Shroud considered.

I. R. Shroud: What do you want, brother Mal, brother-in-charms?
Mal: Must go to live feed. Your match is my fantasy.
I. R. Shroud: Going live! You would leave my

purview — perv-view — my pay-per-view.

As mentioned, "going live" or "going to live feed" is parlance for finding the object of desire. It's the term for dealing directly with the porn star, the video stripper, the centerfold, the model. It means that you are not just a pedophile — which is a person whose sexual preference is for children, but a molester, or potential molester — a person who *acts* on that preference. It means going from the image to the real human, from fantasy to reality. It is much joked about because few deviants have the resources and courage to take this step — and it is seldom done. It represents a graduation of sorts, an escalation from the ranks of the lookers and collectors and masturbators to the company of the peepers, the johns, the buyers of flesh, the stalkers and, occasionally, the rapists and the killers.

I wanted to go live because I needed the girl in the picture. I needed her to tell the truth about what didn't happen.

Mal: Such is the power of your work, Shroud. Dream girl to real girl. I stand humbled and desiring.

I. R. Shroud: Rule One of the Live Feed: Flesh disappoints.

Mal: Rule of Mal: better disappointed than eternally un-cum.

I. R. Shroud: Flesh is risk; image is answer.

Mal: But image has inflamed. Only flesh will immolate. You have my humble request. Make real the angel you pictured with me.

I. R. Shroud: Shroud needs to consider. Mal needs to consider considerable expense. Mal must now be considered by most an unreasonable risk.

Mal: But consider Mal's record to date. A more forthright partner none could find. Test Mal. He will be found neither tightfisted nor wanting.

I. R. Shroud: What if he wants the item to disprove the image?

Mal: Experts will exonerate. Image damage is done in public eyes. Reality of dream is all that can move me now. I inhabit the lower depths.

I. R. Shroud: Back in ten.

I knew that the odds of Shroud coming back on-line were small indeed. Yes, he was arrogant. Yes, he felt secure in the ether of his computer. Yes, he wanted my money along with my soul. But he had gotten his whiff of Terry the cop, and he was going to play it safe. I looked at the blank screen.

Then, to my genuine surprise, he was there.

I. R. Shroud: Mission feasible. Object obtainable. Must vet you closely now, Mal. Reasonable and customary fee is ten. You will be asked to perform. Problems?

This was a very real ten thousand dollars that was being asked of me. And after I gave it up, there was no guarantee The Horridus would deliver the girl, no recourse if he failed.

Mal: Punishingly extravagant.
I. R. Shroud: Worth every penny?
Mal: Will need time to gather.
I. R. Shroud: Follow, then this simple formula: Walk the serpent field, Moulton at Laguna Hills Road, 10 A.M. tomorrow. Hug the water. Be in possession of half. Rep. will instruct.
Mal: Five, then, for faith and action?
I. R. Shroud: Correct.
Mal: Thank you, thank you, thank you.
I. R. Shroud: Down, Mal. Talk 2 P.M., PST. Start at Fawnskin to find new room. Will need balance shortly after. And out.

Shroud vaporized. I lurked for a while, listening in, while the deviants whispered about their needs. No gossip about Mal and Shroud. They had heeded his warning, or were at least not talking about us.

Now that I had The Horridus talking again, I needed a way to catch him in the act. Any act would do. Crossing a street would be just fine. Vinson Clay could do it. And maybe, with luck, so could I.

I made careful note of the hour and minute my conversation with I. R. Shroud began, and when it ended. I put it in my little blue notebook, right below the other live chats we'd had.

★ ★ ★

Donna stole into the apartment just before
1 A.M. I heard her key in the lock, then the
vibrations of her feet on the carpet, then the
sharper report of shoes on the parquet wood
of the kitchen. I walked into the darkened
living room. Moving in the half light of the
open refrigerator she looked half real, half
there. She poured herself a glass of wine, put
the bottle back, then turned to look at me.

"How are you?" I asked.

"Terry," she said. She came over and leaned
her face against my chest. "I feel like I've been
in bed with the devil himself. I've never, *ever*
felt what I felt today, when I stood in that little
guest house and smelled that smell. And later,
when Sam showed me her . . . Mary Lou's
. . . *head*."

"A long shower might wash him off you."

"A long shower with bleach and a wire
brush. Two gallons of wine and ten years of
sleep. And I'd still wake up with the smell of
the devil in my pores."

"I talked to him tonight. The Horridus. On
the Web."

"Is he going to procure for you?"

"Yeah."

"The girl?"

"That's the deal."

"Can you get him?"

"I will get him."

"How?"

"I'll see the first link of his chain tomorrow when I make a downpayment. In some field down in the south county. One link leads to the next."

Donna sipped her wine but she didn't let go of me. Her back felt tight to my hand, and the hand she held around my back was filled with the wadded material of my shirt. Her hair covered her face from me, but I was sure she was looking out the window toward the bean field and the freeways.

"I don't like the ugliness of all this. Children and monsters. Pictures and snakes. It makes me feel unclean and far from any God I ever knew."

"It does me, too."

"Will Melinda help you?"

"Why do you ask that?"

"Because she's the expert on the computers, isn't she?"

I thought about her question for a while. "I'm on my own there, except for Johnny, and what I can squeeze out of Vinson Clay. Mel might help. I mean, she'll always do the right thing, because that's Mel. But she's not going to do much for me. I kind of ruined her life, more or less. Humiliated her."

Donna broke away from me and stood back. "Does she know about us?"

"I meant, the pictures humiliated her."

"But I meant, does she know about *us?*"

"No."

"How sure are you of that?"

"I've told you a million times, Donna — she doesn't know. And at this point, what would it matter?"

"Things like this always matter."

"She never knew. She doesn't now."

Donna looked at me in the near dark.

"Well, Jordan Ishmael does."

I waited, a cold wave of nerves breaking over my scalp.

"We talked. *He* talked, mainly."

"Explain."

"Said he wanted to confirm his suspicions about us. Said he was acting on a tip. And, thus confirmed, he wanted to know . . . if . . . I needed help."

"It was a bluff and a come-on. He doesn't know anything about us."

"Well, when he said that, he was standing about where you are now. He knocked. He identified himself. I'll give him that. It was my fault, Terry. I'd come over from Tonello's. He just followed. Or maybe he did get a tip — I don't know. I denied you even knew about this place, but it didn't help much. Not with two mugs on the counter, and that bottle of tequila, and your Sheriffs windbreaker over the chair."

My skin rose up and crawled. "When?"

"Three days ago. You were still in jail."

"Arrested by Ishmael."

She said nothing.

"Why didn't you tell me sooner?"

"It didn't make sense to. I thought you might . . . do something you'd regret."

"So, what did you tell him?"

"That you were a good man and that someone was framing you. And if he wanted to help me, he could do it by helping you. And if he saw fit to speak of our arrangement I'd burn his ass on the news, sooner or later."

I couldn't speak just then. All I could do is feel the blood pounding against my eardrums, a rush that felt like a river.

"He offered to show me the pictures of you and the girl. Girls. If I had any doubt."

"Did you take him up on it?"

"Of course I did. I'm a reporter. They're you, Terry. I know you didn't do what they show you doing, but they're you. They're good."

"But what did he *want*?"

Donna sighed, then turned to face me. I could see the small light reflected by her eyes. "Terry, I honestly believe all he really wanted was to help me. His concern seemed genuine. And he wanted to rattle your cage, too. One accomplishes the other, doesn't it?"

"*Help* you? Did he *touch* you?"

"No, he did not. And if I were you, I'd derail that train of thought before it made a real fool out of myself."

I will admit I felt nothing that moment except the desire to pound Ishmael senseless with my bare hands or, even better, an ax handle, hammer, gun butt, Mag-Lite, irrigation pipe, tire iron, Louisville Slugger . . .

"I know what you're thinking, Terry. And that's exactly why I didn't tell you the day it happened. But God knows, I couldn't wait forever."

There was a long silence while we faced each other in the dark. I could see the distant freeways past Donna's shoulder and the little gleam coming from her eyes.

"Look, it's late," she said. "Take your woman to the shower now, will ya? Suds her up and smooth her over. She's beat up by the world as we know it, and she could use your arms. Can't let some jealous lieutenant ruin your whole day. What do you say, crime buster?"

"All right, Donna. Okay."

She stayed in the shower for almost an hour. When she came out she was in her robe. Her hair was damp and combed straight back and she was clean and fragrant. But I'd never seen her look so tired. So small. Still, I had to know her answer, and that meant I had to ask.

"Would you be willing to testify in court for me?"

She looked startled, then suspicious, then, quite simply, exhausted. "Testify to what?"

"Being with me at the hotel, January eleventh."

She walked up to me and looked hard into

my eyes. She leaned against me.

"Yes," she said.

"I don't think it will come to that."

"But let me tell you just one thing, dear man — someday you're going to have to give back as much as you take."

She walked into the bedroom.

I nodded, not really understanding, but wanting to. I sat up for a while thinking about what she had said. Oh, I owed: I understood that much. I understood that I owed Donna the truth, and hadn't fully offered it yet. Secrets are debts. And the more of them you hold inside, or the bigger they are, the more you owe. I was a heavy debtor. But there was nothing I was proud of in what I could offer of truth. And I believed then, as I had believed all along, that when I paid the debt I owed her, she would leave me. I had long ago accepted the fact that I am not an honorable man. But I wanted her. And lack of honor can't destroy desire. Just ask The Horridus. Or me.

I lay in bed beside her, but I didn't sleep.

Twenty-six

The "serpent field" off of Laguna Hills Road and Moulton Parkway was actually a park. Not a groomed and organized place, no rest rooms or picnic benches, no fire rings or forest fire warnings — just a hundred acres of Southern California scrub on low foothills tapering down to Moulton Creek. The creek was slow and shallow and I could see flags of algae waving in the current just under the surface. It wound around the west side of the park, then passed under a wooden bridge. There was an old asphalt road running through the property, long closed to traffic and used on this fine morning by joggers and bicyclists and mothers pushing strollers. The brushy hills rose up from the edge of the road. I could see some rock outcroppings near the tops of the hillocks.

Hug the water.

I walked a narrow trail along the stream, which was mostly hidden from sight by a thick canopy of bamboo and sumac and wild dill. You smelled water, dead branches, sprouting leaves, sunshine. You heard grasshoppers, the stream moving, cars in the distance and the occasional wheel squeak of a dove doing thirty-five mph overhead. Every few hundred yards was a small clear area of what looked like beach sand, and from those you could see the lazy little creek heading back into the darkness of the bamboo. When you'd push through the foliage and walk out onto a spit of that sand and glance at all the rich green and running water before you, it seemed like an unspoiled little corner of nature. Then you noticed the cigarette butts and beer cans, the candy wrappers and footprints, the dog turds and flies and the pathetic little nests of shredded clothes and newspapers used by human beings desperate for a night's sleep, and you knew better.

I stood there on one of those sandbars with my paper shopping bag containing five thousand cash, my fake mustaches — what a value *that* had turned out to be — my sunglasses and my baseball cap down low. I felt like the bottom feeder I was. The cap was a gag gift from Ardith one year, and it has a ponytail coming out the strap hole in the back. It's not real hair, but it looks real enough. I went back out to the trail and loitered along, waiting for contact.

Ten minutes later I got it, just a quick *hey man* from the dense bamboo along the water. I stopped. I looked toward the voice but saw nothing but the rampant trunks of bamboo and the deep green daggers of leaves that hid the stream below. A spider web stretched across three feet of space in front of me caught the sunlight. In the middle its architect hunkered dark and still in the silver wires. He believed himself hidden.

Hey Mal? That you?

"Yup."

Got it?

"Got it."

Heat?

"Don't feel any."

See that blue-eyed kid in the Dodgers jersey?

"No. You want this or you want to talk all fuckin' day?"

Not for me to touch. See the Bongo Man down at Main Beach. He'll instruct. If you pass the boy in the Dodgers jersey, could you bathe him for me, get out the dirt in all his secret little places?

"Have your own fun."

Oodles of cuddles, Mal.

I heard the rapid-fire chatter of a camera motor drive as I turned away. Never saw the camera. Never saw him.

I sat on a picnic bench in the shade of the eucalyptus trees at Laguna's Main Beach. I listened to the Bongo Man working a pair of waist-high drums, *bit-a-bit-a-DUM, bit-a-DUM, bit-a-DUM.* He was a pale white guy — early twenties, probably — with tan dreadlocks down to the middle of his back and beads braided into the locks and a red tie-dyed shirt with an orange sun on the chest. He had his back to the blue Pacific, of course. Instead, he faced through sunglasses the little playground, where he could watch the boys and girls on the bars and swings and slides, watch them naked in the outdoor shower stalls where Mommy and Daddy rinsed them off before trekking back to the car . . . *Bit-a-bit-a-DUM, bit-a-DUM, bit-a-DUM* . . .

Where do they get these fake Rastas, anyway? He'd set out a glass jar on the boardwalk in front of him for tips. There were a couple of dollars in it — seed money, I guessed — but that was about it.

An old man in a straw hat stopped and smiled at me. He was well dressed: blue oxford cloth shirt, tan trousers, loafers. He had a camera hung around his neck by a strap. I could see the little rods of sunlight that came through the straw mesh and dappled his face. His cheeks were abundant with gin blossoms and his eager blue eyes were outlined in watery pink. His teeth were yellow.

"Fine day, isn't it?"

"For what?"

"Just being alive. Mal, isn't it?"

"Yeah."

"I'm Cleveland, friend of Shroud."

"Lucky him."

"Guess you might want to take a stroll?"

"Whatever's needed."

I headed down the boardwalk beside him.

He couldn't take his eyes off the playground. I studied him and saw that the clothes that had looked so crisp and conservative at first were in fact stained and dirty. He was like Moulton Creek — kind of presentable until you looked harder. A girl and her puppy and mom came toward us and Cleveland knelt down to pet the dog. He smiled up at the mom and told the girl he used to have one like that when he was a boy and it was his favorite one ever. Called him Noggin, because his head was so cute. He stood and crossed his arms paternally, looking down on them. I knelt and pet the dog, too, always a sucker for puppies. Cleveland took my picture with the dog and the girl.

"You two have a wonderful day," he said.

"Thanks," said the girl.

"We will," said the mom. She looked at the old man fondly, and me a little guardedly, then put her hand on her daughter's back and guided her down the walk.

"That's a lovely age," he said.

"Um-hm."

"Going live, eh?"

"I'd like to pay up and get the hell out of here, if you don't mind."

"Oh, I don't touch it. Just be on your way down the sand now. When you get to the wall with the peace signs on it, set your treasure on the rock that looks like an engorged member. You can't miss it. I call it cock rock. Keep

478

walking and don't look back. When you get to the cement stairs, take them up to Coast Highway. Don't look back from there, either. We'll take care of everything else. Just a second, Mal."

He lifted the camera and snapped a couple more shots of me.

I bumped past him rudely and jumped off the boardwalk into the sand. I had him in my mind and I'd come back for him when the time was right — a week from now, a month, a year. I'd come back for him: guaranteed, absolutely, without doubt. And I'd come back for the perv in the bushes at Moulton Creek, too. A hundred yards south I hit the wall with the peace signs, and saw the outcropping of rocks. Sure enough, one of the formations nearest the sandstone cliff looked something like a penis, if you used your imagination a little, if you had an imagination like Cleveland's. I looked around. Some boogie boarders out over the reef. Some sunbathers south fifty yards. A boy flew a kite with a green dinosaur on it. I set the shopping bag down on cock rock and continued down the sand. When I got to the stairway leading up to PCH I took the steps three at a time and arrived on the highway just a few seconds later, with my pulse throbbing hard in my neck and my heart aching to administer justice to Bamboo Man, Bongo Man and Cleveland. I headed north two blocks, then jumped somebody's fence and crept along to the back where his yard overlooked the water. I parted the palm fronds like an explorer and looked down at the beach.

I could see the rock but the bag was gone. No obvious suspects. Nobody at all.

So I went back out to PCH and ducked into a taco joint. I ordered up a shot and a beer to go with lunch. I ate the tacos and felt a little sick. Then I ordered up two more drinks. There. When I came out the sunlight was golden and slower and all things possessed the unique specifics assigned by the Maker in an age more graceful than ours. I watched my shoes advance below me and believed they were guided by moral feet.

I hustled back down to Main Beach but Bongo Man, Cleveland and my bag were all gone.

Melinda's home — my ex-home — was cool inside, redolent with the smells of Mel and Penny and Moe. Moe rubbed against my leg as I stood on the hardwood floor of the living room and looked back out the front window to the lawn, where the FOR SALE had its back to me, and I wondered what had led Melinda to list the place. Money? I doubted that — she had some savings, and I had made it clear I would continue as an investor should things not work out between us. Things clearly were not, and I was temporarily without a job, but she knew I'd be good for the money if she could hold on a few months. Didn't she? Even if the mortgage was that big a problem she could always get a roommate. No, I thought, it wasn't that. All I could come up with was that she and Penny were too traumatized by my accusal to even stay in a home they had once shared with me. I wondered at the depth of the wound I had laid open in them — in the wound that Jordan Ishmael, to be accurate, had laid open in them — and realized that I really had no understanding of its gravity. Had he even thought it through? How could his despising me justify the pain he brought to them? It was beyond me. I did not understand. It was more than sad to see that for sale sign there, a sign that said to all passersby: this life failed, these people ruined, this house ready for the next suckers eager to try.

"I don't know, Moe," I mumbled.

He rolled over onto his back and wagged his tail. My wasted bird dog, reduced to a shameless household pet. That's what happens when you don't hunt a hunter. I guess I couldn't blame that on Jordan Ishmael.

I knelt and pet him for a while, thinking about the life I had once had between these walls. A woman who loved me, a girl who had come to like me, a job, a dog. And as if my sudden passion for Donna Mason was not enough to ruin all that I had had here, there were the photographs that exploded the world all around me — with Melinda and Penny and everyone else I knew in it. And that, I could and did blame on Ishmael.

By two I was back in my apartment, dealing again with I. R. Shroud.

I. R. Shroud: Reports all good. Payment received.

Mal: Don't appreciate the Kodak moments one fucking little bit. Very disappointed by you.

I. R. Shroud: For my peace of mind, TN, OCSD. We want you so badly to be one of us. Took great trust to show you our faces.

Mal: Point taken but unhappy still. Perhaps some shots of you would level the playing field.

I. R. Shroud: Riotous. Use legal letter envelope for balance. Hundreds only. Place envelope in paperback book, one-third of envelope visible. Embark Green Line Metro Rail from Norwalk station on first train after 4 P.M. today. Board last car only. Prepurchase transfer to Blue. Further instructions to come.

Mal: Am wanting results quickly.

I. R Shroud: First things first.

Mal: Will wait with patience.

I. R. Shroud: As do all good patients. Gone.

In my little blue notebook I noted the exact times that our conversation began and ended. I was afraid to look forward to the day when that information would help hang The Horridus, but I allowed myself a mirthful glance into the future anyway.

For the first time since being charged I strapped on my shoulder rig and .45 and put a light windbreaker over it to hide it from the real cops.

I stood on the Norwalk Green Line platform, 4:02 P.M., a paperback copy of *The New Centurions* in my hand, with one-third of a legal-sized envelope protruding from between pages 122 and 123. The May afternoon was bright and almost hot; it felt about eighty. There was just enough breeze to blow the smog out to Riverside. In the west the sun seemed to be sinking very slowly, as if it didn't want to miss the sunset. The train arrived almost silently and I walked to the last car before getting on.

I found a seat, looked at no one and gazed out the window. The train accelerated oddly — more a sensation of brakes being let off than of power being applied. First I was sitting still, then I was going fast. In the faint reflection in the window before me I saw a mustached man in a cap and sunglasses. And I couldn't help but remember the old Naughton, the sun-tanned, happy young father snorkel diving with his kid off of Shaw's Cove in Laguna, with the sun on his back as he floated in blue water and watched through his mask as his boy dove down to claim a shell from the cream-colored sand.

I knew that I had changed and fallen. But exactly how and exactly why, well, these things seemed beyond me. I felt like I had grabbed hold of a dream that had moved along nicely for a while, like a speedboat on the surface of the sea, only to submerge quickly and without warning, taking my outstretched hand with it while everything precious scattered to the waves and the winds of the surface far above.

West along the Green Line, then: Lakewood, Long Beach, Wilmington, Avalon, Harbor Freeway, Vermont. Before the Crenshaw station a thin young man in a beige suit sat down across the aisle, looking frankly at me, then at the book on the seat next to me. He was thirty, maybe, with glasses and limp blond hair. He had a soft, thoughtful face.

"Good book," he said.

I nodded. "I've always liked it."

"Rereading it?"

"Pretty much so."

"Mal?"

"Correct."

"You'll find the light better at the next station. Exit and go to the far west end of it. There's a seat beside a fat man. Take it. Leave the book on that seat and take the next car east, back to Norwalk. You're done, then."

You're done, then.

He stared at me through his glasses, surprisingly direct for such a meek-looking fellow, then stood and went through the door to the car ahead. I never saw him again. Five minutes later I got off at Crenshaw.

The fat man wasn't just fat, he was huge. Big head, curly red hair and beard, massive arms extending from the kind of short-sleeved shirt you'd expect a nerd to wear: shiny poly/cotton, with light blue stripes, pocket, yellowed collar. He was reading a *Travel & Leisure* magazine. I could smell him as I sat down, body odor mixed with a foul breath that could only come from a soul turned to carrion. I could hear his inhales whistling past nose hair, his exhales hissing past his lips. I looked at him directly just once, but it was the same moment he was looking at me, and I saw his pale gray eyes — little things, little piglet's eyes — roving over me. I held them for just a second, but in that second they said to me: we're together, you and me; we share the secret; we're the same. I tried to convey something harmonious back through mine, but all I could feel inside was contempt and anger. When I saw the next eastbound train approach I stood and leaned over to set the novel on my seat. A big soft hand with red hairs sprouting from the flesh closed over mine, and the little piglet eyes shined with joy as he looked at me.

"It's all worth it, Mal," he said. "Going live is what all of us want to do. You've got the courage, the *balls*, to do it. God bless you."

I couldn't look him in the eye, because he would have seen what I was feeling. I nodded contritely, and managed a quick glance down at him.

He was smiling up at me. It was a happy smile — yellow, pink and black toward the back. The stench of his insides puffed against my face and he let go of my hand.

I rode east in the dusk, watching the last of the sunlight fail while the frail lights of humans came on to take its place. I had a bad feeling about the night to come, but I had a bad feeling about most of them.

I. R. Shroud did not respond to my salutations that night. Nothing. Mum. I wasn't surprised.

I'd just been shaken down for ten grand and The Horridus was having a laugh about it. I was financing his career in serial abduction, rape and murder with money I'd earned trying to catch animals like him. I was so angry my nerves were buzzing and I went to bed to see if they'd stop.

I couldn't sleep. I tossed in bed, got up and roamed the little apartment, tried to watch TV. How many times can you look at a bean field? Tonello's was dark. I was wired but fretful, eager to act but not sure what to do, anxious without knowing why. For a while, at least.

Then I understood that I wanted to drive out to Tustin again, to see who might be stirring at Collette Loach's home on Wytton

Street. The feeling I'd gotten in Hopkin was upon me again, the feeling I'd gotten at Caspers Park, the feeling I'd gotten — however slightly — at the Loach residence in Tustin. The long shot. The hunch. The maybe.

Donna wanted to come. She microwaved some popcorn, which took a couple of minutes, then we hit the road. I slipped a flat little five-shot Colt .38 into my jacket when she wasn't looking. You'd be surprised what space just one less cylinder saves. It was 2:07 A.M. when we got there, though my watch runs two minutes fast. When I rolled down the window I smelled exhaust but it wasn't mine. You get used to the aromas of a familiar car. It really stood out against the smell of the popcorn, hanging there in the moist night air. I parked across the street from Collette's place, two houses down.

We sat in the darkness with a thermos full of tequila and ice, sharing from the little plastic cup. We ate the popcorn from a paper shopping bag. I looked at the formidable wall of the Loach house, the big black sycamores guarding above, the neat little bungalow next door, where the rose fancier lived out the last days of his life. A faint yellow light issued from behind the wall — an outdoor bug light was my guess.

We made small talk while we watched the wall, covering the events of the day, as anyone who spends time with Donna Mason must be

487

prepared to do. She is interested in everything and everyone. Perhaps too much interested in some things, but who am I to judge?

We sat in silence after that. I felt like I should talk to her.

"When I get like this, Donna, I just want to explode. I've been run all over the state by this guy. I'm out ten grand as part of a practical joke. He's done things to girls that go against everything I am and everything I believe in. He's got the key that can clear my name. I'm all ready and there's nothing to do."

"Well, you're doing something now."

I watched the house. I felt the tequila pulling me downward and together, toward some yearned for but often evasive center.

"I feel that this guy, no matter where he lives, is going out tonight."

"I hope you're wrong."

"Used to be nights like this, I'd go to the cave. The Horridus feels the same way. Like I do. He wants to bust out of his skin. He watches his snakes do it and it makes him want to do it, too. He wants to emerge fresh. He wants to start over. The reason he wants those girls isn't only for sex. The sex is the drivetrain for what he does. It's the fuel and the engine. But what he's doing, in a bigger sense — is getting back at everybody who ever wronged him. First, he punishes the girls for what they make him feel. What he feels is wrong, and he knows it, though he can't help it. *I've got to change*. And he punishes them for what he thinks the world has done to him — they're sacrificial. That's what the mesh robes say to me, anyway: you are now an angel, so that I can change, *because I've got to change.* He was probably abused as a boy. Physically, sexually maybe, psychologically. That builds a lot of anger, and a lot of self-disgust. *I've got to change.* The closer he gets to taking one of these girls and doing what he did to Mary Lou Kidder, the worse he feels about himself, but he thinks that's the thing that will transform him. He stopped for a year and a half. He gave it a try. But once you go off peaks like that, you don't go back easily. He's not going to settle for the bunny slope."

Donna said nothing for a long moment. "Does he deserve to die?"

"He'll die."

"Early, in a gas chamber or an electric chair?"

"That's God's decision, not mine."

"And if you were God?"

"I'd roast him on a spit."

I took a nice long drink of the Herradura and ice, then ate another handful of popcorn. The minutes ticked by.

"I know I drink too much. I'll stop when I'm ready to. But right now it fuels me and it contains the flame, at the same time. You drink some and it's like adrenaline going down. Then you drink more and the adrenaline turns into something strong and inward. Then you drink more and the something strong and inward melts into your muscles, and for a while you're one, whole, integrated unit. Then you drink more and your body gets heavy and your mind stays light. Then you drink more and you're asleep."

"It doesn't sound all that exciting."

"I'm just rambling."

"You're packing, too."

"You weren't supposed to notice."

"I notice every single thing about you. And I like it when you let your guard down and ramble."

"The alcohol, though. It's not about excitement. It's about . . . well, I'm not sure what it's about, really."

"Maybe what it's about is about wanting to feel different than you feel. Getting around what's happened to you. Getting around yourself, seeing around the corner of you. When I was a kid, my Uncle Pollard out in War, he'd drink in the tool shed because my aunt wouldn't let the liquor in the house. When he'd gotten enough, he started calling himself Jonah. That's who he was when he was liquored up — Jonah. Even walked and talked different. Wasn't crazy or mean or sloppy or anything — just . . . *a different guy*."

"Sounds great. But, what's *War?*"

"Ah, just another little town in another little holler. West Virginia's full of them. War, Left

Hand, Big Isaac, Tad, Pinch, Ida May. They all got reasons behind the names. Like, Left Hand is on the left side of Left Hand Creek. Stuff like that. Anyway, real drinkers, be they in War or Orange County, are trying to drink themselves into being somebody different. Some of you get good results. I think Pollard did."

I thought about that.

"You think I do?"

"No. I don't think you're much different when you drink. You just talk more and hurt less, I guess. Maybe you're not drinking enough."

We laughed at that.

I continued to stare out at the house. Nothing moved in the breezeless night. I waited for the feeling from Hopkin to come to me, but it didn't. I realized there were still more houses listed for sale by women that I hadn't even looked into yet. It's a terrible feeling to realize you've been wrong.

"Can I ask you something?" she asked. "How come you never told me much about your boy?"

Oh, no, I thought. But I'd had enough tequila to feel honest.

"I didn't want you to be a part of him."

"I understand that, but why?"

"Sometimes separation is good."

"Understand that, too. But do you think that I'm somehow not good enough to be

491

connected up with him?"

I felt a little lump way down below my Adam's apple. Donna Mason's deep and genuine humility never failed to surprise me. "No, it's because I didn't want you to be . . . ah . . . part of what happened to him. He ended in death and I want you to . . . not be affected by that."

"Protecting me? Or just protecting your vision of me?"

"My vision of you."

She was quiet for a long while.

"How come you ordered me not to look into his death when I was putting together our interview?"

"I didn't order you not to look into it. I *asked* you not to pry into the particulars of his dying, is all. In front of thousands of viewers. Can you blame me for that?"

It was a very slick and very cool evasion of the truth. A lie of omission. But Donna caught it.

"I don't think it had to do with viewers at all. I think it had to do with me."

"No."

She looked at me in the darkness for a beat. "I wouldn't have done that anyway."

I almost believed her, which meant I doubted her. I felt bad for not trusting her, but my sins against men, women and children have been far greater than that. "I know," I lied. "Thank you."

"You're welcome."

Lies are walls; you hit them and hit them and nothing breaks but you.

"Maybe now you can explain that court date to me."

I didn't lie about that. I just told her about the photogrammetry and what it might prove, if Donna was willing to tell the world what she was doing that January afternoon in the Marriott. She listened intently, and was quiet for a long time.

"Want to just quit?" I asked her. "You can walk, Donna, and you won't have to explain a thing to me — or to any court in the land. There are decent odds that you'd be better off."

More silence.

"Terry, why do I have to fight so hard to tell what's generous in you from what's insulting?"

"I don't mean to insult you."

"I love you."

"I want you to. I'm just trying to find a way to make you."

"That isn't up to you. That's the whole point. Don't you understand? Just the basic things about me?"

She shook her head and sighed. "Well, then you let me know when you find that way. Meantime, I'll consider myself on the edge of something about to crumble."

"I don't crumble."

"Maybe you just should. Terry, love isn't something you have to *force*. It isn't that hard. It's not . . . something you strain to keep up, like a dumbbell with a ton of weight on it."

I thought about that one.

"How come you put up with me?" I asked.

"I don't know," she said quietly. "I just can't seem to scrape you off my shoe."

"Is that a good thing?"

"Terry, I don't feel like I've got much choice in it."

"Let's drink to that."

We did.

I watched an owl float through the yellow light and land in a sycamore. Moths buzzed the streetlamp, the light a busy halo in the thick, damp air.

"I thought he'd be moving tonight. Hunting."

"Maybe this isn't his house."

"He's *out there* tonight, Donna — I'm sure of it."

"Then he left earlier. Or he hasn't left yet."

"I smelled exhaust when we first drove up. Hang in here with me for another hour, will you?"

"You know I will."

"I'm glad you made this popcorn. I'd forgotten, but I always used to get hungry on stakeouts. Starved."

Donna looked out the window to the house. "Strange, isn't it? Pictures of what isn't true, but they look true. Pictures of you taken by your ex-wife, gone missing. Pictures of The Horridus, hanging over the freeways. Moving pictures of you in my interview. Pictures the press snaps. Then, there's all the other kind of picturing going on — you've got a present-day picture of me you don't want altered by your son's past. A man out there is hunting children because he's pictured himself with them. A man with a gun right beside me, hunting him, because he's pictured this as the only thing that can save his sweet, tormented soul. This is one crazy world we're in here, Terry."

I watched her as she stared out the window at the walled house. I wanted to put her body inside my heart. "Donna, this is as corny as it gets, but I'm glad you're in it with me and I love you more than anything on earth."

She smiled. "I love corn. Pass it, will you?"

Twenty-seven

Hypok climbed into his van and leaned over to check himself in the rearview mirror. Even in the pale interior light he was pleased by the transformation: jet black hair brushed down over his head (boyish and dramatic), black mustaches and Vandyke tapering to a neat point (hip and musketeerish), the earring hoop in his left lobe and the long, bottom-flaring black sideburns (piratical and Presleyan). What more could you want? He'd started the shed three days ago, just after the Item #3 flop. It had taken that long for the whiskers to grow out enough to dye the same midnight black as his hair.

He took a giant swig off the generic tequila and set the bottle back in the center console. He checked his directions on the street map again, like a vacationer making sure he didn't get lost: Leeward Place in Yorba Linda, a bit of a jaunt out the 91 freeway, birthplace of Richard Nixon and home to Item #4.

He hit the garage door control, waited the usual eternity for the thing to rise, then backed out carefully so as not to scrape the Saturn. Easy. Then into the driveway and a quick push on the shut button. He made a nifty little high-way patrol–style turn, where you back up, crank hard, then crank the other way to reverse direction without a time-and-space-consuming three-point maneuver. He used another control to open the front gate and rolled confidently onto Wytton Street in the heart of old-town Tustin as the gate slid shut behind him.

It was 2:03 A.M. by Hypok's watch, which, he knew, was two minutes slow. He started the turn off Wytton and his rearview caught the faint headlights coming up his street from way back in the night.

Wytton to B to First. The school, the church, the ball field. Darkness, streetlights and the private hiss of cars. Half a moon. Then the 55 freeway heading north and east to get him to the 91.

Hypok felt strong right now, immensely strong, with the tequila pulling down all his nerves into one big muscle and the one big muscle under the control of his will. Strong fingers on window handle, strong arm as he cranked it down for the cool spring suburban air. Jazz on the radio, syncopated, mindless and happy. That's what he liked about jazz when he was on a predation, the way it never got to the point, never hit the tonic note, just kept mincing along and got you more and more . . . agitated. He let the notes go into his ears and bounce off the knotted muscle of his nerves and imagined what happens when a bird lands on the snout-ball of an alligator submerged in water. Wham!

Up the 55, merging with the 91, low-lying fog in the basin of the river, tracts to the left and hillsides to the right, truck scales closed, the toll lanes offered for 25 cents but empty anyway, fast-food America anchoring the suburbs: McDonald's, In-and-Out, Carl's, Taco Bell. He gazed at his own gigantic face on a billboard and felt proud. *Have You Seen This Man? Call 1-800-647-SAVE.* He wondered for the thousandth time exactly when Item #3, the little toad, had peeked at him. Must be a problem with the hood. The next one could stare at him all it wanted, he thought. The big illuminated rectangle of his face stood out wonderfully against the dark hillsides, and it was the only one for miles, the reigning deity in this little corner of the American night. It didn't look anything like him anymore, he thought, but that was good, like an advertisement for someone else.

Hypok veered gently to his left, flattening a dozen orange dividers that wobbled back upright in the wake of his van, then he sailed along in the toll lane for a few hundred yards just to see what it was like — he'd never used it and this was his chance — but at this hour with so few cars what was the benefit except the satisfaction of feeling those rubber stanchions bending under you like helpless pygmies and the comfort of knowing you were breaking the law and getting away with it? He trampled another ten pylons and settled back into the no-pay fast lane, jazz low on the radio, fog triangulated in his headlamp beams, generic tequila harnessing the tracers of his imagination and tamping them down in his brain like gunpowder.

He thought of the Item and its mother waiting for him on Leeward: ditzy blondes, both of them, the mom maybe thirty and the Item maybe seven or eight, with long spindly legs and lots of hair. Met them at church months ago, talked to the woman at the Single Parents meeting afterward a few times, Chloe the Item and Margo the mom, very trusting as you would expect people at church to be. He'd regaled Margo with tales of his beloved "Mike," age five, living with his mother back in Texas. Even showed her a picture of him, courtesy of some Bright Tomorrows moron who'd foisted it off on him in a burst of motherly pride. *My son, Alexander.* He'd filed Chloe and Margo under the port-in-a-storm category, because they weren't easy to research, like the Bright Tomorrows Items, and it took him two prowls into the assistant pastor's office to view the Rolodex long enough to get the address and phone number, because Margo wasn't listed in the phone directory. He kept maybe a dozen port-in-a-storms catalogued in his head, reserved for a situation just like this one: billboards of his face on all major county freeways, a composite drawing (not bad) distributed to post offices, neighborhood markets, health clubs, police stations, school offices and thousands of homes throughout Christendom; cops getting closer to him, pressure, pressure, pressure. The pigs called it proaction — that warthog Ishmael spelled it out, right on TV — and proaction was exactly what he was going to give them, courtesy of Margo, Item #4, Neighborhood Congregational Church — Praise the Lord! — and the port-in-a-storm file.

It was hard to keep his excitement contained. Hypok thought about the ten grand, delivered to him that night by one of the Friendlies. What a sweet, secret delight it was to know that he had been instrumental, first in ruining the reputation of Crimes Against Youth sergeant Terry Naughton, and now in fleecing him out of ten thousand more bucks! And that on top of the $30,000 Naughton — Mal — had coughed for his original customs. Talk about a smiley face. That money would go a long way now, especially with his snakes no longer eating up a hundred dollars' worth of vermin a week along with the occasional boxes of kittens or puppies he'd get free in the classifieds, so long as he promised a good home for them. After quitting Bright Tomorrows, he'd live on Mal's money. A cop's money. Tax free. He was commissioned. He was golden. He was changing. He was *there*.

He really was there. He pulled onto Leeward and proceeded west to the correct number. It was easy to find because they were right out there on the curbs, in reflecting black and silver paint: 239. He drove past, made three right turns and pulled alongside a little park to settle himself. He cut the engine and got out the bottle. He liked the way the liquor warmed up in the center console, down there where the engine heat seeped through the plastic. He thought about Mal again. What would the inmates do with him if he went to prison? It was hard to imagine the wrath. He took another drink. Idea: would law enforcement *pay* for information on the continuing exploits of T.N.? What if he contacted this Ishmael fool, for instance, the one on the TV press conference, the proactive prick, and told him he had additional information on the accused? Interesting. But would the cops pay up enough to make it worth his while? Idea: take it one step further. What would Mal do if he threatened to expose his latest request to the Sheriffs? Maybe *that's* how to get the last few drops of blood out of Naughton. Wait until he finds out who his dream girl is. Make him sweat awhile. Daydreams can be so exciting, he thought, especially at 2:38 A.M. on a damp May morning.

He took another swig, for luck, then worked on a pair of latex gloves and started up the van.

Thirty seconds later he was sitting outside Item #4's house, engine off, neighborhood still, moon low over the uniform roofs of uniform houses, his heart slamming inside his chest like a dragster with a blown rod. He put some cinnamon drops on his tongue. He pulled off three eight-inch lengths of duct tape and stuck them inside his jacket. The glass cutter and toilet plunger, the rim of which was smeared with petroleum jelly for a sure fit on the window glass, sat in his lap. He put the Hiker's Headlight on and arranged the lamp up on his forehead, equidistant from each eye, a snug, cyclopean organ just waiting to illuminate prey. He knew the Item's room was in the back and he knew they didn't have a dog. It was just a matter of getting over the gate without waking up the world, then he'd be home free. He got out and quietly pressed the door shut, nudging it into its latch with his hips.

Fifteen steps to the gate, arms at his sides and plunger tucked up under his armpit. Calm strides, but assured ones, the stride of a man on familiar ground. Then the gate getting closer, closer now, closer still, Hypok running the last five steps, long eager steps like the high jumpers take in the Olympics — *one, two, three, four, five* — then the swing of his right leg and the heave of his left, plunger held before him for balance, and he was atop the rickety grapestake fence, pausing for just one moment like a sentence delayed by a comma, then he shifted his weight and drew himself together to spring off with hardly a sound, just the brief swoosh of a body falling through space then the muffled air-cushion tap of athletic shoes on concrete as Hypok landed apelike and crouched on the side walkway by the trash cans, his eyes adjusting to a new gradient of darkness, moonlight only, his ears tuned to every sound in the night, his heart pounding hard and a voice inside snickering, *clean.*

Eight steps, right turn: window. Plunger on. Cutter scratches a loose circle around the suction cup, pane rasps quietly as it breaks away. The hole is clean. Michael Hypok: craftsman. His latexed hand reaches inside for the slider latch. There. Up unlocks, so he eases up. The window slides in the channel with hardly a sound if he does it slowly, and he does it very slowly so the Item can remain in dreamland, and when the window is finally open and a brief pause tells him that no one is stirring not even a mouse, he hoists himself into the opening and in the faint white moonlight his supple body pours to the bedroom floor like cream dispensed from a pitcher.

He turned on the Hiker's Headlight and found the bed. Item #4 was sleeping deeply, lost in a comforter, just its little head with all that blond hair showing. He looked down and admired it for a long minute: all the innocence, all the joy, all the magnificence it would inspire. But, work to do.

Then he heard something in the darkness to his right.

The light blazed on and he stood there looking at this *thing*, Margo Gayley, Christian single mother, in the doorway wearing a pink robe and a terrified expression, holding something small in her hand.

She pointed it at his face. He had already begun to crouch and coil when he heard an aerosol hiss and saw the red mist jet overhead. He leapt just as she lowered the can, but he was already up, midair, and he took a load of the stuff on his neck.

His eyes burst into flames just as his hands closed around Margo's throat. He drove forward. He couldn't open his eyes because of the heat. She made an awful gagging sound. He felt both their bodies slam back into a flimsy panel that gave way and let him fall down on top of her, hands powerfully locked on this thin throat, and he felt a bunch of what had to be clothes falling on his back as he forced her head down as far as it would go. He focused every cell of his burning, outraged strength to drive his thumbs all the way back to his fingers. He put his weight into it, his neck and back, his hips and legs, everything dedicated to the meeting of thumb pads and fingertips. They were already close to touching. He'd never heard a sound like she was making, part whimper and part screech but mostly this dry clicking sound like muscles flapping against each other. He released his thumbs for just a second to move them higher up, where the bones and glands were, then smashed down again with ferocious force. He felt her fingers on his wrists, but they had no power. She was kicking up violently with her knees but he'd landed between them and all he had to do was keep his groin jammed up tight against hers and her knees couldn't even touch him. He could hear Item #4 screaming and feel it thrashing his back with something, but neither mattered a bit right now, only the *rrr . . . rrr . . . rrrrrrrrrrr* coming from his own throat. Then a sudden muted crunch and his thumbs almost met his fingers and the woman relaxed so Hypok throttled her still harder until there was no resistance left, just accepting flesh and this screaming thing behind him lashing his back with what felt like a belt.

He whirled. The Item shot out the door and into the house. Hypok rose with shaky legs and followed it. It ran down the hallway and around a corner. Hypok made the corner in three long strides, just as it flew out the front door. Hypok followed it into the little front yard, into the misty morning air, but he stopped short and thought about the van. How far away from it could he get — his life force, his escape, his freedom? Fuck it, *get the Item!* It was hauling down the sidewalk, loose T-shirt rippling and tiny feet a blur beneath it, like how the chickens used to run when his mother chased one down for dinner. It wasn't screaming, it was just moving and moving fast. *Get the van, then get the Item!*

Ten steps and he was there, flinging himself through the door, turning the key in the ignition where he had left it, throwing the tranny into first and gunning the gas all at once. The van jumped forward. He hunched over the wheel and flipped on the brights. There it was, flailing straight down the sidewalk, growing larger in the bright beams, shirt waving like a flag at a ballpark, hair flying out everywhere.

The van ate up the distance. The Item looked back, eyes dark and shining. It looked like an animal just before you run over it. Hypok lurched past it, then threw the van into park and slammed through the door. But it cut across the lawn on a diagonal, away from him. He heard its scream pierce the heavy air. It screamed again. A light went on in the house it had passed, the house on the lawn of which Hypok now stood, eyes burning and heart pounding, watching his future scooting away from him like a rabbit. Like a bad dream. Then another light, one house back of him. Then another, from the house it was running to. Like every damned household in suburbia knew he was here. Up the walkway to the porch it scurried, while Hypok could only watch in mute, furious heartache as the door opened and Item #4 vanished from the moist darkness into the warm welcoming light of a cozy Orange County home. After the Item was inside, two heads appeared in the doorway, looking at him. Then the man stepped onto the porch and crossed his arms. Ward Fucking Cleaver in boxers. The woman was probably already on the phone.

Hypok walked back to the van and drove away, unconcerned that Ward would remember his plates, stolen months ago from an out-of-commission Audi near the Bright Tomorrows building in Irvine.

He was a mess. His eyes burned, his lips and nostrils burned, his neck burned, his right thumb was sprained and he had absolutely nothing to show for himself. He held up his right hand and looked at the latex glove, fingers torn and peeled back, a yawning hole over his palm. Same with the left, but no palm hole. He noted that his lucky snake bracelet was gone, fuck, probably ripped off in the disagreement with the mom. God knew how many fingerprints he'd left behind, but he was clean, they couldn't match prints with nothing, the pinheads. Margo Whatsername wasn't going to be fingering anybody for a while, either.

Driving slowly, he signaled his occasional lane changes, trying to get his nerves to settle a little. He drank more tequila, but that did the opposite of settling nerves, it just taunted him with its warmth and courage and it made him feel again that consolidation down there in the naughty zone, morning wood, which he'd been hoping to deal with in some depth before the sun came up. It made him want sex; it made him want . . . well, *everything*.

He headed east on the 91, out of Orange County, where he figured some kind of APB would be on the cop waves. Not enough traffic on the roads to feel safe, yet. Just before the county line he saw another billboard of himself. It really wasn't a bad rendition of his old look. He thought it might actually be a help to him now, transformed as he was into dark-haired, hip and poetic sideburn and earring man. It was a decoy. He watched himself watch himself until the sign turned to reveal the insipid stop smoking announcement on the other side. He wondered what the names of the bones were he'd crushed in the mom's throat. Whatever. That thumb was sore.

Getting off on Maple Street in Corona, he then went north to the park. Hypok had scouted the place as a possible Item release site, but it was too crowded, too many people, no privacy. Of course it was closed now, but he parked anyway and wandered across the damp grass toward the drinking fountains and rest rooms. Stooped over the fountain he let the water loop up into his eyes and blinked them a lot until the burning eased up. Then lips and nose. He pulled off the gloves and rinsed them, then poured some of the wet gravel from the fountain bed into them and tossed them on top of the outhouse. Then he giggled.

He sat on a picnic bench for a while and listened to the park birds. He yawned. Then he climbed up onto the table and stretched out on his back, with his elbows on either side of his head and his fingers laced beneath it to form a pillow. Let the traffic get going before you head back home, he thought. Another hour or two.

Then his little cowboy pj's were down around his knees and Collette and Valeen half hidden under the sheet were giggling and oohing, inspecting, probing, playing. All he wanted to do was relish their touch and his feeling, lie there and pretend he was sleeping though they all knew he wasn't. Yes, that would be enough, to just stay there forever, enfolded within the smells of his sisters and the sheets and the bewildering wonders of being four years old and loved so much and feeling so sweetly, deliciously, mysteriously *good*, peeking out the window where the Missouri sky held a full orange moon and, one night, a pretty little rat snake on the sill illuminated by the porch light looked through the screen at him.

Hypok woke up, startled and aroused. He watched the traffic heading out Maple to the freeway. The headlights were still on but the first light of morning had turned the world gray. This wasn't Missouri. He looked down at his pants and rolled over, trying to hide what could not be hidden forever, imagining a way to express what had to be expressed. Fully expressed. Soon. He was sad, frustrated and furious.

A few minutes later he was back in his van, heading for home. The traffic was heavy from Riverside into Orange County and there wasn't a way on earth they would spot him.

About halfway there, he got an idea.

No time for a long predation. No time for the port-in-a-storm stuff. It took weeks to get those right.

But he wanted action and he wanted it now and he was going to get it. God, he needed it. He was aching: heart, head, balls, thumb. When they've put your face all over the freeways, you know your time in that place is short. You've got to *act*. Hypok decided to just go get some live bait and go hunting. Like back in Wichita, but simpler, something irresistible. He'd had the idea before.

He brought out the tequila and took a long, warm gulp. Most good. Then he turned the jazz back on low. He imagined the big County of Orange Animal Shelter, right off I-5. He'd shopped there occasionally for free dogs and cats for Moloch, but he hadn't been there in months.

How much is that doggie in the window?

Twenty-eight

Johnny Escobedo called me at six the next morning to tell me that The Horridus had just moved again. APB on a white van, stolen plates, description of UNSUB male pending. One terrified girl, okay — she got away. But her mother was strangled while she escaped and The Horridus had slithered back into the dark. Johnny said it looked like the mother had heard something and surprised him. I wasn't at the crime scene, but I could have told you that.

For the next seven hours I'd sat by the phone, waiting for his updates, feeling more foolish, helpless and impotent than I had ever felt in my life. It just frosted me, because I *knew* he'd be out that night and I'd missed him. Finally I blew up. I threw a full beer bottle through the TV screen — though it wasn't even turned on. Then I smashed my fist into a kitchen cabinet that splintered like the cheap wood it was. So much for my deposit. Neither helped. There were white splinters in my knuckles.

In the early afternoon I took a break to meet Melinda at her house. She'd taken the day off

511

work to have an escrow officer put a rush on the papers that would allow us to sell the place and split the money. Neither one of us had expected a sale so quickly. She had some documents for me to sign. She was wearing an old yellow sweatsuit she used to work out in, with her hair pulled back in a ponytail and a brooding look on her face. She looked underslept, pale.

I was in a foul mood when I got there, and a fouler one still when Melinda held up the papers, said "sign these" and with a sigh held them out to me. Moe looked at me and slunk away.

"Thought I might get consulted before *we* decided to sell," I said.

Her look was sharp as a paring blade. "Don't."

"Sorry. But I'm having trouble figuring out why I'm doing real estate deals while *The Horridus is out there killing people and chasing little girls.*"

"It'll take two minutes. Then you'll be back on the case."

Pure sarcasm.

"Just sign and get out?"

She smiled wanly and shook her head. Then, our standard peace offering: "Coffee?"

"Hell. Why not?"

In the bright Laguna kitchen we watched the coffee drip into the carafe. When it was ready we took our cups to the sundeck outside and sat in the shade of a silver-dollar eucalyptus. The day was warm and it was breezy there in the canyon, as it often is, and I felt again the loss of it all. My home, though it wasn't really mine. My woman, though she wasn't really mine. My daughter, though she wasn't really mine. I guess I had borrowed a family after losing my real one and now it was time to return it. My frustration and fury melted away when I felt that loss. It just blew away in the breeze and it left me with a heightened sense of what was here for me now: nothing. She set the papers on the patio table and put a rock on them so they wouldn't blow away.

"I wanted to get a few things straight with you," she said. "One is, I don't think you did what those pictures showed, but I also know you don't remember a lot of what you did, back when we were drinking so much. I don't either. But that doesn't really matter. You've made Penny's life extremely difficult. She refuses to believe anything that's on the TV or in the papers, but that isn't enough to save her. She's taunted at school, she's ridiculed by friends, she's been disincluded by loving parents who think their own children might be . . . contaminated by her contact with you."

"It doesn't make sense to shun her for something I *didn't* do."

"Men believed the world was flat for centuries. That didn't make sense either."

"Well, now that's really —"

"— But more to the point, Terry, you've humiliated me. You can't even imagine the looks I get, the things people say — some of them trying to help, I know — just the way people are. You might be the alleged monster, but I'm the bride of Frankenstein. Well, I'm sick of it. That's why I'm leaving. For Penny, and for me."

I didn't speak. I could see by the flush on Melinda's broad, pale cheeks that she was angry and hurting.

"I've already made an offer on a place up in the Portland area. Good schools. Nobody knows us. So I'd appreciate your cooperation on the sale. According to the joint ownership either one of us can impede a sale, and I'm asking you not to."

"I won't."

"I'm settling for a little less than I asked. It's still a buyers' market and I want out. So, thank you."

"What are you going to do for work?"

She looked at me and smiled just a little. "You wouldn't believe it if I told you."

"You're going to use that old credential and teach school."

She nodded. "I just can't do it anymore, Terry. The filth we shovel. The people we deal with. We're just garbage collectors — human garbage. I'm sorry, but I'm bitter and I'm burned out and I'm finished. They'll get The Horridus and another one will crop up to take

514

his place. Anyway, there's openings in some of the Portland districts. I'll get something."

"How's Penny taking it?"

Melinda's eyes bore into me. "She wants to stay."

There was a long silence then and I listened to the cars hissing past on Laguna Canyon Road.

"You know, Terry, you did something more than humiliate me to the world. You humiliated me to me."

"You know I'm innocent."

"Of the children, I believe so. But how innocent are you of Donna Mason?"

I watched her sip her coffee. There are times when a man wants to crawl down a hole, and times when he *is* the hole. This was one of those.

She chuckled. "You can tell me I'm wrong and I won't bring it up again. I'm not after confirmation. I'm past that, to be honest."

"Well, yes. There is that."

"How long?"

"A few months."

"I'd flattered myself that it was more recent. I suspected. When I saw the interview I realized she was in love with you. I just *knew*. So, when were you going to get around to telling me?"

"I'd been thinking about . . . how to do it."

Her face was flushed now, but Melinda still had the interrogator's calm that had worn down so many creeps over the years. "Noble of you, not to rush things."

"The same way you thought before you left Ish. I hurt you, Melinda. I cheated and I lied. But you're not righteous either. Nobody is."

"I feel very put in my place. I apologize for asking you when you were going to tell me you were cheating on me. I stand corrected."

"I was wrong in what I did. I know that. I wasn't expecting what happened."

"And what, exactly, happened?"

"I just met her and fell. I thought we'd be right together. I fought it. I did what I could because I knew someone was going to get hurt. I did fight . . ."

"For whom?"

"You and me."

We were quiet a moment while Melinda stared at me.

"What about us? Were we right?"

"I don't think so."

"Oh, Jesus Christ. Don't. Don't start listing my faults."

"Most of them were mine."

"I've got no interest in them, now."

"Do you want me to get up and walk, or sit here and bleed?"

"Sit and bleed, sonofabitch, because I'm not done with you yet."

My turn to offer the olive branch:

"More coffee, then, hon?"

"Sure, *cakes*."

When I got back with fresh cups, Melinda

had her knees up and her arms wrapped around them and her head sideways on her kneecaps. Her ponytail hung down behind them. I walked into her field of vision to set down the cup, then walked back out of it and sat down again.

"I knew we weren't right, too," she said. "I knew it from the first. But I did it anyway. That sounds like I settled for something less, but really it was just the opposite. I was getting more than I thought I deserved. I thought you'd make me feel young and beautiful and happy again. I thought you'd wrangle me into having another kid, even though I told you I wouldn't. I felt old, Terry, when we started seeing each other. And I do again, now. I feel old as owl shit. I look in the mirror and I see a face made out of old, dry owl shit. For a couple of months you made me feel like a woman again, then it was just back to being dried-up old me. You're one of those men that gets older and a little crazier, maybe, but you hold your looks and your body keeps up with your desire, and you do okay for yourself. I knew the drinking would pass. And when it did, I knew your vision of me would pass, too, and you'd see me for what I was. Owl shit. So, no, I'm not arguing with you when I say we weren't right. We weren't. Of course, then, nobody is, really, especially at our age."

"God, Mel — you talk like you've got a foot in the grave."

"I feel that way, Terry. Sometimes. I really do. How can't you, in the kind of work we do?"

"I don't know. Maybe I do."

"And maybe you compensate with a twenty-eight-year-old television bombshell from Dixie."

"West Virginia stayed Union."

"Who gives a shit what West Virginia did?"

I watched one of our neighbors — former neighbors — driving along the gravel road. She craned her neck, having seen my car out front, trying for a look at a real child molester, the kind of guy they're going to start chemically castrating in the golden state of California soon. (As head of CAY I was in favor of the old-fashioned, actual castration, but it is considered cruel and unusual. As an accused child molester with a trial date not yet set, I had to admit to some uncertainty on this issue.)

"Maggie brought me cookies the day she found out you'd been arrested. There was a plate of them for you, too."

I said nothing. Melinda unwound from her pensive position and leaned back against the railing of the deck.

"So, sign the papers, Naughton. I'll let you say good-bye to Penny sometime, but I don't want to make too big a thing out of us leaving. I'm putting a happy face on it. And I'm determined to look happy if it kills me, which it might. I'm talking to Wade and the personnel people tomorrow. Thought I'd give you the scoop. Is that what Donna Mason called it, when she sat you down for that interview?"

She actually waited for an answer. "They call it an 'exclusive,' I think."

"Well, Terry, you'd just had sexual intercourse with her, a few minutes before, so *you* must have felt pretty exclusive, yourself. It was written all over your pathetic little face."

"Mel."

"Mel fucking *what?*"

"Enough."

"Yeah, enough. Take a hike, old friend, but sign the papers first. See you in the next life."

I signed the papers.

On my way back to the apartment all hell suddenly broke loose. Very quietly, but it broke loose just the same.

First was a call from Loren Runnels:

"Terry, they've got Tim Monaghan from the FBI here to talk about those photographs. Will's flying in from Boise, should be landing in an hour. I can't get a read on Zant, but he wants to see us at three, up at County with Wade and the photo boys."

"Holy, *holy*, shit."

"Don't get your hopes up."

Next was a call from the second-to-last person on earth I expected to hear from:

"Terry, this is Jim . . . Jim Wade. I've got some people we need to talk to at three today.

You'll be here, won't you?"

"You know I will."

"How are you?"

"I was worse the day my son died."

"We've got some things to talk about. I'll see you then."

My heart was pounding so hard I could feel my chest knocking against the shoulder restraint. The luck was back, man: the stinking Irish luck was coming back to me. I felt it. I knew it. I *was* it.

So I called Johnny and got him at the Gayley crime scene.

"Anything good there?"

"Skin and blood under her nails, hair all over the place, fingerprints galore — who knows whose. He's made at this end, Terry. All we need now is a suspect. We could use your eyes, boss. It was bad, what he did to her."

"The Bureau's here to pow-wow with me and Wade. I'm smelling the finish line."

"I'll say a prayer for you."

Then I called Vinson Clay at PlaNet and wouldn't stop talking to his secretary until she put me through.

"I need Shroud," I said.

"Naughton. Look . . . we're considering. I took it to com-mittee. It's the only way to cover our own asses around here."

In committee. Lawyers, lawyers, lawyers.

I went back to the metro apartment to

shower and shave before my meeting with the FBI and the sheriff. And there was part three of all hell breaking loose, a user-group posting from I. R. Shroud:

Mal — Sorry for delay. Been busy as a bee. If you're going live, call Chet for the feed. He'll direct. It'll be worth every penny you donated. Tee-hee-hee.

And that's when I realized who the girl in the photographs was.
Of course.

I could feel the heat of eyeballs on me as I walked into Sheriff Jim Wade's office at 2:58 P.M. that day: Ishmael from the hallway; Woolton and Vega from their desks; Burns from his chat with Jim's secretary; and Frances, who stopped her conversation with a deputy I didn't recognize to stare at me rather blankly as I made the long march to Wade's door.

When that door closed behind me there was Jim and Rick Zant, my lawyer Loren Runnels, Will Fortune and a large, athletic man who could only be Tim Monaghan. Monaghan was with the Special Photographic Unit. I shook his hand and we sat around Wade's desk.

"They're fake," Monaghan said. "They're the best I've ever seen, but they're still fake. They're digitized mockups, reshot with a film recorder. Several ways we can tell this, but I don't think I need to go into detail right now. Basically we knocked them on three points — physical anomalies, replicated edge marks and contradictory patterns in the grain matrix. I can testify in court if you want, but one of the reasons I'm here is to keep it from coming down to that. I think we all might have better things to do. We want to talk to the guy who made them. I know you do. We'll give you our help if you want it. Will, you have anything to add?"

"Not one word."

Talk about a golden silence.

Two hours later I was sitting in a conference room, uncharged, reinstated, apologized to, put back in control of CAY and gathered with my unit — plus Wade, Woolton and Burns, the six deputies temporarily assigned to us, plus six more brand spanking new ones that Johnny said were a welcome-back present. Monaghan left us with two FBI agents he must have been storing in his briefcase. Our only task was to accelerate our search for The Horridus. We had to light a fire under his ass so hot he'd jump right out of his skillet and into our pot.

Oh yes, Ishmael was there, too. He was the only deputy on the whole floor who wasn't lingering around Jim Wade's office when we came out, the only guy who wasn't standing there clapping and smiling when Wade said he'd just had the rare experience of being able to help correct one of the biggest mistakes of his life.

Ish just stood there in the room acting like he had business with a telephone, staring at me with his green cat eyes and a look of spiritless revulsion on his face. Then he turned his back to me and kept on talking.

Twenty-nine

"I'm looking for a puppy for my daughter," Hypok said to the animal control officer. "She's four."

The officer — a dour hag of perhaps thirty — told him where the puppy run was, and if he didn't find one he liked there, he could try the kennels out back for a slightly older dog. Hypok knew the drill here, but he asked all the standard questions anyway. It had been six months or so since he'd hit them up for Moloch chow. The officer on duty today was one he'd never seen before, but it paid to be careful when your face — former face — was on a freeway billboard not two miles away. It was really kind of a thrill to glide through the world with a new look, but you didn't want to press it.

Hypok thanked her and walked back to the puppy run. He tilted a little on his way in — all that cactus juice flowing — but it was a good tilt, kind of a personal slant on things. Part of the new look. He was fresh from a shower and change of clothes — khaki pants with pleats, an almost matching cotton long-sleeved shirt with plenty of outdoorsy, all-

American looking pockets and epaulets on it, manly gray socks and a pair of work boots. He'd put a pen in the pocket of the shirt. He felt trustworthy and animal friendly, the kind of guy who ate granola and would be happy to let you touch the cute little pup he was walking. But his psoriasis was flaring up — it always did when he got close to a predation — and even the cool, clean cotton was a torment against his skin. He'd gotten a fresh tube of Lidex goop delivered by the pharmacy, though the new delivery bimbo was too dumb to just drop it in his mail slot as usual. But the Lidex helped. And the tequila helped, too.

The puppy room was small and square. It had cages on three levels, and it echoed with the whines and yelps of puppies and the cacophony of the big dogs outside, and the occasional metallic slamming of doors. It was surprisingly loud. It smelled of dog shit and piss. There were other puppy lookers there with him: a family of five with a chubby but rather sexy daughter who looked to be about three; and an elderly couple made up of a man who probably weighed a hundred and a fat woman who weighed at least twice that.

Hypok stepped to the cages and stopped eye to eye with a black puppy about the size and shape of a shoebox. He looked mostly lab, with something smaller and curlier mixed in — cocker spaniel, probably. He had deep brown eyes, the brightest of white teeth and a little pup weenie with a whip of damp hair curving off it. The label said he was an "All American," one of the shelter's euphemisms for mutt. He was expected to weigh between thirty and fifty pounds as an adult. He licked Hypok's finger through the bars. A very cute dog. There were three more just like him in the back of the cage asleep, neat as a row of socks. Next was a beagleish unit yapping quite loudly, paying Hypok no attention at all. Hypok wasn't a fan of the beagle, though Moloch had eaten one about a year ago, a full-grown dog he'd gotten here for free. It had been a sullen thing, didn't like Hypok, didn't like the ride home in the then-red van, didn't like the guest house or the "last supper" he was offered, didn't like it at all when Hypok led him to the cage door in the back of Moloch's world and tried to guide him in. The beagle had wheeled twice and bitten at him but Hypok remained in control. He kept the stubborn little hunter lined up with the open door and kicked it through. The dog had cowed in the corner a minute, then was tentatively exploring the front glass when Moloch hit him like a bolt from Olympus and ten minutes later the ungrateful hound was nothing more than a slow lump. Hypok moved down the row: golden ones, black ones, calico ones; furry coats, short coats, straight coats and curled coats. Even a Dalmatian mix — spots intact — which Hypok knew wouldn't last long in this market. The older, out-of-proportion couple seemed charmed by a Doberman–golden retriever mix with nice eyes and good confirmation. "You can tell he's intelligent," the huge woman noted. Her skinny mate muttered, "All dogs are dumb." Hypok continued.

Then it was love at first sight. She was a tiny, furry little thing — a failed Lhasa apso, by the look of her — roughly the size and appearance of a fluffy bedroom slipper. He could hardly tell her face from her ass, her eyes just barely visible behind the sprouting brow hair, which was a direct mimic of the tail hair at the other end. A reversible dog, Hypok thought. Her whole tiny body wiggled as she wagged her tail and licked Hypok's finger. The sign said Yorkie-Lhasa mix, but it could have said anything, because Hypok had made up his mind. He quickly toured the rest of the puppy room, then marched back to the front desk to register his claim.

The old hag gave him the standard lecture and made him fill out the standard forms. He used his Warren Witt fake California driver's license with a picture from years ago. It showed him with the short dark hair but no Vandyke or mustaches. The animal control officer seemed to somehow disapprove of it, or him, or something. Maybe it was his breath that she didn't like, though the tequila and cinnamon drops seemed to be keeping his outlandish inner smells from coming out his mouth. He coughed quietly into his hand and waited for the results: not really that bad at all. The cost for the pup was $47, which included a $25 "altering deposit" that he would get back when he had the thing sterilized. Fat chance of that. He remembered a dog pound back in Missouri — or was it the one in Arkansas? — where they'd give you a puppy *and* a can of dog food for five bucks. He paid cash, breaking one of the nice hundreds delivered to him by the Friendlies from Naughty Naughton, then dumped the change into a donation bottle.

He named her Loretta. It was the kind of name he liked — kind of country/traditional — not like the sadly ambitious names that girls have now. She sat on the bucket seat next to his, not really scared, lifting her small buttish face to the air conditioner breeze that parted the long strands of her eyebrows to reveal her BB-sized eyes. Her face was kind of smashed in — from what you could see of it — but her white-and-tan-splotched hair was gay. The grim crone of an animal control officer had offered to tie a bow around the dog's neck, and Hypok had chosen white with black paw prints. "What's your daughter's name?" the officer demanded.

"Nan," he'd said with a proud smile.

Now he was heading back out the 22 toward the 55, giving serious thought to where he should start. He took a generous gulp of tequila and held up the clear plastic bottle: one-third left. It was 5:45 P.M. Friday, with all sorts of good possibilities at the malls because working moms like to pick up their daughters at day care after work and go spend money on Fridays. The amusement parks were always good. The supermarkets would be good, too. The beach would be okay but not great because it wasn't quite warm enough yet. Same for the public swimming facilities, though the one down in Mission Viejo had showers and was active last spring. The parks were always good, especially if you liked Latins, which Hypok neither liked nor disliked more than any other ethnic brand. Obviously, it was too late in the day for schools or bus stops. The trick was to be where the kids were numerous and the parents lax. A lot of it was just luck, too, though. The tequila consolidated him in a wonderful way, compressing him into a single, purposeful unit of acquisition. He was back in the hunt. The first order of business was to stop at a pet store and get a leash and a little collar, and maybe some of those little poopie tissues that come in the round plastic eggs like the rubber snakes in the vending machines used to. He had once purchased a realistic rubber coral snake for a quarter.

"You girls can get expensive," he remarked to the dog.

Loretta yawned, then looked at him and wagged her tail.

Hypok looked out at the traffic-swelled County of Orange as he crept down the 55. It wasn't his idea of a good place to live, really, because it was expensive, fast paced and filled with successful, hardworking, narrow-minded people. They wanted it all, and believed they deserved it. Real consumers, reeking of entitlement. One of the upsides was that there was plenty of work if you needed it. The other upside was that these "master-planned communities" were dandy breeding pens for middle-class human beings, who tended to produce attractive, healthy offspring. So, it was a trade-off. But compared to Missouri or Arkansas or Georgia or Florida or Texas, Orange County was pretty good. The parents here were a lot more careless than you might think, which he attributed to a general arrogance in baby boom adults who were themselves just older, privileged children. They thought they owned the whole fucking world. He thought about his next place, wondering if a more rural but growing metropolitan area — like Portland, Oregon, or Denver, Colorado — might give him the sense of nature that he really liked, along with a suitable population base for successful work. He briefly entertained an old fantasy: sell house and most belongings, buy big pickup with camper on it, buy small trailer to tow behind the pickup and go around the states taking choice Items into the camper bed, allowing them to enjoy his company, then letting them have free run of the trailer for as long as they could until they met up with Moloch — the full-time tenant of the trailer. He loved the idea — it was the RV lifestyle they were always talking about on the radio, with a wrinkle. But he knew he'd miss the comforts of a true home. That's why he'd retracted Collette's listing, because of the comforts of Wytton Street. But the current fact of the matter was that the heat was on here in OC, and he'd either have to move, quit or get caught. His days of carefree anonymity were over. Another Item or two collected, and that would be about it. There was no reason to press something when the odds were growing against you. But that was easy to say and harder to do, when every cell, nerve and corpuscle in your body was screaming out for the same thing: love, touch, *release*.

Hypok continued down the 55 to the 405, heading for Fashion Island, an outdoor mall in Newport Beach that had a pet store. He could kill two birds with one stone: get Loretta outfitted properly, and troll for Items right there in the mall until security threw him out for having a dog. If he explained he just bought the dog at the store, it might buy him a little leeway. Fashion Island was a ritzy place, not as crowded with kids and moms as a run-of-the-mill suburban mall, but it had some things going for it: (1) parking places very close to some of the store entrances, (2) dozens of entrances/exits as opposed to the limited number — usually four to six — found in an indoor mall, (3) the pet store, (4) an outdoor, relaxed, adult-oriented atmosphere that distracted parents with products and made them lax, (5) healthy, nutritionally advantaged Items, and (6) plenty of single guys around for cover. This time of day wasn't a good one for Fashion Island, Hypok conceded, but if he didn't have any luck by six-thirty, the movie theaters, amusement parks, stadiums and entertainment arenas would be heating up by then, as well as all those wonderful fast-food restaurants that featured playgrounds for the kiddies.

He cruised the parking lot near the Robinson's/May store, a prime place to be if he got lucky. Circling the two best rows for the third time, Hypok suddenly felt a jolt of anger passing through him: a tensing of his muscles, a dimming of his vision, a huge desire to strike or throttle something living — the dog next to him, for instance — then it was gone as quick as it came on and he calmed himself with another swig of warm tequila as he waited for a fat-assed Japanese luxury sedan to vacate a space so he could pull in.

He ran a tender hand over Loretta's tiny hairy head. She shivered. He licked his finger and offered it to her. Lick, lick. *Ohhh . . .*

Out of the van, lock the door, Loretta held to his side like a football. Just a few steps and he was into the sensual cloister of the mall, all perfume and product and groomed human beings, corporate America pandering to the bored and prosperous, Hypok's natural instincts isolating the blonde with the stroller; the frizzy-haired brunette with a daughter on each hand checking the curios in the From Russia with Love booth; the portly third-world nanny guiding a young son and daughter behind a speeding mother who was already through the doors of the Express store offering 33 percent off swimwear and a buy-two-get-one-at-half-price deal on "summer casuals." Hypok noted the five-year-old Item (red dress, ribbon in hair) nearly a hundred yards ahead of him; the seven-year-old (pink shorts, pink blouse) trailing its father into a department store; the four-year-old (denim pants and matching oversize jacket) standing alone by the leather sandal booth and looking very enticing indeed. He approached. He stopped about ten feet behind it. He set down Loretta and started cooing at her. She wiggled, jumped up to lick him, then began to wander away with a precarious sideways puppy canter that brought a smile to Hypok's face.

"Loretta!" he ordered calmly. "Come back here, little girl!"

The four-year-old turned as if on command — they often responded to a masculine voice at that age, especially if their parents were already divorced — and it looked quickly at

Hypok, then at Loretta. Its face broke into a smile bright and warm as a Death Valley sunrise. It slapped over to Loretta in its little sandaled feet and bent down, oversized jacket covering most of its pale, chubby legs. Dinosaur Band-Aid, lower right calf, freshly applied, no peripheral dirt buildup yet. Loretta was jumping up to lick the Item. Her tail wagged over her back. Hypok sighed and walked over to them, taking a knee a few feet away to watch the precious Item/canine encounter. He looked directly at them from behind his sunglasses, showing no interest at all in who — if anyone — might be the Item's keeper. Loretta sprang up and down like a ball attached to a rubber band attached to a paddle. She scooted away. The Item lunged after her and fell to its knees: white thighs, a flash of something whiter between them. Loretta wiggled toward it. Hypok knelt on one knee with his left elbow resting on his kneecap and a hard, ferocious heat annealing his guts. Something of Valeen and Collette in this one, he thought, in the way its eyes shine. He doubted if this Item had the unabashed carnal curiosities of his older sisters at age, say, ten, but that was hardly the point. There were ways around that little problem. Then, the almost inevitable happened. Hypok sensed it before he saw or heard it, and he knew exactly what it was. Suddenly, a large intrusive figure barged into his field of vision and squatted down next to the Item and Loretta. It was like a dark cloud passing over the sun. Human male: forty-something, polo shirt, shorts and deck shoes, no socks, one of those come-late-to-familihood dads who were a whole lot more vigilant about their brood than the twenty-something kids who started early. He was actually gray haired. He looked at Hypok with a neutral expression, nodded, then reached out to the puppy. Loretta dropped her flag of a tail and cowed, then approached him reverently. He pet her. She peed. Hypok moved up and forward and swept the still dribbling Loretta up into his arms. He smiled down at father and Item.

"Be careful of the wee-wee," he said. He expected security to lock onto him at this point. Things felt wrong.

"Come on, Lauren," said the old gray-haired, idiotically dressed daddy boy.

Hypok moved toward the pet store. Another Lauren, he thought. Chloe, Lauren, Jessica, Joy, Tiffany, Charlie: when will Americans stop naming their daughters after perfumes?

On to the pet store now, Hypok carrying Loretta under his left arm, scanning the shoppers for Items — a little redheaded siren by the bookstore; a plump temptress walking with its plump mother, same chunky legs, a miniature version of the physical mold it'd come from; a sultry, pouting Item of perhaps twelve — too old, but that looked brazenly at him as he passed by and he caught the aroma of perfume and shampoo coming off it. Into the store, a brief notification of the clerk concerning his intentions, then to the collar rack, way down at the bottom where the smallest ones hung upon display hooks and he brought out a pink, a yellow and a blue for Loretta to sniff as if the tiny fool really cared what color she wore. He picked a light blue one that sort of fit, though a long piece of it protruded beyond the buckle when it was snug enough not to slip over and off Loretta's head. He picked a leash to match it. In the food section he found a small box of puppy treats for very small dogs. At the cash register he paid with one of the twenties given to him by the harpy at the animal shelter, the bill a limp but direct descendant of the crisp hundreds paid to him by a perverted cop who couldn't live without pictures of himself and girls not yet into puberty. What a world. The woman at the checkout counter was big and horsy looking, perhaps nineteen. When she smiled she looked like John Elway with long hair. She pet Loretta with an enormous freckled hand.

"She's *so* cute."

"For my daughter, Nan."

The Denver QB stared hard at him. Ready to call an audible at the line, Hypok imagined.

"Are you on TV?" she asked Hypok.

"No, I'm in advertising. Billboards, actually."

"You look like *some*one I know."

"And you look like someone *I* know, too, but I can't think who."

"Probably that football player," she said, smiling and looking down. "That's what all the guys say, anyway."

"Say good-bye, Loretta."

"Loretta! That's my mom's name. 'Bye, Loretta!"

Back into the evening now, the darkness complete, the lights of the shops bright and alluring as diamonds, the dog collared and leashed, flouncing back and forth in front of him. Past the gleaming storefronts and the central courtyard, past the benches and the planters and the fish pond, through the booths again, winding through Fashion Island like a snake on a prowl, alert to danger and opportunity, attuned to every odor on the breeze and every nuance from the bodies of the mammals all around him, Hypok himself the head of the serpent, the ultraviolet eye, the heat pit sensor, the aroma-gathering tongue, the collating brain in a secret hunt among the privileged and prosperous, the harried and the careless, the vain and the ignorant, the innocent and the pure.

He stopped at the intermittent fountain, a kid pleaser at all times of the day and night. His brain panted.

Hypok receiving: two twelve-year-olds unattended and perilously brash looked his way with admiring eyes, old as they were it sent a ripple of electricity up his back. A tandem stroller for two-year-old twins in pink, just a hair too young. A petite Indian girl in a sari, dark and mysterious as the Ganges of which Hypok was reminded, picturing crocodiles taking down Hindu bathers in diapers and turbans.

Then, his senses all ratcheted up a full degree and his breathing shortened as a five-year-old pigtailed seductress in overalls and black tennies spotted Loretta and angled straight toward her, its hair tawny brown in the lights, its arms thin, its face a littoral of light and shadow but a mask of pure happiness to be sure, white teeth and red lips and eyes dark as tidepools at midnight — an Item so absolutely perfect and compelling that Hypok's breath shallowed out to almost nothing, snagging against his throat like a skiff on a Key West flat, and he breathed in deeply now and fumbled for his cinnamon drops as he knelt and fed out leash so Loretta could wobble out to greet this radiant, approaching Item.

He watched the Item sit cross-legged, with Loretta climbing all over its lap. The Item grabbed the puppy's head gently, steadied it while looking into Loretta's face, then kissed her on the nose.

"You smell good!"

Its voice was thin and high and very clear, made you feel like you were breathing mountain air, or amyl nitrite poppers.

"Her name's Loretta," he managed.

Breathe in. Breathe out. Expand lungs. Relax.

The Item looked at him for the first time, and Hypok knew that its first reaction to him would make it gettable or not. He waited like a disciple for a miracle, or a revelation from his master. Then, an ocean of warm optimism rolled through him when it smiled and said, "Mine's Ruth."

Ruth! A genuine name! The Book of Ruth!

"Here," he said, "you can offer her a reward."

"What did she do?"

"She's being nice to you."

Hypok cracked open the box of doggie treats and held one — shaped like a tiny hot dog — out toward the Item. It leaned forward, still sitting, still smiling, and took the biscuit.

Loretta got a whiff of it and jumped toward the Item's hand, then tried to climb its arm.

"She's hungry!"

"Hold the treat over her head, tell her to sit, and tug gently on the leash." Hypok felt the warm, surging seas inside him starting to settle and solidify. The breeze against his ears suddenly felt cool and instructional: *get it to the van*. "Tug *gently* on the leash."

When Loretta felt the tug, she wheeled left, then right, trying to locate her torment. Then she stopped, looked up at the Item's lowering hand and leaped, snatching the treat midair and dropping it to the ground. She whirled around, trying to find it through all her hair.

"Ohhh!"

"That's all right, Ruth. She's got a lot to learn. Just like her brothers and sisters."

"How many puppies do you have?"

"Well, there's Mommy, Daddy and five others. Loretta is the happy one, because she knows she's staying with me and her parents. The others are sad. So I left them in my car."

"Sad why?"

"I'm taking them to the shelter. Hopefully, they'll find homes, but you never know. Puppies understand that kind of thing. They understand when they're safe and when they're not."

"Ohhh. That's sad."

"It's very sad. It breaks my heart, actually. So I stopped here to get a box of treats for them all. I'm just looking for excuses not to drive to that animal shelter."

"I wish I could take them."

"I doubt your parents would be very happy about that."

"No. We have a cat."

"Where are your mom and dad, by the way?"

Ruth looked at him, then turned and pointed to a crowded restaurant lobby. The place was packed — people standing outside, inside, everywhere. "Getting dinner to go."

It looked like a long wait.

"Which ones?" he asked.

"Oh, they're in there somewhere. We do this *every* Friday. They let me watch the fountain because it takes so long, and Daddy can have wine, but he can't bring it down here."

Loretta had rolled onto her back while the Item scratched the dog's hairy little belly.

"You know, I'll bring the box out, and you and your mom and dad can at least look at the others," he said. "No harm in that, I guess. Who knows?"

The Item smiled again, lifting Loretta up into its arms and staring into her hidden puppy face. "Could I have this one?"

"She's mine! But I'll let you see the others. All right?"

"Great!"

Hypok stood and walked toward the Item, bending down to take Loretta.

"Can't she wait with me?"

"Well, I should keep her in my sight."

"But I'll watch her."

"No . . . I really can't let her be away from me like that. Let's see . . . why don't you . . . you know, my car is just right over there, so if you want to take the leash and walk her for me, that would be okay."

"Can't leave the fountain, Dad says."

"Well, that's understandable," he said, softly.

Hypok set Loretta down and held the leash.

The Item looked sadly at the puppy. He said nothing for a long, punishing moment.

"Actually, I won't be able to bring them out, I guess, because I have to carry the box, too. Someone else would have to take Loretta."

He smiled, then offered his most contrite and penitent expression. It was good enough to make God believe him. He held out the leash.

"It's right over there. We'll probably be back before your dad even *gets* his wine."

The Item smiled too, and stood, then scampered toward his outstretched hand, reaching for the leash.

"Let's go fast now," he said.

"Come *on*."

"I'm right behind you."

A quick pivot of scaled head toward the restaurant lobby: a chaos of happy, hungry humans, the smell of food, white lights against the blue-black springtime sky of Southern California.

Ruth!

Thirty

You stand in a room where a person was murdered hours ago and the room feels different than others. It feels ashamed. It feels violated. It feels guilty. You tell yourself it's just in your mind, that you're projecting yourself into the space, but places like that are different, even if you can't tell why. They scream, but the scream is silent. They offer proof, but the proof is hidden. They wait for you to make things right. So you listen, and you look and you hope.

I'd gotten out of the department building as soon as I could, after reorganizing some of the CAY task force responsibilities and huddling briefly with Wade over the question of the media and my new exonerated status. We decided not to hold a press conference and not to release the story through Public Information just yet, hoping that The Horridus would continue his computer transactions with me. There was only a small chance that he would, we agreed, but it was a chance worth taking. There was still a small chance, too, that Vinson Clay over at PlaNet would do the right thing and finger I. R. Shroud for us — *if* I could get him back on the line. The Bureau had talked to Vinson, throwing their weight behind our plea. For myself, I would simply remain for a few more days as the accused child molester I had been, with few people outside the department much the wiser. Easy. At my insistence, The Horridus task force room was going to be staffed twenty-four hours a day with investigators and deputies assigned directly to the case. I had the feeling that The Horridus was about to rampage soon: he struck and failed and he wasn't going to wait another thirty days to try again.

Wade, uneasy at the prospect of what might happen, agreed to keep the force working around the clock.

"The proaction was dangerous," he said bluntly. "We got a mother killed."

"We didn't kill her," I answered bluntly back.

"But if we'd left things well enough alone, Terry?"

"With The Horridus out there, sir, things will never be well enough."

He sighed. "All right."

Then he got up and closed the door to his office. You could see the heads turning again. He didn't even bother to sit down.

"I'm hearing the rumors. You think somebody here had those photos made up?"

I told him I was sure of it: I. R. Shroud had been the supplier — perhaps the creator —

544

and someone using my Web name, Mal, had made the purchase.

"Who?" he asked.

"Ishmael talked to Shroud thirty-two times in the last seventy-four days. I've got that from two different sources, sir, and it's easy enough to check out."

"How would he know your Web name?"

"It's not a secret around here. I've written it down a dozen times at least, in my reports. Hell, Frances and Louis have both used Mal to lurk in the chat rooms. Ish could pick it up without working too hard."

Jim Wade colored deeply. He crossed his arms over his chest and leaned against his door. "You two bastards," he said quietly.

"I kept mine within the rules, Jim. He didn't."

"This is all an angle to move up the ladder?"

"It's all ambition, jealousy, pride and suspicion. It's human nature."

"Well, I know a lot of human beings, Sheriff deputies among them, who don't resort to this kind of shit on the playground."

I shrugged. "It's about Mel and Penny, too, and Ishmael helping me get on here twenty years ago. I don't know, sir — ask Ishmael. He made the overtures to Shroud. Ask him what the hell they were talking about, if it wasn't pictures."

"I will."

"And I'll be curious to know what he says."

"Maybe it's about Donna Mason, too."

It didn't surprise me that Ishmael had ratted out my living arrangements to Wade.

"She's one thing I'd like to keep out of this," I said. "We're sharing an apartment. On the salary I've been entitled to for the last two weeks, it's about the best I could come up with."

He looked at me and shook his head. "She's turned down Ishmael three or four times, on story ideas. She's covered you like you were the risen Christ. Did you tell *her* your Web name?"

To tell the truth, it had felt far more natural and innocent to tell Donna my lurker's name than it did to admit to Wade that I had done so. My stomach shifted a little. "Yes."

"Who's the girl in the pictures?"

"I'd rather not say just yet, sir. I'll get to her when I can."

Jim Wade looked at me with his cop's face, not his politician's face or his public servant's face. It's a wise old face when he wants it to be, filled with a remarkable combination of doubt and hope.

"All right. You know, that special Mason did — the Texas connection — there were some things in there that shouldn't have gotten out. That was our stuff, Terry. And I know she got it from you."

"Guilty. Sir, I'm in love with her and I trust her. She's the only one who didn't drop me when those pictures hit."

Wade smiled without happiness. "Her and Johnny."

I said nothing.

"What I'm saying, Naughton, is that you aren't a CNB employee who happens to have an office here."

"I understand. I've been trying to help us."

"You've been trying to help yourself. Just in case you didn't know, the woman you lived with until a week ago gave me her notice today. She's had enough of all this."

The Gayley crime scene was bloodless, but grim in its own matter-of-fact way. John Escobedo and I let ourselves in at 6:05 P.M. that Friday night, some fourteen hours after the death of Margo and the attempted abduction of seven-year-old Chloe. It was like the other scenes in the telltale ways: suburban, middle-class, ground-floor residence, no man in the house, single working mother and young daughter. And when we walked into Chloe's bedroom, there it was, the silent scream.

Johnny walked me through, though there wasn't much question about the sequence.

"He came in through the window, used a glass cutter and a bathroom plunger to hold the glass. Reilly couldn't get anything off the plunger, so far. Anyway, he moved the latch up to unlock it, then slid the window back and climbed in."

I could see the carbon powder on the windowpane and the rectangular shapes where the acetate lifting tape had been applied, then removed.

"The window was crawling," said Johnny. "Frances is running them through CAL-ID and WIN with all our parameters on The Horridus."

I looked glumly at the dust and glass, knowing The Horridus was wearing gloves when he came through.

"Gotta try, boss," he said.

I turned and looked at the closet. It was easy to know where Margo had been standing when she surprised him because the room was small — not much space between the door and the closet. There was a chalk outline on the carpet in the shape of human legs, continuing into the closet, then the outline of a head against the far wall inside. Some of Chloe's little-girl clothes were piled to either side of the silhouette. Beneath and beside the clothes were Chloe's shoes. Mixed in with the shoes were those things you might expect in a seven-year-old's closet that hadn't been organized lately: dolls and drawing tablets, books and markers, stuffed animals, plastic horses, balls. Obviously, the sliding closet door had been open and Margo had reeled backward with The Horridus on top of her, probably with both hands locked on her throat. I knelt down and looked in.

"What did you take?"

"The pepper spray container, two books for prints — even though it's a long shot — and a couple of shiny leather shoes that he might have touched. It was hit and miss, boss. There wasn't anything that looked too good. The CSI's really combed through for hair and fiber, though. There's a lot for the lab."

"No dust. Did you ALS the wall here inside?"

"We did. Nothing."

"Coins, keys, pens, nail clipper, Chapstick — anything he might have lost from his pockets?"

"Not unless he carries Little Miss Makeup."

"Loose button, thread?"

"Come on, boss. We'd be all over something like that."

"Yeah, I know that . . ."

My voice trailed off, like it was consumed by the closet in which Margo had fought and died.

"The blood and skin's our payoff," said Escobedo. "If we get a suspect we can make him all the way."

I turned and wondered what Chloe was doing while her mother fought for her life in the closet. Escobedo read my thoughts.

"The girl used a little Indian bead belt on him, she said. We've got the belt for fiber. She said when the guy was done with her mother, he stood up and she ran for it. Out the door, down the hallway, around the corner and out the door. She said he never touched her."

"But no description?"

"Black hair, average, average. She only saw him from the back, half covered with the clothes that had fallen down. When he chased her through the house it was dark. She left the lights off as she ran, thinking ahead. Bright little girl. Outside she saw him when he gave up the chase. Dark too — couldn't see much at all. No help there, boss, except the dye job on his hair. Black, she said. Not dark brown — black."

"What was he wearing?"

"She was too scared to notice."

I thought for a moment. "Latex might tear in a struggle."

"That's why we dusted the living shit out of this place."

I knelt again and picked up one of Chloe Gayley's shoes. It was a white canvas tennis shoe with some purple cartoon characters on it. I lifted it, turned it over and shook it: just a few grains of sand, and that was all. I couldn't help but wonder at the tragedy of it. Just a day earlier, Margo and Chloe Gayley were a struggling little family unit, trying to pay the bills, get the grades, have some fun, do things right. Nice little apartment. Church-goers. Good people trying hard to scratch out a life from a marriage that didn't work. Now, Chloe was without a mother she had seen murdered, Margo was dead forever and their life was destroyed. Would some good come out of it? Maybe someday. But was that good anything like the good that might have come if this had never happened? No. This was just a loss, pure and simple, all caused by a monster's appetite. An appetite as yet unsatisfied.

"He'll move again soon," I said. "He's moving now."

"What if he lies low, licks his wounds, figures he's on a cold streak?"

"Pray for that one, Johnny. Pray for Margo Gayley to stand up and walk again too, while you're at it."

I lifted Chloe's clothes off the closet floor and set them aside. Then I went through every one of her shoes, turning them over or feeling inside.

"Terry, what exactly are you looking for?"

"A miracle."

There were no miracles in Chloe Gayley's shoes, except that she would walk in them again. Survival as miracle.

My cell phone rang against my hip. I'd forgotten what a pleasure it was to feel a call coming through and know it was probably from my people at the department. It was Frances, who, alone among my CAY brethren, had neither welcomed me back to the fold nor acknowledged that she had been wrong about me. Frances too, I thought, who had found the pink envelope in Alton "Chet" Sharpe's den and hand-delivered it to Jim Wade.

It was strange to recall my words to Wade, just an hour earlier, with which I had admitted that Frances, too, was well aware of the Mal handle, and the terrible access that name was granted in certain private chat rooms.

"Terry," she said in a flat, businesslike voice, "we might have something useful here. We just got a call from an animal control officer up in Orange. Says The Horridus was at the animal shelter about two hours ago. She thought he looked familiar when she talked to him, but couldn't place the face. Then she drove past the billboard on her way home."

"Describe."

"Black hair. Facial hair too — mustaches and those little sharp beards the kids are wearing, a completely revised edition. But she says it was him. She said his breath was bad — and she *hadn't* seen Ish say so on TV."

A current of joy buzzed into my heart. I thought about The Horridus at the animal shelter.

"What's his name?"

"Warren Witt, a Santa Ana address, deputies on the way."

I could see it. I could see him. And the logic behind his visit to the animal shelter came clear. "Did he take a puppy?" I asked.

"Yes. For his daughter."

"He's using it for *bait*, Frances."

"I know he is, Terry. The officer made the

552

van for us, because the guy was so weird — white, late-model Dodge, Cal plates 2JKF869. Plates stolen off an '89 Toyota three weeks ago in Irvine — a little side street off of Von Karman, a business area."

"Give me his residence address."

Frances did.

"We'll be there in twenty," I said. "Before you leave, get Amanda Aguilar and the animal control —"

"— I already did. They're on their way here."

I was still holding one of Chloe's shoes in my hand, a little suede hiking boot with a red flannel lining. When I turned it over, nothing whatsoever came out.

We got there in less than twenty minutes, and just as I had suspected, it was not a residence at all. Instead there was a tortilla factory that had been in business, the owner told us, for forty years. No Witt. No Warren. He gave us each a sack of fresh tortillas, the no-lard, low-fat kind the gringos like. He was just about to lock the door for the day.

We stood in the twilight outside the shop. You could hear the mariachis a few doors down, and taped music coming from a record shop up the street. Friday night in the barrio: good music, good food, goodwill toward men. It sort of made you want to stay there and forget about the world outside.

"Frances," I said, "get started on the body shops, will you? Get a couple of the new deputies to help you. Somebody painted that van in the last two weeks and we need to know whose it is."

"Goddamned Witt, probably," she said. "And every one of them will be closed by now on Friday. He's driving around out there, Terry. He's got that damned little dog and he's going to get a girl with it."

"Try anyway. While you're at it, we'll plaster this bastard's new face all over Christendom."

"That'll take time."

She looked at me for a long moment. "Terry, I just wanted to say how glad I am to have been wrong about you. I . . . wasn't sure what to do with what I found. I'm glad to have you back and I'm glad to call you boss. I don't know what happened, but I . . . I hope we can find out. I know the last few weeks must have been hell for you."

High as I was on the adrenaline of closing in on The Horridus, my heart still warmed at Frances's words. I had always liked her and thought her judgment sound, and the fact that she had so quickly taken sides against me was not the least of the thousand arrows I had felt.

I nodded and gently touched her arm. She pulled it away and hugged me.

"It means a lot," I said.

"I'll help you get to the bottom of it," she said. "That's the least I can do."

Johnny drove. And I called Donna Mason

at CNB, then all three networks. Then I called two local L.A. stations, and both the big papers in Orange County. I told them all we'd have a new face for them in about an hour.

I've never seen a group of men and women work as hard and as fast as we did for that next hour. Joe Reilly and his lab techs were still there, three of them working the hair and fiber for matches with evidence from the three earlier abductions; two were lasering the objects collected from Chloe's closet for prints; one still making the Hae III enzyme cuts on the flesh and blood DNA from under Margo's nails; while Reilly himself was hybridizing the first of the high-weight nucleotides, which he'd cut and blotted earlier in the day. Joe looked at me briefly as I passed through, his thin black hair flying like a man in a wind. We had yet to broach the topic of Joe being on a witness list against me in a case that was dropped. I wondered if we ever would, and what good it would do.

"Get me a body, Naughton. We're solid state at this end."

"Coming up, Joe. What about the latent on the snake scale and prints from Gayley's —"

"— We've got a match. We know it's The Horridus. Now do your job and bring him in."

In the task force room — it was christened Room Horrible — we had a deputy on each of the three 800 lines; Louis double-checking the statement from the neighbors to whom Chloe had fled; Frances briefing Amanda Aguilar and the animal control officer before they were sequestered in a conference room to do the sketch; one FBI volunteer on a CAY computer lurking the chat rooms for any gossip about I. R. Shroud; the other Fed in conference with an L.A. Sheriff sergeant who was part of the joint-agency SAFE group working child sex out of the Federal Building in L.A.; three deputies collecting paint-and-body-shop numbers from a stack of phone books a yard high; Rick Zant from the DA's office trying to convince the corporate lawyers for Bright Tomorrows that a release of their employee and subcontractor list might save a life; Woolton on the phone to half the police departments in the county; Burns on the line to the other half; two young deputies trying their best to track property ownership, DMV records and credit information on the ten remaining Eugene Webbs and the eight remaining Eugene Websters in three huge Southern California counties; a young deputy checking out-of-state phone companies for one Collette Loach; and Jordan Ishmael hovering over the room like some kind of mute god, seeing all and saying nothing.

And that was just in Room Horrible. We had twelve more deputies in the field, assigned specific tasks: two who were reinterviewing fabric store and pet shop employees, in case

The Horridus had made another purchase in the last week; another pair dispatched to the home of the regional manager of the county's largest auto paint chain, which, we had learned, kept computerized records of work they had done; one deputy assigned to each of the three release sites The Horridus had used; one staked out at each of the residences he'd already hit, to make sure he didn't try to take a good thing twice. We even had a team following my footsteps at the behest of I. R. Shroud, moving from Moulton Creek to Main Beach to the Norwalk Green Line station in hope — slim at best — of encountering one of The Horridus's allies. Besides those, there were ten units cruising the obvious places where The Horridus might hunt that night — amusement parks, malls, theaters showing kids' movies, entertainment complexes — and two helicopter teams shadowing them from above, strafing the same haunts with search-lights and glassing the world below for a white van. We'd already pulled over nine vehicles by then, with another few thousand to go.

Jordan Ishmael stood in the conference room. We were both getting ready for the press. He was checking the mike at the podium when I walked in. We looked at each other across the empty chairs.

"Congratulations, Naughton. You beat the rap."

"Thanks."

He turned the mike on and spoke into it, his voice amplified into the room: "YOU'VE MESSED UP A LOT OF LIVES, FRIEND. YOU DESERVED WHAT HAPPENED, WHETHER YOU DID THOSE GIRLS OR NOT."

"It was a nice try, Ishmael. But you left a big fat trail, and I'm not the only one on it. See, the way it works when you mess with me is you get messed with back."

"NO IDEA WHAT YOU'RE TALKING ABOUT."

"Next time you invite yourself over to my apartment, make sure I'm home."

"WHY WOULD I WANT TO DO THAT?"

"So I can kick your ass back out the door."

"NOT LIKELY, LITTLE FELLA."

"Going to be a long ride down, Ish. Bring Dramamine. I've got you."

"WHAT YOU'VE GOT IS MAGGOTS IN YOUR SOUL. I CAN SMELL THEM FROM HERE. ONE GOOD THING ABOUT MEL AND PENNY LEAVING IS THEY WON'T HAVE TO SMELL THEM ANYMORE."

"I think the volume's about right."

I heard the mike click off and looked at Ishmael studying me from behind the podium.

"I. R. Shroud spells Horridus, Ish. How could you be so goddamned thick you didn't see that?"

"Why would I?"

"Because you talked to him thirty times the last two months, while he was out there taking girls. That's why."

"You're one mixed-up little leprechaun, Naughton. Donna suck all your brains out, too?"

"I'm saving you for another day, Ish. It's going to be a good one for me. Count on it."

I heard the door open behind me and Frances stood there with a sheet of flimsy fax paper in her hand. On top was a shot of the rear end of a white van. The bottom shot was from the side, and showed a blur of a driver, a dark-haired male with facial hair was about all you could say for sure.

"Motion-activated cameras shoot toll lane violators and they get tickets in the mail," she said. "They got this at 2:19 this morning. White Dodge, plates 2JKF869, eastbound on the 91 toward Yorba Linda. One of the Fas-Trak people saw our press conference, knew about the van, thought we might use this. It's our van."

"Can Reilly's people enhance the driver?"

"The prints are being messengered over right now."

"Talk to Joe. Tell him what's coming in and we need a rush on it. If we can get an enhancement for Aguilar and the girl to work from, it might make things a whole lot more convincing."

"Can do."

In the doorway I literally ran into Rick Zant.

"I finally got the Bright Tomorrows attorney

to come around," he said. "They ID'd him from the press conference composite. He was there, shooting video for members. David Lumsden — home address in Capistrano. Dawn Christie was kind enough to follow suit if we'd offer a specific name. Bingo — he shot videos for them, too. Same name and address. Woolton has four men out of the Capo substation on the house."

"There won't be a house."

The old fury surged through me as I stood there, realizing that cracking an alias hadn't helped us much at all. He was still out there — The Horridus, I. R. Shroud, Gene Vonn, David Lumsden, Warren Witt, David Webb, John Q. Public, what did it goddamned matter — and we were still in here, waiting for *him* to make the next move. I felt like a fly caught in a web, trapped by the silk and knowing that the spider was moving in.

So I kicked the wall of the hallway. My foot went through the plasterboard. When I brought out my shoe it was covered in white dust.

"That hurts," I said.

"I can see that it might, Terry. Maybe if you smash up your other foot too, it will help us catch this guy. You can't expect him to go around town using his real name, can you?"

I kicked another hole in the wall.

"Nice to have you back, Terry!" someone piped from Room Horrible.

"Get to *work!*" I yelled back, already dialing the home number for Sam Welborn on my cell phone. I told him I was back in the hunt. He said he was happy to hear that, and I told him we had two more aka's and bad addresses, a botched abduction and a murder. What I needed now was anything he could give me on Collette Loach.

He was silent. Then, "Who in hell's *that,* Terry?"

"One of Wanda's daughters or sisters, I'm hoping."

"Well, I've already got the sisters checked out and Collette ain't one of them. But her daughters, those girls were grown and gone by the time Wanda bought that place in Hopkin. All's they did was visit sometimes."

"Ask around, Sam."

"I have been. That's what I'm telling you."

"Maybe someone out in Hopkin remembers her. Forget the phone company — we've already struck out with them."

"What is it you want to know about her?"

"If she's related to Wanda. And if so, exactly where she is. I need a phone number and an address and I need it soon."

"I'm on it."

Within the next fifteen minutes, CNB, all three networks and two L.A. stations had reporters and camera crews set up in the conference room, along with writers and photographers from the *Times* and the *Register*.

Amanda Aguilar and the animal control officer had completed their collaboration and a blown-up version of the sketch now sat on an easel beside the podium. He looked like one of those hot new actors — a smart-ass with a Vandyke and a wispy mustache. I stood at the back of the room with hope in my heart, a hard glance at Ishmael and a secret smile for Donna, who didn't notice me as she stood on the dais and completed a sound check with her shooter.

Everybody else noticed me, however. Their heads turned as if my name had been announced when I came in. They stared hard, disbelieving that the accused perv was back on Sheriff Department soil. Then they started toward me.

I held out my hands toward them, palms up, shaking my head.

"Talk to him," I said, nodding over at Jordan Ishmael. "He'll have the story for you. Part of it, anyway."

With that, I retreated to Room Horrible.

Louis stood and faced me as I walked in. "The deputies just made the Capistrano address for Lumsden," he said. "It's the public library."

Thirty-one

Hypok walked across the parking lot toward his van, Ruth and Loretta out in front of him, the lot filled with the bright bodies of expensive cars and the clean beams of their headlights. We're quite the family unit, he thought — beautiful daughter, protective father, happy pup. He stole another glance over his shoulder: all clear.

"Here, I'll unlock the back — the box is too big to take out the side doors."

"How many again?"

"Three brothers and three sisters."

"Before you said five."

"No, it's six. They're unbelicvably cute."

He swung open the back door of the van. Luckily, the interior light was weak and unrevealing. He deliberately blocked its view with his body as he climbed in. He reached down into the console next to the tequila and brought out a Mag-Lite, the heavy aluminum, four-battery job with the adjustable beam. Shining the light in front of him, he looked over his shoulder at the Item: two feet from the doors, Loretta in its arms, trying to see past him to the desired box of puppy delight.

"Oh, wow, they're all sleeping now! You've *got* to see them." He knocked the flashlight against the seat back, reached forward and tugged at the console with one hand, then made a soft grunting sound. "Oh darn, I can't get the whole box past this thing here. Just climb in and take a look."

"Kind of dark in there."

"I've got the flashlight, no problem. Come on up, but watch your knees on the cabinets — they're hard. Here, I'll take Loretta and you can climb in."

Hypok kept the light trained in front of him, but he pivoted at the waist and held out one hand, palm up, for Loretta. He smiled at the Item and looked past it, toward the mall, but nothing at all seemed out of order.

Come on . . . hand the puppy to her master . . .

The Item hesitated. He could feel the doubt coming off of it in quiet, uncertain waves. The way a mouse looks before a viper hits it.

Loretta whined.

"Oh, *here,* honey," he said, reaching further, his voice filled with sympathy and accusation.

Then Ruth gave in, leaned into the van and lifted the puppy toward him. Hypok reached just past Loretta and caught the Item by its wrist, yanking hard. The dog hit the floor. The Item sailed over the transom toward him. It yelped. It was midair and starting to scream when Hypok slammed the flashlight into its oncoming head. A sharp and heavy crack and

564

it landed on the van floor, limp and silent as a dropped blanket. He hurtled over it and landed in the parking lot. He looked once more over his shoulder as he slammed the van doors shut, then walked around to the driver's side slapping his hands together like a carpenter dusting off, and got in.

Two minutes later he was half a mile away, at a stoplight down on Jamboree, waiting for the light to turn, plotting the quickest course back to Wytton Street, Loretta on the seat beside his.

The Item was completely silent. He got out his bottle and took three nice long gulps — almost gone. He didn't bother to turn on the radio because the chorus of voices singing in his head now was more beautiful, deep and resonant than anything he'd heard in a long, long time.

Down Jamboree in the comforting darkness, to Redhill Avenue heading toward Tustin, past the old blimp hangars of the Marine Corps Air Station looming in outrageous bulk against the sky — largest wooden structures on earth, Hypok had heard — then into the fringes of Tustin, a quiet little town for the most part, middle America, familyville, good schools and churches, the kind of place where young people bought the homes their folks and neighbors used to own and settled in to give their own children lives remarkably similar to the ones they had had, the kind of place where a Lumsden, Webb, Shroud, Horridus or even Hypok could quietly lose himself with appropriate behavior and never so much as raise an eyebrow, but could hunt a delicious young Item or two or three when it became necessary and still remain safe against the world in his little walled home, his nerve center, his headquarters, his lair — was Item #4 stirring?

He looked behind him for just a second, training the Mag-Lite beam on its jiggling head. Nice, the way the hair and blood shined in the light. Far out in dreamland. Not too far out, Hypok hoped: both he and Moloch preferred live prey. He tapped the light against his crotch then, listening to the solid thump of it against his risen self. Clunk, clunk clunk. Funny. It was going to happen tonight, he knew, the complete act, the full circle of desire and satisfaction and the transformation of one strong human into an organizing God, another lowly human into a lofty angel; the human molt; the private pageant symbolizing the power of life over death, immortality over sin, need over shame. He checked his speedometer against the 35 mph sign whisking by on his right, and let off the gas a little. No time to be careless now, he thought, not on this warm night in May, blessed, bountiful May, when all reptiles move in earnest to eat and mate and assert themselves in the private darkness away from man.

Onto First Street, follow it into old town.

Past Wytton once, and quick look down toward his house to be sure there was no trouble, then an assertive cruise past it once again. He made a quiet U-turn at the intersection and reached up for the garage door opener — deluxe model, a two-hundred-foot response radius — and pressed the open button. He saw the towering sycamore beside his garage accept the softly growing light from below. He used the gate opener and timed it perfectly so the gate had just slid to its furthest point when the nose of the van slipped past and before he was even through he hit the close button. He rolled slowly into the garage, then pressed the control again and brought the front tires to rest against the railroad tie he had bolted into the cement to keep him from cracking into the wall, keeping as far away from the Saturn as he reasonably could. There. The door closed behind him and Item #4 stirred very quietly — just a dreamy whimper — and Hypok knew that all of his preparation, his versatility, his conviction and confidence had paid off again. He wiped a tear of gratitude and happiness from the corner of his eye as he swung himself into the back of the van, lifted Item #4's head by its warm, damp hair and shined the flashlight at its face. Beauty, he thought, a true angel's beauty, once you get the blood wiped off. Its eyes opened slowly and it whimpered again.

"There, there," he said sweetly. "The worst

is already over." He got Loretta and put her down by Item #4 and Loretta licked its sticky face. *"Ohhhh . . . let's get you inside and cleaned up!"*

Hypok sat in the chair by the old bed and ate the ravioli out of the pan. The Item lay on the bed with the black hood over its freshly washed head and face, and one of Collette's old sundresses — a pale blue background with clouds and cowgirls atop white bucking broncos. He had taped its hands together in front of it, and its ankles, too, and of course, its mouth. Loretta lay beside it. Moloch knew something was up; he watched Hypok from inside the big dollhouse, his head visible through the "dormer" window that protruded from the roof. Tongue out; wobble in the air; tongue in. Motionless silver eyes with the black vertical cut of pupil; armored head; scales, bone, muscle.

He took a neat gulp of cactus juice and looked to the bed again. Item #4 wasn't a fighter. Either that, or it wasn't scared. It didn't struggle like the others, though maybe the flashlight conk had something to do with that. All it did was moan *"Hmm-mmm-MMM!"* every once in a while, and quiver some. He'd cleansed the wound and blotted most of the blood out of its hair, and it was a nasty cut all right — an inch long and deep, and widened out like a smile from the tautness against the skull. Other than that though, it was in near mint condition.

Time now to daydream a little, as he always did when he had an Item in place and ready. A sense of accomplishment overtook him, coupled with a rising frazzle of anticipation. Have to keep the two in balance, he thought — a little reward after work well done, and a little something to look forward to in the next hours. A working man's Friday night. He couldn't help but think about his first full human transformation, the Item back in Hopkin, and how he was so nervous he hardly knew what to do. Stage fright. He wasn't sure if Moloch would even be interested, though withholding food for two months probably helped. The next time, when he offered up his mother, things didn't go smoothly at all: sophomore jinx. He thought back, fondly now, on the rigorous diet he'd enforced upon wretched Wanda, the Ultra Slim Fast shakes and no-salt, no-fat crackers, the way he had to gag and tie her in the basement for the last week while he made sure she was edible. Then, Moloch still wasn't sure what to make of the naked, trembling old crone released into his Eden, hungry though he was. Moloch had watched her for a long while, then manifested himself next to her, his big shoebox-sized head across from hers, looking her right in the face. Must have terrified him, tasting the scent she gave off. She had backed into a corner, for

569

what good it might do. But Moloch swerved away and redistributed himself into the play-house, looking somewhat morose, Hypok believed, at the prospect of an edible item smelling so bad. But his mother's bad smell hadn't thrown him for more than a second, no: he went to the freezer, got out some frozen rats he used for his big *horridus* and microwaved up a couple of large ones until they were piping hot. A pair of scissors and off with their feet. Click, click, click, into the waste-basket. Then he'd entered Moloch's realm — very warily — and smeared his dismal shrew of a mom with warm rat blood. It came out like ketchup from a plastic packet, except thinner, and steaming. Then he retreated outside and watched as Moloch, keen to the smell of rodent, slid his four hundred pounds of appetite over to gagged and bloody Wanda, then grabbed her by the shoulder, looped three times around her skinny little body and did the tighten-up. Hypok would never forget her bug-eyed stare. Of course, she seemed to be blaming *him* for her fate, but that was hardly a surprise. You could predict that. He couldn't be sure exactly when she died, because her face was purple and her eyes popping with blood but her superfluous white fingers strained against Moloch's armored bulk for a full five minutes or so. Then Moloch let go of her shoulder and nosed around his catch for a long lazy while, tongue berserk, finally deciding to start with her head, as big constrictors usually do. She stuck in his throat for a second, quite literally. It figured. Then Moloch unhinged his jaws and loosened up his neck — the narrowest part — and the plates of his pale mouth crept methodically down, and the next thing you knew Wanda was gone up to the shoulders. Hypok remembered standing there on the other side of the glass, intrigued by the spectacle, noting the way Moloch's throat widened even more as he started in on the shoulders, his dark green scales parting widely against the pale pliant grout of underskin, the way they looked like counter tiles set casually apart. To be honest, Moloch had looked pretty funny with Wanda's shoulders inside his neck, like he had these wings inside that were trying to press through a wall of gristle to get out. After that, it was fairly routine: the slow mechanical advance of unhinged jaws, half an inch of Wanda at a time, no hurry, an occasional rest, then another effort. Her head and shoulders started out as a dramatic lump inside him, but they eventually blended into Moloch's massive bulk. There was a moment — Hypok's favorite — when the snake's mouth had advanced all the way to his mother's white, drippy little rump and Moloch raised his head and Wanda's ass and legs lifted skyward in the cage, scissoring apart rather lewdly, and Hypok wondered if Moloch was concerned about the lack of a tail. Apparently not, because Moloch stayed like that — his head upright, probably six feet off the cage bottom — while Wanda's shriveled butt disappeared and her legs slowly came together like in water ballet and a moment later her ankles and up-pointed toes were going down in the slowest of motions, like a diver disappearing into a pool of pink tar.

You could just lose yourself in the past, thinking about good times like that.

"Hmm-mmm-MMM!"

"True," he said.

Time now to change into the good skin. Hop to.

He stripped down, then got the shimmering, scaly suit out of the bedroom drawer. Cotton backing; polyester/acrylic overlay. He'd handwashed it in an expensive detergent for wool products since his last shed, and it smelled fresh. He glanced just once at his sores — festering now, always giving him fits at times like this — but he chose to ignore them and just try to be the best he could be, like in the army. Legs and arms, squeeze in and close the big zipper up the front. Booties and gloves. Hood. Blue, silver, white of pearl, indigo, violet. Oil on water, abalone polish, faceted, changing, shifting always. For a while he stood in front of the mirror in the darkened room, only the lamp to illuminate his new self, and admired his transformation. Gone the frail, blistered man, gone the human cursed by God, gone the reeking mortal meat of Hypok. Look *now*, though — at the shine of scales, at the glimmer of limb, at the svelte metallic repto-hominid poised here at the peak of evolution. *Look now*, he thought. Here I am — Future Man But More Than Man: *Homo hypokithicus.*

Give me my mate.

Thirty-two

I retreated to Room Horrible while Ishmael began the conference in the press room. Strange, to sit in the eye of that hurricane and feel the reach of my senses — the eyes of the choppers flashing through the county skies, the men and women on the ground, the voices of our people gathering information from all points in the universe — but to know I was still waiting, still looking, still hunting in the dark.

Then it happened.

Johnny turned to me from his desk, holding the telephone down at his side.

"He took a girl up in Newport twenty minutes ago," he said. "Used a puppy to get her away from the parents. Dark-haired suspect, facial hair, white van."

"Get there."

"*Gone.*"

And he was gone, while I got Dispatch to send out the word to all units, praying the van was still on the road. I called the helos myself and told them to concentrate on west Newport and inland of Fashion Island.

"*That's a white Chrysler-Plymouth-Dodge, late model, over.*"

"We know that much, over."

"Then goddamned find it!"

"Eyes wide as always, Terry . . . and out."

Five minutes. Frances intercepted the messenger carrying the photo from the FasTrak toll road people and ran it down to Reilly in the lab.

The press conference was only five minutes old when a young deputy manning the 800 lines got our first call of a sighting of the new Horridus. The deputy explained to me that a young man claimed to have seen The Horridus drinking a piña colada in a Huntington Beach bar just last night — 1:30 A.M.

"He was at the Gayley house in Yorba Linda," I said. "Forget him."

Ten minutes. Sam Welborn called from Wichita Falls to say that Wanda Grantley had three daughters, according to some old-time Hopkinites who knew. None had any idea what their first or married last names were. Collette Loach didn't ring bells. Still working.

Fifteen minutes. One of our Newport units found a witness who saw the van eastbound on Jamboree about the time the father called in. It tracked with my hunch that he'd move inland, away from the coast.

The piña colada deputy said he had another caller on the 800 line: she had seen this revised Horridus exactly one week ago in a supermarket in Irvine.

"He hadn't revised himself by then," I said.

"He still had the white hair. Forget her."

Eighteen minutes. Chopper Three called in with a late-model Plymouth van moving south on Pacific Coast Highway at MacArthur, just entering Corona del Mar. Two Sheriff units were less than half a mile away, and three Newport Beach police units were already in pursuit. I slapped on the radio headset and identified myself.

"We're right over him now," said the Chopper Three sergeant, "not going to let him out of my sight. I can see NBPD coming up behind him now . . . lights on . . . doesn't see them . . . *there* — he's pulling over. We're on him, Terry . . . over."

"Stay up. Over."

"Couldn't bring me down with a missile. Will advise, over."

Another young deputy working the 800 number said he had a caller on the line who claimed to be The Horridus.

"Ask him where he is," I ordered. The deputy did.

"He laughed and hung up."

"Talk to Frances or Louis first when you get a call," I said. "I don't want these assholes wasting my time."

"Yes, sir."

Piña colada appeared beside his young partner. "Sir, caller on the line says The Horridus lives in the apartment next door to her. Very old woman, sir, says he drives a black pickup truck and delivers papers —"

"— Well, he doesn't. Talk to your buddy here about screening these through CAY — got it?"

They turned and marched back to their phone bank.

My heart was thumping hard as I put down the headset and turned to the sound of someone coming through the door in a hurry.

Some things get your attention when you see them out of context, like your dog curled on the forbidden couch, like a movie star in the airline row across from you. They catch your eye and you know that something is different.

And that's what I was thinking when Joe Reilly came through the Room Horrible with his hair askew and a strange smile and an evidence bag held up before him. Joe Reilly, scientist, rarely seen out of his native lab habitat. Whatever he had, it wasn't an enhanced photo of a toll road violator.

"Something in here you should see," he said. "It fell out of one of the shoes we were getting ready to laser for prints. One of the shoes from Chloe Gayley's closet."

Joe handed me the plastic bag and I set it on the desk. I flattened it with my fingers to deflect the glare of the overhead lights and stared down at the small shiny object.

It was a bracelet with a simple stainless-steel chain and an oval plate in the middle. The lobster-claw clasp was twisted open, unlockable now, ruined. On the front of the plate was an engraved serpent wrapped around a leafless branch. The words MEDIC ALERT were engraved down each side of the snake.

I flipped it over.

Allergic to Sulfa drugs
Call Collect (209) 669–2450
6548369

"It could have come off in the struggle," he said. "Either that, or it's the girl's, or maybe her mo—"

I handed the bag back to Reilly and dialed the number on the badge. When the receptionist came on I gave it my best:

"Dr. Terry Naughton out at UCI Med Center in Orange, California. We've got an ER admission here with your bracelet on, sulfa drug allergy, a-ok on that. Thought we'd get anything else and an ID — no wallet, no nothing on him, looks like a drug OD. We might lose this one."

"Number please?"

I told her.

"Just a moment, please."

Thirty-seven seconds: I timed it on my watch.

"Dr. Naughton, that's strange, because the bearer would be Mary Lou Kidder, last address is Wichita Falls, Texas. Now, I can —"

I hung up and stood. I was ready to crush something, anything. If one of the 800 deputies had approached to tell me about another bogus Horridus sighting, it might have been his last day of walking upright.

"It belonged to a girl back in Texas," I told Joe. "The one he fed to his goddamned snake."

Joe's countenance fell, and he nodded.

Dispatch told us the Newport Beach police had already let the white Plymouth van go — family of five on their way to dinner.

Frances edged past him and took my sleeve. "Terry, sorry. Look — one of the guys has a girl on the 800 line who says she tried to deliver a prescription ointment to The Horridus. I know it sounds kind of funny, but she's watching the press conference and she's positive it was him. I don't know, she sounds honest and credible."

"When?"

"Yesterday morning. He came out and yelled at her. That gave her a damn good look at somebody, boss."

I thought of Strickley's speculation about a skin condition that would make him unsure of himself. Something you might need prescription ointment for.

Well, now.

"Give me the phone."

"You'll have to walk to it, Terry — some of them still have cords. Her name is Tamara and she's seventeen. We've got her stats already."

I picked the phone off the table and identified myself, told her not to hang up, then asked her to tell me what she saw.

"I'm like the new delivery person for Sloan's Pharmacy in Santa Ana. And I went to take the delivery to our customer? And he came to the door and yelled at me because we're just supposed to put it in the mailbox. But I didn't know that? But he was the guy on TV tonight. It's a rilly good drawing. Earring. Everything."

"Do you remember his name, or the name of the street?"

"I'm really sorry but I can't remember either one, because I'm new like I said and I don't know the route yet? I mean, I can call the owner, Mr. Sloan, and he could probably tell me, but I thought I'd call you first. But I think he goes to bed pretty early. Either that or we open at nine in the morning."

"The house was in Santa Ana?"

"No. We deliver in Tustin, too."

"Tustin."

"Yeah."

I felt the little chill traverse my scalp.

"Old town?"

"What's that?"

"Over by the high school."

"I'm not sure where that is. I'm new to California."

"Wall around the house, trees?"

"Definitely a wall. I don't remember any trees, though."

"A gate to drive in and out of, that slides?"

"Yeah. There's a few of them in that area."

"Tamara, think hard about the street name. Forget about the guy. Just let your mind relax and let the name of the street come to you."

If she would just have said Witmer or Whitman or Wymer or, God forbid, Wytton — I would be there in five minutes. I looked at Frances while I waited, my eyes wide but not seeing anything, looking right through her. Then I closed them. I tried to will that street name into Tamara's mind.

"Like it's hard to relax when you're talking to a cop?"

"My girlfriend says the same thing."

She giggled. She was quiet for a long beat.

My heart was beating so hard I could feel my ribs hitting my shoulder holster.

"I'm feeling like really stupid."

"You're not stupid. Let it come."

"It won't."

"Okay. All right, Tamara. Answer this for me and the street name will come to you. What medicine were you delivering?"

"I'm sorry. I don't know the names. It was some kind of tube of something. Like a cream or ointment."

"For the skin?"

"I don't know. Wait. The street was something like Lomsdale, or Plumb Stem or Lump Street maybe?"

My heart sank. Then it recovered.

"Lumsden?"

"Yeah, how did you know?"

"That was your customer's name, Tamara. You're getting close. He uses that name all the time. It's a fake name and he usually gives a fake address to go with it. But he gave his real address to you, because you had to bring him something he needs. You're close. Think about that *street* name —"

"— But you're making me like rilly nervous again and —"

I could feel the pulse in my neck, going about a thousand beats a minute. "I'm sorry, Tamara," I said as meekly as I could. "I just get excited, too. I apologize."

"That's okay."

"Hey, while you think, I was wondering about this. I'll ask you this while you think of that street name, okay? Now, you said he came to the door. That's good, but how did you get past the gate?"

"I *meant* he came to the gate. He came out because we're supposed to drop the delivery in a slot in the wall and not ring the bell. Not *bother* him 'cause he's so *important*. And he came out and like yelled at me 'cause I didn't know. Like I already told you?"

"What did you do then?"

"I'm drawing like a total blank on the street.

I could take you guys there. I know right where it —"

"— *That's too slow for us now, Tamara!*"

"God, I'm just —"

"— I'm sorry. Really, I didn't mean to snap. I apologize again."

"You were more like yelling."

"I'm just getting so much pressure here at work to get this guy, you know? I take it personally. All right. I'll be cool. I promise. So, can you tell me what you did when he came out and yelled at you?"

"Oh, and he had rilly bad breath."

Heart in my ears. Beating like it was trying to fly. Scalp tight and mouth going dry. The pen in my right hand snapped and left a splotch of dark black ink on my fingers. I dropped the pieces on the floor and wiped the ink on my pants.

"Good! Great, Tamara. So . . . what did you do after he yelled at you and you smelled his breath?"

"Oh, well I threw this flower at him and walked off. I don't have to take that kind of —"

"A rose?"

"Totally! This old man like lives next door? He had this rose and he says he grows them and asked me if —"

I cupped the phone and turned to Frances.

"It's 318 Wytton Street in Tustin. Get Johnny and two of our units there ASAP, but keep them a block back until they get a go-ahead from me. But first, Frances, get Chopper Two to pick us up on the roof. *Now!*"

A minute later we lifted off the pad, the Civic Center receded beneath us, then the bird banked hard and threw my head back as we climbed fast toward the southwest. Stansbury was the pilot. Frances radioed Johnny down in Irvine and about-faced him to Tustin. I could hear his voice over the rotors and the deep roar of the engine.

"Unit 83 to Airborne Two, Frances, I'm running under lights and siren, still six or eight minutes out. Okay."

"Stay the course, 83, we'll be less than five."

"Dispatch has me holding a block out. I'm unmarked, man."

I told Frances to let him onto Wytton, but to hold until we put down, then find us.

"Unit 83 reads, over and out."

I asked Stansbury if his piece of shit chopper went any faster. He just smiled and eased onto the fuel, shooting us across the black Orange County sky and into Tustin. I navigated us in by the map, then by my memory of old town. We were spiraling down along First Street when I saw Wytton, then, in the sudden beam of the helo's searchlight, the towering syca-mores over David Lumsden's guest house.

"No lights, Stan!"

"Just making the ID, Terry. Fret not."

"Put us down on the street behind Wytton," I said. "If he's there, I don't want to spook him."

"I'll drop you down his chimney if you want."

"Behind Wytton, far end of the block."

"You're there."

Then the chopper dropped like a rock and my stomach bounced off the roof of the cockpit. Frances said "Woooh," and steadied herself while she drew and readied her sidearm, then reholstered it under her coat.

"If he's not there yet?" she asked.

"We'll wait."

"This thing is making me sick."

"Think pleasant thoughts."

"That's why I checked my Sig."

The helo swept into a big semicircle and came in low onto Hurst Street, just behind Wytton.

"Put us down at the far end," I said. "We'll go over the fence."

"Roger," said Stansbury. "So it is written, so it is done."

I dropped to the asphalt of Hurst Street, road gravel stinging my face as I ducked the rotors and made for the sidewalk. Frances ran behind me. Johnny Escobedo and two prowl cars pulled up silently to the curb. There we were, a magnificent seven.

We huddled while I used my notepad to sketch the general layout of the Lumsden place. I ordered one deputy around to the main house to block the drive with his car, jump the wall and take the front door. Another one at the back of it, and one on each side of the guest unit. Johnny would follow me in, then Frances.

"Vests and shotguns," I ordered.

Hypok lay in the half light on the bed and ran his gloved hand over the pale blue dress, over the hip of Item #4. He lay behind it, but not too close, turned as it was toward the big cage. He remote-shot a couple of images of them on the digital cameras tripoded behind and above him. The smell of years came from his mother's old red wool bedspread and Hypok felt like his mind was anchored not in the present at all, but free to skip back and forward in time, a nimble, lively little water bug glancing upon the tops of things. Shoot. Shoot. Shoot.

"Valeen?"

"Umm-mm-MMM!"

"There you are! I'm here, too. What's Collette doing in the potty?"

Hypok, propped on one elbow, looked across the Item to Moloch's world, pleased to see him curiously tasting the air with his tongue, patrolling one wall of his cage with excruciating patience. He looked down at himself, pressed out hard against the new skin like a shiny tent. He began the undulation.

"What's Collette doing in the potty?"

"*Hmm-mmm-MMM!*"

He giggled. "Umm-hmm. She *is?*"

Movement. Rhythm. Touch. Loretta asleep at his feet. Back to Missouri and the warm humid nights, back to the smells of his sisters around him, the room that somehow retained the smell of bacon and gardenias, back to the knowledge that his body was growing into feelings he already possessed, that he was soon going to experience them as he was born to. So close so many times, almost there, almost to the brink, almost to . . . what was it . . . release? An explosion of some kind? Undulate. Then back to the farmhouse in Arkansas and the terrible days of Ernie Mears and his mother locking him in the storm cellar for "things" undone with Valeen and Collette, for the neighbors' rabbits he stole from the hutch and strangled, for just about anything at all that would keep him locked away while they drank and yelled and mounted each other all over the house like animals, actually found them once on the kitchen floor with the soup boiling over and Ernie's overalls down around his boots and Wanda on all fours with her face glazed toward the window, *reaching for her beer on the floor beside her.* Then, onto better days for sure, those back in Hopkin when he began to truly know himself and what could happen if he could only arrange things correctly, and he discovered with Item #1 just how to direct the scene to excite and satisfy himself, how the pageant needed to be acted, how the final tableaux he had photographed with the cheapie Kodak burned in his mind like an eternal coal until he could muster his wit and stamina enough to begin the whole production again. Puxico. Fordyce. Hopkin. Tustin. Point to point, memory to memory, past to present and back again, all tied up into one. He clicked the digital camera again, capturing the present for the future.

Undulate. Closer.

Girl smell. Girl warmth. Girl touch. Contact.

"Nmm-nmm-NMM!

"No? Are you sure? Collette's getting a *what* from the bathroom?"

Then the sudden flash of light outside the windows and the sudden realization of what he had heard but not heard in his excitement — the faint overhead drone of an airborne machine coming closer, going past . . . coming back again?

Loretta stood on the edge of the bed and whined.

Then the light was gone and Hypok lay frozen.

Listen. Undulate. Listen.

But even with the windows closed against the cooling spring night he heard that machine coming closer again, sneaking through the night as if he were too stupid to notice something that fucking obvious; he was sure of it now, the faint, fast *botta-botta-botta* of blades in air and he rose from the bed and parted the blinds enough to see the lighted craft settling to earth somewhere on the street behind his.

Up with the zipper.

Although Crotalus horridus can be a ferocious foe, he will gladly flee if given an opportunity.

He let go of the blind, went to the bed, lifted Item #4 and took it around to the side of Moloch's world. Moloch watched him. He stripped the hood off it, then opened the door, unslung the struggling thing from his shoulder and dumped it in. He fetched Loretta from the bed and threw her in, too. Then he slammed the cage door shut and locked it with the key he kept hanging on a nail by the cage and dropped the key down the toilet and flushed it.

Finally, he got his .44 magnum from under the bed, opened the front door, locked it behind him before slamming it, then he slipped around to the side of the guest unit, up the fire ladder he'd installed there for just such an occasion, onto the roof and into the dark sturdy branches of the sycamore tree through which he climbed onto the rose fancier's roof, then down to the lowest part of it before he dropped to the ground and began weaving through the backyards of the houses over fences and hedges with the dogs barking but it didn't matter, he was light afoot and armored in his fresh skin, in possession of a lethal fang, not so much immune to the night as a part of it.

Let them try to find me.

We jumped the wall at 8:02 P.M. There was a light on in the guest house. One of the deputies shone his flashlight beam against the door as I ran up the stairs onto the porch, took three short steps and lowered my shoulder. It took one more charge to break the thing open and I flew through its unresisting swing, rolling to the floor and up with my .45 out front and my finger finding the trigger, Johnny and Frances beside me in a heartbeat, all three of us screaming and my nerves fried.

When I burst into the back room I could hardly believe what I saw. A glass cage took up the whole wall. There was a snake in it almost as big around as a man, too long to even guess at. Part of it was looped around and over a dollhouse. The other part was spilled out to the cage bottom and coiled around a little girl. Her head and neck and shoulders stuck out from the rolls of muscle at a strange angle, like she was rigid. A hand protruded from between two massive coils. Her mouth was taped shut but she looked through the glass at me with huge dark eyes. Her face was pale purple. I couldn't tell if she was alive. The snake had its mouth over her shoes and ankles, about halfway to her knees.

"God in heaven," said Frances.

"Mother of Jesus," said Johnny.

The girl blinked.

"You *bastard!*" screamed Frances. She knelt and emptied her 9 mm into the glass. All the bullets did was punch little holes through it and knock puffs of dust off the drywall behind it.

"Door's fucking *locked!*" yelled Johnny.

I zipped up my jacket halfway, held the left side over my head and jumped through the glass. I think I bounced off the tree inside. I landed in gravel, on my back, my legs up. I righted myself and stripped the jacket back. The snake had already disgorged the girl's feet and his head was about two feet off the ground, his tongue loping out ahead of him as he moved toward me. I shot him between the eyes. His head dipped like someone had slapped it. Then he rose up palebellied above me and I could see the jagged exit hole in his jaw. I shot him twice more, up through the bottom of his head. He writhed higher, coils loosening on the girl and his green body twisting to expose the plated yellow stomach. His mouth gaped. I stepped under the head and tugged on the girl, with the pistol still ready in my right hand. The huge reptile body rolled away from her — green revolving into yellow, then into green again — and I lifted the girl up and out and hugged her against me. Something small and brown fell to the ground but

I couldn't see what. I looked to Frances, waiting just outside the shard-toothed hole I'd made, her arms reaching through.

"Give her to me, Terry. Here!"

I'm not sure why I didn't. Why I couldn't. It was like I wasn't supposed to, like she was mine and there wasn't anywhere in the world she could be safer than in my arms. And though I'd had that thought before in my life and been wrong, some things are born into a man and you can overrule them but you can never make them go away.

"Terry! Give her over!"

I stood there for just a moment in the ocean of twisting scales, with the girl held tight to my chest, then I passed her into Frances's waiting arms. She was light, and loose as a beach towel.

Johnny helped me through to the other side. I looked back and saw a small dog scratching up against the glass, trying to reach the hole I'd made. Johnny reached in and scooped it out.

Two paramedics rushed through the doorway, then ran to Frances. One of the deputies charged in right behind them with his shotgun lowered and I thought for a second he was going to blow everyone there to smithereens. "House is empty, sir. Grounds, too. There's nobody here but us."

"He's in the neighborhood," I said. "Everybody door to door."

"You're bleeding," said Johnny, and when I looked down at myself I could see the slick red soaking my shirt and pants. I felt like I'd been punched in the ribs. In fact, I felt great because I knew I'd just done a good thing, whether the girl made it through or not. I felt lucky.

Louis pushed his way past the uniform and held up his radio. "Terry, he's down in the flood canal behind the street. Stansbury was strafing south with the light — guy wearing something shiny was hauling ass north. Suspect stopped under the bridge and hasn't come out."

I heard a gasp, then a gentle male expletive from the other side of the room. Frances looked up at me from the paramedics. "She's breathing."

I approached and looked down at her, a skinny little girl wrapped in a blanket. Her eyes were terrified, but she was drawing breath deep and fast. Someone had gotten the tape off her mouth. I took a flashlight from one of the uniforms.

"Let's go get him."

The flood control channel ran behind Hurst Street. Louis kept up radio contact as he led us through a backyard and over a cinder-block wall. The lights in the houses were coming on and I could hear dogs barking from the yards on either side of us. A quarter mile south I saw the chopper hovering and a bright cone of light flaring down to earth. We climbed the chain link and landed heavily on the other side.

In the dim moonlight I could see the ditch was deep, with high, sloping, concrete walls and a flat bottom to carry the floodwaters out to the Pacific. Stansbury held the helo low over the street, a few hundreds yards away. It looked like the bird was held up by the stanchion of its own white light. I heard Stansbury's voice rasp over Louis's radio: *still under the bridge here, haven't seen him move in over a minute . . . I'd get on him if I were you flatfoots . . .*"

"Johnny — can you make it down, then up the other side?"

"Done."

"I'll take the center. Louis, take this bank."

In an instant Johnny was down to the bottom, through the slick of water, then scuttling back up the far side. The last twenty feet of embankment was dirt, not cement, and for a moment he was tearing at it with all fours but sliding down at the same time, going nowhere. Then he found a foothold, got himself moving and made the top. He righted himself, flicked his flashlight beam once and drew his gun. I slid down the dirt on the soles of my shoes, and when I hit the rough cement I leaned back further and rode it down. When I hit bottom I was moving fast but kept my feet under me, ran up the other side a few steps to slow down, then started trotting through the brackish stream toward the chopper. I wedged the flashlight under my left arm, brought out my .45 and reached it around to my left hand, chambering the first round.

The middle of the channel was slick with mud and algae, so I tried to stay left or right. The bridge came at me out ahead, illuminated by Stansbury's fierce spotlight, and I could see the shining sides of cars parked on the overpass behind the fence. The pale concrete of the channel narrowed, then lowered in perspective, disappearing into the darkness under the bridge.

I stopped about thirty feet short of the entrance. Even from there I could hear the sounds from inside: the lazy chime of running water; the clear and surprisingly loud *doink, doink . . . doink, doink* of a drip that must have had its source high up; and the strange, metallic *whomp* of the chopper condensed in the tunnel then echoing out at me in odd angles from the darkness. Louis stood to my left, above me, and looked down. Turning the other way, I could see Johnny in a crouch, waiting for me to call the play. I wasn't sure. It looked like a good way to get shot, if he was armed. I wanted him. I wanted him for myself, almost as bad as I'd ever wanted anything in my life. He was mine and I was going to take him. I looked in front of me to the dark yawning mouth of the overpass, moved to the far left side so my gun hand would be free, turned on my flashlight and looked in. As soon as I put my head into the opening, the echoes of the rotors hit me not only from both sides, but from ahead and behind, too. It was like having four ears. But I could navigate the invisible world of sounds by the steady *doink* and the minor sibilance of the running water.

The shiny little creek meandered along the bottom. There were large concrete blocks set in the floor of the culvert, just a few feet apart, to keep the large storm debris from going further downstream. Each one was almost a yard high and a yard wide — just big enough to hide a man. Three rows of three. I ran the light around them: branches caught lengthwise, mud and trash, a car tire. I held the beam just over each block and looked for shadows on the water. For movement. For a shape. For anything not quite right. Nothing. Nothing but the thump of the helo above.

I stepped back out of the tunnel and waved Johnny to go across the street, then back down again. He nodded and sprung onto the fence. Less than a minute later I saw the beam of his flashlight coming toward me from the other end of the tunnel. I waited until he was near the opening, then started in. Three steps. Four. I remembered something that Joe Reilly had once told me — *always look up*. So I aimed my beam to the ceiling and followed it up with my eyes. Rust-stained concrete walls. Steel girders supporting the street from below. Bird nests and the dusty remains of spider webs long tattered and unused. I ran the beam down the wall to my left. It was sheer and clean except for the runoff tunnel that slanted up gently through the wall toward the street. The opening was about four feet off the floor of the channel and just big enough for a man to crawl into. There was another runoff line opening on the same side, about twenty yards further down toward Johnny. On the wall to my right I could see the black openings of two more, directly opposite.

Hypok lay in the cool barrel of the runoff line, feet slanted above him in the gentle uphill rise, both arms extended with the .44 firmly in grasp, barrel resting in a pile of debris through which he could easily see, elbows braced, his face recessed within the tunnel but his line of sight quite clear and unfettered. The nice wad of pine needles, leaves and trash not only hid him from flashlight view but gave him a steady brace for the gun.

His sores burned beneath the fresh skin. But he could scrunch backward into the deeper darkness of his hole, or forward toward the opening rather easily, using his elbows, knees and toes. He was tubed. It was like being born. Or like hunting if you were a snake, deeply penetrating the space of your prey, stealthy and silent, cunning and deadly. He rested his chin on the cold concrete and gazed down the length of his fine-scaled arms luminous in the near dark, to his pearlescent hands wrapped devoutly around the fat grips of the .44, then down at the shiny blued barrel waiting in the loose barrier of detritus. He could see the white post of the front sight and the generous rear notch into which you must center the post before you place it upon the target, pull the trigger and blow a hole the size of a softball out of any living thing on earth. He'd gotten the cop killer ammo, of course, Glaser Blues with the compressed #12 shot and the plastic, round-nose design. Guaranteed full knock-down on any hit or your money back.

The flood control channel was a great place to hide, he thought, unless it was raining. He'd found it months ago on one of his evening prowls. If the chopper hadn't surprised him, bearing down low, spotlight igniting the ground around him like napalm and he just fifty yards from the protection of the bridge, he might have hidden down here for days. Then used the change of clothing, cash and ID he'd stashed in the runoff line across the ditch, and gotten himself to an airport or bus station. Now he was basically fucked, he told himself, though the idea was far less distressing now than he had imagined it would be during his many years doing the things he'd done, knowing that someday it would come to this. California had the death penalty, but they also had good lawyers and lenient juries. No, it wasn't time to give up yet. If he could get himself out of the tunnel, back up the channel and into the cover of suburban backyards, he might be able to lose the chopper long enough to break into a house, fade a homeowner or two and get their car. Maybe they'd have an Item for him to take.

Through the loose wall of flotsam in which the barrel of his revolver lay, he could clearly see the main channel down in front of him. He could clearly see the white post of the front sight. To his right, a light came into view, playing along the creek bottom, then sweeping back and forth. They have no idea where I am, he thought. He wondered if it was the cop he helped pull the trick on, Naughton, the little hothead weirdo on Donna Mason's show. Mal. Hopefully. Cops were all basically the same, though. The light became brighter, tapering back to its source. He could hear the slosh of feet in water, very quiet, but still audible, magnified by the hard concrete tunnel. *Slishhh* . . .

Then the beam veered away to the far wall. He watched it focus on the mouth of the runoff line across from his. A dress rehearsal, he thought. He watched the cop. He couldn't tell if it was Naughton or not. The cop got right up close to the wall. His flashlight was in his left hand. He spread his legs and lowered himself into an amusing, ready-for-anything stance. Hypok could see the gleam of a firearm in his right hand. Then the cop leaned forward and aimed his beam up the opening. He didn't look in. Hypok watched as the tunnel filled with light, saw the stained brown walls of concrete, the loose archipelago of flotsam and jetsam scattered inside. But the cop still hadn't put his snout into the hole for a good honest whiff of things. Then he knelt down, quickly, some commando move he'd learned in school. His head was just under the opening and the light went off. In the darkness Hypok couldn't see what he was doing, but he guessed the man was having a lights-out preview. Ten seconds. Then the tunnel went bright again and the beam had moved to about a yard inside it and Hypok could see the dark silhouette of a head looking in. What a sight. It was a lot like one of those paper targets at the indoor range, but no shoulders, only head, a perfect silhouette. He got the white post of his front sight settled into the notch of the back one and held it steady in the middle of the target. It was easy to do with the barrel on the bed of debris he'd built. A brain shot. Maximum stopping power. Guaranteed knockdown with any hit. The light raked the walls, held steady for a long while, then went out.

The next thing he knew, Hypok was looking across the channel at the flashlight aimed directly at him, weaving a little bit, but coming his way.

The cop veered to Hypok's left, out of sight. Who wouldn't? But Hypok could see his light and hear the gentle footfall of shoes on concrete, then the *slishhh . . . slishhh* of the dead man crossing the water, then the sucky sound of wet soles on dry cement again. Silence. Hypok imagined: he gets the light in his left hand and shines it in. And it happened. Next, he shines it around in here, but he doesn't look in yet. That happened too. Bright. Hypok closed his eyes. Then, the cop turns off the light for ten seconds while he looks up here and tries to see me in the dark. The light, in fact, went out, and in the next eight seconds Hypok watched the scarcely visible outline of a human head not six feet away from him, not four feet from the muzzle of his revolver, becoming more distinct with every thunderous beat of his heart.

The shot was almost unbelievably loud. The echo bounced around the canal at me. I flattened myself against the wall and looked back toward Johnny, offing my light. I heard something land in the water. *"John!"*

Then I heard the sound of a body against the concrete, doing what, I couldn't say.

"Okay, Naughton! Creep down!"

"Hold there, Johnny! Hold!"

"Holding! Holding!"

John's voice? He rarely called me Naughton. His light went on, shining my way. I turned

601

on my own and held the beam down in front of me to light the ground. But I felt wrong, something felt wrong and when I looked up to Johnny's light I saw it hadn't moved, it wasn't moving at all — why wasn't it on our man? — so I veered out of its path and ran down the middle through the water toward it.

When I got there, the flashlight lay in one of the runoff openings, held in place with a rock. Below the opening was Johnny. Johnny, on his back with his head in the mud, his widow's peak collapsed over his eyes and smoke rising from his mouth. Far ahead of me now, moving along the bottom of the channel was a figure faintly opalescent in the moonlight, vanishing fast. I brushed Johnny's cheek with my fingers, then moved out.

Louis had already slid down into the channel bottom to give chase. A uniform came jangling down from the other side, skied the last ten yards on his boot soles and fell in behind Louis. I caught them quickly, muttered something about nailing the fucker once and for all and shot past both of them. I am light boned and quite fast, and have much more stamina than a man of my personal habits deserves. But if I had been fifty years old and thirty pounds overweight it wouldn't have mattered, because I could still see Johnny's gone face back there in the ugly little stream and I would have willingly run myself to death to avenge him.

I couldn't outrun the chopper. Stansbury roared past me overhead, raking The Horridus in his light, then banked and tried to stay over him. In the brief moment that the beam caught my prey I saw a scintillant flash of blue silver, like a marlin breaking water in the Sea of Cortez. I raised my knees and *ran*.

Out ahead, crisscrossing his way across the ditch, trying to avoid the beam above him, The Horridus was a glimmering phantom gliding from darkness to light then back to darkness. He was blue, then opalescent, then violet, then almost invisible in the night. He was fast, but he wasn't as fast as me. His hundred-yard head start shrank to eighty. I was flying over that channel bottom like a hawk over a city street.

When I was about sixty yards away, he looked back. The chopper beam grazed him and I could see the bright reflection of his eye, straining around to see me. Then an orange-white jet of flame cracked in the darkness ahead and the booming report of a handgun quaked along the channel and passed. I hit the water with both hands out and slid about ten yards. Then I was up again, quick as a seal, and I saw Stansbury's light capture him in a bright wide halo, with the water splashing up around his shiny legs as he sped down the center of the culvert.

Suddenly he angled up the embankment and scrambled over the last ten yards of rocks and soil without a slip. I realized that using the high ground, he could loop back and shoot me like a duck on a pond — quite literally — so I clawed up the concrete side and fought my way up the loose sharp rocks to the top. God bless Stansbury, who now hovered over The Horridus, drenching him in the full beam of his flood. He just stood there in the center of the light, his metallic body heaving, his metallic head bobbing up and down as he labored for breath. I took a knee and drew down on him, but as soon as I got my sights in line he was off. As he loped out of the light I could tell he wouldn't go much further: his back was bowed, his arms loose before him, his legs heavy. But the big gun was still in his hand. I tracked him down the barrel of my .45, then stood and started after him again.

Stansbury's light caught up with him. The Horridus was at the far side of the channel cut, hunched, facing the chain-link fence. I stopped fifty feet short of him and lined up my automatic on his heaving, shimmering back. Just behind the fence was a cinder-block wall, separating someone's backyard from the flood control easement. He was bent, hands on his knees, looking back over his shoulder at me while he breathed fast and shallow. His breath was an urgent whistle, in-out, in-out, in-out. I could see the revolver still in his right hand and the glint of his eyes behind the fish-scale shine of his hood. He turned his head away slowly, lifted one leg and worked his foot into a toehold in the chain link. He looked back at me again. Then he heaved himself up and reached with his free hand for a grip on the cinder block. He grunted and slipped. Hard. His foot dropped free and his left wrist snagged on the sharp metal X of the fence top. He danced on his tiptoes, writhing around to face me, his left wrist still impaled above him, the big black handgun in his grasp. He brought it up. I shot him once in the face for Johnny and four times in the chest for me. He hung from the fence. Then something gave and his wrist popped loose with a metallic clink and he fell to the dirt.

Thirty-three

The department mandates a thirty-day home leave for deputies involved in fatal shootings. I spent the first day sitting around the apartment, filling out paperwork brought over by Louis and Frances. Really I spent it thinking about Johnny Escobedo and the family he'd left behind. I called Gloria and all she could do was cry. I cried with her. She asked me if I'd talk about him at the funeral and I felt my heart burst and flutter like a balloon. My chest ached for hours so I went to the emergency room and got checked out. Nothing wrong with my heart, they assured me, just pain from the cut in my side. I knew better.

All day I kept running through those last few minutes in my mind, wondering if I'd made the wrong call, wondering if there was some way we could have shaken The Horridus out of there without costing Johnny his life. The answer is, as it often is in our line of work: yes. Yes, I could have waited for more officers. Yes, I could have held back for daylight. Yes, if I'd known he was lying like a viper in a cramped tunnel we could have called a fire engine to flush him out. Yes, I could have chosen to investigate the runoff lines on the other side of the channel myself. But I didn't. I did what we thought was best and right, and it had gotten Johnny dead. I paced the little apartment, sometimes picturing him in my mind. Sometimes it was Johnny alive; sometimes it was Johnny with his head in the water. More memories to love and hate, more to protect and abhor. I dread all things that are gone. I always thought my biggest opponent was the future, but it has turned out to be the past.

I talked on the phone, napped fitfully but with vivid, inexplicable dreams. I ate some canned peaches and half a pack of cookies. Every once in a while I ran my fingers over the bandage covering the tight twenty-five stitches in my side, courtesy of the snake tank I'd run through. The cut was long but not deep because of my ribs, which had done their job and sheltered what was inside. They ached profoundly, but nothing like the heart behind them.

Late afternoon on that first day, I called Alton Allen "Chet" Sharpe and told him I was coming by to talk to the girl I'd paid $10,000 to meet. The girl in the pictures. I was ready to go live.

He and his wife, Caryn, were at their main residence — a place I'd never been to. It was evening on a quiet street in Anaheim, one of the thousands of Orange County avenues

607

where just about anyone can live and be left alone to do whatever it is they do, so long as they do it quietly. Such is the blessing and the curse of suburbia. All the notoriety surrounding the selling of their daughter for sex and the suicide of their customer during a police sting had been focused on the Sharpe rental in Orange, miles away. If Chet and Caryn's Anaheim neighbors even knew who they really were, there was no sign of it. In fact, the door was open when I got there and a cute little girl of about six was standing there, holding a stuffed bear, waving at me.

She watched me come up the walkway and onto the porch.

"Hello, Sergeant Naughton," she said with a smile.

"Chet home?"

"He's expecting you."

She giggled, pleased at remembering her lines. Chet appeared behind her, with his Chet-likes-Chet grin. He set a hand on the girl's shoulder and shooed her out past me. I noted the little swept-up ends of his freshly manicured fingernails. I noted his pressed shirt and smart necktie, and the pen in his pocket.

"Neighbor girl," he said. "They always seem to take to Caryn and me."

I looked to make sure the girl was out of earshot, then turned back to Chet. "You take to her, and I'll kill you."

"I know you would. You're good at killing. Come on in."

I turned again to watch the girl disappear into the front door of what I truly hoped was her own home.

Chet led me inside. The place was decorated in the past tense — green shag carpet popular twenty years ago, heavy furniture, some busy wallpaper in silvers and greens. Lots of children's toys lying around for girls like the one who met me at the door. Mirrors everywhere. It smelled like fried food. We stood in the den. There were cartoons playing on the TV. From the open doorway I heard the sounds of someone knocking pans in the kitchen and a rising hiss from the stovetop.

"Made your bail, I see."

"Always save for a rainy day. I talk to Linda every morning, at Orangewood. Getting a good education, some therapy she likes."

"You're pure slime, Chet."

"We'll be reunited. She'll be back someday. You can't tear apart the American family that easy. Have a seat?"

I looked around the miserable room. I looked at groomed Chet. I looked through the doorway to see Caryn with her back to me, getting something out of the refrigerator. She had on a denim dress too short for her and her big hair was done up big as usual, lacquered into swirls that looked stormswept.

"I thought at first it was your daughter," I said.

"Thought who was?"

"The girl in the pictures."

"Well, I never saw those, so I wouldn't know, would I?"

"But you knew what I. R. Shroud was using them for."

"I found out later. He just wanted some old stuff that maybe hadn't been shown around for a while. Something that might *look* new. If I'd known he was having some fun with you, I'd have had them to him a lot quicker."

"You make some money off them?"

"Nope. We enthusiasts trade back and forth. It's fun — not profit, Deputy."

"It's a crime."

"*Making art* with pictures that old isn't a crime. The statute of limitations ran out a long time ago. You know that, or you wouldn't be here without your storm troopers beside you and your six-gun blazing."

He smiled at me, rather prissily, as if he were genuinely offended by me.

I considered Chet for a moment. Though it rankled my soul to its core, Chet was basically untouchable now. Yes, he had a trial pending on a multitude of charges, ranging from child endangerment to pandering a minor. Yes, the evidence was compelling and Chet was about to take his first hard fall. But it was his first, and that would be a big factor. Caryn's first, and Linda's, too. I'd already heard from Loren that Chet and Caryn were going to argue that Linda's services *as a model* were being offered to me, *not* services as a prostitute. Loren said that a legitimate modeling portfolio belonging to Linda was going to help their case measurably. In court, I foresaw the my-word-against-theirs case shaping up, and my job would be to convince a jury that I knew the difference between buying photo time with a girl and buying her body. Chet would try to convince them of roughly the same thing. Of course, Caryn could not be made to testify against him. Linda, as a minor, could. But I knew where her loyalties were and I knew she'd be hostile all the way to the verdicts. It was going to be a long and ugly thing.

And the fact that Chet had trafficked in child pornography for years wouldn't get him much — such possession was legal in this country until just a decade ago. The fact that he had possessed certain pornographic images and supplied them to I. R. Shroud years later was past the statute of limitations — four years. The girl in those pictures was now a woman close to thirty-five years old. I looked at her again. She was still in the kitchen, cooking his dinner.

"How old was Caryn then?"

"Seven."

"Who was in the original picture with her?"

"Her old man's best friend. Her old man.

Some other guys. There wasn't just one."

"You must have been in heaven when you met her. Daddy's sex toy, all trained and broken in."

"She'd retained everything good about the human spirit in her, Deputy." The Chet-loves-Chet smile again. "She was made for love, and love is all you need. We never hurt Linda, you know. We all made love. We adored each other and we brought pleasure to each other and we respected each other's bodies. It's not what guys like you think it is. Guys like you call it a sin because you don't have a word for anything that good and natural. You're not honest. You got to be honest, like us, to live outside the law."

Right there is everything I hate about the child molester. They rationalize the urges, and they look to others just like them for what psychologists call "validation," whatever in hell that is. Then they spin these theories wherein they are natural and loving and help their young charges develop into wise, tolerant and satisfied adults. Into people like Chet.

It was a dumb question, but I still had to ask him. "How come you told the investigators that you got those pictures of me off the Web? They were the only thing in your whole collection you were actually innocent of."

"Well, they were in my possession, so why deny ever having seen them? No one would have believed that. Especially when the nega-

612

tives were found, though I had no idea *that* would happen. So I told them everything in my collection was taken off the Web. It's true. More or less."

"Not the magazines from Holland, or the books from Denmark."

"Well, that stuff was completely legal to make, you know."

"It isn't anymore."

Chet looked at me. I could see the thin blade of his viciousness, the tiny little sliver of something he would probably call courage. "Really, I figured anything that would hurt you would help me. They found evidence against you at my house — well, good. I'll take you down with me as far as I can. We hate cops."

"We hate you."

He was smiling again. "I thought it was really endearing that you'd fallen for Caryn. And paid up good money to meet her in the flesh. Some of that money is going to our defense. Well, go in and talk to her if you want. Go live, Naughton. You paid for it."

Maybe Caryn got the psychic waves coming from us, because she turned and looked our way. She must have known I was there. She looked neither surprised nor distressed, neither curious nor concerned. The look on her face was the same look I'd seen on a hundred young victims, and later, on their adult faces. It's a look not so much of something missing but of something missed.

"See you in court, Deputy," said Chet.

"I'll be there."

I walked across the street to the little girl's house and rang the doorbell. She answered it and I asked to see her mom or dad. A moment later they were both standing in front of me, two thirty-year-olds still dressed for work, a nice-looking couple, the woman with a dishrag in her hands and the man with his shirt sleeves rolled up and a pair of glasses resting crookedly on his face.

I told them who I was, showed them my badge and they invited me in. They didn't have to be told to get the girl into her room before we talked. She still had her stuffed bear. When the mother came back, I told them who Chet and Caryn were and what they were charged with and what had happened over in Orange that day. They'd heard about the case, but hadn't seen any pictures of Chet or his wife or girl, and had no idea they were living right across the street. The woman's face was pale and I could sense the physical threat coming off that man, even so mild a man, from across the room.

"Call me immediately if you have any problems," I said, rising. "And let your neighbors know the score."

"We'll handle it," said Dad. There was actually steam on the inside of his glasses.

And that, in a nutshell, is why I do what I do. Because the devourers of innocence are always around us and always have been. Because when one goes down, another pops up to take his place. Because the price of liberty is eternal vigilance. But somehow we have forgotten what vigilance is, or never learned it in the first place. There's a stream that trickles through all of us. It's always there. It's evil and we know this, so we force it to mix with the larger river inside us. We let it be consumed by the greater flow of good. But when the good in the river runs dry and there isn't enough of it to dilute the stream, then the stream flows faster and harder, uncontrolled, and it finally floods one life, then another, then another. And it's always the innocent who are easiest to pull down. It's always the innocent who are standing there on the banks and looking in, curious and trusting and sometimes, maybe, even a little brave. The innocent never know. They need someone with an eye for evil, someone who sees it coming before there is anything at all to see. They need people who know the stream. They need people like me.

I didn't see Donna until very late. She stayed at the studio to edit what she'd shot that day: 318 Wytton Street and environs, interviews with the mothers of the first three Horridus victims, the dating service employees who'd worked with him; interviews with Frances, Wade, Ishmael and Louis; a brief conversation with Gloria Escobedo; and a long talk with Daniel and Sara Freedman, parents of Ruth. I know this because Donna called me three times that first day, to keep me informed. I missed her and resented her working instead of nursing me, which, in turn, I resented myself for feeling. But I was too exhausted to harbor that sour emotion for long, and by the time I was expecting her to crawl in bed with me — I'd waited up as long as I could — I was longing for her company, her voice and her presence. She arrived, as she often did, just as I was beginning to dream, and her arrival was as close to comfort as I would get for some weeks. I remember her outline as she stood in the doorway in the near dark. I remember smelling her as I fell back into my waiting dreams.

Early on my second day off duty, Louis brought me all that I'd requisitioned from Sheriff Wade, and, surprisingly, been granted. The department phone callout lists for February, March and April. The Computer Crime and Fraud log-ons and IRC records once collected and organized by Melinda and soon to be taken over by her temporary replacement — Jordan Ishmael. Time cards and expense sheets for the entire CAY unit (a decoy) as well as for Ishmael, Woolton, Vega and Burns (all decoys, too, except for one). It was a lot of material, but there was a lot I wanted to learn. I pored over it and started to piece together the activities of Ishmael for the last three months. I was looking for the smoking gun, the link that would lead from his thirty-something log-ons to I. R. Shroud to the pictures of me in the cave with Caryn Sharpe. When the tedium got to me, I dozed and dreamed about that muzzle flash in the darkness of the flood control channel and I kept seeing Johnny standing up, arranging his face back into place and looking like he felt sorry for me.

At noon I joined the search team of the home on Wytton Street. What a haul. We pulled eighteen boxes of child porn from a spare bedroom of the main house — photos, books and magazines, 8 millimeter and video, even printed booklets with long ornate faux 19th-century narratives of firsthand sex with children and no pictures at all. A lot of it was stuff I'd never seen before, things he'd created or collected over the years, most of it old, but some of it quite new. There were digital images of all three of his Orange County victims. They all showed him, too, mostly from the back and above, completely disguised in his scaly suit. In the manner of most pedophiles, The Horridus had organized and catalogued the stuff with great care and thoroughness. He'd even cross-referenced the girls and boys according to their physical appearance and whatever names they might be given, in case

617

he wanted to follow a certain "career." There was a fascinating collection of "photographs" depicting celebrities with various children, in various poses — all of them very convincing. If it wasn't the president of the United States, you wouldn't laugh.

Of greater interest to me, and to the FBI people who helped us, was the equipment on which he had created some of the images. There was a studio in one of the main house bedrooms. It was neat and organized, just like his library was, and we guessed he had over eighty thousand dollars invested in a big fast Apple, a good scanner and digital ESP, all the Adobe software you could buy, and good printers — about fifty grand's worth of machinery — which gave him the ability to reproduce the finished images so accurately. Throw in a film recorder, which would turn the final image from a digitized work of "art" back into a photograph, and you could do whatever your skill, patience and time would allow you to. He had done up some pictures of me with other girls and boys, too. Likely, they were practice runs for the ones he finally printed, photographed and passed along to Ishmael. There were also pictures of the cave interior — without me or anyone else in it. Had he taken those himself? Or had they been supplied to him? Remembering Will Fortune's lessons on the camera anomalies, I studied the negatives on one of the film editors and made a mental note of the edge marks on the film and the anomalies of the camera that originally captured the image. I also carefully pocketed three of the pictures of myself — two of them with Matthew — that had been stolen from Ardith's home. I would lift the fingerprints off them myself, and run them against Ishmael's, on file in personnel.

Of course, Ishmael was there, helping to oversee the search. It took me a while to find the right time, but while he helped load the printers into one of our vans for transport downtown I got a financial ledger out of the box it was already packed in and took it with me to the bathroom. I shut the door and locked it and sat down on the pot seat. It didn't take me long to crack his bookkeeping, because The Horridus hadn't done anything much to disguise it. His handwriting was neat and careful:

2/12 RC. M. 15$/5I/DN.5

My translation: Received from Mal $15,000 for five images, half down. This was back in February, on the twelfth. It truly impressed me — although a man sitting on a toilet can be thought of as impressionable by circumstance — that Ish would go to such expense to embarrass me. Had he hoped to get more for his money? Certainly, and he almost had. The Horridus was a busy craftsman:

2/16 RC. A. 1.5$/3I/DN.5
2/23 RC. S. .5$/1I F
3/08 RC. F. 2$/5I F
3/15 RC. D. 12$/6I/DN.5

I made a careful replication of these entries onto my own small notepad, then wondered if the financial ledger might disappear from the evidence room, just as the pink envelope containing my damnation had disappeared a few weeks ago. I thought the chances were good. So I unbuttoned my shirt and slipped the ledger in, where it could ride up against my stomach for the next few hours and remind me what I was after. I looked in on my bandage and felt the itch of the stitches underneath. Stitched and bandaged human flesh has an indescribable smell. I went back out and helped log and load evidence, carrying the burgled box myself, nodding at Ishmael on my way to the van.

On a bookshelf in the guest house we found an adult human skull. I understood it instantly to be his mother's, though I wasn't happy about my wisdom. Some thoughts you just wish you never had. The front mandibles had been lipsticked bright red in a ridicule of womanhood, or perhaps of all life itself. It was perched up high, and aimed down to look at the bed where her son took the girls. Beside the skull was a whole femur, most of a small human foot, and a complete left hand on which a wedding band was affixed. Joe Reilly wandered around the scene without saying much, except to caution the techs about handling the evidence. He looked gray in the face, but so did everyone else. Joe reached down, touched the red wool blanket on the bed and looked at me, nodding.

There were notebooks with descriptions of his encounters with Pamela, Courtney and Brittany, though he referred to them throughout as "Items" "1," "2," or "3," respectively. He had kept a log for his time in Arkansas (two "Items"), Indiana (two more "Items") and Texas (one "Item" I knew as Mary Lou Kidder). I spent enough time reading them to see that FBI profiler Mike Strickley had been right — he had "scared himself" to California, where he let his first two victims go for unknown reasons and his third escaped rape and death because we interrupted him. There were graphic descriptions of five earlier rapes, and five "transformations" involving his anaconda. In the handwritten narrative there was some evidence of a troubled conscience, though not nearly as much as you might expect. He addressed the damnation of his soul and how his mother had "born and suckled Satan" — meaning himself. I read his self-analysis with some interest because I'm always intrigued by how people get to be the way they are, and because, strangely enough, they usually know. He had one quality I especially admired: he hated himself. He knew what the stream was all about, and he couldn't beat it so he finally gave up and let it have him.

A small notebook was dedicated to phone numbers and Web sites. The names attached to the numbers and descriptions of the sites were "coded" only by The Horridus's own shorthand: "494–4698 RS." During my brief perusal I recognized only one, that of Abby Elder. But because it was small and fit easily in my pocket, and because I desired that it implicate Lieutenant Jordan Ishmael, I took the notebook, too. There was more than enough to convict The Horridus of helping frame me, if he'd been alive to convict. A drop or two to seal the fate of a corrupt cop wouldn't be missed in the larger bucket of things, and the bucket, of course, would never be missed in the stream.

We had more trouble with the big snake than with any other piece of evidence on the property. Apparently the monster had been undead after my three shots, and when the last deputies had left the guest house the night before it had moved out of its cage, through the broken glass and into the house. Deputies sealing off the scene the next morning found it stretched across the floor. But when we entered the guest house for the formal search a day later, it wasn't there. We assumed it had been taken away. I found it in the bathtub, layered upon itself high up past the rim, with one huge section of body pressed against the bathroom wall and its tail trailing across the room where it stopped, just barely out of the doorway. Its defeated head was poked between two coils. Six men and three women spent the next hour (1) determining that it was dead, (2) unwinding it out to the living room, (3) holding it as straight as possible (not very) while Joe Reilly himself used a twenty-foot tape to measure it. Even with the death curves still in the body — no amount of manual weight, strength or force could get them out — I was surprised how long it was. Every time someone lost his hold the snake would move slowly as its muscles tried to reclaim their final shape, and we'd jump like fleas. Our screams and curses would flood into the air and nervous laughter would crackle through the room like electricity and we'd have to start again, pulling on the thing and trying to hold its powerful — even though dead — body still again. It seemed like the damned thing would never stop moving, and so far as I saw, it never actually did.

Joe finally looked up, using the second twenty-foot length of tape, his thumb on the inch mark, and said, "Thirty-one feet, seven inches, *not* including postmortem rigor." I learned later in the week that it weighed in at 545 pounds. A local mortuary did us a favor and cremated the animal, all five sections, no charge. It was rumored that one of the crematorium workers skinned it before it was cut up, and rolled the skin up like a carpet and took it home. I wouldn't have done that myself. I wouldn't want that skin within a thousand miles of me. I don't know where the ashes were disposed of, and I don't care. But I know they'll end up back in the stream.

Surprisingly, the hardest task I had was to find out who The Horridus really was. I found six complete sets of identification, which included CDLs, birth certificates and Social Security cards: Gene Vonn, David Webb, Warren Witt, Mark Yost, David Lumsden and Michael Hypok. He worked for the dating services as David Lumsden. He dealt with PlaNet as Mark Yost. He dealt with utilities and the phone company as David Webb. I found Gene Vonn on three bank accounts; David Webb on four more; and Warren Witt on three others. Two for Lumsden right here in Orange County. A total of twelve accounts at different banks in four states.

But it was only when I read his notebooks further that I learned who he was, at least to himself: Michael Hypok. I first came across the name in his notebooks, in third-person references. I thought at first he was writing about a friend, and I thought, oh shit — here we go again. He used the name only occasionally. It was suddenly, casually interspersed with the simple first-person "I," so it took me a while to catch on. But after a while it was clear that he himself was Michael Hypok — at least sometimes — and those times were when he was at his most grandiose. When he wrote of "transcendence" or "transformation," or got on a tirade about how stupid the police were, his voice shifted to a third-person narrative starring Hypok. *Hypok knew that the authorities, stupid though they were, were getting close.* I found no evidence that he'd used it as an alias. In fact, I couldn't prove that he'd ever uttered the name out loud to anyone but himself. I wondered if it was just a name he liked. Then, at the bottom of a kitchen drawer in The Horridus's home, I found a limp, stained envelope containing a Texas driver's license and a Social Security card belonging to a Michael Hypok some twenty years older than The Horridus.

Over the next few days I checked that name a thousand different ways. There were Michael Hypoks in forty-seven of our fifty states — but I couldn't find a single hard fact that linked any one of them to Michael Hypok of 318 Wytton. The closest I got — thanks to Sam Welborn's tireless combing of north Texas — was an oil rig worker who'd worked up around Wichita Falls back in the mid-seventies. After that he'd dropped from sight, vanishing from the area like a played note of music. A fingerprint comparison between The Horridus and the Michael Hypok whose Social Security card and license I found in the kitchen showed them to be altogether different men. But I wondered. Had Gene Vonn taken his name? Or that of another Michael Hypok altogether? Why? Had he known him and admired him? A buddy's dad? A mentor? A character from a show or book? A name he had dreamed? There was no telling. No one knew and no one cared. After a while, neither did I.

It was easy enough to find Collette Loach. Her number was written down in several places because she was his sister. I got her by phone at her home in New Hampshire. She was genuinely surprised that her brother had been the number-one suspect in a series of violent sexual acts against children. She sounded concerned that he was now dead, but not bereft. She told me she never really understood why Gene wanted her to buy a house using his money — but she would have been a fool to turn down that kind of offer. She figured Gene was just shy, as always, just a little to himself, a little secretive, but a real sweet boy. She'd never heard of anybody named Hypok. She asked me if I'd be interested in cleaning out the house and renting it for her — she'd make it worth my while.

I spent most of my downtime studying the log-ons and phone activities of Ishmael, comparing them to what I had learned about I. R.

Shroud. Shroud had been on the Net during all the times Ishmael, as Mal, had been. Mal, of course, was a name usable by anyone, but I used our log-on and IRC records to trace each call to the specific origin terminal. In every instance that corresponded to Shroud's activity on-line, the Internet provider linkup was made from Ishmael's computer, located behind the heavy doors of his office. Most of his chats with Shroud were early morning — 5 to 6 A.M. — or late evening, between seven and nine. Some were as long as eight minutes; others as short as thirty seconds. As might befit any complex business transaction, the longer ones came first, followed by the shorter nuts and bolts of delivery, approval, payment.

So far as money went, Ish spent $30,000 to commission ten images of me and seven-year-old Caryn Sharpe (née Little). I was almost unbelieving that he could hate me that much. Thirty grand will buy you a lot of good things, and you can enjoy hatred in private for as long as you want. It's free. I wondered if Shroud had put him through the paces at Moulton Creek, Main Beach and the Green Line Metro Rail, as he had to me. I thought not. He'd only tested me because he suspected me of impersonating the original Mal. He had smelled a cop, so he had wanted cash, and my picture taken as insurance.

It seemed to me that some kind of bank wire transfer of funds would be easier, so long as customer and provider trusted each other. I confirmed this idea through Gene Vonn's bank statements, which showed two deposits of $15,000 wired direct. The bank manager gave me the name on the payer account, though my heart gave a little jump when she first said it. The account belonged to Melinda and Jordan Ishmael. It surprised me that Ish had left it joint so long after the divorce. Then I wondered if he'd used it at other times for other purposes: a safe, forgotten slush fund always at least half attributable to an unsuspecting ex-wife. Why not? And to have it surface in the financial records of The Horridus was a fate that Ish, even in his deepest, most prescient nightmares, could not have foreseen. You get not only what you pay for, but who you pay for it.

It took over a week to finally nail down my tormentor with something absolutely convicting: fingerprints on the pictures stolen from Ardith's collection. Reilly took his sweet time in processing those latents because I told him quite frankly they weren't part of any active case, and because I was quite casual about my request. I didn't want to bring attention to myself or to a lieutenant who was my superior. So Joe put it low priority and I had to call him twice a day to see if he'd ID'd the prints.

It was late on a Friday — two weeks after the death of The Horridus — that I went to the lab to shake loose my final piece of evidence against Ishmael. I still wasn't quite certain, even then, exactly what I was going to do with it.

Joe looked at me over his glasses and pretended not to know why I was there. When I told him he changed the subject to the new ultraviolet/infrared analyzer that he had created to examine various materials, mostly inks. It was a funny-looking contraption with two different light sources and an ingenious system of adjustable wooden eyeshades to protect the examiner from ambient light. It sat on a corner bench with two stools in front of it. Joe's people had nicknamed it Ugly Box and he assumed I'd want to give it a whirl.

"Joe, all I need is your make on the fingerprints, if you've come up with one."

"We'll get to that."

Then a long pause.

I didn't have to acknowledge that I'd put him in a tough position — helping condemn a fellow deputy against whom he had no personal or professional grudge. Also hanging in the air of his lab at that moment was the fact that Joe had been ready to testify against me on the mocked-up images. I'd decided to say nothing to him about it, and I didn't. He was only doing his job, saying what he thought was true about the photographs he'd examined.

"I'll run them through myself, if you'd like," I offered, meaning I'd make the calls to the various print banks — CAL-ID, FBI and WIN

— though I am not a fingerprint expert and wouldn't really know what to tell them to look for. At least it would take the onus off Joe and his people.

He looked at me rather sadly with those cool blue eyes and said no, he'd done the work once so there was no sense in me doing it again. He shrugged. The expression he gave me was that of a doctor about to reveal a rare disease. Or a father whose son has brought some inadvertent disaster upon his family and friends.

"They're Melinda's," he said.

Thirty-four

Melinda and Penny were home when I got there, packing for the move. The doors and windows were all open and so was the garage, stacked with boxes. I stood on the front porch and looked in through the open door. Moe jumped all over me, then flopped to his back and wiggled for attention. Melinda stopped in the middle of the living room with a stack of old 33's in her arms, offering me a challenging look that tightened to hostility when she saw the expression on my face. She was dressed, as often, in her old sweats, and her hair was up inside a Dodgers cap. Penny came from the kitchen carrying a produce box. When she saw me she smiled, blushed and looked down, then came alongside her mother.

"Hi, Terry."

"Hi, Pen."

"Come to say good-bye to us?" asked Mel.

"Not exactly."

"Do it anyway. It's the last chance you'll get. Penny, go to your room and get those posters off the wall. We've waited long enough on them."

"— I —"

"— *Now*. Put the kitchen stuff down."

Penny looked over her shoulder at me as she exiled herself to her room. Her face was flushed — embarrassment, I believed — but she still gave me the right-in-the-eye look that she had begun to offer me, just before my fall. Our Look. I returned it. I heard her door shut loudly.

Melinda carried the albums past me and I followed her out to the garage, petting Moe as he wagged along beside. I stood at the entrance, just under the door, and looked out at the canyon. Our "June gloom" had arrived early, as it often does, leaving the afternoon sky a humid, eye-squinting white, and muting the colors of the hills and houses. The eucalyptus trees, which always seemed to me to be perfectly suited to Laguna (they're actually Australian), were languid and somnolent in the warm spring haze. I heard Mel set down the box of records somewhere behind me.

"So," she said. "What's the news?"

"I knew it was Ish," I said, still facing the little street and the hills beyond.

"What was Ish?"

"Who set me up with the pictures."

She said nothing.

"Did you count on that?" I asked.

"What on the face of the globe are you talking about?"

"Why? I mean the whole thing. *Why?*"

Her voice came, flat and not a little angry.

"Have you spun out again? Like the good old days with the booze and your grimy little cave? Life's pressures made you nuts again? I can't be there for the rescue this time. Tell me what you're talking about because I can't read an addled mind."

"There's a lot we can just skip if you want to."

"We could skip this whole conversation from the sound of it."

"Things do need saying."

"Then you're going to have to explain yourself."

"Okay, Mel. You took the stills of the cave with my camera. But you didn't know that cameras leave tool marks on a negative, like a gun leaves marks on cartridge. The tool marks matched up perfectly, once the Bureau and Will Fortune got my old Yashica into the lab. It seemed to confirm the theory that I took the pictures. But I knew better, and I began to wonder who had access to it. I was pretty sure it was Ish, until Joe found your fingerprints all over the pictures you stole from Ardith's notebooks. Those were still at Wytton Street."

I waited for her to say something, but she didn't. When I looked back at her she was leaning against the garage wall with her arms crossed, head tilted down a little, but her eyes fixed straight on me. It was easier to accuse her to the hills than to her face. I wanted her to defeat my case, shatter my evidence, provide me with a surprise but ironclad defense. But she didn't and I knew she wouldn't. So I turned back to the oblique spring haze.

"It was easy enough to get the pictures of me — the raw material. You just took a day off, had a couple of drinks maybe, and played burglar while you knew Ardith was at work. It probably took you fifteen minutes, once you decided to do it. You knew those shots were somewhere in Ardith's possession because I'd told you about them. Well, maybe it took half an hour — they were up in the closet. The hard part was getting to Shroud on the Web, fishing around as Mal. You knew it was one of my handles, and you did the fishing early or late, before work, and after everyone else was gone. You used Ishmael's terminal. It took you close to forty conversations, once you were referred to the proper creator. I'd be willing to bet you did some horse trading right here at home, too. The artwork cost you thirty grand, because you wanted good stuff, real convincing, state-of-the-art images. You put them in the pink envelope and slipped it into Chet Alton's house the night after we took him down. Ditto the negatives from the film recorder. Not really too difficult — you knew we were about to sting a creep so you were ready. All you needed to know was where he lived — easy enough to find out, with your terminal linked up to everybody else's. But that's why you came home late and headed straight into the tequila — lots of nerves needed cooling by then. Kind of a celebration, too. You figured Chet would have to explain away those pictures of me to cover his own pathetic ass, like all the other stuff he'd collected. They were just a handful out of a million pictures at that point, so when he said he'd never seen them before, nobody on the planet would believe him. Of course, he couldn't argue away the negatives, too, could he?"

One of my former neighbors drove slowly past and rubbernecked me from his car. I waved like a suburban dad: all systems normal, family life rolling along. "Amazing how your neighbors ignore you until you're an accused child molester," I said. "Then you could write a book and they'd line up at a mall to buy it."

"The whole world's that way."

"Want me to keep going, close my case?"

"Do what you want."

"You paid on your old joint account, which you never closed out or took Ish's name off of. I don't know why. Maybe you thought if I traced things that far, I'd figure it was Ish for sure and challenge him to a duel or something. But you didn't have two payments of fifteen grand sitting around, so you got an unsecured loan at God knows what rate, figuring you'd cover it with what you could get out of the house equity here. You settled for a lousy deal because you needed the money sooner than later. Plus, you understood by then that you were helping to finance The Horridus, not some closet perv named Shroud. That made things kind of hot, especially inside your soul. Time to quit the game and get out. According to the papers I signed, you'll get less than twenty of the original thirty you paid up for this place. Same with me. But that was enough to borrow against, keep the cash flowing and get you up to Portland. I could go on with more details, but I think you get the drift."

Silence.

I turned. She had picked up one of Penny's aluminum softball bats. She had the handle in one hand and the barrel in the other. She appeared to be studying the logo. Then she looked at me, her face glum but her eyes charged with something I had never seen in her before. Her irises were black. She fixed me with a look of pure fear and fury, and I understood what I was to her. I was a monster standing in the mouth of her cave. If I hadn't turned to look just then — would she or wouldn't she? A cold shiver blossomed across the middle of my back because I didn't know the answer.

Then, motion to my left.

"Mom?"

Penny's face was uncomprehending as she looked at her mother. As uncomprehending as mine must have been.

"Are you guys —"

Mel looked at her as if Penny were a stranger. Then the rage passed and the pale gray returned to Melinda's eyes. She dropped the bat back into the box like it was scalding hot. "We're okay, honey. Just ugly adult stuff that you don't need to hear. Go back in."

Penny's doubt was mollified just enough that she could glance at me, then back at her mother, and pretend she hadn't seen something that would stay with her forever. She looked down and absently petted Moe. "I can't find the . . . the tubes we had for the posters."

"Under your bed."

A pause. Another look at me, then at her mother.

"It's okay, honey," said Melinda. "Go back inside."

But Penny looked at me before she spoke. Her voice was soft, so girlish, but it was built of conviction and forethought. "I'm going to say something, whether you guys say I can or not. I liked us all here together. You both drank too much because you were totally sad but you were getting over it. You guys were trying. Everything was going to be all right. Things started going pretty good. Then this thing happened and it all got worse. I knew you didn't do what they said you did, Terry. But I wish you would have told me that yourself. And I wish you two would, like, get your shit together, because it's *definitely* not. And if it's not, you're just going to ruin everything again for everybody around you, no matter where you go."

Then she looked again at her mother before coming over to me and throwing her arms around my neck. I smelled the hot sweet tears on her.

" 'Bye, Terry."

"I'll miss you, Pen."

"Then call."

She looked behind at her mother again as she walked back to the house. Moe tucked himself up close to her and followed her away. Then she was gone and I had the thought that it would be many years until I saw her again.

"Proud of yourself?" Mel hissed. *"That's* what I never wanted to happen, and it did anyway. You came here and you took her heart and you left. You fell in love with your TV cunt and you did exactly what I knew you'd do when we started out. I loathe you for what you did, Terry, but I loathe me even more for knowing it would happen from the very goddamned *beginning."*

"I had higher hopes than that."

"High as a kite, I'm sure. Like you were."

"Then why did you even let it get started?"

She was silent, and some of the ferocious anger rose again in her eyes. I'd never really known, until that moment, how much of Melinda's considerable willpower was tapped to keep a lid on the furies in her blood.

"For *me*. To make *me* happy. To make *me* feel good again, like I was something of value. I'm too goddamned old to need a man to make me feel valuable. I know that. But it doesn't do any good to know you shouldn't feel a way you feel. You pushed my buttons, Terry, you hung my moon for a while, and there wasn't a lot I could talk myself out of. And you know something? I did it for you, too. I did it for your secrets and your son and your sadness and all the crazy, crazy shit you were going through when I first got to know you. You needed what I had. Hell, you needed *everything*. And it made me feel like an angel to give it."

I looked at her. The flesh of her face was red and sagging and she looked, in spite of her anger, defeated.

"You put me back together, Melinda."

"But I liked you better in pieces, because you were mine then. And I'll tell you, if I wasn't going to keep you, no snot-nosed newscaster was going to get the man I fixed up, either. That's a hateful thing to say, and what I did was a hateful thing to do. But I'll stand by them, because that's the way I *felt*. So I acted accordingly. By the time of your birthday I was ready to move. You deserved to have your cute little world busted up some, for what you did to me. That's the thing about men,

Terry — you take things and really don't think of the consequences. You take and you take and you take, and you don't think about what it's costing. And when the bill comes due, you try to walk away. Nobody walks away from Melinda Vickers. I do the walking, when it's time. So get out, and do what you want with what you know. I'm giving you something valuable here, Terry. I'm giving you the luxury of being thrown out. Take it. Feel wronged. You can remember me any way you want, but don't suck up to my kid anymore. You don't qualify as a part of her life. You're just history we're going to forget."

I looked at her a long while.

"Well?" she asked.

"I'm sorry for what I did."

"I'm not, for what I did. I wish you could have sizzled on the grill a little longer."

"You lay it on pretty thick, Mel."

"Life with you was a bag of shit, Terry. What's it matter how I spread it?"

I nodded and walked away.

Thirty-five

"Am I poisonous?"

"As in harmful, or as in fatal?"

"Poison is poison, Donna."

"You're serious, aren't you?"

"Yes."

"Let me consider that a moment while you swerve to avoid the mule."

We were thirty clicks south of the border, between Tijuana and Ensenada, Donna with five days of vacation ahead and I still on leave. Donna, per usual, was shooting video, having never been to Mexico before. We were in her convertible and the top was down, so that made it easy. She had a polka dot scarf over her head. The morning was late and warm and the coastal fog was breaking up to reveal green hills and a hard blue Pacific. The dark highway flowed by under us, divided by a center railing of black and white posts that blurred if you tried to watch them up close. The road is good and wide and encourages velocity. I moved toward the center line on the sweeping down-hill curve. The mule's ears flapped in the slipstream of the car. The roads down here are better than they used to be, but shoulders are not a Mexican concern.

I was driving fast and hadn't said much, until then. I was anxious over what we'd do with five days together, because we'd never had more than twelve hours straight. Donna's presence put me in a state of agitation so intense I couldn't imagine five days with her being anything but good. But I have been misled by passion before, or, maybe, passion has been misled by me. More to the point, Melinda's verdict was echoing loud in a soul made hollow by Johnny's death. But I had not asked Donna to Mexico to lose myself in her, as I had tried to do in Melinda — to my shame, I know. What I wanted to do was find myself. And hopefully, to be able to stand the man I discovered.

"First of all, I don't think you should shoulder more than your fair share of the blame," she said.

"For what?"

"For anything. You see, that makes a man unhappy, and it makes him feel sorry for himself, and he hogs the road because he's taken on such a wide load. It's arrogant to take all the credit for good things, right? Well, taking all the blame is pretty near the same thing."

"You're telling me I'm not poisonous."

"Naw, Terry. All of us choose what we drink. Except the children and the feeble-minded, I suppose. They can get suckered."

"I tried not to misrepresent myself."

"You're pretty obviously who you are."

"But then I messed up and had to lie about it. About you."

"That truth would have been told."

"Yeah. But I don't know what I could have done about Johnny."

"Then don't convince yourself that you could have done anything. Just mourn him, Terry. Don't add him to a list of mistakes you made. That doesn't do John or you any good."

I held up the bottle of Herradura we'd bought back in Tijuana. Good dark gold. It was still a little early in the day for power drinking, but I was considering a nip to build an edge, make things festive. Donna had suggested the liter rather than the quart.

"You haven't had much to drink the last couple of weeks," she said.

"Pretty light."

"Feel a bender coming on?"

"Yeah."

"Pull over. I'll drive. You can take on spirits, prod your conscience all you can stand."

I always liked being a passenger. You get to see more.

Donna is a very good driver, fast and alert and aware. So I sat back and inhaled the perpetual trash-burn smell of the Baja coast and watched the blue water hit the black rocks and felt the unhurried sunshine on my neck and legs. Rosarito. Puerto Nuevo. Calafia. La Fonda. We pulled over at Teresa's, a restaurant that stands alone at the edge of the rocks and has windows looking down a hundred feet to the violent shore. It was just before noon on a weekday so the place was empty of customers, just Teresa's husband and one of her sons, and Teresa, who does the cooking.

We took a table at the window. Teresa's has pink walls with posters of bullfighters on it, and lots of Mexican beer advertisements. I've been here a lot. This time of day the pink warmth of a room built by hand meets the cool blue of a coast indifferent to human effort, right there at the windowpane beside you. This border shimmers with a collision of forces old as time itself. It's like the glass is the only thing that stands between the one thing and the other. You sit there and feel very mortal, which is to say very alive. Somehow blessed, too.

And Teresa's slender husband starts you off with a curt *buenas días* and a shot of good tequila. We sipped and stared out the contested window glass.

"You're beautiful," I said.

"You're not even looking at me."

"I don't have to."

"Why, thank you."

"True story."

"All your stories are true, aren't they?"

I thought about this.

"No."

"Should I know the difference?"

"That would take time."

"Do we have that?"

"I'll give you mine if you really want it."

She looked at me and rested her hand over mine on the tabletop. What a nervy shiver that woman could send through me.

"So," she said, "if we have time, where should we start? What stories of yours shall we vet?"

"There's a lot to choose from."

"I want a specific one."

"Which?"

"The one you always think about. The one that's bigger than you. The one that eats at you all day and every day. The one that the tequila gives you the courage to face, and the comfort to avoid."

"Ah." I looked at her dark bright eyes, her brown hair released now from the polka dot scarf and curling forth around her face, her pale skin.

Just then, Teresa's husband came to ask us our preference: small, medium or large lobsters. We got large. He poured us two more shots and Donna asked him to leave the bottle.

"I can see where this is going," I said, looking at it.

"Drink it up, Terry, if that's what it's going to take."

I poured another shot and sipped it half down. Here we go, I thought.

"Don't you have some questions about the

cause of Matt's death?"

"No."

"Why not?"

"Because you told me he drowned and that was good enough for me."

I looked at her for the slightest sign that she was lying. I saw none at all. A dishonest man never trusts someone else.

"You didn't read his death certificate?"

"You asked me not to. So I didn't."

"I asked you not to do a story about what happened to him."

"Well, we can argue semantics all day. Fact is, I didn't mention your boy. I did everything I could to make you look good and strong. That interview was a ten-minute love poem to you, whether you understood it or not. Maybe I'm no poet. But I went to some lengths to keep the original out of my boss's hands. You know, I could take some offense here. I'm trying not to."

"No, no. Please don't."

I tilted back the golden liquid and poured more. I could clearly feel the warmth of our pink room and the cool of the Pacific just behind the glass and the roiling border zone between them where Donna and I sat and waited for the truth to be told. A squad of pelicans coasted by the window in formation, no movement of their wings at all, just big brown birds resting heavily in air. I thought of Matt. I thought of Johnny. I thought of Mary

Lou Kidder. I heard a lovely twinkling sound and when I turned to it a girl in a pink dress stood beside the table with some curios to sell. Paper calla lilies in her left hand. An open box of Chiclets on a platform tied around her neck. And a mobile of small onyx birds connected with string in her right. She lifted the birds and in the invisible turmoil of our zone they moved and chimed sweetly against each other.

"No," I said.

"Here, for all," said Donna, and put down a twenty on the table. The girl smiled and set down the lilies, then the box of gum, then handed Donna the stone birds. She said *gracias* and ran for the stairs.

"I like these," she said, holding up the mobile. She hung it over the window latch beside us.

I drank until the ocean outside was impossibly bright, every silver shard owning a specific life of its own, every flash a minor history. The least I could do was offer back a history of my own.

"If you read the certificate of death it refers you to the coroner's report. I wanted an autopsy because I really wanted to know what happened. On Matt's, the immediate cause says 'respiratory arrest.' The next line says 'due to' and the examiner wrote in 'drowning.' The third line says 'due to' and the examiner left it blank."

Donna listened and studied me. "So?"

"So, I know him because we both work for the Sheriff-Coroner department. He likes me. He . . . well."

Donna nodded and waited.

"When Matt and I were at Shaw's Cove, it was a lot warmer than this," I said. "It was late September, with the Santa Anas blowing hot, and I took him out of school because the weather was so good and you could see underwater about fifty feet. No divers there, except us. I remember the sand stinging my ankles while I was putting on my wet suit. I remember real clearly zipping Matt's up from the back, with that black piece of cord they put on. Matt's suit was black and yellow, made him look like a bumblebee. I was real proud of him for taking to the water so well — he was just five and not at all fearless — but he knew what he could do and couldn't. There were so many other things he was afraid of. The dark. Closets. Under his bed. Car washes, the way the vacuum hoses make all that noise and coil up on the racks like big snakes — that scared him out of his wits. Scared of dogs and bugs and buses. But not the ocean. We spent a lot of time together down at Shaw's Cove, it was kind of my thing with him. His mother, she wouldn't go out past her knees, and I used to worry that would ruin it for him. Ardith was afraid of anything she couldn't see under the water, which is a lot. But that fear never got into Matt. We sat on the beach and put our boots and fins on, got our masks ready. I let him go in first like I always did. But I was only a few steps behind him, like I always was. The waves were short and crisp and it was just beautiful, Donna, the way the Santa Anas held up the faces and blew spray off the tops. You looked through the silver mist and then you saw blue sky and then a long low bank of orange brown way out there, which was Catalina with all the smog blown up against it. I remember thinking how great the sunset was going to be that evening. It was cold when I first went under. The water gets down into the suit and your body heat warms it up, that's how a wet suit works, but that first dive under always gets you. I came up and put my mask on and dove back under and I couldn't believe how clear it was. Matt was out ahead maybe all of ten yards. That yellow wet suit really showed up good, and his fins were blue and I remember thinking what a perfect little human he was. So we just swam along the rocks on the north, that's where you see a lot of stuff, right up close to shore like that, octopus and skates and rays, all the surf fish and the little bass that aren't safe out with the big boys. And up close to the rocks you get the grass, which is green and sometimes straw colored, swaying all together, and all the purple urchins and the green-gray anemones big as dinner plates, and schools of baitfish that look like stainless steel in the sunlight, because there's plenty of light up by the rocks there — you're only in, say, three or four feet of water, Donna, at the most. You can see the sun slanting in past the surface, looks like raindrops slowed down and stretched out. This big school of baitfish came up from behind us and we were there in the middle of them, thousands of fish hauling ass past us in perfect unison. Then this dark shape after them, really fast, and it's this little black cormorant just swimming his heart out under three feet of water, chasing down his food. When I came up for some breath he was sitting there on the water about ten feet away like he'd been there his whole life. Matt was on the other side of him looking back and smiling, and I remember that smile real clear because when you smile with a mask and snorkel on, your mouth looks distorted and Matt looked funny to start with because the mask was so big for his face. You know? Then we followed the edge of the rocks out to where it's deeper, maybe ten feet, then twenty, about. Matt came over and he said he wanted to show me how deep he could go and I said go right ahead, I'll watch. So he dove down and came up, then I dove down a little deeper and came up, and he went deeper than me, and like that. We maybe dove five or six times each. I wasn't straining or anything. I didn't think Matt was either, because I kept watching his breathing and how he was doing. It was a contest, but it was a friendly one. Then, I went down the last time and gave a kick or two extra, and when I looked up at Matt he was floating up there looking down at me real peaceful and I drifted back up and broke the surface with a big spit of breath and drank some more air in. And Matt was still floating there, looking down. So I said hey, what's to see down there, young man, but he didn't answer. So I swam over and poked his shoulder and he didn't notice me and I knew it was a shallow-water blackout. So I grabbed his wet-suit collar and lifted it out of the water and his head dangled down on his chest and I slapped him across the face, not hard, but hard enough. That didn't do anything. So I got his head out of the water and tried to tell if he was breathing, but that's hard when you're treading water for two and everything's wet and moving around, plus the wind blowing you in the face. I couldn't tell if he was breathing so I got his head locked up between my hands and breathed for him and kicked harder than I'd ever kicked in my life to get him in. You can really move out with those big fins on. Next thing I knew we were on the beach past the waterline and I had his wet-suit stripped down to his waist and I could see he wasn't breathing so I did CPR. Every cop knows CPR. And you know what happened? He coughed and spit up a bunch of water and started breathing. He was just barely awake, though. There was a flock of seagulls right over us and I thought they were mocking me. Matt's eyes kind of opened and he was looking at me and the pupils were dilated so big his eyes looked black. He was terrified. But he was breathing. So I got that wet suit the rest of the way off and mine, too, and I took him in both arms and started running. I knew there was a walk-in clinic up Coast Highway and I was going to make it there faster than humanly possible. You know, the way I remember that run isn't always the same. Sometimes I think it took a long time because all these details come at me, and the details are always standing still when I see them, like this pink hibiscus blossom hanging over a fence by the sidewalk along Coast Highway. I mean, when I think back I can still see that thing, the white stamen in the middle and the yellow pollen stuck to it. Or I can remember the coldness of Matthew's body against mine, the exact smell of his hair, which was salt water, like you'd figure, but with boy and a little shampoo still in it. I remember holding him tight — I'll never forget that. Then, other times all I remember is a blur of cars and people and lowering my shoulder into the door of the clinic. I do remember knocking into the examination room where the doctor was, with the nurse talking loud at me, and the look on the face of the lady the doctor was with. I remember it was kind of a struggle giving Matt up. It was like the doctor was pulling away part of me. And I remember lying

Matt out on the table and thinking how hopeless he looked. And I remember yelling and the doctor ordering me firmly to get a blanket out of the other exam room, then locking me out. And, of course, the nurse leaving Matt's room a few minutes later, walking away from me down the hallway, crying. It was five days before we found out what happened to him. We thought the truth would make us feel better. Well, you know how that can go. First, he had an embolism that knocked him out while he was in the water. Then, he almost drowned because he was unconscious. I saved his life at that point. Then, well, Donna, what happened was he was alive when I started off with him up Coast Highway, but when I laid him on the table, he was gone. While I was running, you know? Because of the way I had his head up against me? Because he was cold and I didn't want to drop him? He didn't drown. What happened was, I suffocated him."

There was a silence as the zone along the windowpane hummed where the pink room met the blue sea. The onyx birds turned slowly.

My eyes burned and my heart was trying to hide. Or was it trying to be found?

Donna's voice was a whisper.

"I'm sorry for you, Terry. And for Matthew, too."

I couldn't speak right then. I heard the faint sound of the Virginia hollows in her voice and

I believed for a moment that I was back in one of them, surrounded by green hills, a continent away from the Pacific I love and hate.

"You've never told anyone?"

"Ardith."

"You're a magnificent and stubborn man."

"Now you."

"Yes. Now me."

"Never tell?"

"I can't tell what isn't mine to tell, Terry."

"Forgive me?"

"I can't do that, either. You can."

I thought about that. It would be the end, and the beginning of everything.

The employees of Thorndike Press hope you have enjoyed this Large Print book. All our Large Print titles are designed for easy reading, and all our books are made to last. Other Thorndike Press Large Print books are available at your library, through selected bookstores, or directly from us.

For information about titles, please call:

(800) 257-5157

To share your comments, please write:

Publisher
Thorndike Press
P.O. Box 159
Thorndike, Maine 04986